THE THREE GRACES COLLECTION

LAURA DU PRE

WHO'S WHO AT THE FRENCH COURT

The Royal Family

Catherine de Medici, Queen Mother of France, wife of Henry II.

    Charles, King of France, Catherine's son

    Elizabeth of Austria, Charle's wife

    Henri, Duke of Anjou, Catherine's son

    Louise of Lorraine, Henri's wife

    Francis/ Hercules, Duke of Alençon, Catherine's youngest son

    Margot of Valois, Catherine's daughter

The Bourbons

Jeanne, Queen of Navarre, first cousin of Henry II, due to France's Salic Law, she cannot inherit the French throne, yet her descent through a male relative means any of her male decedents can.

    Antoine, King of Navarre. Jeanne's husband

    Henry, King of Navarre, Jeanne's only surviving son and heir

    Catherine of Bourbon, Henry's only sister

    Henri, Prince of Conde, Henry's first cousin

Marie of Cleves, Henri the Prince of Conde's first cousin and his wife

Henriette of Cleves, Duchess of Nevers, the eldest of the Cleves sisters and close friend of Princess Margot of Valois.

Louis Gonzaga, Duke of Nevers, an Italian who became a naturalized French due to his association with Catherine de Medici. He inherited the title Duke of Nevers from his father-in-law.

The Guise

[Descended from Claude, a younger brother of the Duc de Lorraine, the family retains the epithet "of Lorraine," and strong ties to their Lorraine cousins.]

Anna, Duchess of Guise and Nemours, a granddaughter of Louis XII.
  Francis, her deceased first husband and the second Duke of Guise
  Mary of Guise, Francis's sister and mother of Mary, Queen of Scots
  Henri, Duke of Guise, Anna's eldest son and heir to Guise dukedom
  Catherine of Cleves, Henri's wife and older sister of Marie of Cleves. Became Princess de Porcelian through her first marriage.
  Catherine of Lorraine, Duchess of Montpensier Anna's only daughter
  Louis II, Cardinal of Guise, younger brother of Henri
  Charles, Duke of Mayenne, brother of Henri

The Court

Simon, Baron de Sauve, Catherine de Medici's secretary who rose to become one of Charles IX's Secretaries of State.

Charlotte, Baroness de Sauve and later Marquis of Noirmourtier, his wife.

❧ I ❧

L ouvre Palace, Paris, 1572

I CANNOT KEEP THE RIBBONS FOR THE QUEEN'S DRESS FROM tangling as I walk. It is as if they are conspiring to knot and defy me. Amused at my predicament, the Queen's guards nod at me and try to suppress a smile. I try to hurry to my mistress' chambers, but the extra effort sends a wave of air and what progress I had made tangles into a loose braid.

Entering the Queen's antechamber, I bob into a curtsey, "I'm sorry, Madame, they seem to have gotten the best of me." Like the guards, she cannot suppress a giggle at my frustration. Recovering herself, she shrugs her petite shoulders.

"Perhaps it wasn't meant to be, Marie." She answers me in Latin, our shared language. Since coming to the French court, Elisabeth of Austria has attempted to speak French, but she has as much difficulty as I have found in maintaining her wardrobe this morning. "If you would, please fetch my gown."

Thankful for the reprieve, I place the ribbons on the nightstand and quickly forget them. As Queen of France, we would usually expect Elisabeth to rule over the court, but we all know that the true Grande dame is her powerful mother-in-law, Catherine de Medici. A quiet, pious and studious young girl, this arrangement suits Elisabeth well and she appears at court whenever the circumstances warrant it.

This hot August morning, her presence is certainly justified in court, as is mine. My cousin Henry, the young King of Navarre, is about to be married and we are eagerly awaiting his arrival in Paris. The bride to be is the king's sister Margot, the Princess of France and one of the most celebrated beauties of Europe. At first glance, their match seems perfection, but as the bride and groom do not share the same faith, the betrothal has been fought with difficulties. The largest hurdle the two have faced, was the lifelong hatred between their mothers. Their hatred is due in no small part to my Aunt, Jeanne, the formidable Queen of Navarre.

I should not speak ill of my aunt; she took me in after my mother's death and my father's inability to raise his youngest daughter, a girl of nine. Married to my mother's brother, Antoine of Bourbon, Jeanne of Navarre did not hesitate to send for me and offer to bring me up within her home. Of course, life with my aunt came with certain conditions, amongst them the requirement that I follow her Reformed faith. Unable to imagine what to do with me on his own, my father readily agreed, and I was packed off before my tenth birthday to an unfamiliar home with its odd and alien faith.

So I was raised, like my cousin, the King of Navarre, as a Protestant, although little of the Reformed faith appealed to me. My loyalty to my aunt meant that I followed her religious instruction, and I have spent my life as a Protestant. My older sisters, Henriette, who is eight years older than I and our middle sister, Catherine, five years older than I, were raised in the Catholic faith. As a result, my family feels very alien to me sometimes. After ten years with my aunt, I returned to the French royal court to become a lady-in-waiting to the new Queen, whom I found an easy mistress to serve.

I had not seen my aunt in months when she traveled with my cousin, Catherine to Paris to negotiate the marriage between Henry of

Navarre and Margot of Valois. Our reunion was tense, as I felt she judged me for falling from the faith she had instructed me in since childhood. Within weeks, however, my aunt died I had lost the second mother I had known in my short life. Aunt Jeanne was determined to see her children married well and safely, while furthering the reformed faith and that included not only her son's marriage to a Catholic princess. My aunt had seen that I also married well and married within her faith.

My aunt chose my other first cousin, the Prince of Condé, to be my groom almost a year ago. Condé's Christian name was "Henry" in honor of the king's father. I had known my cousin since I came to the Navarrese court, as he also came to court as a motherless orphan adopted by Jeanne of Navarre. Many people criticized her for being harsh and calculating, but one could never say Jeanne of Navarre abandoned a child in need of a motherly figure. Rather than hold her generosity over our heads, she seemed to relish her opportunity to be the mother of more than the two children of her body.

Because of her generosity in taking me in, I felt obligated to go along with the match she had made for me. Protestant princesses were rare in Europe, Save the foreign ones from German principalities. It was a foregone conclusion, therefore, that I would marry and become the Princess of Condé as we forged a new Protestant dynasty. Despite any misgivings I might have about our marriage and mourning the death of my surrogate mother, I went ahead with our ceremony this past July and Condé and I married according to Protestant rites.

Now, almost a month later, I struggled with adjusting to married life. My royal mistress, herself, married for less than two years, became a genuine friend and a source of support for me. Elisabeth was in the final months of her first pregnancy and as her stomach expanded, we worked to expand her gowns. As I placed the rose-colored one she had selected for the evening's reception on the bed, my wedding ring hung on the silk of the bodice.

"I'm sorry, Madame," I grimaced and looked at her helplessly.

"It's all right; you aren't used to wearing it. It will become second nature to you, eventually."

"It feels heavy," our time together had taught me that I could be honest with her without fearing her judgment.

"I miss wearing mine. It's been months since I've been able to get it on my finger." Her hand went to her belly absentmindedly. All of France eagerly awaited the birth of the royal heir. Like any other woman, Elisabeth only hoped for the birth of a healthy child.

"I suppose it won't be long before I'm in the same situation." I tried to keep the edge out of my voice, but looking at the expression on her face, I knew that I had not succeeded in doing so.

Elisabeth smiled at me, the compassion showing on her face. Like me, she had no control over the man she married. She fulfilled her duty as a royal princess and her current condition was a fulfillment of her obligation to supply an heir. Unlike me, she accepted her role without complaining, a choice I secretly envied.. Although officially separated by our religious beliefs, the devoutly Catholic Elisabeth never held my faith as a strike against me. We were inseparable most of the time, except for the times we worshiped our Lord. The Queen accompanied the king to Mass daily while I attended sermons from the leading Protestant preachers who were allowed to remain at court.

As soon as I entered my private apartments within the vast Louvre palace, I removed my hood and attempted to smooth my brown hair. I had wanted a few quiet moments alone, but as I entered the bedchamber, I saw that my husband was already sitting beside our bed. Since going from cousins to husband and wife, our interactions had been awkward. Every new bride must take some time to adjust to married life, but I felt as if my adjustment period took me more time than most.

I was determined to work to make our marriage a success, but the truth was that my husband and I were very different people. Like my Aunt Jeanne, he had taken to the Protestant religious with relish and embraced the dour and restrained nature of the most ardent followers. As a result, his character was often dark and brooding, which made it difficult for us to connect with one another. A life stripped of the gaiety and spontaneous nature of most Frenchmen seemed an empty life to me. I was determined, however, to do my duty to make our marriage work, if not for our shared for faith, then for our family's sake and to honor the memory of my Aunt Jeanne.

"I've just come from the Queen's rooms; we've done all we can to prepare for Navarre's arrival. If he decides to come at all."

I raised an eyebrow, "Do you think that he will back out of his mother's promise?"

"If he knows what's good for him, he will. None of the Papists can be trusted to keep their word."

I held my tongue, choosing not to remind him that my closest friend at court was a Papist. I had no desire to pick a fight that moment, exhausted as I was from the continual preparations for the upcoming wedding.

"We are expected to be at the Admiral's house this evening to hear the Reverend Challoit." His imperious tone grated on my nerves and this time, I chose to say something.

"When have I failed to join you for a sermon at court? Do I not come faithfully as a believer and as your wife?"

He shrugged, and I imagined that he got some thrill out of bating me. "I sometimes feel as if you are not as sincere about our faith as I am. One might think that the Catholic flavor of the court is rubbing off on you."

Would that be so bad? In my mind, toleration was better than the extremism that my husband seemed doggedly determined to display. The king himself was willing to allow those of both faiths to worship without molestation at court. Both the king and his mother had encouraged toleration amongst the two groups of Christians within France and within the court. Still, men like my husband seemed determined to provoke hostility between themselves and the moderates of the court. Sometimes I felt as if my fellow Protestants only wanted to play the part of the persecuted party to garner sympathy abroad. From what I had seen so far, my countrymen enjoyed an unusual degree of religious freedom.

"We both serve at the pleasure of the king and his mother; we cannot forget that. Attempting to incite hostility between the Catholics and Protestants does nothing to help either side."

He snorted, "Now you sound like Catherine."

I shrugged, weary of his baiting. "Perhaps she is right."

I fidget in the room, as always, feeling uncomfortable. In front of me, another "preacher", whose name I struggle to remember is droning on and on about "atonement" and other lofty concepts that I have heard since childhood. These meetings and prayer nights are a stripped-down version of the Mass that the Catholics attend daily and officially, they are meant to encourage discussion and personal understanding of the word of God. I have never confessed this to anyone, but for me, these meetings are more like being scolded for being a naughty child. The men who run them seem angry and spiteful, and I rarely feel the presence of God during them. Instead, I feel as if I were watching a performance or lecture. After the man designated as the "minister" concludes his sermon, the congregation is encouraged to speak of their sins openly and confess them to one another. I am far from a shy woman, yet the idea of having my privacy violated in front of virtual strangers horrifies me.

The entire experience feels more like an excuse for a gossip session like those that run rampant amongst the lords and ladies of the court, except this is supposedly sanctioned by God. My bit of rebellion is to list demurely some shallow "sin," such as loving my shoes too much or feeling as if I am unable to return my husband's love that he gives me.

This ploy seems to satisfy the overbearing men who run the meetings and for a few moments at least, I am left alone.

Still, I long for an hour of solitude to be alone with my thoughts and for the blessed quiet to hear God's voice, not that of a preacher whose performance is scheduled for a given night. I wonder what it would be like in the hushed halls of a Catholic mass. But of course, as a Protestant princess, I am not allowed to know. I am not allowed to confess even that I am curious to learn. If I were to ask the Queen to allow me to accompany her during Mass, she would leap at the opportunity to bring her dear friend along, but she is wise enough to never put me in the position of "violating" my professed religious beliefs. Without any other options, I am forced to wince as the noise and din around me swirls until the meeting is over.

৩৵৩

CONDÉ AND I TAKE OUR PLACES IN THE MASSIVE THRONE ROOM OF the Louvre palace. Navarre and his gentlemen have finally arrived in Paris safely, and to our relief, the formal betrothal will be held as planned. The ceremony demonstrates the tangled web of relations and religious preferences across the country; while the groom is Protestant, his cousin is the very Catholic Cardinal Bourbon, who will conduct the betrothal ceremony and the strange wedding ceremony that is to come. In deference to Navarre, they will be wed on a platform erected outside of Notre Dame Cathedral. After their vows, the new Queen of Navarre will be escorted by her brother the Duc d'Anjou, known as "Monsieur," who will stand in the groom's place for the Catholic Mass that will follow the ceremony.

I cannot help but flash back to my wedding ceremony a month earlier, as Condé and I were wed in a thoroughly Protestant ceremony in the formidable Chateau Blandy near the village of Melun. Navarre had stood nearby while I was wed and now I would watch as he likewise was united in matrimony. Like the ring on my finger, our marriage had failed to settle upon me, being more of an intrusion than a comfort. I hoped that as time passed, this would no longer be so. I wished the same for Navarre.

The appearance of so many new people in Paris had also meant that the court had been reshuffled in our housing arrangements. My husband and I were allowed to move out of the Louvre and lodge in my sister's home with her husband, the Italian Duc de Nevers. Henriette was the heiress of our family, our elder brother having died a few years earlier, and her husband took her title, but not the management of her finances. Thanks to Henriette's wily use of her financial assets, she was fast becoming one of the most important creditors in France.

Perhaps every new groom is uncomfortable being lodged with his new wife's family, but I sensed that my husband tried little to integrate himself with mine. Henriette and her husband, Louis were devoted Catholics, like our other sister, Catherine and that brought no small amount of scorn from my husband. I would have thought that the idea of having so many fellow Protestant allies in Paris weeks after meeting for our ceremony would make Condé happy, but he seems so dour and determined to be quarrelsome that I doubt anything could make him happy. Even during our shared meals, he took the opportunity to criticize my sister and her studious husband.

"Must we sit here while the two of them continue crossing themselves?"

"Husband, it's simply in thanksgiving of their food. We should all be grateful for the bounty of God's providence," I quoted a minister's lecture from a few weeks earlier, hoping that he would use the parallel to find some common ground with Louis and my sister.

"It's idolatry," he sneered, poking at his fish.

"Making the sign of the cross is not creating an idol. We all revere the cross as the instrument of our Lord's torture and resurrection. Surely we can all agree on that?"

"I will be glad when this spectacle is over and we can get back to our regular lives."

"And back to our rooms at the palace?"

He shrugged, "As far away from Paris as we can get."

My husband's sulky attitude notwithstanding, we all felt

the uneasiness surrounding the two factions stuffed into Paris that hot August. The stifling heat, bereft of any rain or wind to bring us relief, and the overcrowded streets turned the city into a tinderbox. I waited on Queen Elisabeth as best I could, but the crowds and our continual obligations to attend banquets, fetes, masquerades and dinners meant that I rarely had time to speak with her. I had hoped to be with her when her child came and like me, she had hoped to go into confinement in quiet.

The Queen's quiet descent into confinement was not to be; her sister-in-law's marriage demanded her attendance and despite their different natures, the two women were close friends. No matter how many demands pregnancy or decorum placed on her body, Elisabeth was determined to attend as many events surrounding her Margot's marriage as possible.

As I had suspected, the wedding ceremony was odd, to say the least. The platform gave the half-Protestant half-Catholic wedding a cobbled and confusing flair, and the fact that it was held outside meant that the atmosphere was more like an open market than a solemn rite. We held our breath as the vows were said, Navarre readily agreeing to the marriage and Margot holding her tongue. The King in his anger pushed her head forward, forcing her to give her assent to the marriage. In a typical wedding, this would have been suspect, but this was far from typical. Rumors abounded that Catherine had resorted to trickery and bribes to attain the dispensation from Rome for the close cousins to marry and few, if any of us, had seen the supposed letter from the church.

At last, the Cardinal Bourbon pronounced his kinsman and the Princess of France man and wife, and Navarre stepped aside to allow his new wife to celebrate the marriage mass. Dressed even more splendidly than the bride, the Duc d'Anjou led his sister into the cathedral and out of propriety, we Protestants in the assembly waited outside until the mass was over.

"Let the pompous boy take her inside. That's half an hour that I won't have to spend looking at him." My husband mumbled in my ear and I turned to glare at him.

"This is hardly the time to resurrect old quarrels."

He looked at the Duc de Guise, whose eyes were on Margot instead of my sister, his wedded wife. "Tell that to Guise."

After the ceremony, we all sighed a sigh of relief that the feared violence that could stop the wedding from happening had not occurred. The streets of Paris stayed blissfully quiet through the following evening. Perhaps the Protestants were silly to worry that they were in danger.

❦   3   ❦

The Sunday evening following the wedding we were all invited to a banquet given by the King. Given the Reformed faith's belief that to be joyous on the Sabbath was disrespectful, none of the Protestants accepted the King's invitation. Yet to decline the invitation was to insult the King himself. When I heard that they had planned to risk offending the King, I was horrified.

"You cannot just refuse to go," I trailed after my husband as he stumbled around our bedchamber, looking for last minute items before he left. I shoved his hat and shoes into his hand, impatiently waiting for him to finish dressing himself.

"We have gone above and beyond in our willingness to be polite to the King and we have the right to attend our services. This debauchery is against our beliefs and we will not compromise on them in fear of offending an earthly monarch."

I exhaled a sigh. King Charles had been more than accommodating towards his Protestant guests and now they were thumbing their noses at him. As one of the Queen's ladies-in-waiting, I could ill afford not to attend the banquet. As far as I was concerned, my husband was acting rude and downright childish.

"I will attend the banquet while you attend the service at the

Admiral's house." Compromise seemed better than continuing the argument. My husband was intransigent as always.

He snorted in response, raising my ire even further. "Absolutely not—you will not attend an event without me there beside you. I will not have it said that my wife is a wanton woman."

"And I am to offend both the sovereign and my mistress?"

"You are to explain that your husband commanded you to accompany him, as any dutiful wife would."

❧

AT THE MEETING, I SEETHED AND DID MY BEST TO AVOID CONTACT with my husband. What would the King think of our absence? I was sure that his arrogance would place both of us in danger. During the seemingly endless sermon, I turned over in my mind what I would say to the Queen to explain our absence.

Afterward, Admiral Coligny took my elbow and asked to speak with me. Despite his decision to become a firm Protestant, unlike my husband, the elderly admiral was willing to work towards reconciliation between the two faiths. In fact, the King considered the Admiral to be a close friend and mentor, calling him "father" after the death of the King's actual father. It was difficult not to like the admiral; while he was an accomplished soldier, he was also a fair and kindly man. He was one of the Protestant leaders I had always had respect for, going back to my days as a child in Aunt Jeanne's court when the Admiral would visit.

"I hope that all is well between you and the Prince of Condé." Such an innocent question, spoken without malice, caused me to wince. Unwilling to upset him, I chose to lie. "I think that we are still getting used to one another. We'll take time to settle into married life."

He nodded, whether out of an understanding of what I meant or simple kindness, I could not tell. "It was your aunt's fondest wish that her family remain united in marriage. She had high hopes for both of you and your marriage was one of her triumphs. I'm sure she is looking down from Heaven, smiling with pride at both of you."

Guilt coursed through me. Had I been acting with ingratitude and judgment towards my husband? Was it just as difficult for him to adjust to married life? Was a being disloyal to my Aunt in my constant unhappiness about my marriage? After all, few women were allowed to choose to marry for love and perhaps I was also being unreasonable.

I looked at the admiral who in turn looked at me without a hint of judgment in his eyes. "I think that I am asking too much of my marriage so far. Perhaps I'm being too harsh on Condé."

"Ah, we are all sinners with a multitude of faults. Thankfully, we can ask our Lord for forgiveness." He winked at me, "Even for a Bourbon princess."

I laughed at his joke, thankful to have a moment of levity. "Still, I worry that our absence today is going to be seen as a sign of stubbornness and disrespect. The King has been a close friend to you and as Protestants, I fear that we are trying the limits of his goodwill."

He nodded, "King Charles has proven to be a generous monarch towards us and it could be that we are acting paranoid at the supposed threat in Paris towards those of our faith. His mistress is a devout Protestant, and he willingly gave us the freedom to worship two years ago."

"Shouldn't we be doing all that we can to work towards reconciliation?"

"I will speak with the King and assure him that we meant no insult by missing the banquet." He squared his shoulders, "As an elderly man; I can attest that I am almost worn out from the endless fetes surrounding the King and Queen of Navarre's wedding. Perhaps the Catholics have more stamina than we do."

That evening, I resolved to be more generous towards my husband. Motivated in part by the shame I felt in neglecting to appreciate what my aunt had done for me, I thought of ways to repay her. After all, those acts were motivated out of concern for my welfare. Also, I had neglected to show compassion for my husband who felt as ill at ease in our marriage as I did. We had one another to depend on upon and perhaps I should try harder to be his helper in our marriage.

THE FOLLOWING WEDNESDAY EVENING, THE COURT HELD ANOTHER ball and masque and this time, the Protestants had no objection to attending. Mindful of the strain the event would place upon her in the late stages of her pregnancy, the Queen had decided to sit by her husband and preside over the banquet. "I'm pleased to see that our Protestant guests will be here tonight," she squeezed my hand and for the moment, I was assured that the King had not felt slighted by our absence.

Still, despite the King's efforts to bring the two sides together, most of the Protestants sat in a corner, dour and grimacing at the celebrations laid out before them. They seemed poised to find insult and offense at every corner, and I had no doubt that they would eventually find it. Perhaps it was the influence of those angry, brooding men in black who had influenced my husband in his dark nature. If I put my mind to it, perhaps I could use our time at court to show my husband that life could be brighter by moving him away from their heavy influence.

Despite the Queen's assurance that she and the King bore me no anger for missing the ball on Sunday, I felt as if I should do everything that I could to tend to her, particularly since she had two scant months before her child and the heir to the throne was born. I resolved to remain seated beside her and attend to her every need. I was accompanied by Madame de Sauve, the wife of the King's chancellor, who had been called out of town for state business. As married women, we enjoyed a bit more freedom in our movements than the unmarried girls who formed the Queen's household.

"Princess, you should take a break and enjoy the masquerade. I can sit with the Queen." Although Madame de Sauve's offer was made without a hit of artifice, I was reluctant to go. I still felt that I had to make up for my earlier absence.

"Yes, do Marie. While I am barely able to move and Madame sits here in Paris bereft of her husband, there is no reason why you should not enjoy yourself."

Unwilling to offend the Queen for the second time in a week, I rose and made my way to the dance floor. As this was a masquerade, I wore a masque depicting the Queen of Hearts. Scanning the ballroom,

I looked for my husband to ask him to dance. After several minutes, however, I realized that he was not to be found in the cavernous ballroom. Feeling foolish, I decided to return to the Queen.

"Madame, you must do me the honor of a dance." The lilting voice beside me caused me to turn. I saw a man richly dressed and sporting Lion's head for a mask.

"I must return to the Queen, Sir; she will be expecting me." Embarrassment mixed with annoyance at my inability to find my husband when I most needed him. I had no intentions of fighting off unwanted attentions from another man to add to my problems of the night. I looked desperately at the Queen to try to catch her eye; to my horror, I found that she was being attended to quite sufficiently by her other ladies. My heart sank as I failed to come up with another excuse.

"Ah, I see that the Queen is well taken care of. Excellent, you must dance the next dance with me." Taking my hand, he led me to the center of the ballroom where the couples were already lining up to begin the next dance. I was trapped.

❦   4   ❦

Despite my initial misgivings, my partner turned out to be a welcome diversion. We spent the dance in amiable conversation and he even managed to get a few laughs from me. By the time the dance had ended, I was sorry to see him go. With a courtly bow and a chaste kiss on my hand, he reluctantly left my side. I began to scan the room again for my husband and eventually, my eyes alighted on him. Stalking towards him, I grabbed his hand and pulled him away from the men he had been speaking to earlier.

"I believe that we should spend at least one dance together tonight."

"Now? I am in the middle of a conversation with the Seignior--"

"Henry, we both have duties to perform and I think that one dance is not too much to ask of my husband." I could hear the angry edge in my voice and no doubt the men he had been speaking with earlier could hear it as well. I cared little for their opinions, however, as our standing at court was more important than whatever he was talking about with them.

He gave a heavy sigh, "Very well. Gentlemen, if you would excuse me." I gave a coquettish courtesy and allowed him to lead my out onto the ballroom floor. As he methodically led me through the dance, I

noticed the man in the lion mask dancing in the corner with his partner. He gave me a slight nod which caused me to blush. I tried to cover
it, but not before my husband noticed it.

"What is the ass doing now?"

"Who?

"Anjou. He's taunting me, just as he did with my father."

Thankfully, my mask hid my surprise. I had no idea of the identity
of the man I had danced with earlier. Part of me enjoyed the mystery
of not knowing who my gallant partner was. Now I knew that it was
the King's younger brother who had partnered me. Despite myself, I
felt a thrill that he had chosen me out of all the ladies at the
masquerade for a dance.

"Stay far away from him; there is no telling what kind of mischief
he is up to."

"At a ball? I hardly think that he is plotting as he dances."

My husband snorted, "There is talk that he is plotting an assassination of one or more of the Protestants in Paris."

I rolled my eyes, weary of the plotting and paranoia. "You have
been convinced that there is a plot going on for days and we have seen
no evidence of it. I am growing tired of all of this." My husband said
nothing, choosing to end our argument at the point. We spent the rest
of the dance in silence and he returned to his place with the black-clad
men for the rest of the evening.

I, however, marched straight to the Queen and sat beside her,
determined not to leave her side for the rest of the night. Waiting on
the Queen could hardly lead to any trouble, or cause my husband to
object to my behavior. I would play the part of the respectful matron
to perfection. My resolve lasted for about an hour until I saw a tall
figure walking towards the raised dais and straight towards the Queen.
My heart sank as I noticed the lion's mask covering his face.

"Your Majesty," he sank to his knees before the Queen, giving his
sister-in-law a courtly bow that would put the most ardent actor to
shame. When he rose, I noticed the wide grin splitting his face. To my
horror, he plunked down beside me, taking the seat that Madame de
Sauve vacated eagerly. I was trapped and decorum dictated that I could
not ignore the King's brother.

The Duc turned to the Queen and began a lively conversation that made her smile. Perhaps he was not there merely to speak with me or to cause mischief, which caused me to relax in his presence. "Sister, you are at quite a disadvantage. How do you feel?"

The Queen fanned herself and exhaled a long breath. "I feel unwieldy, waddling and sitting constantly. The heat is not helping my discomfort; I would be happy once my condition is over, to be truthful."

He crossed himself and took her hand tenderly. "Would be to God that your son is born soon and all of France can rejoice in his birth."

I was touched by his kindness and concern for the gentle Queen. I was in the midst of deciding that I had misjudged the Duc when he suddenly shot to his feet and bowed again to the Queen. "You look parched; I will get you some wine." He bounded off and for a quarter of an hour, we had a respite.

"Majesty, do you feel up to staying? I can help you back to your apartments." If I could convince the Queen to retire early, my problem would be solved. To my chagrin, however, she simply patted my hand and fixed a smile on me.

"Absolutely not. I will remain here to support my husband. And as you were deprived of the opportunity to attend the last ball, I will not force you to leave early."

I opened my mouth to protest, but the Duc appeared suddenly in front of us, cutting off my response. In his hands, he carried two cups, one for the Queen and another for myself. Once again, decorum dictated that I could not be rude to the Duc. "Thank you, Sir," I replied, trying to keep my voice as level as possible.

"Madame, I don't believe I have had the honor of introducing myself." He once again settled next to me and by his behavior, it was obvious that he was determined to carry on a conversation with me.

"You have been on the battlefield for the King, your brother, is that not so?' The rivalry between my late father-in-law and the Duc was an open scandal and I hoped that bringing it up might cool his enthusiasm. Anjou led his armies against Protestant strongholds, including the city of La Rochelle, against my family members. One of those armies surrounded and fatally wounded Louis, the previous

Prince de Condé. To be fair, Anjou did not do his duty purely out of bloodlust. Despite the King giving us freedom to worship across the kingdom, some Protestant enclaves like La Rochelle were unwilling to bow to royal edits. We were on very different sides and I hoped that chasm would discourage him from attempting to continue to flirt with me. Earlier, I had the excuse of ignorance of his identity, but now I could not claim to Condé that I was unaware of who I consorted with as I sat beside the Queen. I hoped that my husband would storm to the dais to reclaim me and remove me from this awkward situation, but once again, my husband was nowhere to be found. For all I knew, he was out planning a counter strike to answer the feared attacks by the Catholics.

"Yes, we have been dealing with rebellions against the throne for some time and my brother has entrusted me with putting down any insurgents. It would seem that no matter how many concessions the King makes towards the Protestants, they are determined to show no loyalty to their King."

That had my ire up, I may not be the most dedicated to the Reformed faith, but his casual retelling of the royal attacks on Protestant strongholds was going too far. "I beg your pardon, Monsieur. Some of those 'insurgents' are my kinsmen." Ignoring decorum, I glared at him, daring him to say anything more offensive.

He was immediately contrite, "Forgive me, my lady. It is the extremists that I am talking about. And the Protestants are not the only ones who suffer from extremists." His gaze alighted on the Duc de Guise, my other brother-in-law, who held a view that rabid Catholicism was the only way to unify France. Guise and my husband continued to circle warily around one another, but Catherine and I had no idea how long their uneasy truce would last. Or when Protestant would decide to attack Catholic.

Still, I refused to concede any point to Anjou. Snapping my fan open, I began to wave it wildly, moving his flowing golden brown hair out of place. "I take it that you agree with your mother that moderation in both faiths is the best way for all Frenchmen."

"Aye, I do." He said it with such a soft voice that I could not help but look at him. His expression was contrite and gentle. His bravado from a moment earlier was gone. I immediately felt guilty myself for being so harsh with him.

THE DUC D'ANJOU WAS DETERMINED NOT TO LEAVE HIS PERCH beside me, although he took pains to appear as if the reason was that he was loath to leave the King's pregnant wife without a male champion to take care of her. He kept her plied with wine and sweetmeats, feeding her from his own plate. From all appearances, we were simply seeing to the Queen's needs and her comfort.

The truth was that the more time I spent with Anjou, the more I grew to enjoy his company. He was solicitous and kind to both of us, seeing to our every need as if he were a suitor. Despite my earlier reservation, I found myself laughing at his quick jokes. Perhaps it was the mulled wine that went to my head, but in his presence I relaxed more than I had in the previous months. Unlike my husband, the Prince of Condé, Anjou was a lively and quick-witted man, one more than capable of flattering a young girl looking for attention and appreciation. The longer we sat together, the more I began to resent my husband in his treatment of me. I had brought some prestige to our marriage and unlike Condé, my family was well connected at court. My position as a lady-in-waiting to the Queen furthered our position at court. If my husband were unwilling to appreciate me, perhaps other members of the court would be willing to do so.

"Heavy thoughts, Madame?" Anjou cut into my reverie and I blushed at the thoughts that had been going through my head.

"No, I was thinking about how difficult it would be to make it to her majesty's chambers early tomorrow morning after tonight's festivities." I smiled at him despite myself and I was rewarded with a laugh from the Queen.

"You are dismissed until tomorrow afternoon, Marie. I could not ask for a more attentive servant tonight."

"And what am I? Simply a decoration?" Anjou's mock offense caused both of us to laugh and the Queen rolled her eyes at him in mock disgust.

"Well, you did get us some refreshments, so I believe that you have been somewhat useful. But not as useful as my ladies."

"Perhaps I should visit your rooms more often, Sister, to learn how to serve you better. It appears you have the best attendants in France." The meaning of his words was clear, and I felt a sharp sense of foreboding. I would do nothing to encourage the King's brother to visit me on such a pretense, but once again, I was trapped and had no means of extricating myself from the situation.

We spent the rest of the evening in easy companionship, as I tried desperately to downplay Anjou's obvious ardor. Finally, at two in the morning, the musicians played their last dance, and we were all instructed to remove our masks. The moment was quite anticlimactic for me and I used the end of the festivities as an excuse to find my wayward husband.

I found him once again scowling, but this time deep in conversation with the King of Navarre. While my cousin took pains to greet me, my husband barely spared a glance at me. "Well, I see this bit of frivolity is finally over."

"I am glad—attending the Queen in her condition is quite challenging. She was kind enough to allow me to join her later in the afternoon." I motioned for my husband to place my cloak on my shoulders and as he spun around, he caught the eye of Anjou.

Anjou inclined his head as if the gesture were for my husband, but I knew it was intended for me. I balled my hands and drove my fingernails into my palms as I waited for his Condé's ire. "I wonder what Anjou is up to now." His comment, made so casually, made me realize that he had not noticed the hours that we spent in each other's company. For now, at least, I was safe.

"I have no idea," I tried to appear as disinterested as possible.

"We'll find out soon enough; I'm sure of it."

❧ 5 ☙

Despite the extra hours of sleep, I struggled to make my way from the Hotel Nevers to the Louvre Palace in time to begin my service to the Queen. Upon entering her rooms, I found that she looked even more exhausted than I felt. I felt a bit of relief in that fact; if the Queen did not feel up to attending any more events, then perhaps I could avoid running into Anjou altogether.

The Queen and I spent an hour together as she and her Catholic ladies embroidered altar cloths for the churches of Paris. As a courtesy to my Protestant faith, I was excused from working on the altar cloths, although my skills with a needle were quite good. I was tasked instead to read from the Psalms as the rest of the Queen's suite continued their work. While the Queen took great pains to keep me from feeling like an outsider, activities like these still caused me to feel isolated from the rest of her household.

A few hours into our work, the Duc d'Anjou swept into the Queen's inner rooms, just as he had promised to do the night before. As was just my luck, there was an empty stool beside me and the Duc quickly settled upon it. "Ladies, I believe that I would like to begin my education on the proper attention to be paid to a Queen this very day."

Elisabeth's slight eyebrows shot up, "Would that have anything to do with your election to the throne of Poland?" Faced with an unstable government, the Poles had made overtures to Anjou to take the throne and strengthen the ties between the two countries. Once upon the throne, he would need to marry and secure a Queen of his own. His departure from the court would be a welcome occasion for my husband and the other leaders of the Protestant faith.

"Ah, the negotiations are going very slow, I'm afraid. My mother fears I will never find a throne upon which to sit. Besides," he shot a knowing look in my direction, "the process of finding a suitable bride is not the easiest of tasks."

"And what would your highness be looking for in a bride?" The words tumbled out of my mouth before I could stop them. I don't know if jealousy or stupidity motivated them, but there they were, hanging in the air for all to hear.

He stretched his legs out in front of him and crossed them at the ankles. Appearing to be deep in thought, he scratched his chin. "Well, I would prefer a well-bred French bride to all others, of course. .Alas, I would have to be of one religion and the Poles are Catholics like us. If I were to order her from Heaven, I would wish for a small woman with dark hair, a fair complexion. If it pleases God, I would like a well-educated wife who has no trouble with gaiety. I would need her to preside over our court, of course."

One of the teenage demoiselles let out a peal of laughter. "Good heavens, Monsieur, that sounds like our Marie!" A furious blush covered my entire face and I could have slapped the stupid creature.. I stood up to avoid looking at her or anyone else in the room.

Sensing the tension in the room, the Queen quickly put in, "Yes, but alas the Princess of Condé is married. Brother, you will have to find another ideal woman to be your Queen."

She turned to the ignorant girl and waved her hand to the ones sitting near her, "Girls, would you do me a favor and pick some roses out in the palace garden? I would love to smell them this afternoon." The girls rose and quickly filed out of the room. My gratitude to the Queen for relieving me of the presence of those quacking geese was immeasurable.

Anjou broke the silence moments later, "Madame, I hope you won't think me too forward, but your piety and grace is a standard that any great lady would be wise to emulate." As he spoke, he took olives from a tray and popped them one by one into his mouth.

How did he have the ability to put me completely ill at ease, then follow with a compliment that threw me off balance? The combination was maddening, but I would be lying if I claimed that I did not enjoy his presence. Sensing he had the advantage, he pressed further. "Tell me, Princess, how do you enjoy being at court?"

The subject was a safe one, and I was thankful for it. "I have been lucky to win the Queen's friendship. France is lucky to have such a generous and humble lady." Elisabeth turned to smile at me, embarrassed a little by the compliment.

"Marie has the opportunity to get to know her older sisters. She grew up under Jeanne of Navarre's loving care," both she and Anjou crossed themselves at the mention of my late aunt. "Now she has time to get to know her family."

"And you are living with your sister, are you not?" I was surprised to hear that he knew so much about my living situation, but I suppose the court's penchant for gossip meant that no topic was off limits.

"Yes, my husband and I have happily moved to the Hotel de Nevers during the wedding celebrations so that we can relieve the strained accommodations in the palace." The Duc's grandfather, Francis I had decided to turn the former fortress of the Louvre into a palace and his son and grandsons worked constantly to bring the structure up to royal standards. That work meant continuous construction and half-filled rooms that could only accommodate a typical sized court. The amount of wedding guests in Paris that August had spilled out of the city's walls and into the surrounding countryside.

"I do so enjoy spending time with both Louis and Henriette. In fact, I don't think that I spend enough time with them." I held in a breath—was he once again making plans to rendezvous with me for less than honorable purposes? I prayed not. When my husband caught wind of Anjou's plans, he would be furious.

"I'm afraid that their home is bursting with people right now. You would be lost in the crowd. My husband is entertaining members of our faith and some of our other relations."

"Yes, space is at a premium in Paris these days." His comment seemed so offhand that I barely took any notice of it. It took most of my resolve to keep the blush that crept up my face from spreading to my hairline and betraying my discomfort. The fair complexion that he had praised earlier worked to my disadvantage.

❧

WHEN I RETURNED TO MY SISTER'S HOME THAT EVENING, MY husband met me at the door of our bedchamber. He paced the room, and I prepared for a lecture. Did my husband know I had spent the day with Anjou? To my surprise, his agitation was not directed towards Anjou or me. "Marie, I insist that you stay home for the next few days."

"Whatever for?"

"We have heard rumors today that there is a credible threat towards Protestants. We don't know who they will target or when they will strike. For your safety, you must remain in the house at all times."

I wanted to protest that he was becoming more and more paranoid, but my relief in his failing to discover the time that I spent with Anjou led me to agree to his absurd demand. I could not control whether Anjou pursued me at the palace, but perhaps he would not make good on his plan to visit me at my sister's home. A few days apart might cool his ardor and I would no longer have to worry about his attentions towards me.

"Fine," for once, I decided that there was no need to argue.

$$\text{❄} \quad 6 \quad \text{❄}$$

To my horror, my husband's prediction turned out to be correct. Only two days later, the following Friday, an attack on a leading Protestant did occur on the open streets of Paris. As the elderly Admiral Coligny walked from a worship service to his lodgings, a shot rang out. The bullet grazed him, but fearing for another attempt on his life, his men dragged him inside and to safety.

No one knew for certain who fired the shot, or in whose interest the assailant acted, but most placed blame at the feet of my brother-in-law, the Duc de Guise, and his mother, Anna. The Guise blamed the Admiral for the death of the previous Duc de Guise and Anna had many times been overhead threatening to take her revenge on Coligny. Whether the Guise had a hand in the assassination attempt or not, this put our family in a delicate situation that we had been dreading for months. While my husband considered Coligny a close mentor, my sister firmly stood in defense of her husband and his family. Henriette and her husband fell in the middle, with both sides eying each another with distrust.

As soon as he heard of the attack, my husband went with Navarre to check on the admiral, staying throughout the night. I would learn later that the leading Protestants formulated a plan to go directly to the King and ask that the guilty party be punished for wounding Coligny. It was short work to discover that the signor De Maurevert, who Coligny had learned months earlier was working undercover for Guise, was the man who fired the shot. The fact that the shot came directly from a window of Guise's mother, implicated him further. As soon as Henriette and my brother-in-law heard of this, they insisted that I remain in their home and admit no guests whatsoever. As I planned to avoid Anjou for the sake of propriety, I readily agreed.

The next morning, the twenty-third of August, Henriette received a message from my husband that Coligny's wounds did not seem to be life-threatening and after a quick amputation of parts of his fingers he should make a quick recovery. Condé added that he and Navarre were meeting in Navarre's chambers to discuss what they would say to the King and not to expect him. By that afternoon, I felt terrible, and I went to bed, caring very little what went on around me. My lungs felt heavy and congested, a problem tha had plagued me since I was a child. Usually, this condition occurred during colder months, but the excitement, stress and lack of sleep lead me to feel weak. I was asleep before the sun set on that day, oblivious to what was transpiring at the nearby Louvre palace.

❧

HOW CAN I DESCRIBE THE HORROR THAT TOOK PLACE THE NEXT morning, that Sunday, as the people of Paris were supposedly going to church? In truth, I can tell you nothing about it firsthand. I witnessed none of it, shut up in my sickbed as I was, but later I would hear the gory details from both Protestants and Catholics alike. I think that both exaggerated, but from what I can reason out, the King that we had put our trust in to offer us safe passage and hospitality turned on the Protestants and ordered the mass killings of those of our faith.

Why did he allow it to happen? His mother and her allies were later blamed; the guilt having passed from Guise alone to the woman who wore her son down with the threat that the Protestants would quickly kill His Majesty in retribution for the attack on Coligny. There were many whispers that Catherine and even Anjou were behind the plot against Coligny; and to Save Catherine, Coligny and his followers were slaughtered. Whatever the truth of that day, when I heard of the Protestants cut down without regard to their age or sex, I wept and my condition worsened by the day. I may not have been the most ardent follower of the Reformed religion, but no man or woman deserved to be slaughtered on the feast day dedicated to St. Bartholomew.

My first concern upon hearing of the slaughter, was to enquire about the condition of my husband. Henriette came to my bed and wiped my brow. After turning to give me a sip of water, she held my hand. "Condé and Navarre are safe; in fact, they are both in the King's bedroom for their protection."

Relief washed over me. "Thank God." I sank back in the pillows.

"Dearest, they aren't completely out of danger."

That caused me to worry anew. I struggled to sit up. "What do you mean?"

"The King has offered them a choice: they can convert to Catholicism, or they will be executed."

My blood ran cold. "The last thing that I expect Condé to do is to convert to Catholicism. Do you think Navarre will?"

She shook her head, "I have no idea. Guise and my husband argued for both of their lives and hopefully, in gratitude, they will agree to take the King's offer."

"Gratitude? You think that denying their beliefs is a show of gratitude? What about their souls? Are they to sacrifice them to the wishes of a King who betrayed them?"

Her expression darkened, "Careful, Marie—there are countless bodies of Protestants lying in the streets of Paris. Even some Catholic nobles have been cut down. Now is not the time to speak against the King."

Too weak to argue with her, I instead asked her when I would be allowed to see my husband. No matter how strained our marriage might be, I desperately wanted to speak with him, to hear from his lips of the unimaginable choice that he faced.

"Officially, they are under house arrest and are not allowed to speak with anyone, especially a Protestant. You will most likely not be allowed to see him until either he or you convert."

There it was—I was also to be offered the Devil's bargain. Would I take it, or would I remain steadfast in my professed faith? Would my husband stand firm or would he Save his life at the expense of his soul? Worse still, what if one of us took the offer while the other refused? The hangman's noose might not part us, but we might never meet in Eternity.

※ 7 ※

I spent the next few days begging ill health as I awaited news from my husband. Before, I had chafed at the idea of him ordering me about, but after the massacre in the streets of Paris, I wished for nothing other than to ask his advice. I could not stand the idea of us being parted at such a time.

My days in my sickbed were not without incident—I was treated to the unexpected visit of my sisters' confessor, an Italian priest who made every effort to sit with me and spend part of the day discussing issues of faith. At any other time in my life, I might have welcomed the opportunity to satisfy my curiosity about the Catholic faith, but separated from my husband and worried as I was about his safety, I deeply resented the intrusion. I was not a stupid woman, and I knew that his "visits" were initial efforts to convert me.

August turned into September and I finally received word that my husband and the Navarre were safe, but both were stubbornly refusing to abjure their faith. The word came by my sister Catherine, who unlike Henriette decided not to mince her words with any hesitation. "Marie, the King, is growing angrier each day—and if they do not give into his demands, they may both be killed."

"But I thought your husband and Henriette's both argued that they should be Saved."

"Yes, Saved so that they be given the chance to convert. This was the only reason the King agreed." I knew that there was more to it. The King's reasoning couldn't have been so simple; he and his mother wanted to keep the senior members of the Bourbon family alive to balance the growing power of the Guise family.

"If he does not convert, am I never to see my husband again? Surely the King could not be that cruel."

She hesitated as if unsure of her next words. "Perhaps the Queen could appeal to the King to allow you to see him. We could argue that you could talk some sense into him and Navarre."

"But how could I get word to Elisabeth?" Stuck in the bed as I was, I was in no shape to attend upon the Queen.

"I will have Henriette speak with Queen Margot. They are close enough that Margot will get the message to her."

THE QUEEN RECEIVED THE MESSAGE THE NEXT DAY AND BY THE TIME we sent it, Catherine and I had a solid plan. I would receive instruction in the Catholic faith and would do my best to encourage my husband and cousin to do the same. The King and Queen were relieved that I was willing to convert and sensing that I could influence my fellow Protestants to do the same, I was allowed to speak with my husband in private at the Louvre.

When I found Condé, he looked haggard as if he hadn't slept in days. Likely, this was the case as I had heard that both Bourbon cousins had been harassed to convert almost continually. He sat in a chair, his body deflated.

"Are you hurt?" I kneeled at his side and studied his face. The same face that had annoyed me in the past two months was now a welcomed sight. He gave me a rare smile which reassured me somewhat.

"You know what they are threatening to do to us? Recant or die—as if we were simply some cult of pagans." He banged his fist on the arm of the chair as he spoke.

I took his head in my hands and tried to soothe him. Once I had his ear close to my lips, I whispered to him. There was a guard at the door and I was sure that he was there to hear our every word. "I have agreed to go through with the instruction in the Catholic faith. I have no desire to lose my life or yours. I suggest that you do the same until you can find a way out of this nightmare."

He jerked his head away from me, "You would willingly betray all that our Aunt has taught us? With so little provocation?"

I lost my temper, "Little? Do you know how many of our faith are lying dead right now? Do you not realize that had I not agreed to listen to the catechism, we would continue to be separated? Come to your senses, for God's sake."

"I cannot stand to speak to you. You have broken my heart and if Jeanne of Navarre were here, you would have broken hers as well." He placed his head in his hands and began to sob.

I stood, once again exasperated at my husband's shortsightedness. In a loud voice, I proclaimed, "I am being realistic. You may choose to remain a prisoner, or you can agree to reconcile yourself to the King. It would serve you well to look at your present circumstances before you make your decision." With that, I nodded to the guard and swept from the room. I had no doubt that the guards would make all haste to report my words to the King. God willing, I would be allowed further opportunities to "convince" my husband to convert. Our very lives depended on my ability to do so.

❦

ONCE WORD SPREAD THAT I WAS AMIABLE TO CONVERSION, I HAD several additional visitors to my sister's home. The confessor assigned to me came on a daily basis and despite myself, I enjoyed learning from him. The longer we spoke, the more I identified with the beliefs and practices of the Roman church. I had never been given the opportunity to question my faith before. I found the relative freedom I had to examine my true beliefs for the first time in my life refreshing.

Other visitors to the house caused me more distress, in particular, the Queen Mother and the Duc d'Anjou. Rumors spread that these two Valois were the real architects of the bloody events on St. Bartholomew's Day, but I had little way of knowing if the rumors were true or not. Regardless of their truth, I felt uncomfortable with Anjou's numerous visits. It was not that I felt his presence distasteful; on the contrary, I very much enjoyed his company. I questioned the propriety of his visits to me and the fact that he offered to be a sponsor when I was received into the Catholic Church. I politely refused and asked Louis and Henriette to stand for me.

On the ninth day of September, the King became so enraged by Navarre and my husband's refusal to convert that he dictated a decree for their death. Once again, the Queen heard of his plans and intervened, despite her advanced pregnancy. I knew that I had to act and do so in a decisive manner. Five days later, I was received into the Catholic Church, a penitent and a true believer. My decision had an almost immediate effect of lifting the suspicion of me. I was allowed to return to the Queen's service, which I did as soon as possible. Her child was due in October and I had no desire to miss being there for the woman who had supported me on so many occasions.

Returning to the Queen's service also restored my life to some semblance of normalcy. While the court generally broke into camps of victorious Catholic radicals, moderate Catholics and Protestants, in the Queen's presence, I had a kind of buffer. After my conversion, I spent more time with her as I was allowed to attend daily Mass at her side and to stitch the altar cloths with the rest of the ladies in her retinue. We became closer friends, if that were possible, and during our long hours of conversations, I confessed to her my fear for my husband.

"I cannot thank you and the King enough for your compassion, but I am afraid that my husband is digging his heels in on remaining a Protestant."

She nodded, as always saying little, but understanding everything. "I believe that he must come to the point that his heart sees the way to the church. Perhaps it is a longer road for him, nein?" She had reverted to her native German and her voice broke with genuine emotion.

"I hope to continue my visits to him and to aid in the instruction of the church. It is my fondest wish that we are united together in

Paradise." I had initially resented my conversion, yet the more time I spent with the Catholic faith, the more I drew comfort from it. My words were not merely to assure the Queen that I was no threat to the King's reign. On the contrary, I thought that I could cause Condé to see reason more than a priest ever could.

❧ 8 ❧

My belief that I could convince my husband to convert proved to be a naïve one. Condé remained as intransigent as ever, mocking my conversion as a ruse to stay at court. "How am I to aid the King of Navarre in leading our people if you have gone over to Papistry under my very nose? What kind of resolve does that show, wife? What kind of faithfulness? You spend a few months at court and your head can be turned by fripperies and baubles?"

My face hot, I shot to my feet. "As always, I offer you an opportunity to Save your life. It is no fault of mine if you are too pigheaded to see the truth. The King has kept his resolve for so long; I'm sure that he will be willing to keep you here." Both he and Navarre were still being held under close watch a month after they were given the choice of death or conversion. The longer they held out, the more I feared that even my powerful brothers-in-law could not protect him.

Standing before the door, I turned to face him. His face was as resolute as ever. "Do you want me to become a widow? It's less than a year since your father passed. You do not even have an heir to which to pass your title. What would become of me?'

He released a heavy sigh. "I'm sure that you will manage without me." He said no more, but I waited for a few minutes. Fed up with his sullen behavior, I knocked on the door and marched out the door. He would not see the tears that welled in my eyes.

⚜

THE TRUTH WAS, I COULD DO VERY WELL WITHOUT HIM. A wealthy, titled Catholic widow was a much sought-after commodity at court. Like Navarre and my husband, I was a Bourbon and Catherine was determined to keep at least some of us alive to check the Guise power. During the last King's reign, the Guise had run roughshod over Catherine and her eldest son, virtually ruling the country and she never forgot them for their coup. Before Admiral Coligny's fall and death, the Coligny family had provided a Protestant counterweight to the Guise, and we Bourbons were the only family left that could compete with them for power and influence at court.

If I was a cynic, I would assume that this was the reason why the Duc d'Anjou was determined to spend so much time with me. My sister, Catherine had been previously married to a major Protestant Lord, widowed young, then snatched up by an influential Catholic. Why would Anjou not assume that I was just as ripe for the taking? As, I am not that hard-hearted, I assumed that the feelings Anjou displayed towards me were as sincere as those that I was developing for him.

Within the quiet walls of Elisabeth's apartments, we sat, the Duc as solicitous towards his sister-in-law as he had been the night of the banquet. Perhaps motivated by so base a feeling as jealousy, I decided one day to probe the Duc's plans for his marriage.

"I am told, Monsieur, that you have in the past courted the Queen of England, is it not so?"

He nodded, a wistful look in his eye. "It's true—Elizabeth, and I were very close to becoming man and wife."

"So," I plucked a stray thread from the altar cloth the Queen and I were working on, "why did you not go ahead with the ceremony?"

He raised his eyebrows dismissively, "Well, for one, she is not of our faith. I cannot be united with a heretic."

"But your sister was."

"She is not in line to the French throne, as I am. Until the birth of the King's son," he swept to his feet and gave the Queen a very courtly bow, "I am heir to the throne. France must be secured and cannot be ruled in any way by a woman."

"And it was Elizabeth's religion and her status as the Queen that barred you from marrying her?" My voice sounded high and tight, even to my ears. I cursed my inability to keep the jealousy out of my words.

"There are too many women in France who are her superior, many of them found under my very nose." He gave me a look that promised more than mere friendship and I knew at once his intentions were more than flirting.

"And will you search France for a bride now?"

He threw up his hands. "I would prefer a French wife, how could I not? But as my dear sister knows, for a prince, it is not the easy to pick a wife."

"True, I knew as a girl that I could be shipped off to the furthermost corners of Christianity and I could say nothing about it." The Queen tried to keep the wistfulness out of her voice, but in her condition, her moods would suddenly swing. To break the dark turn the conversation had taken, I rose to get her a drink. After assuring that she was fine, I returned to my seat.

"If my mother would simply see that it is best for me to choose my wife, she would make my life much easier." He tapped on his knee with his finger, the motion almost hypnotic.

"Ah, is there another marriage in the works?"

"Yes." he spat out, suddenly petulant. I did not like this side of him. He seemed less of a man and more of a toddler at this sudden change of mood. "She is determined to make inquiries of the Swedish court. The entire country is a frozen block of ice and I have heard that the women are barely more than simple farmers." He shuddered at the thought.

I thought back to the day I saw him standing beside Margot, the splendor of his outfit almost outshining the bride. A simple-minded wife would drive the Duc d'Anjou to the point of madness. Despite myself, a giggle escaped my lips. He turned to me, outraged.

"Forgive me, Sir—it's just the idea of you being shut up with a woman wearing coarsely spun wool seemed perfectly ludicrous to me." I held out a hand to him in an attempt to sooth him. "I would never wish an unhappy marriage upon anyone, even my enemies."

He looked at me, the sparkle returning to his eyes. He was up to some mischief, but I could not tell exactly what. "Indeed, well, at least I can count on your support, Princess."

THE DUC'S VISITS CONTINUED WITH REGULARITY AND THE QUEEN prepared for the birth of her child. October opened with only a faint break from the oppressive summer heat, although we all welcomed a respite from the suffocating humidity that had hung over Paris since that bloody August.

I moved my lodgings from my sister's home to a suite of rooms adjacent to the Queen's at the Louvre. We knew that at any moment, her labor could begin and she was determined that she would have Madame de Sauve and myself near her when the time came. I had no further contact with my husband, although the confessors the Queen mother sent to him gave me regular updates of their attempts to convert him and Navarre to the Catholic church. The death threats from the King changed into a waiting game. Either the King would relent and allow Navarre and Condé to be released, or they would be permanent residents of the royal prisons.

Luckily, my status as the wife of a political and religious prisoner of the King did not prove to be a handicap in court, thanks to the influence of my sisters and the Duc de Anjou. I was received with every courtesy and even the notorious gossips of the French court refrained for the time being from making me into a scandal.

In mid—October, the Queen's labor pains began. As she requested, Madame de Suave and I were present along with the midwife and the Queen's chambermaids. After an exhausting labor, the Queen delivered her first child. Despite our hopes, the first child of Charles IX and Elisabeth of Austria was not to be the heir for which France had prayed. The tiny baby was a girl, and the Duc d'Anjou remained his brother's heir and the first gentleman of the court.

AFTER THE QUEEN RECOVERED FROM THE BIRTH AND WAS churched, I returned to my sister's home at the Hotel de Nevers. We had not made any plans about my lodgings after the wedding of Margot and Navarre and without a husband by my side, I had little option other than return to my sister's home. Thankfully, both Henriette and Louis were more than willing to take me on as a houseguest.

I had assumed that by staying at Henriette's home, it would make it difficult for Anjou to make regular visits to me. On the contrary, he made daily visits to me, stopping for the flimsiest and most obvious reasons. At first, he claimed to be interested in my progress as a new Catholic, but I knew exactly where his true interests lay. Louis considered the Duc a protégé and began advising him in governance if the Poles decided to make him their new sovereign. The more time I spent with Anjou, the more I realized what we shared in common. In place of my dour and plain husband, the Duc chose to dress in the most fashionable clothing of the day. He carried an air of elegance and authority that Condé never could. Anjou looked like a prince. Despite myself, I fell in love with him during those days. In my loneliness, my tongue loosened around him and Anjou became my confidant during those long weeks that I worried over my husband's fate.

"I have lost my ability to influence my husband. We are not married a year and I would have more luck speaking to a stone wall." Anjou kept pace with me as I marched through the gardens of the Hotel de Nevers. I enjoyed his boundless energy during our walks together.

"Perhaps it is for the best. Perhaps fate has intervened to send you towards a greater destiny?"

His words caught my attention, "What greater destiny?"

"If it is Condé's wish that he end his days mired in heresy, it is best for his soul that he be delivered to his Lord. You would be free to make a more suitable match with a loyal Catholic Lord."

I shook my head, "No, I made my vows between God."

"But that was in a Protestant ceremony. In the eyes of God and the Church, the two of you are living in sin. I beg you, sweet Marie, have a care for your soul and ask His Holiness for an annulment. Given the circumstances, you are in; he will not deny you a release."

Guilt pricked at my conscience. "But what about Condé?

Anjou took my hand, encircling it with is larger, warmer ones. His touch sent a thrill up my spine. "Condé will have to answer to God for his sins. If he chooses to die as a heretic, he has no right to drag you to the depths of hell with him."

Was he right? Would my husband drag my soul to hell? Or by giving up on him, was I the one Condémning him to hell?

❧ 9 ☙

Scarcely a week after my interview with Anjou, as October slid into November, a messenger arrived at the Hotel de Nevers bearing a message for me. Expecting a letter from the Queen or perhaps a note from my husband, I shut the door to my bedchamber and opened the missive. What I discovered caused me to pause. I beheld a poem, written by Phillip Desportes, a noted poet and a favorite of the Queen Mother. The poem told the tale of Eurylas and Olympus and carried the title of "A First Adventure." I could not fail to notice that the two characters in the story were meant to represent Anjou and I, and despite myself, I felt a pride in knowing that someone had put our relationship into verse.

While the poem carried all the characteristics of Deportes, there was no doubt that Anjou himself had commissioned the work as a veiled way to declare his feelings for me. This must be what a genuine courtship felt like. I was not unaware that both my sisters had lovers, but I confess that before that day, I could hardly understand why they did so. I felt giddy and a warm glow spread throughout my body. It was like standing in a sunbeam, but the warmth of the sun was contained within my body. This, happy feeling, then, must be what being in love with someone must feel like.

Did I feel guilt in those early days? I must confess that I did not. Anjou's warning that Condé and I both faced the wrath of hell for our illegal marriage caused me to fear for my soul. My husband may not have worried about the fate of his soul, but I was terribly concerned for mine.

A royal prince felt love for me. Dare I hope that I could begin another life with him? What would life be like with a man who cherished me, adored me and gave all outward signs that he wished to spend his time with me? Such a marriage would be so unlike the one I had with Condé. I began to resent the fact that the marriage with Condé had been forced upon me by my aunt and with no more consideration for our compatibility than our shared religion. Now that singular reason was no longer valid, and I had the opportunity to grasp happiness for myself.

It was this promise of future happiness that caused me to indulge the Duc d'Anjou wholeheartedly in his pursuit of me. Did I consider the scandal that my behavior would cause? My husband had lingered in a royal jail since the end of August, holding my status at French court in limbo. Also, if Anjou was correct, and the church did not recognize my marriage to Condé, I was guilty of no transgressions against a man to whom I was not lawfully wed.

My husband was by no means ignorant of the goings on outside of his prison within his apartments in the Louvre. The Queen Mother herself took joy in telling him of my happiness in converting and I have no doubt that either she or another mentioned of the time I spent with Anjou. By the beginning of November, Condé started to fade from my mind as if he never existed. Anjou and I began to see one another in more public places, chatting at the tennis court or walking alongside one another as we exited Mass. Buoyed by his suggestion of an annulment, I began to picture a life with him more clearly. As our recklessness grew, however, so did the resentment of the rest of the court. Our affair came to a head one crisp day in early November.

The Duchess of Montpensier, only sister of the Duc de Guise, became the unlikely catalyst for the open scandal of exposing our relationship. Although the entire court knew of Anjou's visits, none dared to speak of it openly until she dared to do so. Linking her arm in

Catherine's she called out in a singsong voice. "Ah, the sweet honeyed lips of my love, which doth rain kisses down my neck. Like the warmth of your arms, encircling me in my bower."

I stopped cold; I had heard those words, but there was only one place that I could have heard them from—the poems composed by Desportes. When I read them, they seemed poetic and romantic, but their words were very much divorced from reality as neither of us had made an attempt to make our attraction physical. They were the words of an admirer to his lady. Coming from Montpensier, they sounded lewd.

Turning, I faced my sister and the foul woman beside her. The only way that she could have heard those words would be if my room had been entered and my private papers rifled and stolen. My immediate suspicion fell upon Catherine, but once I looked at her face, I realized she was just as horrified as I was.

My sister pulled her arm from Montpensier and clapped her hand over my shoulder. "Come, dearest, don't' make a scene."

"It already is a scene," my face hot with embarrassment and anger. I had been betrayed. The assembled group in the garden fell deathly quiet as if none of us knew what to do next. Montpensier, however, took the opportunity to continue.

"I wonder what Eurylas' poor lord and husband would say about Olympus sneaking into her chambers every night while he lingered away, chained up in the King's, that is, the gods' prison. One might say that Eurylas delighted in the opportunity to cuckold him."

Before I could say a word, Catherine stalked towards her sister-in-law, "Silence, you snake! I'll have you whipped and sent off to the country-side before you can say another word." To her credit, Montpensier blanched, but while the exchange diverted attention away from me, I felt it moments later returning to me. Still, in my horror, I had lost the ability to speak and Catherine pulled me away, out of the garden.

Catherine acted immediately, calling in her husband. In her bedchambers, she railed against Guise's foolish younger sister. "It is one thing to humiliate my sister, but is she ignorant enough to alienate the Duc d'Anjou in public? Is our marriage not enough to Save the

Guise family from the hangman's noose? Must your sister put your entire family back in line for execution at every turn?"

Guise exhaled a long sigh. "My sister is not the smartest woman at court. I'll grant you that. I will speak to her."

"That is the least I expect you to do, as you are the head of her family. I told her I would have her whipped and I think that in this case the action is warranted."

He threw up his hands, "So what would you have me do?"

"Tell your insipid sister to stop provoking Anjou and to stop doing it by humiliating my sister."

"She's only following my lead; the spoiled boy has heaped humiliation upon me for years."

My sister's face turned a shade of red I had never seen before. Whirling to face her past few months husband, Catherine spat, "And that 'humiliation' includes having to marry me to Save face when you were barred from marrying Margot, no?"

That last jab hit Guise in a most tender place. We all knew that Guise would be Margot's husband had the Queen Mother not checked his power play in attempting to marry into the Valois family two years earlier. Despite the separation of the former lovers, my sister still harbored a suspicion that Margot and Guise remained lovers.

"We all do what we have to, to survive at court, my dear," he gave a sarcastic bow to his wife, whose face still looked murderous.

"I believe that my family has done more than enough to Save the Guise from destroying yourselves. I won't have my sister drawn into your feud with the Valois."

"And what are we to do about Anjou?" His question hung in the air, one that I had not found the answer to during the heady past weeks of our infatuation.

Catherine exhaled a long sigh, "I doubt that there is much we can do."

The next day, The Duchess of Montpensier departed for the Guise lands to the east and I exhaled a sigh of relief for her absence. Catherine and I had assumed that our silencing of Montpensier would be the end of the scandal, but instead, it pushed it further underground. When I entered rooms, I noticed the gossip stopped, and as I waited on the Queen, I noticed prying eyes upon me. I was no longer an object of pity; I was a topic of scandal.

The unfairness of it all infuriated me, I had made no moves to start an affair, and the verses were at his urging, yet the court viewed me as a harlot. For his part, Anjou seemed unmoved by the court's behavior, and he continued to visit me on an almost daily basis. For my protection, I insisted on having either of my sisters beside me at all times, hoping that the fact that Anjou and I were never alone would silence the wagging tongues of Paris.

As Catherine and I walked one early morning from Mass, I looked down to see that our pace was in rhythm, something that young girls would do at play. "No matter what the gossips may do to me, I am relieved to have an excuse to spend so much time together."

"Was it so bad in Navarre with all of those Protestants scolding you?" Regret at the fact that we had not had the opportunity to grow up together washed over me.

"Actually, no. Aunt Jeanne was incredibly loving towards me. It was hard to tell that I wasn't her daughter."

"Given her penchant for sermonizing, I'm surprised she didn't take every opportunity to tell you how grateful you should be for her taking you in." As soon as she said it, she winced. Before she could apologize, I stopped her.

"Protestantism may not have been for me, but I never lacked for a mother in my life. Now, a beautiful older sister, yes. Cousin Catherine was a wonderful younger sister, but to find someone to boss me around, I had to come to France."

She threw her head back, laughing. "Henriette is that good at ordering you around? I shall have to tell her that." I squeezed her hand, and we fell into a companionable silence.

"Your Highness!" One of my pages called to me. Turning, I saw the boy running at full speed.

"Whatever is it?" Visions of my husband marched to his execution flashed in my head and I felt momentary guilt for our levity a moment earlier.

He handed me a message, and I hurried to unfold it and read its contents. It was a letter written by my sister's confessor. Of his volition, my husband had decided to convert to the Catholic faith. I stared at the message, rereading it several times.

"What is it?" Catherine's face was grave, her concern showing in her eyes.

"He's going to become a Catholic." I was unable to keep the disbelief out of my voice.

Catherine tried to force cheerfulness, "So, I guess he will be returning to you, then."

"Yes, returning to me..." But, did I want him?

My husband and Navarre had had a change of heart, and

both had decided to embrace the Catholic faith. Like me, they received instruction in the catechism and in late November, both were received into the church as repentant sinners. I have no doubt that my Aunt Jeanne's heart broke at the sound of both of them renouncing their affiliation to Protestantism since unlike me, their devotion to Protestantism seemed to be genuine.

I attended the service in a daze, worrying how Condé's reappearance in my life would affect me and what I would do about Anjou's attentiveness. For that matter, what was my relationship to Condé, since we had married as Protestants and not as Catholics in good standing? Were we to remain man and wife? Did I have the freedom to choose another marriage? Could Anjou and I be together? My heart leapt at the thought.

After the celebratory Mass, I hurried to speak with Anjou, to tell him of my thoughts. I found him standing next to Condé. As I approached, I could not make out their words, but once I was within earshot, my heart sank.

"Ah, now that you are a part of the True Church, nothing is barring your way to serve the King in his fight against the Heretics."

My blood froze, was Anjou suggesting that a Bourbon make war against his own people, his own family?

My husband turned his face away from me, his voice tight. "I would never give His Majesty reason to doubt my loyalty or my sincerity."

"Loyalty? My brother will be pleased to hear that you value loyalty so highly." Anjou's voice became a sneer and I could feel the hatred between the two men. Neither of them turned to acknowledge me.

"Yes, without loyalty to one's vows, what are we? No better than a crude animal rutting in the pasture?" His meaning was clear, and I began to seek a way to escape the two of them.

"You might find your dedication misplaced, My Lord, given the events happening in Paris these days."

"Doubt it not; I plan to hold on to everything that is mine and defend it against anyone who would dare take it."

I caught the Queen's eye and hastened to her side. So, Anjou's flirtation with me had been nothing more than a way to get at my husband. I had been making a fool of myself, daydreaming that his feelings for me were genuine. Tears stung at my eyes.

"Marie, isn't it wonderful?" Mistaking my tears for those of happiness, the Queen embraced me.

"Yes, it truly is."

"I am so relieved that your troubles are over. Our prayers have been answered, yours and mine."

✦

THAT EVENING, I SAT IN OUR BEDCHAMBER AT MY SISTER'S HOME, attempting to garner some heat from the fire. A click alerted me that my husband was entering the room, and wordlessly, I rose to greet him.

"As part of my bargain with the King, I have written Rome on both our behalf to seek the Pope's forgiveness for marrying outside of a Catholic rite."

"Does that mean that I am still your wife?" I could not tell if the idea comforted me or not.

"We are to marry in two weeks according to Catholic rites. The King has given his permission, and I see no reason to do so with any delay."

"Are you to depart with Anjou's army, then?" I wrung my hands, desperate for any change of topic.

"We leave in January. For La Rochelle."

"Henry, you cannot be a part of a violent assault on your own people!"

"You forget, Madame, that we are both Catholics. Is it not our duty to exterminate Heretics?" He lingered over me, his voice growing higher with every word.

"If you had no desire to recant, then why become a Catholic?"

He snorted. "It was my only option. My wife was here, playing the whore with the Duc d'Anjou. I figured I might as well get out of prison before she gave him a bastard."

Had he slapped me, he would have wounded me less. I turned my face towards the fire so that he would not see my tears. "I have played the whore with no one. You can ask my sisters. I remained faithful to you, even when you left me vulnerable while you stayed imprisoned by your own stubbornness."

He pounded the table with his fist, "And now I am out of one prison and into another one. Perhaps I Saved my life, or perhaps not. I doubt not that I failed to Save my own soul."

Word spread immediately through the court that we were to remarry and in the intervening time, my waking hours were spent with Condé close by my side. Determined to show to the world that I was his, he accompanied me to every ball and event, not once allowing me to leave his side. I appealed to the Queen that I was failing in my duties to her, but mistaking my pleas for the false protestations of a bride in love, she only told me "Marie, you deserve to spend time with your husband. After your separation, it will do you good to get to know one another again."

I had worried that Anjou would take the opportunity to stroke Condé's jealousy by openly flirting with me or by a few well-placed poems, but I heard nothing from the prince. Perhaps I was right and his attention towards me was merely a ruse to stir up mischief against Condé and the Bourbons. Anjou's time was devoted to planning the New Year's siege of La Rochelle and I scarcely even saw him in the days before my second wedding.

The day of the ceremony dawned, cold and black as if Heaven itself voiced its objection to our second union. The Pope had readily sent his blessing for the ceremony and the Cardinal de Bourbon, our kinsman, was to perform the ceremony. Unlike our day in Blandy, there were a few of our lifelong friends in attendance and I carried none of my naïve hopefulness as I walked down the aisle. Looking back on that day, I believe that my husband's motivation for our remarriage was from a desire to exact his revenge upon Anjou, who was responsible for the death of my father-in-law and who had seized the title of Lieutenant General from the Condés.

A confident part of me stood at the altar, wishing that Anjou would appear suddenly to object to the ceremony. If he would not do it out of love for me, at least he would do it for spite. Anjou would twist the knife in the ultimate revenge upon both Princes of Condé. I convinced myself that if he did love me, Anjou would Save me from this fate. His silence would indicate that he did not love me, after all. I realize later what a ridiculous bargain I made with destiny and with God as I stood there, but I clung to any hope that I could back out of our marriage.

To my disappointment, however, no one voiced an objection to our vows, not even my sisters. I knew well what they both thought of Condé, but they sat behind me, silent as statues. When I heard only silence, I resolved to go ahead with the ceremony. Voicing my assent, more so than Navarre had at his ceremony to Margot, I, once again, became the wife of the Prince of Condé. If Anjou tried to catch my eye after the ceremony or during the banquet that evening, I pointedly ignored him. I realized that I had been holding my breath the past weeks, waiting for a declaration of love from him, yet he had artfully given no concrete demonstration of his feelings towards me. His words were simply hollow and meant to perfume the air between us. Not only was I twice-wed to a man I did not love, but I had also foolishly thought myself in love and during the ceremony I had the proof that my feelings were not reciprocated. At least I had my husband's wealth and title to comfort me. As we were now Catholics, he could not be barred from any further favors from the King. As a close friend and lady-in-waiting to the Queen, I would work with him to strengthen our position at court. If we could not be lovers, we would be partners.

We had little time to celebrate our renewed marriage, as

the King commenced a siege of La Rochelle in the bitter cold of December. If the King wished to strengthen his ties to the newly Catholic Bourbon princes, his decision to send them to wage war against their friends and allies was a curious way to do so. I would have thought that forcing them to attack the city would be the perfect excuse for both my husband and Navarre to defect, but apparently, the King was determined to force them to prove that their conversion was genuine. Denied the opportunity to spend time with my husband, I was also unable to move into the Hotel de Bourbon, which was my due as Princess de Condé. I remained at my sister's home as the guest of Henriette and her husband.

"Cheer up, Marie—at least you won't have the pressure of being a new bride on top of running a new household." Henriette's breath puffed in the stark light of the afternoon. Despite the cold, I was determined to walk outdoors and nothing that my older sister said could dissuade me. I was determined to be as obstinate as the rest of the court.

"How am I supposed to begin life, living on my family's charity and sitting in Paris, all but abandoned?" I could hear the self-pity in my voice, but I set my teeth in defiance. Hadn't I been through enough in the past few months?

"Think about it another way: with Henry gone, you have the opportunity to bend the King's ear without Condé's blunt manner souring things." My sister did have a point—my husband purposefully spoke in the most undiplomatic way possible.

"You're suggesting that I use my friendship with the Queen to our advantage?'

"Of course," her brown eyes sparked, "everyone does and you have an opportunity most wives would kill for—the ability to speak without a clumsy husband undoing your efforts."

I considered her words for a moment. My sister had spent more time at court than I and unlike me, she was not bogged down with the moralizing of the Navarrese court. At the thought, I instantly felt guilty. My aunt had taught me the best she knew, in line with her own principles. But here at the French court, I would need to use different tactics.

Before I could respond, a servant approached with a letter. He handed to the Henriette, who broke the seal open. Her eyes widened as she read. A few seconds later, she blushed. "Ah, this is for you, Marie. I suggest that you read it in private." She quickly folded the letter back into its envelope and slid it under my forearm, looking for all the world like a naughty school girl caught snooping.

"Fine, I'll read it later." I had no idea what kind of missive my husband has sent me, or what he planned to complain about, but I had no desire to read it immediately. Lost in my feelings of self-pity, a coughing fit overcame me and I was unable to stop it from shaking my body.

Henriette shot a look of disapproval. "See, I told you that going out in this cold, dry air was bad for your lungs."

I waved away her concern with my hand. "If I stay inside all day, I'll go mad. Do you want that—a madwoman sharing your home?'

She shrugged, "In this court, it would be a novelty."

The letter from La Rochelle sat on the table where I had thrown it earlier in the afternoon. It was not until I readied for bed that I remembered to look at it. The only thing worse than being cursed with an absent, quarrelsome husband was being cursed with a letter from that absent, quarrelsome husband. Suddenly, I longed for the moments when he seemed much further away from me. My shoulders sagged, and I allowed a long sigh to escape my lips as I opened the letter to read its contents.

The letter was not from my husband, after all. It was instead a love letter from the Duc d' Anjou. Anger burned within me as I read the letter which was filled with professions of his love for me and apologizing for his inability to stop my remarriage to Condé. He feared that I did not return his love, he wrote in the letter, and his feared his mother's wrath if he did try to break up my marriage.

Despite his fear, he continued, during the season of Advent, he could not stop himself from professing his true feelings for me. After reading the last line, I stood and crumpled the letter in my hand. A hearty fire blazed in my bedchamber and in my anger, I threw the letter into the fire. As the parchment blackened and crumpled, I felt a sense of self-satisfaction. Anjou had squandered his opportunity and I would not be tormented with declarations of love that came too late.

Determined to remove all thoughts of Anjou from my mind, I decided to take Henriette's advice and use my position at court to advance our own fortunes. In this, Henriette's proved to be a capable role model. Upon becoming my father's heir, she had inherited a large amount of our family's debt and through her shrewdness, had changed it into a substantial fortune. My title of Marquess d'Isles, given me at birth, came with it some property, but my father had done a poor job of managing it. With the Queen's intercession, I secured the King's help in collecting the rents due to me. By the time the New Year came, I was on my way to becoming a wealthy woman in my own right.

The week before Christmas, I received a letter from my husband, filled with his characteristic complaints and criticisms. The siege was going terribly, a fact that Anjou had tried desperately to hide from his brother, the King. Condé related with pride the ability of the populace of La Rochelle to withstand the bombardment from the Catholic army. I was glad to hear of their bravery, yet at the same time, I did not like his recklessness in sending such blunt reports to me. Beneath the pages of my husband's complaints, I noticed another page, written in a familiar hand. I held my breath as I read, but I laughed when I recognized my cousin Navarre's handwriting, thanking me profusely for the pairs of woolen hose I had packed for the both of them.

The winter raged on, bitterly cold and loath as I am to admit it, during those cold nights, I even missed my cold husband. The King granted an increase of my pay as a lady-in-waiting and the Queen and I visited the little Princess Elisabeth as often as possible. As the girl was not the heir to the French throne, there were few restrictions over her upbringing. Despite her reputation for stringently supervising her children's households, Catherine de Medici allowed her daughter-in-law to manage the princesses' household.

In February, the Queen and I sat, playing with the Princess, whose easygoing manner even managed to attract Queen Margot, who willingly played the part of a doting aunt. "Marie, have you heard from your husband?" Margot braced as her niece made a play for her diamond brooch.

"In his last letter, he stated that the siege would likely go on for months."

Margot sighed, "I guess then we will be forced to endure Paris on our own for much longer." Her joy in being left to her own devices was obvious. For my part, I was anxious to begin my marriage, no matter how ill-considered it had been. "I wish I could enjoy my freedom as much as you do, Madame. I think too much time in the Navarrese countryside made me needy for company."

Margot shuddered, "I don't know that I would long for the countryside of Navarre. After the French court, I likely would find it boring. Still," she glanced at Elisabeth, "it would be nice to spend some time as Queen for once."

"I would hate to see you go," a sigh escaped Elisabeth. "I'll still have Marie here for company, though."

Margot nodded, "It's likely, Sister, that we will be forced to enjoy Paris for many more months."

⊗⊱⊗

THROUGH THOSE COLD MONTHS, I CARRIED A SECRET. I HAD BEGUN corresponding with Anjou, despite my initial anger in his letter at Christmastide. Loneliness finally wore at me and I gave into a girlish infatuation with the romantic Duc as he sent me love letters and poems that made my heart soar. Some letters came to me from La Rochelle, while others were apparently composed at court, featuring the same romantic imagery of Desportes. Unable to resist the flattery, I began responding to the Duc, once again, finding in him a confidant and ally.

Finally, in late April, as I returned from Mass, my sister Catherine met me and bowing her blonde head, whispered in my ear.

"Is it true that the Duc d'Anjou, and you have begun a friendship?" My furious blushing gave her all the response she needed.

"How did you know?"

She slowed our pace as we walked out of earshot of the rest of the court. "My husband told me that the Duc recently bragged that he planned to make you his lover. Have you given him any promises?"

I shook my head, "No, we only exchange letters." Deep, passionate letters that made my day when they arrived each morning.

"That is wise—while an affair is nothing at court, I would not advise you to stroke the anger of the Protestants. Their views of 'morality' are, shall we say, extreme?"

I rolled my eyes, "You needn't tell me that."

"Does Condé know about the Duc's letters?"

"If he does, he has not mentioned in his own letters. They are full of petty complaints as usual."

Catherine nodded, understanding my frustration with the dour Condé. "if the Duc returns soon, do you plan to do something to deepen your relationship?"

That was what ate at me. While part of me wanted to explore the passion the Duc offered, still I worried what the decision to enter into an affair would cost me. "What do you advise?"

She smiled, "Henriette and I can give you pointers of managing a jealous husband and a passionate lover. And in your case, your lover will one day become King of France. You could not reach higher. I suggest that you continue to encourage the Duc in his affections." True, my sisters had grown up in the French court, while I was still trying to make my way within it. With my husband constantly enumerating his complaints, it would be wise for us to cultivate a friend within the Valois family. Besides, my heart fluttered at the idea of starting a relationship with the dashing and romantic prince.

Henriette, in particular, proved to be willing to help me in my long distance relationship with Anjou. In those early days of our friendship, I had not made up my mind how far I was willing to allow our interactions to go and I convinced myself that by sheer will, I could resist his physical advances. I suppose it was arrogance, but part of me thought myself morally superior to those who had grown up in the Valois court. I suppose it was an echo of my Aunt Jeanne's teachings. Still, watching several other women fall prey to their attractions to men to whom they were not wed made it easy for me to do the same thing.

Anjou and I fell into an easy pattern, his letters arriving alongside those of my husband's. Convincing myself that I was being somewhat loyal to Condé, I read his dour letters first and after enduring them, I cheered myself up with those from Anjou. At Henriette's suggestion, Anjou addressed his letters to her, the official explanation being Anjou's constant need for loans from my wealthy sister. While Henriette was more than willing to keep Anjou in her debt, even an impoverished Valois prince would not possibly need the amounts that would require the volume of letters that came to the Hotel de Nevers. Eventually, even with Henriette's help, the court learned of our relationship.

⊗

I CONSTANTLY READIED MYSELF TO DEFEND MY FLIRTATION WITH Anjou. We had exchanged mere words, after all, and the court could only accuse us of a passing infatuation. My words to Anjou were measured, hardly the proof of adultery. Even I was appalled, however, at how casually the court looked at our relationship. If anything, it seemed as if most of the nobles supported it. For one thing, Anjou was the Dauphin, likely to inherit the throne as Queen Elisabeth continued to fail in producing an heir. Her misery could be to my advantage and it was only the idea of giving her heartache that caused me to feel guilt in my relationship with Anjou. No one wished to deny the next King of France what he wanted, particularly a King who held Catherine's de Medici in his youthful palm.

Perhaps it was simply that we slipped into the morass of illicit behavior around us. Each week there was a new scandalous relationship and most of them were more illicit than ours. We could not provide the court with jealous screaming as we were stationed on opposite corners of the kingdom. Any angry or jealous words would have to wait until the siege of La Rochelle was over.

In mid-March, Catherine called me to her private apartment, where I dreaded the dressing down I would receive for my conduct with her favorite son. As I curtsied low, memories of the accusations of witchcraft and debauchery Aunt Jeanne had hurled at this formidable woman swirled in my head.

"I am told, Madame Condé, that you enjoy a close friendship with my son, Henri. Is that so?"

My mouth felt thick; many had walked unwarily into the spider web that Catherine wove. My next words would likely determine the rest of my short life.

"His Highness has been kind to me since my conversion to the Catholic church. I am grateful to his and your kindness this past few months." With any luck, throwing myself at her mercy would soften whatever punishment she had in mind for me.

She paced the room, as if lost in thought. "I must say, your sincerity is a model for your husband. It is sad that Condé seems to treasure his soul so lightly."

"His sincerity was to the Reformed faith; it would seem." What was the point in lying to the Queen Mother of France? She knew more than most that my husband came to his conversion virtually at the point of a sword.

"My son writes to me daily," the Queen deftly turned the topic of conversation. Although I was grateful that I would not have to defend my husband further, I knew that the time for a lecture and warning had finally arrived. I held my breath as she continued.

"He tells me that the rigors of war are wearing on his soul. Quite the soldier, my Edouard Alexandre," her voice took on a dreamy quality. "Yet he says that your letters buoy his spirits on a daily basis." At his compliment, I smiled and quickly tried to hide it.

"I see you enjoy speaking with my son, is that not so?"

"Other than my sisters and the Queen, I have few friends here at court. Any friendly face is a comfort to me." I would continue to be honest with her. Too many unwary men and women had fallen into the spider's trap, weaving their way to their death before they were aware that they were in trouble. I would be smarter than that.

"I must say, I am not thrilled at the idea of my son conversing with a married woman. As you know, I deplore immorality in my court."

Her last statement stretched credulity. Catherine de Medici was well known for demanding an outer facade of morality while employing members of her Flying Squadron to seduce any man Catherine deemed a threat to her. My father-in-law had fallen prey to her ladies, yet Catherine would happily deny that she employed a spy network at all. This fluid morality was the duplicity of the French court at work. Was I seconds away from walking into a trap?

"Madame, The Duc and I have a friendship that is as chaste as the one I enjoy with the Queen. Neither of us is guilty of infidelity or any other kind of immorality. When compared with other members of the court, The Duc and I are practically as innocent as babes. I was under the impression that Renee de Rioux was His Highnesses' paramour, not I."

At the mention of the woman who had openly and wantonly thrown herself at her favorite son, the Queen Mother bristled. "The woman's lack of discretion led to her decision to return to the country."

"I would also add, Madame, that the Duc has initiated all of our meetings, not I. I can assure you that I am not a huntress out to snag a royal prey. As with my service to your daughter-in-law, I am ever willing to render my respect to the Valois family."

Had I gone too far? Would Catherine think that my last words were impertinent? I had no idea why I said them, other than weariness from the months of accusations from the members of the court. Defensiveness made me bold, I suppose. On the other hand, I had spoken the truth when I said that neither of us had committed any sin against my wedding vows. Still, given the Queen Mother's reputation, I stood quietly until she decided to respond.

Several minutes passed. Catherine rubbed her chin, ruminating over everything that I had said. Suddenly, she shot to her feet, and I rose to mine in deference to her station. "My son has assured me that his feelings for you are pure and that you are the most chaste of women in France. It is his wish that I keep an eye out for you while you are at court. With your mother and your beloved aunt gone," she crossed herself twice, and I hastened to do likewise," the court can be a dangerous place."

The suspicious woman was gone, replaced by one who more closely resembled a maiden aunt. I had passed a test with Catherine de Medici, but what that test might be, escaped me.

Eschewing a coach, I walked back from the Tuileries to the Hotel Nevers, turning over what had just happened before my eyes. That the Queen Mother had given her blessing for me to continue my correspondence was shocking enough. What was almost beyond my belief was the fact that I had stood my ground before the most powerful woman in France. Apparently, the months alone and without my husband had done some good for me.

Before I realized it, I was standing in the courtyard of my sister's massive home, a stone bench before me. Taking a seat on the bench, I began to formulate a plan. With Condé halfway across the kingdom, he was hardly in a position to stop me. I knew my sisters well enough to know that they would support me. As Catherine had told me months ago, I was in a unique position to further the Cleves and Condé fortunes.

Lost in my thoughts, I barely heard the shouting behind me. "What on earth are you doing out here in the cold? You'll harm your lungs, you silly creature!" Henriette rushed towards me, a gray cloak in her hands. I blinked up at her, an apparition complete with curly blonde hair waving in the Spring wind as she ran. Henriette rarely ran; she mostly glided from ballroom to ballroom. I started to giggle at her, thinking that perhaps my sister was right and I was mad.

She threw the cloak across my shoulders and began tucking it in as if swaddling one of her children. Clucking her disapproval, she tried to pull me inside.

"I need your help," I murmured.

"Yes, you do, you ignorant girl!" She pulled me to my feet and began dragging me inside. Had I spent more time with an older sister, I probably would have rebelled, resentful at being bossed around. Instead, I found it touching. She continued to chide and lecture me as she pulled me into my antechamber. Once she had me inside, she began rubbing my hands and arms as if to warm me.

"Thank God—you aren't as cold as I'd thought. Did you walk all the way from the Tuileries?" As she spoke, she shook her blonde curls even further askew, and I was unable to keep from laughing at her comical appearance.

"Yes, I did. And it's not that cold out, even for April. I've just come from meeting with the Queen Mother."

She expelled a long sigh and took a seat before me. "And what did Catherine say?"

"She gave me her permission to continue corresponding with Anjou."

Her eyebrows shot up. I really must find a way to keep laughing at my eldest sister, but she was making things difficult for me. "Really? Margot told me that she was hard at work getting a Swedish princess for him. I would think that she would be determined to wipe away any trace of scandal."

"Maybe what I told her convinced her that I was not a disgrace." I stood and began to pace the room. Henriette's took my shoulders and shoved me down to a sitting position, determined to make me sit down.

"I would think that Anjou has Catherine in quite a bind. She can never say no to him, no matter how outrageous his behavior. It's more likely that he told her in no uncertain terms that he will have you as his mistress and there is nothing that she can do to stand in his way."

"She would agree to that?"

"He is the Dauphin. He is also the only child that she has been unable to rule. Even Margot is afraid to defy her sometimes. If Catherine alienates her favorite, and he becomes King, she will lose her position as the power behind the throne. So what will you do?"

That was easy, now that I had made my decision. "Since I have spent so many months having to bear the ill effects of gossip that I am the Duc's mistress, I think that I will start to reap the rewards of being his lover."

She cocked her head to the side, "Are you the kind of woman to spend her evenings in another man's bed?"

"I don't know." It was true; I had never considered going through with it. But with Anjou also halfway across France, there was no bed into which to hop. "I could just encourage his feelings and when we see one another, there may not be any feelings. Then our relationship will be as chaste as ever."

Henriette broke into a laugh, "Good God, sister—you're even more devious than I am. I hadn't thought of that."

"The court has forced me to this, branding me a courtesan when I've done nothing. As the Dauphin's mistress, I would be able to control who has access to him and who gets the favors given to the nobility. If he were to become King," I choked at the idea, realizing that if he were to ascend to the throne, Elisabeth would lose her station. She would most likely return to Austria, perhaps to a second marriage.

She grabbed my hand, "Charles has been sickly since birth. His lungs aren't strong, and if he dies without an heir, that is entirely out of your hands. Elisabeth knows this and I doubt that she'll resent you for taking her place. She would hardly begrudge you for taking Marie Touchet's place."

I rolled my eyes to heaven at the name of the King's mistress. At any moment, the woman would give birth to the King's second child and if it were a boy, it would give Elisabeth more heartbreak than my affair with Anjou would. Still, I had no desire to add to her misery.

"You said you needed my help, Dearest. What do you need from me?" The big sister was back, and she searched my face.

"I would love it if you would hold some salons here at the Hotel. Be sure to invite as many members of the court as possible."

Henriette burst into laughter. "I'll speak to Margot and the Duchess de Retz. We'll throw the most dazzling salons that Paris has ever seen."

❧ 13 ❧

As I had assumed, the gossips were more than willing to attend yet another salon thrown by Margot and the Duchess de Nevers. Unlike me, Henriette's husband, Louis was more than prepared to allow the court to roam the halls of his home. A consummate politician and a pragmatist, Louis knew that a well-connected and popular wife meant advancement that constant warfare could hardly bring to their family. Unlike warfare, most of the combatants in the salons survived until the next morning.

The Queen Mother's tacit approval of my relationship with Anjou led to an immediate rise in my status. I quickly gained new "friends" at court and with their dubious friendship came more influence at court. Although the King rallied in late Spring, the court followed the fickle winds of power. The Dauphin was in the ascendency and to curry his favor, one must go through me.

One evening, at a banquet given for the Polish envoys, Catherine clucked over me as if I were one of her children. Henriette took my elbow and led me to an alcove. "She is worried about losing his love and since you have it, keeping you happy is the key to keeping him in her hands."

"She has to be scared of you as well." Catherine gave Henriette a glass of wine. "They've started calling Marie "Reinette.'" *The Little Queen*, now the court looked to me as the leader of the French court. They had called Mary of Scots that when she and Francis II came to the throne. A throne that the Guise family controlled. Was it a sly reference to my sister, the Duchess of Guise? Was I said to be in the employ of the Duc de Guise?

THREE DAYS LATER, I SAT AT THE SIDE OF THE QUEEN MOTHER. THE three matrons accompanying us made us the picture of domesticity, a young girl and her three aunts. As the days passed, Catherine took to treating me more and more like her child. I had no shame in basking in her attention. I was starting to enjoy the power and the immunity that came from her favor. It was a pleasant surprise to find that far from the fire-breathing dragon I had imagined from my aunt that the Queen Mother was instead inclined to be a maternal figure. I started to think of myself as her surrogate child. Perhaps it was easy to do so because I had been the same to my Aunt Jeanne years earlier.

A page appeared at the doorway. "Forgive me, Majesty. An important message from the Polish court." Startled at the news, Catherine dropped the embroidery in her hands. She opened the letter and read quickly. "Get my secretary at once!"

Alarmed, I looked at her face, afraid that something had happened in La Rochelle. Instead of fear, her face beamed. As Catherine's private secretary scurried in with a paper in hand, she clasped her hands together. "It has happened! Nostradamus' prediction has come true! Three crowns for the house of Valois!"

I understood her immediately; the Duc d'Anjou was the new King of Poland.

MY HEART THRUMMED IN MY CHEST AS I STOOD IN THE COURTYARD of the Chateau de Blois. The heat of early July beat down on the lords and ladies assembled that morning, but I cared little about the heat. The Queen Mother stood in front of the group, clasping her hands and craning her neck in the most un-royal fashion. She cared little for decorum; her beloved son, the Duc d' Anjou was finally coming home from La Rochelle to take his place on the throne of Poland. The King had bowed to his mother's wishes and hastily signed a peace accord with the Protestant armies to bring his brother home that much sooner. As the drums and trumpets sounded, we knew that Catherine's work had finally come to fruition.

"Thank God! Thank God and the Holy Virgin, he is home!" I half expected her to jump and clap her hands in glee, but she curbed her enthusiastic behavior before doing so. The gates flew open, and Anjou, at the head of a large and weather-beaten army, rode into the courtyard on a white horse.

"He never does anything halfway, does he?" The King shifted, impatient to get the ceremony over with a soon as possible. The haste with which he arranged the peace was not due completely to his desire to please the Queen Mother. The rivalry between the King and his flamboyant younger brother would resume with Anjou's return to court. The sooner the King delivered the King of Poland to the Poles and out of France's, the happier he would be. Before he could do that, however, he would have to endure his brother's triumphant return.

Drawing his mount directly in front of his mother, Anjou leaped off of his saddle and raced towards his mother. The two embraced, Catherine kissing her son's hands. She cooed loving words to him, oblivious to the rest of the court standing nearby. As the two continued with their private reunion made awkwardly public, the rest of us began to shuffle our feet awkwardly as the King had done moments before.

"Brother, I assume you will want to begin preparations for your trip to Poland?" I heard a barely concealed snort behind me. The King was more anxious to rid himself of his brother than we had thought.

Anjou turned from his emotional mother to face his older brother. Waving his hand, he chuckled, "I still have the dirt of the road on me. And the army," he gestured to the exhausted men behind him, "will need to be taken care of before I go." Striding past the King, whose face had started to redden, he pulled his mother to the side of the assembled crowd.

With Anjou greeted, attention turned to the rest of the men who had entered the courtyard. The awkwardness of the royal brothers was palatable, so it was a relief when Navarre stepped forward and bowed to the King. "It's nice to see the beauty of the Loire again." He bowed to Margot, who barely acknowledged him. Then he turned to wink at me, "there is much to be missed at the French court."

I blushed so furiously that I could hardly meet my cousin's eye. I knew that he was merely teasing me, yet his flirtatious remark made me uncomfortable. Against my will, I began to search for my husband. I found him inspecting a horseshoe with his long-time page. Determined to rid myself of the feelings of embarrassment, I threaded my way past the men.

"Henry, are you all right?" Our meeting would be awkward, no matter how it occurred. I would take the initiative and break the ice between us.

"As well as can be expected." He glowered at Anjou, whose back was turned to us as he accepted the congratulations of the court.

"I can't imagine what it was like, having to go back there; and as the aggressor."

"It was part of the devil's bargain that we made, remember? The one you suggested that I make?" I bit my tongue, determined to avoid getting into an argument with him in front of the entire court. I had hoped that we could reunite and display some level of civility towards one another, but my husband was just as intransigent as always.

I glanced over at my sister, Catherine, who was deep in conversation with her husband, the Duc de Guise. Their marriage was just as strained as ours was, but I was jealous of their ability to put their animosity aside to discuss business. The Guise stuck together as a united front, something that we Bourbons had yet to learn.

Catherine caught my eye and shot me a sympathetic look. I felt an overwhelming desire to grab my older sister and hide under her skirts. Had I been years younger, I would have done so. I was a grown woman, however, and a wife and I did not have the option of hiding from my problems.

A long sigh escaped me and at the sound, Condé turned to look at me with a puzzled look. "You look unhappy, wife. I can't imagine why, since your dear friend, Anjou has been returned to you."

"My husband has been returned to me as well." I hissed in his ear, unwilling to let anyone hear our conversation. How my husband could manage to get my anger up so quickly was beyond me. "Now I would like to return home and begin our lives together."

Condé shot another angry look at Anjou, who was still oblivious to him. "Our household may be a little crowded. Is there even room for me?"

There was no chance that I could keep my cool had I remained standing next to him. I stalked off from him and headed towards Queen Elisabeth. "Madame, if you'll excuse me, I need to return to my apartments."

Perceptive as always, Elisabeth squeezed my hand and looked me directly in the eye. "Marie, I think that heat has gotten to you. I order you to lie down until you feel better." With her permission, I walked into the chateau, willing myself to walk as slowly as possible so that no one could detect my anger. I would have to deal with my husband's childish taunts later when I managed to regain my senses. We were off to a terrible start, indeed.

❧ I4 ❧

The reunited court took a while to get used to one another
once again. When the Protestant princes, the Duc de Guise
and Anjou were gone, most of the tension between the
factions of the court were gone. With them returned, the court
returned to a boiling point, as if it was moments away from spilling
over into violence. As always, there was scheming and illicit behavior,
yet we had enjoyed a brief season of quiet while the Siege of La
Rochelle raged on halfway across the country.

As childish as it was, I endeavored to avoid my husband as much as
possible. Pleading sickness or headaches, I retired to my bedchamber
before my husband finished his daily activities. During the day, I regularly stayed at the Queen or Queen Mother's side to discourage my
husband from isolating me and picking a quarrel. He could not legiti-
mately accuse me of spending an inappropriate amount of time with
Anjou. On the day of his return, I was careful not to be seen with the
Duc. In the days after the army's return to Blois, Anjou spent his days
behind closed doors, meeting with the Polish envoys. Overwhelmed
with his new duties, he scarcely had time to write me any letters,
chaste or otherwise.

Early on a July morning, Condé marched into my bedchamber, startling me. "What do I owe the pleasure of your visit?" I laid my hands in my lap and tried to wait patiently for him to begin.

"I have been appointed the new governor of Picardy. I am to leave for Amiens immediately."

"The King gave you a governorship? That's marvelous!" I meant what I said; the income and influence that came with a royal governor-ship were something of which to be proud. My work to raise our status at court those past months had paid off handsomely.

"You won't be going with me," he added bluntly. "Apparently, the King is concerned that I will use the position to raise an army against him. You are to stay here as a hostage of the sort." He grimaced at the word. I was not sure if he was angrier at the idea of his wife being used as a hostage or to the idea of my staying behind at court.

"It's probably best that I do stay. Catherine's child will come soon." My sister was again pregnant, but given her penchant for taking lovers, I was not sure if the child was her husband's. I wondered if Condé had heard the rumors of the child's parentage. Perhaps he had not, given how quickly the Protestants rose a cry at the loose morals of the French court.

❧

On a sweltering July afternoon, I bid goodbye to my husband in the courtyard of the Chateau St. Germain as he prepared to leave for Picardy. Although the court usually fled the heat of Paris during the Summer for the Loire Valley, the King had returned to Paris. Given the rivalry between the King and his younger brother, it was likely due to the King's determination to remind Anjou of who ruled France and who would soon be packed off to the cold hinterlands of Poland.

Determined to speak to my husband before he left, I took his arm and led him to a quiet spot behind a balustrade. "Henry, I know that you believe that I am your enemy, but I do have both of our interests at heart." I had always tried to be honest with my husband and this was no exception.

To his credit, he did look shamefaced for a moment. Taking the advantage, I pressed further. "I've done my best to keep us in the King's favor these past months and I will do the same while you are in the countryside."

He glanced at Anjou and drew me closer. To an outside observer, we were a loving couple enjoying a few last stolen moments together. "Navarre and I are convinced that I'm being sent there to check the power of the Guise."

That came as a surprise. I knew that Picardy bordered land owned by the Guise. "Is the King softening his stance against the Protestants, then?"

He snorted, "Hardly. He's determined to balance the power of both religious camps and keep the Guise in check."

If that were so, it would make things awkward between my sister Catherine and myself. We Cleves were distant cousins of the Guise, as were the Bourbons. This was the French court, however, and family ties could quickly be disregarded in the quest for power.

"No matter where I worship, my loyalty will always be to my friends and relatives. I hope you realize that."

He turned to me, shocked. "Are you volunteering to act as a go-between?'

I nodded, "Yes. If you would trust me, I can be of value to you. I have the Queen and the Queen Mother's ears."

My husband could hardly doubt the truth of my words. "Very well, I could use a spy in the French court. I'll write to you when it's safe."

His men signaled that it was time to leave and with the briefest touch of my arm, he walked away from me. Perhaps I had managed to get through to him finally. My victory could only help our faltering union. For the first time in almost a year, it looked as if my husband and I had come to an understanding and were finally on the way to becoming true partners.

THE MORNING AFTER MY HUSBAND'S DEPARTURE FOR PICARDY, I entered my brother-in-law's study to discover that he had a visitor. It was the Duc d'Anjou, and the two were deep in conversation. Not wanting to disturb them, I turned and started to leave the room. Seeing me, he and Anjou rose to their feet and gave me a brief nod. "Marie, you're a welcome distraction," Louis winked at me and Anjou gave me a hungry look.

"Monsieur, I had no idea you were here." I gave him a brief curtsey. I had gone into the study to borrow a book, but finding Anjou there made a little uncomfortable. Mindful of my offer to work with my husband, I had no desire to give him the impression that I would cuckold him the moment he left my side.

Anjou's white hands absentmindedly traced the papers he held in his hand. I tried my best not to notice them, but I failed. Seeing the direction of my glance, he gave me a broad smile. "Louis is advising me on my new role as sovereign of Poland. Living in a foreign court can be challenging, as Louis well knows. His advice has been very helpful to me."

"France's loss will be Poland's gain." I tried to keep my voice neutral, but the tremble gave me away. The more I tried to adopt a formal tone towards Anjou, the more I failed in my attempts. I was giving myself away despite myself. I had missed him those long months, and it was evident to all of us.

"The process of setting up my rule has taken longer than I had hoped so that I will need Louis' advice."

"Then don't let me interrupt your meeting. I only came to borrow a book." I turned to leave the room and Anjou hastened to follow me to the door.

"We've finished our business for the day. I can't monopolize Louis' time any longer today." Anjou gave him an elegant bow and Louis responded with a nod of his own. Placing his hand on my forearm, Anjou started to lead me out of the door.

"Highness, I don't want to give you the idea--"

"Idea, Madame de Condé? Whatever idea are you referring to?"

"I don't want to become another man's mistress. My husband and I are completely mismatched, but as a twice—wedded wife, I do plan to honor my marriage vows."

He took my hands in his larger ones. Staring directly into my eyes, he was silent for a moment. "Marie, I have no desire to turn you into a harlot. My feelings for you are honorable. You can rest easy that am not planning to lure you into my bed. There is no need to be afraid of me. Your virtue is too important to me."

I felt at that moment that he was sincere and I relaxed in his presence. The fire between us still burned, but perhaps he was right. We could simply remain as chaste friends and I would do nothing to betray my marriage vows.

"I enjoy being around you and in this court, it's hard to find a woman who does not use her body to advance her prospects at court. The fact that you are different is what drew me to you. It is one of the reasons why I value your friendship."

"I would be honored to count your Highness as my friend, as long as that is all that we will be."

❧ 15 ❧

Satisfied that Anjou would do nothing to blemish my reputation, I continued to relax in his presence. With his return to court, I remembered how easy it was to talk to him and to share my thoughts. The Queen Mother continued to treat me as a beloved daughter and in her presence, the Duc was the powerful portrait of decorum.

Mindful of his upcoming coronation, the court remained in Paris to aid Anjou as he prepared to leave to rule Poland. The King continued to be impatient with his brother's lackadaisical attitude towards leaving France and gossip began to spread that I was the reason for Anjou's reluctance to leave for his new kingdom.

I paid little attention to the gossip, confident that Anjou would do nothing to damage my reputation purposefully. I began to dread the day that Anjou would leave and I would feel more alone than ever. With my husband halfway across the kingdom, our relationship began to thaw, and he sent me a cipher to use during our correspondence. Taking advantage of my position as the unofficial second lady of the court, the Protestant-leaning courtiers and the Anti-Guise factions began coming to me to ask for my husband's support.

As I had feared, Condé's presence in Picardy created a rift between my sister, Catherine and I. While we were always outwardly cordial towards one another, we rarely shared any confidences.. The relationship between both of my older sisters began to disintegrate, as Henriette and Catherine began to argue over our inheritance of our late father's estate. Since I continued to live with Henriette and Louis, Catherine began to assume that I was firmly on our eldest sister's side when it came to their conflict. Alienated from my family, I began to spend more time confiding in Anjou about my troubles.

As we walked back from morning mass late that July, he turned to look at me. "There are storm clouds in your face, Marie. Can I relieve some of them for you?"

"I don't think that I am used to having siblings. Are they always that much trouble?"

He burst into hysterical laughter. I glanced at him, shocked at the uncharacteristic show of emotion. He was usually calm and calculating in his behavior.

"I'm sorry, you are asking a Valois if having a family is trouble? We are experts in causing trouble for one another." He wiped the tears from his eyes and continued to struggle to contain himself.

"Then, how do you suggest I deal with the arguing?"

He pursed his lips and blew a long burst of air out of them. "Move to Poland? I'm sorry, that was in bad taste. If my years at court have taught me anything, it is that your best and only ally is yourself. Others may swear to have your best interests at heart, but no one can watch out for you better than you can for yourself."

"In the end, we are all out of our self-interest?" I tried to sound more innocent than I felt. After all, I had volunteered to be a go-between for my husband and the Protestants left at court. Anjou could never learn that fact and certainly not from me.

He nodded, "Granted, no one schemes more than my family, yet the court is a dangerous place for the innocent and unwary. One grows up quickly here."

My shoulders slumped. Anjou took my hand in his and patted it. "I think that is why I enjoy your company so much. You are not as jaded as the women who have grown up in the French court."

I smiled; perhaps more of my character was due to my Aunt

Jeanne's teaching than I had realized. My husband would laugh to hear that my Protestant upbringing had affected me more than he had initially suspected. Even now, as a devoted Catholic, I could not turn my back on my childhood. Wherever Jeanne was, I was sure she was smiling down on me.

I returned to my suite at the Hotel de Nevers to find a letter from my husband. The cipher he had devised was complicated, yet I was sure that once I had studied it, I could manage to use it successfully. To safeguard our secrets, he suggested that I hide the cipher and burn his letters upon reading them. Both of my sisters were married to powerful Catholic lords and Condé had no desire to risk someone discovering his plans. Given the tense situation between the three of us, I agreed that it was best that I hide my deepest secrets from my sisters.

I spent the rest of the morning practicing our code, frustrated at the beginning, but eventually I managed to compose a letter that would pass by undetected yet be legible once my husband received it. I was under no illusion that my status as a favorite of Anjou and the Queen Mother would place me above suspicion by the spies in the court. No matter how safe I might assume I was, I would have to be vigilant.

In the afternoon, my maid announced that I had a visitor. I frowned, knowing that I hadn't expected to receive anyone. "It's your cousin, My Lady," she bobbed a quick curtsey.

I looked up to see Navarre stride into my room. "This is a surprise!"

"Forgive me, Marie—all those months of war have caused me to forget my manners." His face broke into a wide grin, a boyish behavior that he frequently employed to keep himself out of trouble, or at least to keep himself from being blamed for the trouble he caused. His ruse worked with everyone, including me.

Embracing him fondly, I motioned for him to sit next to me at my desk. "I can help you regain your social graces unless you're beyond all hope."

Crossing his legs at the ankles, he drummed his fingers on the wooden table. For a moment, he was silent, as if considering his next words. "I have been told that you are in contact with Condé."

"Yes, we're communicating much better these days. I had hoped that our relationship would improve, and it looks as if my wish has come true."

He nodded, falling silent once again. "It is refreshing to know that some people at court are happy with their spouse." He was referring to his icy relationship with Margot, a relationship that had not thawed since his return from La Rochelle in June.

"Considering how hard I worked to Save his life, it would hardly do for me to give up on our marriage completely." I could tell that my cousin was working his way towards telling me something, but I did not yet know what that thing was. As children in Navarre, we had been friends, but we rarely shared confidences. I could no more read his expressions than I could a stone wall.

"Would it be unreasonable for me to think that you are corresponding with him during his time in Picardy?" He continued to test me and I decided to wait until he told me the actual reason for his visit.

"We discuss things that any spouses do, cousin." I lifted an eyebrow and looked him in the eye. Folding my hands in my lap, I continued to wait for him to confide in me.

He leaned forward, lowering his voice. Although we were completely alone, I could understand his caution. The very walls of the court had ears and in his position, he could never be too careful with his words. "Condé told me that you offered to send word from Paris to Picardy if need be."

We had at last arrived in the actual reason for his visit. "Yes, I told Condé before he left that I could be of use to him in Paris. Given my position here at court and especially under the Queen Mother's protection, I think that I am more valuable here at court."

"Have you spoken to my sister Catherine lately?" His abrupt change of topic drew my interest. I shook my head, feeling a momentary bit of guilt at the fact that I had been remiss in my correspondence with the Princess of Navarre.

"Catherine has always had my best interests at heart and I think that is something that you both have in common."

I gave him a smile, "Would you like me to write to Catherine?"

He nodded, "Yes, I am sure that my sister would love to hear from you. Princess Catherine must be quite lonely with all of us here in Paris. Sometimes, she does write to me, but I think that my letters are under too much close inspection."

I nodded, continuing to follow his reasoning. "As far as I know, my letters are not being read surreptitiously. If you would like, I could send word to your sister from time to time."

Noticing his expression, I added, "Or I could pass on a message from Navarre to Picardy. Would you like that?"

He brightened at that, "As a matter of fact, Marie, I would be in your debt if you would do so!"

$$\text{❦} \quad 16 \quad \text{❦}$$

While I worked to remain the secret go-between amongst the Protestants in Paris, Navarre and Picardy, not all of my time that sweltering, humid summer consisted of gathering and disseminating information. With Anjou returned to the court, I indulged in his company as often as possible. We both knew that his time in France was limited and we were determined to spend it in one another's company.

The seemingly endless rounds of balls, banquets and fetes held in honor of the upcoming Coronation, gave us the perfect excuse to enjoy our time together. I had feared that Anjou would press to make our relationship sexual, but unlike his contemporaries, he seduced with words and actions, not his body. To the amusement of the court, we continued a relationship of the mind in stark contrast with the clandestine couplings that others indulged in amongst the darkly lit corridors of the palaces of Paris.

As Anjou led me around the ballroom of the Louvre one humid August night, I noticed the Polish envoys standing awkwardly against a wall. "They look severe," I tried, but failed, to catch their eyes.

"They're more boring than the Protestants," he pulled his face into a scowl. His misery was palatable.

"Are you dreading your trip to Poland?'

"It tears me away from you, from my mother and France. How can I do anything other than resent it?'

His admission surprised me. Since hearing of his election to the throne, I had assumed he saw it as a stepping stone to power and the place that he and his mother had always hoped for him. Fate might not give him the throne of France, but it had delivered the kingdom of Poland.

"I hate to see you in such misery," I squeezed his hand, desperate to lighten his mood. "I hated leaving Navarre for Paris after I married Condé, so I can understand how much you will miss France."

He expelled a long sigh, never breaking in the steps of the intricate dance. "Oh, Marie—it is your compassion that I think I will miss the most." He looked deep into my eyes as if preparing to say more. At that moment, the dance ended, and he led me from the dance floor to the dais where the King and Queen Elisabeth sat. The King's face was hard as a stone and he gave his brother a stern look. For his part, Anjou acted as if he was oblivious to the King's anger.

"Back so soon, brother?" Although the comment was meant to refer to his return from the dance, we all knew that the King referred to Anjou's continued delay in leaving France for his kingdom.

"It is my duty to return the Princess de Condé to the Queen," he fixed a courtly bow to Elisabeth, who returned his gesture with a nod of her head.

"Ladies, would you like refreshment," opening his arms wide, he gestured to the Queen and me. His charm was, as always, irresistible. As the King scowled at his brother, the Queen gave him a warm smile.

"Brother, I believe that we have been here before. The only difference is that this time, I can see my feet." Elisabeth was right; it was almost exactly a year since the masquerade ball when Anjou sat attentively at our side. This time, however, I was not so determined to keep Anjou from me. I had grown to genuinely enjoy his company and the knowledge that he would leave me as my husband had been forced to do scarcely a month earlier, filled me with a sudden sadness. There would always be the endless rounds of balls, receptions and masques of the court, but the person who made them all worthwhile for me would soon be gone. I spent the rest of the evening trying to keep my expression cheerful, but I knew that nights like this would soon be a thing of the past. France's loss was my loss, and I resented the Poles for taking Anjou from me.

SEPTEMBER BROUGHT THE CHILL OF AUTUMN AND THE REALIZATION that Anjou could delay his departure for the cold nation of Poland no longer. As the ceremony officially crowning him King grew closer; he became more and more melancholy. His meetings with my brother-in-law, Louis took on a more intense tone and by mid-September, I began to worry that he would work himself until a serious malady.

On the seventeenth of September in the Cathedral of Notre Dame, we stood as the Duc d'Anjou officially became an anointed King. The ceremony, while simple, was beautiful. Catherine de Medici wept throughout the ceremony and I used the event as an excuse to let the tears flow from my own eyes. I was not ready to let the man who had become my closest friend and confident leave me. I gave into my selfishness and my resentment of the uncultured Poles deepened into pure anger.

Dressed in cloth of gold, Henri I, the new King of Poland, looked resplendent. Adding to my misery, I suddenly realized that he would once again start to look for a wife and queen of his own. Unfortunately, I would not be that woman. I was doubly married and the Pope would never grant me a divorce from Condé now. As I stood in the packed cathedral, jealousy for a lady who did not yet exist boiled within me.

After the ceremony, the court celebrated with an additional round of banquets and balls. Adding to my misery, I began to notice that with his elevation to his throne, the new King became less of my friend and more of a divine being from whose presence I was barred. I started to panic, thinking that his new subjects saw me like a common whore, one not worthy of their new sovereign. Anxious to set up a new reign and return their country from the brink of chaos, the Polish delegation established the end of September for their departure from France.

Deep in my melancholy, my health began to deteriorate and my childhood problem with my lungs returned. As a result, I was not there when the former Duc d'Anjou left France for what could be the last time. Henriette stayed by my bedside, hovering over at all hours as if I were one of her children. Once again, I was grateful for her overbearing nature and during the hours that she sat with me, we began to repair the awkwardness in our relationship.

"Are you and Catherine speaking to one another?" I fingered the embroidery on the sheets of my bed. Boredom had long since set in and while I knew that it was a sore subject, I keenly felt the need to have a substantive conversation with someone.

She shook her head and pursed her lips, "No. She returned from her estate in Eu yesterday, but I have not seen or heard from her." If my health improved in time, I would join her on her journey to Joinville. The opulent seat of the Guise family, sat uncomfortably close to Picardy and while I would be well-placed to pass information on to Condé, I was nervous about my part in the espionage against my sister's family. Before Henriette could say more, a knock sounded at the door. One of the maids came in, carrying a large wooden box in her hands.

"Delivery from the Chateau St. Germain, Your Highness." She sat the box next to me and bowed as she left the room. Lifting her eyebrows, Henriette looked at the box, then glanced at me.

"What is this?" Grateful for the distraction from our conversation about Catherine, she was more than willing to stick her nose into my business.

"I have no idea. Perhaps it's from the Queen Mother?'

Henriette snorted, "If that's so, then don't touch it and most certainly, don't drink it." I did not appreciate her levity. For years, many people accused Catherine de Medici of using poison indiscriminately to rid herself of troublesome people. I had never been a bother to Catherine, but could she suddenly view me as a stumbling block to her son's new reign in Poland? I hoped not. I expelled a long sigh, suddenly tired. "Just put it on my desk, I'll look at it later."

But my sister would not be swayed, "Absolutely not! This is the most excitement that you've had in days. In fact," she leaned towards me, "it's the most excitement that *I've* had in days."

A cough bubbled up in my throat, taking me by surprise. "Henriette, I'm not really in the mood for mysteries and surprises. As a matter of fact, I would like to sleep now."

She sighed and rolled her eyes melodramatically. "Fine, have it your way. But I fully expect you to tell me the contents of that box as soon as you open it."

I spent the next two days in bed, partly due to exhaustion and partly due to my stubborn decision not to give Henriette the satisfaction of knowing what the box contained. Once I rose from bed, as my maid set my breakfast, I walked towards the table. As I lifted the cover of the box, my mouth formed an "O" as I saw what for myself what was inside.

It was an exquisite rosary, complete with seed pearls. Their milky iridescent colors danced in the light of the early autumn morning. The piece was a marvel of craftsmanship and I stood for several moments admiring its beauty.

Underneath the rosary was a handwritten note, in a hand that I well recognized. "Keep this close to your heart and always within your hands. As you have always done for me, I hope that it gives your peace and comfort. It pains me to know that I will not have your presence with me. Henri, King of Poland."

I beamed with happiness, a feeling that I had not felt in weeks. Anjou, the King of Poland, had not forgotten me. His thoughtful gift meant that my fears that he might forget me in Poland had been unfounded. Oh, how my heart would miss him, but I would hold his beautiful gift close to my heart until I could see him once again.

The melancholy and dissatisfaction were prevalent in court, even touching the Queen. Despite giving birth to a healthy daughter a year before, she was unsuccessful in conceiving another child. Adding to her misery, in October, Marie Touchet, the King's longtime mistress, announced that she carried the King's child. If the child were a boy, the humiliation for Elisabeth would be unbearable. Ever the princess, she soldiered on, not showing her unhappiness to the court.

As we walked amongst the gardens of the Tuileries one afternoon, Elisabeth's absentmindedly playing with the dog jumping at her feet. "I wonder if I am long for this court, Marie."

That had my attention, "Do you think that the King will divorce you?" I could not bear the thought that I would lose yet another friend and ally at court.

"No, I don't know if the King's health will last much longer." She spoke in low tones; to speak of the King's death was treason.

I lowered my voice, and we quickened our pace, so that we could walk together without being heard by her servants who trailed behind us at a discreet distance. "Is it his mind or his body; or both?" There had been rumors that the King was mentally unfit for the throne before his older brother's death, but of course, none of us would speak of it openly. Questioning the sovereign's fitness to rule could endanger both our lives. Yet, Elisabeth meant nothing of it; she spoke as a loving wife who feared for her spouse's health and happiness.

Her shoulders slumped, "Both, I think that his spirit broke on St. Bartholomew's Day. He constantly cries that he hears the screams of the dying. I don't know if it is out of guilt or some madness coming upon him." Throughout his life, the King had been known to experience convulsions and various fits, but none of them life-threatening. Given Elisabeth's concern, there was a real danger that they were becoming life-threatening. She was not a woman given to exaggerations. If she was concerned, then there was a genuine threat to the King's health.

"If I had a son, then at least we would feel safe knowing that there would be a regency. But as things are now," she shook her head.

"The King of Poland is his only heir," the death of the King was the only event that would bring Anjou back to France. I brightened at the thought of his return. As soon as I warmed to the idea, a worrying thought chased after it. As the new King of France, he would immediately need a Queen at his side.

Elisabeth must have noticed the clouds that crossed my face. Mistaking them for concern over the King, she patted my hand. "Don't worry, Marie; perhaps I'm just worrying too much. It is a wife's prerogative, after all."

I smiled at her, determined that she would not know the exact reason for my sudden change in mood. "I think that to be a good wife; one must worry incessantly."

"How is the Prince of Condé? Here I have gone on about my husband and you are here with yours so far away. I'm sorry—I am being selfish."

I shook my head, "Nothing of the sort. We are friends, after all. What worries you, concerns me." That was more than a little lie, but I swallowed the guilt that came with my saying it.

I RE-READ THE LETTER IN MY HAND TO MAKE SURE THAT I understood my husband's request. Condé had readily agreed to entrust me with passing information amongst Protestants, but this was different. He expected me to use my relationship with my sister to spy on the Guise. My husband must have taken leave of his senses.

Furrowing my brow, I read his letter once again, slowly, as if that would help me absorb his instructions. "I have intercepted messages from Eu to Joinville," he began, naming the county my sister had inherited from our father and the chateau located at the heart of the Guise holdings. "Phillip of Spain plans to give the Guise gold to back a coup that will bar the Ducs d'Anjou and Alceon, as well as Navarre, from inheriting. They're tired of the Valois and want to do away with them. They plan to put the Cardinal Bourbon in their place. No concrete plans have been made yet, but I need you to learn what you can from your sister."

Catherine was due to give birth to her child in mid-December and I planned to accompany her to Joinville for the birth. My offer to join her was part of my plan to reconcile with my sister, not serve as a spy in her home. Even if no one discovered my activities, the guilt would show in my face and mar our reconciliation. We were so close to becoming genuine friends, and I resented my husband's plan to ruin that chance.

"Henry, you ask too much of me."

"Madame?" My page came into my study, ready to take a note at my command.

"I was musing aloud. It is nothing." I dismissed him with my hand. A thought came, unbidden to me: was it possible that either of my sisters had spies planted on me within their own homes?

"Forgive me, Madame, but I come with a note from the Queen Mother." A letter from Catherine could not be ignored. Tearing open the seal, I read her missive.

I was commanded to journey with the King of Poland and his entourage across France to see him to his new kingdom. As the Queen Mother knew that I planned on traveling to Joinville with my sister, she and her son eagerly desired my presence when his progress across to the western border towards the Duchy of Lorraine. We would be within traveling distance to the court for a few weeks, a welcome distraction from the awkwardness I would feel while lodging at Joinville.

"Well, I suppose I will be going to Joinville after all." At least I would enjoy Anjou's company for a few more weeks. The despondency I felt at losing him lifted a little.

❧

A COURT PROGRESSION IS MORE COMPLICATED AND EXPENSIVE THAN the moving of armies and this trip was no exception. Along with Catherine and her favorite son, Navarre and the Duc de Guise followed from Paris to Lorraine, where the Queen Mother's second daughter, Claude was the Duchess de Lorraine. Amongst the throng of nobles and retainers, the Duc d'Alceon and his retainers, Joseph Boniface de la Mole and Annibaile Coconnas were to accompany us. To Margot and Henriette's delight, they were allowed to stay behind in Paris as we started the long, arduous trip towards the border.

The court planned to stay in Lorraine for two weeks. Anjou had fulfilled his brother's wish in leaving Paris, but he was determined not to abandon the kingdom for the one he was to rule. At one of the countless banquets given by the leading men of Lorraine, Mole sat next to me, whispering in my ear.

"He thinks that if he tarries long enough, he will become King of France."

Mole's impertinence annoyed me, "Who?"

"Anjou. Did you not hear? The King has been diagnosed with consumption. It is only a matter of time before Anjou is recalled to France to become her King. If he dallies long enough, he won't have to become King of that barbarous court." A Polish noble walked by, close enough to overhear Mole's gossip. I flinched at the thought of him overhearing our conversation.

"I think you assign too many ill thoughts to the new King." I had no desire for Anjou or Catherine to believe I was disloyal to Anjou. My roles as a spy and courtier both depended on it. Mole had somehow determined that I was a likely ally and friend and had spent most of our trip trying to toady up to me. Despite my ongoing efforts to discourage him, he never stopped his efforts to ingratiate himself with me. In Paris, I heard whispers that Henriette carried on a flirtation with Coconnas, his friend. Perhaps Mole thought that relationship gave him unfettered access to me as well. The man was sadly mistaken; he only made me queasy. I wanted nothing more than to avoid him. When I returned to Paris, I would speak to Henriette about her relationship with Coconnas.

Luckily, I caught Anjou's eye at that moment and shot him a pleading look. Ever the gallant, he turned from his conversation and hurried to my side. "Thank you for keeping the Princess company, sir. I relieve you of your duty."

"Thank you," I hissed in his ear, my intimate gesture drawing the attention of the Poles in attendance. Half of Anjou's new subjects were said to be Lutherans and from what I had observed, they followed the strict moral code that Protestants in France did. Likely, they disapproved of my relationship with their new sovereign, but none of them had the courage to say so publicly.

"He's an odious man, that Mole. Mark my words; he will be trouble."

"He has attached himself to me like a leech." I shuddered, the image causing me to think of the King's illness. Was Mole correct? Was I in imminent danger of losing Elisabeth's presence at court? Tears stung at my eyes.

"Marie—I know! I hate the idea of leaving France. I cannot imagine how terrible it will be without you."

The tears spilled down my cheeks. Unwilling to hide my feelings, I let them fall. "I feel as if my entire world is shrinking. Every friend and ally I have in court is leaving me."

He stopped and took my hands in his. "You have my promise, that I will do everything in my power to ensure that you don't feel deserted. I will write to you every day and I will make sure that my mother continues to protect you like her daughter."

"I will hold you to that, Majesty." I curtseyed to him, as his due as a sovereign. He kissed the top of my head as if in a blessing.

❧ 18 ❧

In late November, I had to take leave of both Catherine and Anjou as I settled into the Chateau Joinville to aid my sister in her lying in. "I only have one birth to recommend me," I smiled, referring to Princess Elisabeth, now a year old.

She waved her hand, "Don't worry—I usually go through the process quickly. More than likely, you'll be back in Paris in a few weeks."

"I have no plans to pack up and desert you." No matter what else, I wanted to use this time to connect with my sister. The months I spent as a guest at Henriette's home meant that our relationship overshadowed that of the one I had with Catherine.

I stood and walked over to the nightstand where Catherine's Book of Hours lay and I began to look through it. "The miniatures are beautiful." It was true, the artisanship of the saints was remarkable. As I continued to admire them, however, something seemed amiss. I glanced at my sister.

"Catherine, why do some of these saints look familiar? Do I know the models?'

A furious blush spread across her face and down her neck. I had to know what caused that blush. "Catherine? What is it?'

She bit her lip, "You do know a few of the models. I, on the other hand, have known all of them to a rather remarkable degree." A giggle escaped from her throat. She was up to some naughtiness.

"What do you mean?"

She cleared her throat. "It's a way of remembering them."

"Who?"

"My former lovers."

"Catherine! For shame!"

She waved her hands in the air, "Don't be such a prude, Marie,"

"Prude? Catherine that is sacrilege!"

"Why? All saints were at one time, sinners. I'm merely making that point private."

I couldn't help myself; a giggle burst out of me. "You should be ashamed."

"Marie, it is to your disadvantage that you grew up Protestant. Thank God you converted." She laughed, caught up in her joke. I tried to scowl at her, but failed. Her naughty behavior was appealing, especially because she felt so little guilt over it.

"I do still feel scandalized at court. I thought I would faint the first time I attended a card game."

"So did I, after I married Guise and converted. I had to stop gasping out loud every time I saw something that violated Calvin's teaching."

"How long did that take?"

She counted on her fingers, "Nine, ten months?'

"You are incorrigible, sister." I took her hand, squeezing it.

"It is good to have you here. The politics of court weigh me down. It's much easier to concentrate on one's lover than one's political leanings. Leanings that change by the day, if not the hour."

I thank God that I accompanied her for the birth of her child, because in early December, her labor pains began. Early on the morning of December 3rd, she gave birth to a girl. Although the child looked like an angel, she lived only for a few hours. My sister was despondent, dissolving into a deep melancholy. After giving birth to two sons, one who only lived for two years, the idea of having a girl was a dream that she desperately wanted to realize.

CATHERINE AND I SPENT THE REST OF 1573 CONSTANTLY IN ONE another's company, officially far from the maneuvering of the court. I continued to keep my eyes open for a sign of Spanish gold or the beginnings of a plot, but little came to my notice.

I was determined to make myself useful to her, doing everything within my power to help her mourn the child and work through her grief. Still, my promise to aid the Protestants could not be ignored for very long. Condé sent missives, asking me to come to Amiens to visit him. Winter in the easternmost reaches of France that year was mild, and I made plans to visit him at the end of February. Those plans changed abruptly two days after Christmas day when I walked past the door of the chateau's comptroller. Two excited voices, deep in a conversation caught my ear. Slowing my pace, I started to listen in on their conversation.

"Of course he's still a Protestant! The King was gullible to think that he was genuine and now he's installed himself as Lord of Picardy."

Picardy! They must have been referring to my husband.

"We have friends assembled in Matigny, far enough that he can't go running to his brother-in-law for safety."

I wondered which brother-in-law he referred to, Nevers or Guise? Did Catherine have a traitor in her home, or had a conspiracy been under my nose the entire time? My heart sank at the thought.

"Get this message to Nancy, as soon as possible. We don't have much time to plan."

Determined to avoid being caught, I rushed into a dark corner. With my sudden movement, I could not hear the rest of the conversation, despite the fact that I knew I desperately needed to. Condé would need to hear every precious word of the plot against him, but I could not risk being caught spying in my own sister's home.

As quickly as I could manage without arousing suspicion, I returned to my apartments and began writing to my husband. "Christmas was wonderful, but I cannot stand to be parted from you any longer. I will be there early and I fully expect you to make preparations for my visit."

Calling for my page, I sent the letter to Picardy, knowing that Condé would understand the coded message. Once again, my husband's life was in danger; and once again, I was the best hope for saving him.

❧ 19 ❧

„**Y**our Highness is most welcome!" The rotund rosy-cheeked man greeted me as I entered the small Chateau my husband used in governing Picardy. I was relieved to be there, my toes tingling from the early January cold. I had just managed to arrive in Amiens before a sleet storm and the disagreeable weather would keep me indoors for several days after my arrival.

When my sister Catherine heard of my sudden desire to leave for Picardy, she protested constantly. "You are mad to try to trek across the countryside this time of the year! What possible reason could you have to leave now!" Her recovery from the birth dictated that she stay in bed, but that did not bar her from regaling me with hundreds of reasons why I should remain in Joinville. I was relieved to see that none of Catherine's protests seemed to stem from her involvement in the plot against my husband. Apparently, she was completely oblivious to the scheming going around her. As much as I hated leaving my sister and the bond that we had recently formed, I could not allow my husband to be blindsided in the plot developing in Picardy. I had to do all that I could to Save him.

I half-ran to my husband's apartments, determined to speak to him without delay. Opening the heavy door without ceremony, I looked around the room to find him working at his desk. "Have you learned anything about the conspiracy?"

His face folded into a deep frown, "Yes—it goes even further than you had feared. Apparently, you were just in time. According to Princess Catherine, there was a plot to kidnap or assassinate her in Navarre. Her death would be the end of an independent Navarre, since her brother is unable to escape the French court. Without your help, we never would have made the connection." He looked up at me and gave me a rare smile. "Thank you, Marie. I cannot tell you how valuable you have been to me."

"I promised you that I would help you and our friends, and that is what I did." I returned his smile with a genuine one of my own. The Bourbons were our family, and I was more than willing to keep them safe. The idea of my cousin, Catherine in danger made me sick. Thankful for the new amity between us, I sat in the chair beside him. After so many months at odds in one another's company, peace between us seemed odd. Neither of us knew how to break the awkwardness between us. Unsure where to start, I tried to make conversation.

"My sister, Catherine is doing well. She is getting over the loss of her daughter."

He nodded, "Good."

Having mentioned Catherine, now I regretted doing so. What if Henry had found evidence that she was in on the conspiracy after all?

He squelched my fears with his next words, "There is no proof that Catherine was in on the plot against me. You can rest assured; your sister is most likely innocent."

My entire body shuddered with relief. Before I could stop myself, I crossed myself. "Thank God—we're just now beginning to speak to one another as sisters."

The longer that I spent in my husband's company, the more that the awkwardness between us lessened. That January became a kind of honeymoon for us; one denied us when during the wedding of Navarre and the subsequent massacre in Paris. We were still mismatched as husband and wife, but we developed respect for one another during my days in Picardy. During our nights, to my shock, we began to act as man and wife. Finally, I started to enjoy my status as Princess de Condé.

Our delayed honeymoon could not last forever, however; eventually, I was recalled to court to serve as a lady-in-waiting to Queen Elisabeth. Mole's words proved to be true, and the King was indeed suffering from consumption. Elisabeth and the Queen Mother wrote to me, begging me to return to serve Elisabeth during the King's illness. I could not refuse a direct missive from the Valois, so in February, I was forced to face the ice and cold to make the journey from Picardy to the Tuileries, where the court stayed. Bidding adieu to my husband, we promised to see one another again as soon as possible.

Several unexpected things awaited me at the Tuileries. For one, the Queen Mother assigned me apartments as close as possible to that of the Queen's. This housing assignment was fortuitous since The Hotel de Cleves had closed with Catherine's absence and I felt uncomfortable continuing to impose on Henriette at the Hotel de Nevers. The Hotel de Bourbon had never been my home, despite that fact that I had a right to establish a residence within the vast building.

The other surprise waiting for me came in the guise of a glut of letters from the Duc d'Anjou from Poland. Each letter came directly from the Polish court to the Queen Mother, who held them for me until my return from Joinville and Amiens. Untying the ribbon that held the fat stack of paper, I started to read each letter as Anjou poured his feelings out to me.

Poland and its court were a dull, uncultured wasteland, the worst possible place for Anjou. Virtually from the start, he was miserable and longing for home. Lost in his misery, Anjou began to confess deeper feelings towards me. For the first time, he told me that he loved me and that he had always hoped for a future between us. I had to fight the anger at reading his words; had Anjou professed his love for me before Condé and I had remarried, we could have been man and wife before he left for Poland. I could have stood by his side as his queen as he began his reign.

Anger soon gave way to longing and as I read his letters, I fell further in love with him. In March, I could not control my emotions, crying one moment and the next, screaming in anger at the vicissitudes of fate. Then I discovered that my warring emotions came from another source: I was pregnant.

Catherine and I sat together one evening as I tried to improve my card playing skills. "I have a confession to make."

She put her cards down and exhaled loudly, "Thank God! Finally! You and Anjou are lovers? Well, I must say, it took longer than I had expected." Since her return to Paris, her color returned, along with her spirits. I was thrilled to have my vivacious sister once again.

I shook my head furiously. "No! Anjou and I have never been intimate, but Condé and I were when I went to Amiens. And now I'm carrying his child."

She hastily tried to rearrange her face, but I caught her before she managed to do so. "Well, that's wonderful! You both need a legitimate heir. This is good news, truly. It is." She bit her lip nervously, unable to continue.

"You are a terrible liar, Catherine."

She shrugged her shoulders, "It's obvious to anyone that you and Condé are miserable and that Anjou would be a better match for you."

Too angry and embarrassed to look her in the eye, I laid a card down without looking at it. "I am a married woman and it's obvious now that our disaster of marriage was consummated. If I were to ask for a divorce, there would be no grounds. You know that as well as I do."

"If you were free, then would you marry Anjou?" I could feel her stare, yet I continued to ignore her.

"What exactly are you suggesting? You were only free to marry Guise once The Prince de Porcien was in his grave." As soon as the words were out of my mouth, I regretted them. Catherine had been innocent in the last plot against my husband. Was she really suggesting that I kill my own husband? Was she capable of forming a conspiracy of her own in the mistaken thought that she was helping me?

"Condé is very much like our Uncle Antoine," she said, referring to the former King of Navarre, who switched faiths at will unlike our stalwart Aunt Jeanne whose conversion to Protestantism was genuine. "He never wanted to become a Catholic in the first place. He could argue that you and the Queen Mother coerced him."

"If he chooses that tactic, he loses the King's protection and the governorship of Picardy. It's too important for him to lose." Particularly as it stood between two Guise territories, but I would not say that aloud to my sister. I had no desire to make her into my enemy.

"Catherine, we're talking about things that will never happen. There's no use in going over what could or could not occur." I rubbed my eyes, suddenly exhausted. Between the pregnancy and my sister's prying, I had had enough for one evening.

❦ 20 ❦

"I can't tell you how happy I am for you," Elisabeth gave me a warm hug, uncharacteristic of royalty, but very much in line with the warm woman standing before me. "By all means, sit. You should take it easy until the child comes."

"Don't make too much of a fuss over me." I almost felt guilty for giving her my good news, given the dark circles that appeared daily under her eyes. The king's illness progressed despite an extensive list of physicians who tried to give him relief. Physically and mentally, his body was breaking down. The queen spent countless hours at his bedside, in prayer and tending to him, yet none of her efforts had come to anything.

"The Queen Mother sent to Italy for more experts to help my husband, but I fear that it's for nothing. He keeps telling me to send for Anjou, that he feels his end is near."

I took her hand, sitting with her wordlessly. A lone tear slid down her face. "I'm sorry—I should not have mentioned Anjou."

I shook her head, "Oh, don't be silly. You can talk about anything with me."

"I know that it's uncomfortable for you given the marriage negotiations."

My blood ran cold. "What marriage negotiations?"

Elisabeth looked horrified. Her face drained of color and she pursed her lips tightly closed. "Mein Gott, you haven't even heard?"

"No, Anjou said nothing." He wrote me daily, each letter more passionate and most written at least partially in his blood. He had said nothing about marriage in those letters.

"With the king's illness, he and the Queen Mother think it is prudent for him to marry a princess as soon as possible. If Anjou were to take the throne suddenly, he would need an heir," she looked up guiltily at my face.

I stood up ramrod straight, determined to breathe. The air came from somewhere, yet it did nothing to calm me. I had no right to expect Anjou to remain unmarried. It was selfish and unrealistic given his position. "I understand. A kingdom without a secure heir would be-" I stopped, suddenly aware of how thoughtless my train of thoughts sounded to Elisabeth.

"We've drifted from your happy news, Marie." The official royal tone in her voice told me she wanted to move our conversation from the heartbreaking news to something lighter. "Ladies," she raised her voice higher so that her attendants and maids could hear her, "we will all sew garments for the next Prince de Condé. We have little time, so we will have to work hard. Now, who will start on the embroidery?" She motioned her maid forward and directed us furiously in our needlework.

"Apparently, he was set up from the beginning," Louis wiped his mouth, as we finished the final course of our supper. "Anna Jagiellon made her support of Anjou's election to the Polish throne contingent upon his marrying her. We were unaware of that fact, so I'm sure it came as quite a shock to Anjou," he laughed, earning a sharp look from Henriette.

"Still, few of the Polish nobles want her to be Queen of Poland. From their point of view, she's hardly a strong candidate for a consort.

Apparently, some of them thought he would reject her for marrying... Er, a French lady."

"Are you saying that Anjou wants to develop a relationship with me in order to rid himself of a Polish princess?" My head was spinning, and I tried to process all the new information.

"If Anjou has time to choose his wife yes—I believe that he would much prefer you to any other woman. As far as I can see, he earnestly loves you. But as you know, politics make marriages, not desire."

I snorted at his words. Out of the three of us, I probably understood that concept the most. "Does he have time, do you think, to consider his options?"

Louis looked torn; he had served the current king loyally since coming to France as a foreign prince. Even amongst family, it was dangerous to talk about the demise of a king. As one of Anjou's closest advisors, he would be well rewarded once Anjou took the French throne. "You know, I am no physician. Consumption has no cure; they can only manage it. Illnesses of the lung are often fatal to the sufferer. Besides his lungs, Charles suffered from emotional fits and convulsions since he was a child. His health was never that good. He may die before Anjou could even make the trip to France, much less secure a marriage of his own."

Henriette rose to her feet, breaking Louis' concentration and causing him to jump to his own feet. "Louis, I think that is enough talk of politics for one evening. Marie, I believe that I could go for some fresh air. Why don't you accompany me?" Thankful for the distraction, I followed her lead out of the room and towards the courtyard of the Hotel de Nevers.

⚜

"Marie, I think you still hold to the Calvinists ideas of morality and they hardly serve you in the real world of the French court. No, don't interrupt; listen to me. It is honorable to remain faithful to your marriage vows, but when that honorable behavior makes you and everyone around you miserable, you have the right to look for your happiness." Henriette had with no hesitation, started giving me advice about my situation with Anjou.

I could never understand how similar my sisters could be on their feelings of infidelity yet approach them in such wildly different ways. For Henriette, it was a calculated move while Catherine considered her dalliances to be a romantic adventure. No matter what their approach, they both counseled me to go for the same result.

I placed my hands on my hips, my pregnancy moods making me even more quarrelsome than ever. "If I understand you correctly, you are advising me to take Anjou as my lover. According to your husband, there may be a chance that I could take him as my husband. If I became his wife, I would be Queen of Poland and later of France. Would it not be smarter to hold out for a larger prize?"

"Remember the story of Anne Boleyn? She forced Henry VIII to wait for seven years, then got her king. Once she had him, she failed in her duty to give him a son and he cut her head off. Do you want the same thing to happen to you?"

I scrunched my face, "We aren't as barbarous as the English, Henriette. I hardly think Anjou would have me beheaded."

"You don't know what can happen in a month, a year, or whatever. None of us is immortal. You would be foolish to deny yourself some happiness. Having a devoted lover is a great source of joy."

"I happen to think that I have the time to see how this works out. I am carrying my husband's child and this is hardly time to contemplate a second husband. Once I give birth, I'll see if it's in my best interest to keep the husband I have or replace him."

She was silent, "You know, if you give birth to a healthy boy, your stock as a potential queen will rise. Elisabeth hasn't been able to give the king a son, but if you could prove that you can give a man sons..."

"All the more of a reason I should take it easy during this pregnancy. I've been remarkably healthy this past year and I want to pass that health on to the baby."

She nodded, "Fine, but remember what I told you about the rewards of having a lover."

❧ 21 ☙

L
ooking back on that evening, I should have taken the time to talk to Henriette more about her views on keeping a lover. I would find out later that she and Margot were playing a dangerous game, spending time with the odious Joseph Boniface de La Môle and his friend Annibaile de Coconnas. Henriette took the latter as her lover, either out of boredom or some unknown strategy. As the King's health steadily declined, plots and conspiracies abounded in the court, but I was determined to stay clear of them. Consumed with the determination to get what he considered his due, the young Duc d'Alençon plotted to take over the throne of France right from under Anjou's nose, in complete disregard of the line of succession. As his retainers, Mole and Coconnas formed the heart of the plot, with Margot allying with her youngest brother against Anjou.

"I don't trust Mole, not for a second." Catherine and I were in the Queen Mother's apartments, absentmindedly working on our embroidery well out of earshot of the rest of the retinue. Fear for her son's birthright showed with every movement that the elder Valois made within the court and I noticed that her entourage grew steadily larger as she kept her friends and enemies closer to her.

"What could Henriette be thinking, keeping Coconnas as her

lover? I thought you were supposed to be the impetuous one!" I stabbed my needle into my finger, yelping at the pain. Catherine gave me a sympathetic look and smiled warily.

"Henriette's loyalty, foremost, is to Margot, then to the rest of us. You might think that she's just as calculating as Louis, but she can be reckless." The two had yet to reconcile and their lawyers beat a steady route from the Hotels Guise and Nevers as they fought over our father's inheritance. The Guise were bleeding money heavily as Duc Henri tried in vain to liquidate his father's and uncle's outstanding debts. Catherine's financial problems failed to break Henriette's resolve to fight her for her inheritance.

A messenger rushed into the Queen Mother's antechamber at that moment, cutting off my response. "I must see the Queen Mother!" We rose to our feet as Madame de Sauve rushed to gather her Majesty.

A rustle of skirts announced the Queen Mother's arrival, and we sank to our knees in reverence. "Yes?" Her voice sounded stretched thin as if expecting the worst.

"We have just received news from Picardy." At his words, my head snapped up. My heart began to beat so loudly that I barely heard his next words. "The Prince of Condé has abjured Catholicism and escaped to Strasbourg."

A collective gasp reverberated across the room. I felt every eye upon me, Save my sister's. To her credit, she grabbed my hand and squeezed it to steady me.

"Condé has betrayed the King? So the kingdom is beset by conspiracies after all?" The Queen mother turned her face to me and for a moment, I was sure that she would blame me for having a hand in his betrayal. "Take the Princess de Condé home, Madame de Guise. She is in no condition to hear this terrible news!"

"Yes, Madame." Catherine bobbed a quick curtsey, and all but dragged me out of the room. I barely remember her efforts to bundle me into her coach, or the trip to the Hotel de Guise. To her credit, she never took the opportunity to say "I told you so" to me. She only held my hand and placed my head in the crook of her neck as I sobbed.

THE SHOCK OF MY HUSBAND'S BETRAYAL WAS SO GREAT THAT I TOOK to my bed immediately. The stress of the pregnancy added to my misery and soon my chronic lung malady returned. That was perfectly all right with me; I had no desire to go back to a court rife with gossip about my treacherous husband and my marriage. Catherine hovered over me and she and Henriette made a temporary truce as they worked in tandem to take care of me while I laid in bed.

"It's best that you stay here. The King and his mother see spies and conspiracies everywhere." From the tone of Henriette's voice, I surmised that one of the conspiracies involved her and Margot's lovers.

"If I may offer a bit of advice, I think that you and Margot should stay clear of Mole and Coconnas." I exercised my prerogative as the patient and a pregnant woman to boss my oldest sister around for a bit. Henriette did not take kindly to my switching our roles.

She waved her hand, dismissing my concern. "Oh, Margot and I are fine. We've been at this game for far longer than you can imagine."

"I've lost enough these past few months and I have no desire to lose you as well." Her dismissive attitude grated on my nerves.

"Louis is Anjou's closest advisor and we have no plans to betray him."

"But does the King think that? The Queen Mother? How can you be sure?" Henriette's intransigence was giving me a headache.

A knock sounded at the door, startling us all. My nerves were frayed, and I was in no mood for more bad news. Catherine's young page stuck his head in the room. "Madame, a letter from the Polish court. Her Grace said that the Princess should receive it right away." He placed it in Henriette's hand, and she in turn gave it to me.

"I'll leave you to read it." She smiled and kissed my forehead, as if in apology. Bustling Henriette out of the room, she took her leave.

I looked down at the letter. Anjou's familiar hand made me smile. Opening the letter, I drank in his words.

"My dearest Marie, my heart breaks to hear of the betrayal you have just suffered. Condé is a villain and a fool. I have instructed my court to send word to the Pope on your behalf to annul your marriage. No believer in the true church should remain yoked with a heretic. And no faithful wife should suffer the agony of a feckless, faithless husband.

I await your reply,

❀

HENRI, BY THE GRACE OF GOD, KING OF POLAND AND GRAND DUKE OF Lithuania"

❀

ANJOU'S WORDS COMFORTED ME MORE THAN ANYTHING AND BY THE beginning of April, I felt recovered enough to return to court service. Despite Anjou's offer to help, I worried that the Queen Mother blamed me for Condé's behavior. I tried to avoid her as much as possible, but within days, she called me to her private chambers.

"My dear, my heart breaks for you. No one should have to suffer what you have had to endure! And in your condition. Rest assured, my son and I will do everything in our power to make your situation right." She rose and enveloped me in a motherly hug. My fear dissipated and I melted into her arms. Before I realized it, tears started to flow down my face.

"What is this? No, no tears! I have written to His Holiness and asked that your marriage to that heretic be annulled." She took a handkerchief and wiped my tears away. "All will be put right soon; you have my word on it."

Enveloped in the bubble Queen Mother's protective presence, I lost track of Henriette's dalliance with Annibaile de Coconnas. In mid-April, as I walked down the corridors of the Chateau St. Germain, I heard a horrible commotion directly in front of me. Unwilling to draw myself into another scandal, I hung back and tried to make myself as inconspicuous as possible. A continent of the King's guard rushed past me, swords unsheathed. My heart sank when I realized that they were heading straight for the chambers occupied by Mole. Within moments, their voices drifted into the hallway.

"We found something!"

"Witchcraft!"

"It's an attack on His Majesty!"

I prayed a fervent prayer that whatever the guards found, it had nothing to do with Henriette. Staying rooted to my spot away from the commotion, I could not hear what was transpiring. The courtiers who had rushed past me in a mad rush to see the commotion passed the information along the hallway.

"It's a wax figure of the King!"

"Mole meant to kill the King!"

"My God, he'll hang for this!"

Even in my hiding spot far down the hallway, I could hear Mole protesting his innocence. His words were useless, as the guards placed him under arrest and within the hour, both he and Coconnas were imprisoned. Fear rose within me and I had to get to my sister. If she were in danger, perhaps I could use my influence with Anjou and the Queen Mother to save her.

I found Henriette sitting in her salon, strangely quiet. "For God's sake, what is going on?" I searched her face, but I could not read her expression.

"We had to do it."

"Do what?" Confused, I tried to make sense of her words. "And who are 'we'?"

"Margot and I. The Queen Mother was right. There is a conspiracy. And it reaches far further than she suspected." Henriette's words were dull and emotionless. Even for my usually quiet and methodical sister, her behavior was a cause for concern.

"Henriette, tell me you weren't part of the conspiracy." The implication was too much for me to consider. I would not lose my sister. I would fall on my knees and beg the King for mercy before that happened.

She shook her head, "No. There are Bourbons involved, but I had nothing to do with it." Bourbons. She must mean Navarre. If he was indeed part of a conspiracy against the King and Anjou, his life was in danger more than during the days after St. Bartholomew's.

"What will happen to Navarre? For God's sake, tell me!" I searched her face, but she still sat as if in a trance. Our poor cousin, Catherine in faraway Navarre would never recover the loss of her older brother.

"Margot took care of it. She penned a confession for Navarre. He will escape blame and so will Alceon."

I exhaled a deep sigh. "That's a relief."

"But someone had to take the blame." Snapping out of her reverie, she looked directly at me. "Margot had to sacrifice Mole and Coconnas. The King sentenced them both to die."

I had to know how deep this disaster reached. "Is this due in part to Condé's defection?"

She nodded, "These Malcontents are working together, Protestant and Catholic. Everyone knows that the King will die soon. Anjou is probably months away from becoming King of France. Alceon planned to raise an army and overthrow Anjou. Navarre was stupid enough to ally himself with Alceon. France cannot afford to lose the men who are second and third in line to the throne. So," she let out a long exhale, "Margot decided that Mole and Coconnas would take the blame."

"How exactly?" True, the Valois children could be cold and calculating, but would Margot allow two innocent men to hang?

"Margot penned a letter for Navarre, claiming that he had been 'led astray by unscrupulous people.'" Having implicated the hapless men, the only remaining task was to place the blame on them formally.

"The wax figure, where did it come from?"

"Mole claimed it was to win Margot's love, but the King would not listen to his explanation. He believes it was created to send him to his death. ,"

"Henriette, this is monstrous. These men cannot be held as scapegoats."

She shook her head. "This is the way of the French court, Marie. The ultimate goal is simply to survive."

GUILT ATE AWAY AT BOTH MARGOT AND HENRIETTE, AND THE TWO planned a daring rescue of their condemned lovers. Years of clandestine affairs prepared them for their ruse, during which they would bribe the guards to see the condemned men for a final time. Once their visit was over, the women planned to dress Mole and Coconnas as Margot and Henriette and allow them to walk out of the prison unmolested. When the guards came for the execution, the two would be far from Paris and Margot and Henriette would be in the cell to greet the guards.

Unfortunately, the King caught wind of a plot to free the men and after announcing the date of their execution, he quietly had them executed before Margot and Henriette could make their way to their cell. Henriette was despondent and the guilt she felt continued to eat away at her.

Unable to rescue their lovers, Margot and Henriette made one last romantic gesture. Under cover of darkness, they cut down their bodies and paid to have them buried in unmarked graves. The men's hearts were embalmed, in a sense saving them for all of Eternity. Margot would keep Mole's heart with her for the rest of her life, repaying him for her betrayal in a sense. Henriette's more practical nature meant that her mourning was not as melodramatic as the Queen's, but I knew that she felt her grief just as keenly.

Determined to return her kindness, I went to the Hotel de Nevers and marched into her bedchamber. Amongst the bedcovers, my resilient sister looked frail. Unable to think of anything better, I crawled into bed and held her as while she wept.

WITH MY MARRIAGE IN SHAMBLES, ANJOU DISPOSED OF ALL restraint and began writing to me on a daily basis. His words became more concrete and tender, reassuring me of his love for me. None of his letters contained a proposal of marriage, but given the fact that I was not legally free to marry, he could hardly do so for propriety's sake. Amongst his words of love, he wrote of his continued disenchantment with the Polish court. Upon his arrival in Poland, displaced Protestants from France assailed him, blaming him for the St. Bartholomew's day massacre. Despite his best efforts, he could not install the customs and manners that the French were so famous for. The women were woefully unattractive, "Especially this one ungainly fifty-year-old cow that is determined to make me her husband." I knew from his description that the "cow" he referred to was the hapless Anna Jagiellon. Perhaps his words were a bit mean and unkind to his subjects in Poland, but I was so grateful to have a lifeline to my confidant that I forgave any lapse of manners on his part. He did have a point, after all, in refusing a woman twice his age who expected marriage as her "thanks" for supporting his claim to the Polish throne.

At the same time, I was enraged to find letters from Strasbourg, sent from my wayward husband. He had the nerve to berate me for my correspondence with Anjou and in his letters, he began to accuse me openly of adultery. I do not know if he had heard of the work done on my behalf to annul our marriage, but his hypocrisy at using me to act as his spy and his subsequent betrayal was too much for me. I refused to answer his letters, and I threw each one upon the fire as soon as I finished reading it.

The court continued to be in shambles and within weeks of the executions of Mole and Coconnas, the King succumbed to his illness. Despite the fact that we all knew his death was imminent, the reality of losing the King and his sweet Queen was too much a blow for me. By tradition, Elisabeth was required to remain confined for a month following the King's death to ensure that she did not carry the royal heir. My heart ached for her, given the fact that I knew that nothing would please her more than to give her husband a posthumous heir. I knew more than most how hard she had tried to carry the King's son, but all of their work was to no avail. I had no desire to rub my pregnancy in Elisabeth's face and assumed that she would not want me with her during her confinement. To my surprise, she immediately sent word that she wanted me at her side for the duration of her stay.

"I don't think that there is anything that I can say to console you, Madame." Tears welled in my eyes and I wiped them away, determined not to make a spectacle of myself.

"Your presence here is all I need. I need a friend now, more than anything."

"Where will you go, after His Majesty is laid to rest?" There was no delicate way to ask, so I charged awkwardly ahead.

"I have loved being Queen of France, but I am tired of court life. Once my dower lands are settled, I will go home to Austria."

I had known that this would happen, but hearing her say it, made it all too real. The unbidden tears slipped faster down my face. "I can't imagine court without you."

"That is why I requested that you stay with me; I want my last memories of France to be of time spent with a true friend." Court life without the angelic presence of Elisabeth of Austria seemed like a miserable place indeed.

"What about Princess Elisabeth? Will she accompany you to Austria?"

She shook her head. "No, she will be happiest with her grand-mother. I cannot ask for a better protector than Catherine de Medici."

My heart broke for her. My child had not yet been born, yet I could not imagine living without him or her. If Anjou and I were to marry, I had no doubt that the child would have a devoted stepfather in the new King of France. Impatience rose up within me and I suddenly wanted to see Anjou more than anything. But I knew that Anjou's arrival meant the permanent departure of Elisabeth and I did not want to lose the gentle woman who had been my friend for almost two years.

Elisabeth rose and walked to the dresser. Taking a small box from the dresser, she returned to her seat and placed the box in my lap. "I think that this should go to the next Queen of France." She gave me a knowing smile, and I blushed at the inference.

"I hope you don't mean me. It's presumptuous to think that I could be--"

"Just open it."

Inside the box, a beautiful carcanet, a necklace made to sit below a lady's ruff winked in the light. Rubies framed the delicate floral design of the piece. "It's beautiful. But I cannot take it. It's for too grand of a lady."

"It's perfect for the future Queen of France. And I insist that you take. Every time that you wear it, you will remember me and our friendship." She pressed the box into my hand, an uncharacteristically aggressive move for her.

"Thank you." I could think of nothing else to say.

❧ 23 ☙

Word traveled quickly from Paris to Krakow that the King of Poland was now the King of France. I had hoped that Anjou would come quickly in triumph, and we could once again be together as we had before he left for Poland. Alas, politics meant that things were much more complicated than that.

The Poles had no desire to allow their newly elected monarch to leave for his new kingdom. Anjou was virtually a prisoner in his own court and he was forced to create an elaborate plan to leave Poland under his own subjects' noses. In May, I began to show signs of my pregnancy and I did my best to take the edge out of my anxiety by adjusting my gowns and making plans for my life as a single woman. I decided to take up temporary residence at the Hotel de Guise, although both of my sisters insisted that I live with each of them until I gave birth. The truce between Henriette and Catherine would extend throughout the day that I gave birth, likely in mid to late October.

Without a King and Queen at court, the Queen Mother took over the activities of the court and she made a point to install me as the second lady of the court. She functioned as Regent as Anjou made his tortuously slow way towards France, keeping a low profile and successfully dodging his angry Polish subjects. Sensing my impending change in status, ambassadors began to court my favor, starting with the Spanish ambassador.

"Madame, it is our hope that with your guidance the French court will regain its luster." The man's toadying manner irritated me. I realized that this would be my life from now on, constantly trying to discern the real meanings under every person's words. It would be the price of life with Anjou, but it was a price that I was willing to pay for happiness.

Word also drifted slowly from Rome regarding the status of my annulment from Condé. I had assumed that his status of heretic and renegade from the French crown would make the process progress quickly, but as I was to learn, with the Vatican, nothing happens quickly. Money and influence carried the day, and despite the fact that the new King of France and his mother requested the annulment, Rome continued to delay.

"Look at it this way, Marie. By the time you get the annulment, you'll be fully recovered from the birth. The timing may be more fortuitous than you had thought." My sister, Catherine did her best to cheer me, but thanks to my pregnancy moods and the ongoing frustration, I was in no mood to listen to reason.

As he continued to flee from Poland to France, I heard virtually nothing from Anjou. Instead, he once again, commissioned Desportes to write to me, filling my desk with love poems. The elegies and sonnets were almost as dear to me as the man who commissioned them and I spent long hours rereading them and wishing that he would return to France as soon as possible.

My husband continued to stir trouble, traveling between the courts of the German counts and princes to raise an army against Anjou before he could even take the throne. When Louis told me of how much effort Condé had expended in building his army, I thanked God that the process of my annulment was already advanced enough to keep me from being implicated in my husband's schemes. As before, the Queen Mother bore me no ill will, instead of keeping me in her privy chambers at the Chateau Blois as she held onto the French throne for her favorite son. I had planned to remain in Paris at the

Hotel de Guise for the remainder of my pregnancy, but once we heard about Condé's duplicity, both my sisters and I decided that I would be safer directly under Catherine de Medici's protection. I spent that long summer at Blois, living very much like her beloved daughter as we waited daily for Anjou's return.

With Anjou's continued absence during the Summer of 1574, the Protestants in La Rochelle began to threaten to take advantage of his delay by once again revolting against the crown. Still stung by my husband's betrayal, I turned a deaf ear to the entreaties of Protestant lords at court who asked for my help and support.

In July, the Queen Mother summoned me to her presence. "I have good news, Marie. My son has managed to leave the Poles and is now safely in Vienna."

"Vienna! But that is nowhere near Paris!" I was horrified at the idea that he was so far away from me.

"The Poles refused to allow him to leave without permission from their Parliament. Imagine," she snorted in disgust, "they thought that they could order their King, the King of France, around as if he were a mere stable boy!"

"Will he return to us soon?" I would take any assurance from her that our long wait was finally over.

She nodded, "Have no fear, my dear. Anjou will come back to us." She pulled a letter from her desk, smiling at me. "This is from Elisabeth."

I was thrilled at her letter. I had not realized that Elisabeth would use the occasion to get a message to me. A smile lit up my face and Catherine nodded. "And these," she pulled out a large stack of letters," are also for you." There was no doubt who sent those letters. With an indulgent smile, she dismissed me from her chambers.

The letters were just the encouragement I needed during those hot, restless days. Anjou had spent each day writing to me, but he was unsure how his letters would eventually get to me. In them, he detailed his flight from Poland, from the day that he discovered of his brother's death. He told me about the clandestine meetings with his French lords to plan his escape, detailing the danger he faced. His words concluded by telling me of the day that he finally slipped safely from the Polish borders.

⚜

AUGUST CAME AND STILL, THE NEW KING HAD NOT RETURNED TO his kingdom. The Queen Mother spent each day working to balance the power factions of the cabinet and the Duc de Guise wasted no time in controlling the ultra-Catholic faction. This lead to more friction between them, but my sister and I were spared from the effects of their power struggle. Condé continued to gather more money and more German Protestant troops and he started attacking towns across Normandy. Without a King upon the throne and without a strong military commander to follow his directives, France once again faced civil war.

"This is ridiculous," I hissed to Catherine one day as we furiously stitched clothes for my baby. He's doing his best to tear the country apart." My hatred for my husband had never been greater.

"My husband is doing his best to gather the troops, but the Queen Mother is determined not to give him command of the royal army." The Queen Mother had good reason to distrust the Guise; before Catherine de Medici could assume the Regency for her eldest son King Francis II, the Guise took over the ruling of France and squeezed her completely out of power. The Queen Mother would be foolish to hand over power to the Guise, no matter how desperate the current situation.

"The King is safely in Italy. There's no danger of Spain or even the Austrians capturing him. What possible reason could he have for this delay?" By the end of my sentence, I was shouting and my sister looked at me in amazement.

"The King has to raise money to fight Condé. Your husband," she saw me flinch at the word, "got the better of him in gathering money and troops. Now as King, he has to beg for money from foreign rulers. It's the way of rulers." Once again, Condé stood in the way of my happiness. His self-centered nature truly knew no limits. France was without her King because of him. I could have killed him with my bare hands at that moment.

"I don't know how long his mother can hold on to the throne for him."

"Impatient to become Queen of France?"

"Don't even tease me about that. I've had no offer and I have no desire to curse my chances."

"Ah, so you do want to become Queen, then?"

I sighed. "I want to be happy."

Lost in our girlish teasing, we barely heard the knock at the door. "Come," Catherine beckoned the messenger, whose blanched face sent terror down my spine. Catherine sat with her back to the boy and it was not until she turned around that she noticed his expression. In his hand, he held a letter, edged with black.

She tore the letter open and read furiously. In minutes, she collapsed in tears. "It's from my husband's grandmother. My son, Henry," she could not say any more. Her second child, barely two years old, was dead. Catherine's grief filled the room. Within a year, my effervescent sister had lost two of her beloved children. Although losing a child was a regular part of life, the loss of even one was devastating to see. I could offer my sister little comfort, but I was determined to give her as much support as I could. My impending motherhood made me an emotional mess, yet it also made it easier to relate to the agony that a mother goes through when losing a child.

❦ 24 ❦

By September, I finally understood Elisabeth's comment about waddling everywhere and the inability to see her feet. My own feet disappeared from my sight, seen only when I put my feet up to get some semblance of relief. The pregnancy stretched my body as well as my patience. I cursed Condé for putting me in this position, then abandoning me to it. During the past months, I heard not one word from him, which was probably just as well. I refused to play the part of an abandoned wife. I would not stand for someone to look at me with pity.

Although the King wrote me daily, I had long since given up hope of meeting him for his triumphant return to French soil. Instead of taking the journey towards Lyon to meet him, I settled in the Hotel de Guise to get ready to welcome my child. My sister, Catherine was determined to return the favor I paid her in helping her birth her child almost a year earlier. As we sat, sewing furiously to finish the baby's clothes, on the fifth of September, the new King of France finally returned to his kingdom. The majority successfully made the long trip to Lyon to meet him, foremost, Navarre and the Duc d'Alençon, the new Dauphin.

"You did send plenty of letters with the Queen Mother?'

A smile pulled at the corners of my mouth, "Of course. I told His Majesty that had he returned earlier I could have greeted him in person."

"Marie, it is unseemly to chide the King of France! You cannot afford to be spiteful now."

"I was only teasing him. He knows that I'm teasing him. He also knows that the first chance that I get, I will receive him with all of my love."

I hated the idea of having the man I loved so close, yet being separated by a condition that I brought on by my naivety. Had I not fallen for Condé's ruse, I could have been in Lyons, enjoying the fruits of my efforts these long months. We looked daily for word of my annulment and each day I knew that it was that closer to arriving. As I became less and less mobile, I used the lazy hours of napping to fantasize about the court that Henri III and I would preside over. My sisters, of course, would be my chief ladies-in-waiting. I laughed at that; how they would fuss at the idea of having to serve their youngest sister! Still, there was no one in the entire county that I trusted more to be at my side.

Before that long summer, I had thought that I was a patient woman. As the days passed, I realized just how difficult it was to wait for something that I had wanted for so long. Finally, I would have the loving husband and partner that I had wanted in Condé. All I had to do was sit and wait for him to come to me.

❦

MY CHILD WAS LATE IN COMING. THE MIDWIFE CAME TO THE HOTEL de Guise and declared that we had miscalculated and that it should be here by now. This was not the news that I expected nor wanted to hear. My nerves had been rubbed raw from waiting, both for the birth and the return of the King. Neither seem in any rush to arrive and I had become the most irritable creature on earth. Catherine had borne the brunt of my anger, regretting her offer of hospitality during my laying in period.

"Marie, it always takes longer for the first child. It happened to both of us." In her frustration, Catherine had enlisted Henriette to keep me calm. Henriette was happy to stay in Paris and allow Louis to travel on to Lyon to meet the King. Despite their best efforts to keep me calm, nothing seemed to work. I became more frustrated by the day.

"How long will this child take? Will it ever come?" We all knew that the moment I had recovered from the birth, I would jump in a coach and make my way to Lyons. Nothing either of them said could stop me. Henriette and the King were experts in sneaking off unattended and I was determined to follow their example.

"Marie, the calculation was off. That happens often. Babies are hard to keep to a schedule, even after they are born." Catherine tried vainly to calm me down, but as always, it proved to be pointless.

"Can't we do something to make the child come earlier?" Frustration was wearing me out and I could not wait for the moment that I was relieved of my burden. At that point, I was willing to try anything.

My sisters exchanged glances, "Well, there are some folk cures."

As soon as October came, I was willing to try any unorthodox treatment, no matter how dangerous it seemed. Together, we walked across the courtyard of the Hotel de Guise in the misguided attempt to jostle the child into being born. When that failed, we consulted every maid and midwife in Paris for advice. Soon, we were plying me with copious amounts of wine, which only served to get me very intoxicated.

"Well, she is a bit calmer," Henriette remarked sardonically.

I flatly refused to try the squirrel broth that one midwife prescribed.

❦

FINALLY, ON OCTOBER 6TH, MY LABOR BEGAN. I SENT A QUICK prayer up to God that I was finally going to give birth. After our efforts, I started to fear that I would never have this child. Mixed with my relief came the sudden pain of my contractions. Terrified, I turned to Catherine for support.

"You will take care of this child if I don't survive, won't you? Don't let Condé raise it, for the love of God! Take it to Joinville and put it under the protection of the Guise."

My sister tutted, "Marie, every woman thinks that she is going to die when she is giving birth. This is your first time, so you haven't gone through it. You'll be fine, just try to calm down."

No matter how much she tried to reassure me, I spent the next nine hours in a complete panic. With each pain, I felt as if I were being torn apart. Henriette's confessor came and promised me that he would give me Last Rites if the midwife determined that they were needed. His assurance gave a little comfort, but until the baby was born, I would not be able to relax.

I did find comfort when a message arrived from Lyon, written in the King's hand. He eagerly awaited our reunion in Lyon and I reread the lines of his letter over and over, almost as a litany. His words came the closest to comforting me. Once this ordeal was over, I would finally be free of Condé and we could begin our lives together. I only had to endure the birth.

Finally, the midwife announced that it was time for me to start pushing the child from my body. After the grueling hours in labor, I barely had strength to sit up, much less push a baby from my body. Catherine set her jaw, and all but hauled me up to sitting. "Enough, Marie! It is almost over. You can handle a few more hours at most! Once the child is here, you can rest all you like."

Squeezing my hands as I pushed, we yelled and screamed almost in unison as the baby started to appear. For what seemed like hours, I managed to push until the umbilical cord appeared. "It's done; you can relax now!" Catherine kissed my hair, which by then, was dripping wet with perspiration.

The baby cried almost instantly, signaling to us that it was healthy. After the effort I expended, I would have been devastated to find that it was nothing, and that I had given birth to a stillborn. I fully understood the grief Catherine felt almost a year earlier when she learned of her daughter's death shortly after her arrival.

"It's a girl, Princess!" I slumped back onto the pillows in relief. A girl was fantastic news. Condé would likely never want to take custody of a girl as she could never become the next Princess of Condé. She was destined to live with me and the new King at the royal court. With her fortuitous birth, our plans would be easier to carry out now.

"Your daughter," the midwife handed the tiny newborn to me, her body pink with excretion and blood still clinging to her head. Atop her head was a sparse amount of dark brown hair. I took a moment to look at her. To my relief, she looked nothing like her homely father. This girl would be a great beauty, taking after the Cleves side of the family. A beautiful girl who deserved a beautiful name.

"Hello, Catherine." I smiled at her and touched her tiny pink fingers. She twitched them in response to my touch.

"You've already chosen a name?" Catherine looked at me, amused.

"Yes, for her aunt who helped me survive this ordeal." I smiled at my sister, who beamed back at the two of us.

"Not for the Queen Mother?" she teased.

"Oh, yes—that too. That's an incredible coincidence." We both laughed at that.

❦ 25 ❦

Four days after my daughter's arrival, I started to regain my strength. Catherine was correct; I did think that I would surely die from the birth, but I had survived despite my fears. I was sore, but I felt strong. As soon as I could, I wrote a letter to the King, giving him the news of my daughter. I told him of her beauty, how perfect she was and how she cooed when awake. Most of the time, she simply laid in my arms, content to doze off and make no noise whatsoever.

I talked about how he would love her as I did and that I could not wait until he beheld her for himself. I shamelessly told him that I had named her after the Queen Mother, not wanting to snub either of the senior Valois. It would not do to start our new relationship off with a royal snub and I was careful what I revealed to the King in my letters.

Although it was childish and spiteful, I did not bother to send word to my husband of our daughter's birth. He had cared not one whit for our welfare during my pregnancy and now that I had presented him with a daughter, I was sure that he cared even less. I think that he was suspicious that the child was not his, despite the fact that there was no evidence otherwise. How ironic if he felt I had betrayed him when he had betrayed my loyalty and trust by escaping to Strasbourg and later Geneva? He made his priorities quite clear to me months ago, and I felt no obligation to report my news to him.

Days later, the King wrote back to me, overjoyed at the news of my daughter's birth. He said that he hoped this would be the first of many healthy children and that my next child would most assuredly be a boy. "What a blessing for France that would be! Just think of it, Marie! And how we will love him!" His letters gushed with emotion and each day, I felt more restless at the thought that we could not see one another.

Flushed with excitement over his new reign, he made plans for the court that we would rule over. My sisters would be my Ladies of Honor and he agreed that they would be the perfect candidates. I could not help but laugh at the idea of both of them fetching my needlework as I had once done for Elisabeth. Pangs of guilt crossed my mind as I realized that I would soon take her place, despite her assurances that she thought I was the best candidate to become the next Queen of France.

I spent the next two days recovering, sleeping on and off while I recovered from the birth. So as not to worry the King, Catherine sent word to him that I had a slight cold and that I would join the court as soon as possible. I knew that new mothers were often exhausted, but I had no idea that I would feel that tired. I had expected to feel exhilarated, but other than my pride in my new daughter, I did not feel the euphoria that I had expected to feel. To my frustration, I started to feel dizzy when I stood, so I remained in bed as often as possible.

My sister hovered at my bedside, her face etched with concern. "You've been through a lot these past months. And your first birth is traumatic." She did her best to reassure me, but I could tell that her words were edged with concern.

The Guise's personal physician came to examine me and he determined that I had likely torn something during the birth. Hearing this, Catherine went ashen. "She will heal with rest, correct?"

He nodded slowly. "Given the right amount of rest, the Princess should recover. Her condition is serious, but I think that she can recover."

A week after the birth, I still felt tired and drained of all energy, but as if that were not enough, my old ailment came back to vex me. My lungs started to fill with fluid, choking me and causing me to cough constantly. I called Catherine to my bedside.

"Remember your promise; take her to Joinville and raise her under the Dowager Duchess. I have no desire for her to live with Condé."

"You're acting silly and that is what is wearing you out." My sister's voice was sharp, and I was annoyed. I was furious with her for suggesting that I was overreacting.

"I know my body and I know that it is weak."

She took my hand, "Marie, you are months away from becoming Queen of France. Right now you are being absurd. I won't have that behavior from you." Her tenderness was worse than her bossiness.

"Send in someone to dictate a letter; I want to write the King."

She shook her head, "That, I will not do."

A cough bubbled up in my throat, the rasping sound terrifying her. Without a word, she rose and walked out of the room. A few moments later, her personal secretary came in. "The Duchess said that you wished to send a letter to the King."

I nodded, "My sister thinks that I am silly, but I want to make sure that I can express myself to His Majesty while I am still able."

He nodded, kindness and understanding in his eyes. "Then I am ready."

෧෯

I HOPE THAT THE KING BURNED MY LETTER ONCE HE RECEIVED IT. I told him of my deepest feelings, those that I could not express in person for propriety's sake. I told him what I felt silly expressing to him in my previous letters. If I survived to meet him in Lyon, then I would arrive with his knowing just how much I loved him. He would know for certain that I had returned every desire he had had for me. We would begin our marriage with an understanding and full honesty, something that no other couple at the court could boast of.

If I were correct, and I did not have long, he would know from my own words how much he had meant to me. I told him how he filled a deep longing that my sullen and selfish husband refused to address. He would know for the rest of his life that even if no other woman genuinely loved him, I had done so. Even if every other person in his life were no more than a lying sycophant, I was not. He would have my entire heart and my mind, every last bit of both.

"Hold this letter; my sister will tell you when it needs to be sent." The young man stood, gave me a deep bow and gently walked out of my bedchamber. A few moments later, I was asleep.

❦

My sister is so stubborn that she assumes that she could simply will me to live. If that were the case, I would have done so myself. No matter how strong my spirit, the ordeal of giving birth, combined with my weak lungs, meant that I simply did not have the strength to hold on to this life for much longer. Although my body was weak, I was hardly a weak woman. I had battled my condition for so long that I had finally used up my store of spirit.

Day by day, I could see myself slipping away from the world and feeling less like a part of mortal existence. The only thing that anchored me to this life was the sobbing woman who sat beside me. Every time I awoke, she was there. Most times, Henriette was also there, sadly resigned to the obvious fact that I must leave them both very soon.

I refused to send word to Lyon that I was fading. I would not cause the King grief when he was powerless to do anything to Save me. Even the King of France must bend his will to Providence. I was also worried that if he heard word of my condition, he would ride immediately to my bedside. I had no desire for our final moments together to be filled with tears and regret. I did not want to cast such a dark pall over his nascent reign. Catherine had promised to send my letter once I was gone, when he could not wring his hands helplessly in an attempt to help me.

On October 29th, I knew that the time for Last Rites had finally arrived. I spent as much time with my tiny daughter as possible, telling her things that she could not understand and would never remember. I was relieved that Catherine and the Guise would be there for her since it was obvious that I would not.

The priest came, and I confessed my sins before God and my fellow man. Unlike the public gossip sessions of my Protestant youth, our conversation was quiet and intimate. I was thankful for that, the mercy that the last time I spoke to a man of God, it would be without judgement and end in God's forgiveness. Although I felt no regret for leaving my husband and I had committed no adultery, the act of telling my worries to this man was a comfort to me. Once he left, I called Henriette and Catherine back to my bedside.

"You were strangers to me when I came to Paris and I thank you both for standing by my side when I needed you. I wish that we had more time together, but I can't do anything about that. My daughter will be in safe hands."

Henriette grabbed my hand and kissed it. Placing my palm to her wet cheek, she looked in my eyes. For a moment, Catherine was too overcome with emotion to come forward. Eventually, she sat by my other side, tears falling from her eyes.

"You would have been a splendid Queen of France." Henriette's voice was tender.

"We wouldn't have resented serving you a bit."

I laughed at that, "Yes, you would."

"Well, perhaps a bit."

We spent the next half hour quietly, simply enjoying one another's presence. Gradually, my strength left me and I had to close my eyes. The last sight I saw were their faces as they quietly sobbed and held me.

EPILOGUE

Catherine, Duchess de Guise

I DELAYED SENDING THE LETTER TO THE KING AFTER MARIE LEFT us. I had no desire to admit to myself that she was gone. I knew that once the message left for Lyons, I was all but admitting to myself that my younger sister was dead. Eventually, Henriette convinced me that it was my duty to send word to the King that the woman he loved, the woman he wished to make his wife and queen, was gone forever.

We had sent no word to Lyon that she was fading after the birth because we naively believed that she would recover. With each day's passing, however, she faded more from us. Marie insisted that the King receive no word of her condition because she could not stand to have him sitting near her, feeling completely helpless. Until she told me this, I was unsure if she loved the King or if she was only flattered by his attention.

The Queen Mother broke the word to the King, telling him on November first, All Saints Day. After celebrating mass with Navarre and Alceon, the King was in the midst of writing to my sister and the

Pope of his desire to speed her annulment. He was determined to make her his wife as soon as possible and now that he was within his new kingdom, he was going to act with the influence of the King of France. The few who were present when the Queen Mother delivered the tragic news doubted the sincerity of his grief. He immediately fell into a chair and moments later dragged himself to a couch where he sobbed uncontrollably.

For three days, no one could approach him, even his worried mother. She began to fear that he would take his life in his grief. Finally, with the help of my husband and the King's favorite, Villequier, she barged into his chambers to ensure that her son had not ended his life in his grief. The three forced him to take food, as he had steadfastly refused it during those three days. My husband related all of this to me and while their friendship was at that time non-existent, he genuinely felt compassion for the King's suffering. "When Henri reappeared, no one would have recognized him in his melancholy and haggard countenance. The handsome features, which a few days previously had dazzled his courtiers, were gone. The man who faced us was horrifying."

The entire court went into mourning, giving Marie the status due to a member of the Royal Family as if the two had indeed married as the King planned. The King and Queen Mother draped their private rooms in black and no one dared defy their order to wear mourning clothing. Whereas the King came to the frontiers of France as a buoyant and triumphant monarch, once he finally entered Paris there was little triumph. He entered behind two coffins, those of his brother and the woman he loved more than anyone else.

I kept my promise to Marie and personally took her daughter to Joinville, where my husband's formidable grandmother took over her rearing. To no one's shock, Conde never bothered to ask after her, due I think in part to his suspicion that she was Anjou's child. He had never been a favorite of mine, but his behavior after my sister's death disgusted me. He continued to neglect his firstborn child and I can think of no point when he bothered to meet my niece in person. When I heard of Conde's suspicious passing, I rejoiced in private. His death was no great loss to me.

People scoffed at the King when we married my husband's cousin Louise of Lorraine the following February. The whispers behind fans were that she looked too much like my sister. For myself, I felt a bit of triumph in that fact, because it proves that his love for Marie was sincere. Did it mean that his love for Louise was not real? I honestly do not know. My history and my husband's troubles with Henri III of France make it so difficult to be generous to him. As the years flew past, their relationship became so poisoned that I felt as if the King had always been my personal enemy. But that story is for another time.

I have envied Marie, mostly for the fact that unlike me, she experienced true love. She knew the feeling of being loved back, not the exhortation of being desired by a man for a short time. In that sense, she was the luckiest of all of us. Many bemoan the fact that she never realized her dream to become Queen of France, but I think that even without a crown, she was most deserving of one.

THE END

of

ALMOST A QUEEN

The story continues in **Lady of the Court. Tap here t**o get it now and start reading right away!

Join Laura du Pre's mailing list to receive a **free book,** the latest news about upcoming releases and special offers just for subscribers.

Read on for more books by this author, historical notes, and contact information.

LADY OF THE COURT

❦ 26 ❦

H enriette, Paris, 1573

I HAVE TO HAND IT TO CLAUDE CATHERINE; SHE'S MANAGED TO PULL off quite a gathering tonight. Anyone who is anyone in Paris is packed into her salon, making it much warmer than the crisp October air outside. I slipped outside to take a break a few minutes earlier and by the time I returned; the festivities were in full swing. On this partic- ular night, Claude invited painters, poets, sculptors, writers, everyone in Paris with an artistic bent, and in the midst of everything Margot, Queen of Navarre holds court.

"Madame de Nevers," an undistinguishable woman whose name I cannot place nods at me, a trail of perfume following behind her. This may not be my party, but even the outliers of the court know I am a force to be reckoned with. They say I am the richest woman in France, and I would not deny that fact. My wealth was not simply handed to me, I worked hard for every crown and every sou I possess. Unlike most people at court, if I lost my entire fortune in an instant, I could build it back up with my own efforts. That is what they fear most about me. I rely on no one, not even the King himself.

I stand behind one of the elegant chairs Claude's servants pushed in from the ballroom and glance at the actor standing in front of the crowd. As the Duchess de Retz, she has the money and taste to afford the furnishings that make her Hotel the envy of Paris. I pause for a moment to admire her décor, something she constantly threatens to tear down and replace with something new. Within a few seconds, I look in Margot's direction. She's bored but does her best to give the impression the man has not bored her sleep. Few people would suspect she is anything less than enraptured with his performance.

"God, he's terrible." A male voice slices into my ear and I turn to stare at him. I agree with him, but I don't appreciate the intrusion on my thoughts or my personal space.

Turning, I get a good look at him and lift one expertly plucked eyebrow. The motion never fails to intimidate a man foolhardy enough to try to go head to head with me. I enjoy the challenge of a good conversation and I want to know if the interloper is up to the task.

"You're an expert on actors, then?"

"Madame, I'm an expert on men, and this one can't muster up an authentic emotion to save his life." This was proving to be promising. He could keep up with me so far. I pressed further.

"Then, I suppose you're available to instruct someone on the finer points of acting?"

He gave me an elegant nod, "Madame, I am prepared to give you instruction, any time you wish. He wiggles his eyebrows suggestively. It would seem, however, that the man standing in front of us needs my help more than you do." A good save, flirtatious, the invitation open. He was a bold one. I was about to respond when the performance blessedly ended and a round of polite applause erupted.

"Henriette, sit with me. We're about to have a song!" Margot could barely speak through her giggles. A second later and she had collapsed into them. "Excuse me, Monsieur," I rushed past him to see what had Margot all atwitter. I was disappointed that I could not spar with him any further, but given his performance so far, I was sure I'd see him again soon.

"Aloysius, you must give us one of your poems tonight!" Margot pulled me next to her and threw her feathered fan to hide her face. "Help me, that actor was terrible! We have to do something, or the night is in jeopardy."

She pulled her fan down, her mask of gaiety back. Margot knew better than any thespian in France the benefit of showing an external face. *She could teach acting*, I thought to myself. The thought of Margot Valois, Queen of Navarre starting an acting troupe made me laugh almost as loudly as she had done a few moments earlier. A second thought followed, the realization that in Margot's case, starting a troupe of actors was exactly the kind of outrageous thing she would do. That particular thought had me in hysterics and I could not stop myself. Margot turned to me and pulled a face.

"What on earth is wrong with you? It wasn't that funny!"

I turned towards Margot and covered my mouth with my hand. "I'll tell you later. Aloysius, get up here now!" I gave him my most imperious look and he bounded to his feet in seconds. Some men were so easy to intimidate.

I spent the rest of the evening at Margot's side, both of us determined to keep the actor from ruining the evening by returning to the makeshift stage in front of Claude's massive fireplace. Since her marriage, Margot was determined to enjoy every moment of Parisian society she had left until she was packed off to the countryside to rule Navarre with her husband. I could barely blame her, given what I had heard about Navarre from my own sister Marie. The entire county thrived on misery and boredom. Navarre had converted to Protestantism, a strict flavor of heresy that encouraged a lifetime of dour behavior and sour faces. With their stark black clothing and stripped-down worship services, these men and women took everything enjoyable out of a religious service. Not only were their services dull, they were downright depressing. I shuddered at the thought of having to sit through one of them.

Thank God Marie was safe in Paris and away from the influence of the Protestants. Our Aunt Jeanne would have dragged us all into damnation with her heresy if given the chance. Margot had her work cut out for her, presiding over those humorless followers of John

Calvin and his teachings. Most people would be intimidated by the idea of presiding over a court that did not want them, but Margot was not the kind of woman to be intimidated by the simple fact that she was not wanted.

⚜

I FOUND MARGOT THE FOLLOWING AFTERNOON IN HER PRIVY chamber, lying on a divan, reading. She moved her lower legs to allow me to sit next to her. "Were you distracted last night at Claude's salon? Because I felt like you were distracted."

That was Margot, blunt when she wanted to be; and always perceptive. Many people saw her beauty and her glamorous facade and assumed that she would be stupid, but they were quickly disappointed to find out that she was quite the opposite. Margot never failed to notice anything.

"I was having a conversation before I sat down with you and I was still thinking about it." I hoped that this small lie was close enough to the truth to satisfy her curiosity.

"About what?" She snapped the book closed.

"About starting an acting troupe here in Paris."

She snorted, "As if I had time for something like that. You had an entire conversation about an acting troupe? That sounds suspicious."

Margot then fell silent. She could wait me out until I confessed. She had managed to do just that to me so many times before that I knew it was useless to try and outsmart her. She might be a decade younger than I, but she could outmaneuver anyone.

"It wasn't the topic, it was the tone of the conversation." I sighed, giving unto her insatiable curiosity.

"The tone of the person speaking?" She was splitting hairs, trying to get at the truth.

I threw my hands in the air, "Were you watching me?" She bit her lip like a naughty girl. I had thought that she was engrossed in her own conversation, but she never missed anything.

"I saw you talking with a man and it looked animated. So," she tapped her fingers on the book lightly, drawing me in, "who was he?"

"You don't even know? There are men at the court that you do not know?"

She shook her head, enjoying my discomfort. "No, wait—maybe I do. He's someone in my brother's household. Now, what was his name?" The tapping continued as she played with me like a cat and a mouse. "He's from Gascony and he has some tropical sounding name."

"Coconnas." I was getting tired of her teasing.

Sensing that I was tired of the game, she changed her tone. "Sorry, but as long as I've known you, you have never bothered to take a lover. That's," she waved her hands in the air dramatically, "a little odd for someone in your place. Were I as rich as you, I'd have a line of lovers waiting outside my door."

"Are you saying that I'm boring?" I looked at her with mock horror, which sent her into a fit of giggles. Margot was always up for a bit of fun.

"Yes, whoever heard of a woman who loved and was faithful to her husband?" She shuddered with mock horror.

"I've been quite pleased with Louis, thank you. He's never caused me a moment of trouble and I don't have any plans to cause him a moment of trouble, either."

"But you did find Coconnas attractive?'

"Margot, I'm married, not a corpse." I gave her a thin smile, conceding her point.

✣   27   ✣

I returned home to the Hotel de Nevers, our Paris home, late that evening. Louis met me at the top of the stairs to our bedchamber. "He's not much better." The corners of his eyes creased, and I saw dark bags under his eyes.

I let out a long sigh. "Did the physician say anything about why he's losing so much weight?'

My husband shook his head, "He thinks that it is a malignant tumor, or perhaps something in his blood. Without healthy blood, there can be no vigor."

A better mother would have rushed to her child's bedside to soothe her son. A better mother would know what to say to the boy who wasted away in front of our eyes. A better mother would not spend hours away from her own home because she could not stand the feelings of guilt and helplessness that came with caring for an ailing child. Since my son only had me for a mother, I hid at the Louvre for hours on end to keep from facing the apprehension that cast a dark cloud over our home.

"He's asleep; I would let him rest until tomorrow morning." Louis gently touched my shoulder and I placed my hand on his. None of my money or his favor with the king could help us in this situation. We were simply two grieving parents who stood by and begged God to show us mercy. So far, God had decided not to do so, but we still held out hope that one day he would change his mind. Louis headed back to his study and I drifted to my bedchamber like a wraith.

Frederick was our only son and he had not even made it to his first birthday. When he came into the world, this past spring, he was pink and gave a lusty cry. Getting a child past the dangers of childbirth was dangerous enough and when we both survived the ordeal, I had thought that he had survived the worst. At four months, when his older sisters began to put on pounds and become fat-cheeked cherubs, our son instead became thin and gaunt. We tried every remedy we could think of and consulted the midwives and wet nurses of Paris, but nothing worked. Soon the doctors began to arrive, including the most well-respected surgeons from Italy. Even they could not tell us for certain what was wrong with our son or whether he would survive.

We had two consolations that kept us from falling into total despair, our daughters Catherine, an opinionated girl of five and her sister, Marie who was all of two years old. Unlike her sister, Marie barely gave us any trouble as she was an obedient and quiet girl much like her father. While our daughters were proving to be quite healthy, we could not say the same for our only son.

Margot loves to tease me about my methodical nature, a quality that thankfully my husband shares. We both thought that once we noticed a problem with our child if we attacked it hard enough we would eventually find a solution for it. Our inability to find any relief for his suffering has tried our faith in our own intellect.

Before, we could find solace in our shared ability to use reason, something that sustained our marriage for the past eight years. Louis and I have been very pleased with one another and along with our daughters, we formed quite a team. These days, however, my husband and I pass one another like specters. Faith and reason have deserted us, and I think that we have forgotten how to manage the simplest communications with one another.

THE NOISE AND FRIVOLITY OF THE COURT SOMEHOW MANAGED TO distract me and each day I welcomed the opportunity to escape. While Louis and I engaged in strained pleasantries, the court at large was a haven for pointless and spiteful gossip. It's the perfect place to raise your spirits with its shallow pursuits. This is why I welcomed the opportunity to sit and watch a tennis game one mild afternoon in October.

"God help me, this is boring!" Charlotte de Sauvé, the wife of the Chancellor and the mistress of Margot's husband, the King of Navarre, rolled her eyes. Although her own lover was one of the players, she frequently sighed as if she might well die of the boredom.

Navarre dropped the ball and it rolled into the corner faster than he could run after it. "You stupid little beast!" Navarre ran after it, stumbling gracelessly as he did so. Navarre is my first cousin, although given how ungainly he is, you would not assume that we shared any family ties. Stories abound that he spent his first eight years living in a mud hut and eating insects at his grandfather's insistence. Given how bad he smells, I think there may be some truth to that rumor. Charlotte de Sauvé must be truly desperate to spend any time in his bed. But given the fact that she does so at the Queen Mother's behest, I'm sure that she's paid quite well to do so.

"Baroness de Sauvé, perhaps you would be happier going inside?" Margot turned to look at her husband's mistress and arched an eyebrow. Margot has no ill feelings toward Charlotte, due in part to the fact that Margot has no hesitation in taking lovers of her own. Neither of them came into their marriage as innocent babes, or as virgins. They have an implicit agreement that each is free to take lovers. It's an agreement that most royal brides would envy, and Margot enjoys the freedom it gives her.

"No, it's best that I stay," Charlotte shot a wary glance at Catherine de Medici, who would no doubt berate her spy for failing to keep tabs on her assignment. No one could afford to anger the Queen Mother, especially someone as vulnerable as Madame de Sauvé. Her husband rose under the Queen's patronage and she is dependent on the King's wishes to succeed her father as Vicomte de Tours.

I was once in Charlotte's place; eight years earlier, my brother

James died and there were no brothers left to inherit my father's fortune. King Henry allowed me to become the Duchess of Nevers, but on the condition that I marry my second cousin, Louis and allow him to become the Duke of Nevers. Louis's mother was a French-woman and came with the Queen Mother in her Italian retinue. Upon Louis' grandmother's death, the King allowed him to inherit his grand-mother's estates. In France, a woman could inherit, as long as it suited the King's needs in order to do so. As long as Charlotte plays Cather-ine's game and willingly supplies her with valuable information, she will inherit as I did. The trick is in pleasing the Valois, not angering them too much, and remaining useful to them.

Navarre's opponent in the game was my striking brother-in-law, the current Duc de Guise. Duke Henri stood about a head taller than the rest of the court, towering above even the very average looking Valois princes. Guise's flowing blond hair and his rough good looks broke quite a few hearts in the court, not the least of which was Margot's. The two came dangerously close to marrying until the Queen Mother wrenched them apart. The result of that wrenching was that Guise quickly married my sister, Catherine in a wedding that raised every eyebrow in Paris.

Although Catherine sat only a few seats away from me, we could not even lock eyes. The Guise were hemorrhaging money; and rather than face their creditors, they were determined to cover up that fact by demanding that Catherine get more than her share of our father's estate. I refused to be bullied by a family of spendthrifts, so I refused to give Catherine a sou more than she was due. As a result, she refuses to speak to me.

"Navarre, if it's too much for you, you can simply call the game!" Guise gives him a courtly bow, which would seem chivalrous if we did not know how much Guise despised Navarre. He hid his dislike of my cousin as well as he hid his financial situation. I'm sure that Guise is putting Catherine up to this and I blame him for the greedy behavior more than I blame her. Catherine's passions have always swung from mood to mood and these days, she is more unpredictable than ever. She is due to give birth to their most recent child in December and within a few days, she will travel to Joinville to give birth. Knowing how easy it is to lose a child, I feel guilty that I am being unkind to her. I could lose my sister in childbirth and the thought upsets me so that tears sting in my eyes. "Excuse me, I need to leave." I trip over two of the Queen Mother's teenage demoiselles as I stumble from the court and into the palace.

❦

HEADED FOR A QUIETER PLACE AND ONE FAR AWAY FROM MY pregnant sister, I entered the Queen's presence chamber. The current Queen is a quiet and unassuming Austrian named Elisabeth, who unlike the rest of the court prefers to stay out of sight. I found the Queen and my youngest sister, Marie, stitching altar cloths.

"What did we miss?" Marie held a pin in her mouth, but she still managed to speak. Elisabeth smirked as she looks at her. Neither of them is a gossip and it is slightly out of character for either of them to ask such a question.

"Just Navarre chasing tennis balls and Guise tossing his hair." Marie pulled her lips into a grimace at my bluntness.

"Is Catherine all right? Is she sitting comfortably?" Out of the three of us, Marie does not have any children yet, but she is determined to make up for that lack by accompanying our sister to her laying-in. She's started to hover around her in anticipation of playing nursemaid.

"She's fine," I took a seat and tried to pick up a corner to start stitching. Marie's stitches are impressive. She's making up for lost time as she grew up a Protestant in Navarre with our aunt, the Queen of Navarre. Since converting to Catholicism, Marie is determined to stitch every altar cloth in France.

"I don't miss the last months of pregnancy. I waddled everywhere, and I had to constantly sit down in order to catch my breath." The Queen is known for her kindness and compassion, which is why she has no enemies in court. It is also why she has few friends because she has failed to supply the court with its lifeblood, scandal, and gossip.

"Marie, are you sure that you want to go to Joinville? It's a long trip?" I'm being selfish, I know. I don't want to lose two of my sisters and be left alone in Paris. The court will leave next week to follow the Duc d'Anjou, the newly elected King of Poland and the King's younger brother to the French border to wish the new monarch well. Anjou is completely besotted with my sister and she spends as many hours as possible in his company.

"I promised Catherine I would help her out and I won't go back on my promise. Besides," she blushed a deep red, "I want to say goodbye to Anjou." After saying that, she suddenly became very interested in her embroidery and fell silent.

"My husband is happy to get the King of Poland to his subjects. I think that France is a little too small with two kings." Elisabeth deftly summed up the sibling rivalry between King Charles and his younger brother. Anjou tarried despite the King's efforts to almost move heaven and earth to get him to the Poles. The news of Anjou's election to the Polish throne came while the royal army worked to subdue the city of La Rochelle and its rebellion against royal authority. The king faced a choice of continuing to fund the siege of La Rochelle or pay to have his brother conveniently out of the country for the foreseeable future. The price the King paid in ending a successful siege against Protestant rebels was too high and he regretted paying it immediately.

"Besides, Condé can't complain that I'm being immoral if I'm in a room with a woman giving birth." Marie rolled her eyes and started stabbing the cloth with her needle.

"He's claiming that you're unfaithful? When the entire court knows the opposite to be true?"

"Yes, I can hear him drone on and on all the way from Picardy. Apparently, Paris is a bad influence on me and he thinks going to the countryside and away from bad influences will do me well."

I was the "bad influence" that had Condé so riled up. The rivalry between Anjou and the Prince of Condé stemmed from years of ill-gotten military appointments. The Queen Mother snatched command of the French armies from Condé's father, who in truth was more qual-ified to lead troops than Anjou would ever prove to be. Condé was convinced that Anjou flirted with Marie only to get under his skin. Louis and I had insisted that Marie stay under our roof while Condé left to govern Picardy so that her reputation would remain unsullied.

Nothing could deter Anjou from writing amorous letters to my sister, however. Condé was convinced that since I did nothing to stop those letters from coming into my home, then I must be encouraging my sister to cuckold him. Condé's paranoia was exhausting, but Marie was determined to follow her heart and remain loyal to her husband. How she juggled the two men was beyond me.

"How is your son, Madame de Nevers?" a polite and innocent question, asked by one without malice. Elisabeth of Austria simply meant to be polite, but her kindness caused me to tear up. I would prefer the cruelty and cutting remarks of the court to the bit of kindness that the Queen offered.

I shook my head, "No better. We've called in every surgeon we could think of, but no one seems to be able to help him." The tears overtook me, and I shook with sobs. Marie jumped to her feet and held me in her arms.

"Forgive me, Madame. I should not have upset you." Like her compassion, Elisabeth's remorse was genuine. "I can offer nothing other than my prayers, and you and your family are in them."

God had not deigned to answer my prayers, but maybe he would listen to Elisabeth's. I simply nodded and tried to mouth a "thank you" while Marie held me.

❦

"TONIGHT WILL BE MUCH SMALLER THAN LAST TIME. I CAN'T DEAL with another boring recitation from another subpar actor." Claude Catherine pulled me through the rooms of her vast hotel, a building so massive that it managed to dwarf even mine. I needed this distraction, after several sleepless nights at Frederick's bedside, able to do nothing more than hold his hand. I had thought that by holding a vigil at his bedside, I might prove to God that I deserved to have my son healed. Perhaps God would see that I was worthy of His compassion and He would take pity on us both and heal him. To my disappointment, my bargaining with God did no good; Frederick was no better.

I decided to plunge into the distractions provided by our usual salons to cheer myself up. Avoiding my pain did nothing, nor did facing it head-on. My face must have darkened at the thought because Claude looked at me, "Are you sure that you're up to this?"

I gave her a quick nod, "It's better than crying myself to sleep." I felt isolated and unable to confess my dark feelings to any of my friends. I could hardly tell Margot what I was feeling, as she had yet to have her first child. Try as she might, the princess could not understand the terror I felt in the idea of losing my son. Claude knew little of what I was going through as her children were healthy and robust. Margot had yet to give birth to her first child. I could hardly count on either of them to fully understand what I was going through. Sympathy and compassion were one thing, experiencing the same thing was another.

Claude clapped her hands, "Good! I'll seat you next to some disgustingly handsome man who can carry on a conversation." She winked at me and bounded off to direct the servants in last minute preparations.

28

As it turned out, Claude Catherine seated me next to Annibal de Coconnas, who was more than willing to continue our conversation from the other evening. "Madame, I'm told that you're something of a financial genius," he turned to me. He chose the right form of seduction, if that was what he was doing. I would not be seduced with flowery words about my beauty or grace, but an appeal to my intellect got my attention.

"When I became the Duchess, most of our land was tied up in the Empire and extricating their revenue wasn't the easiest of tasks." This wasn't false humility; we Cleves were faithful subjects of the Holy Roman Emperor and had Phillip of Spain fulfilled his father's promises to us, we would have remained subjects of the Empire. My father, unfortunately, learned how duplicitous Spain could be just before his death and there was little that he could do to get the money due us from our loyalty to the Spanish crown. We were forced to throw in our lot with Francis I, becoming French subjects. My father's marriage to a Bourbon cemented our alliance to the French.

"It's a rare person who can make or keep a fortune these days." He leaned in towards me.

"Are you under the impression that flattery will get you anywhere?"

Was he teasing me? If he thought he was dealing with an empty-headed demoiselle, he was mistaken.

He shook his head, "No, it's not empty flattery. I'm impressed with what you've done."

"Then, I suppose I should return your compliment? Mine don't come so easily." I smiled at him, determined that he would understand my warning that I would not be an easy conquest.

He fingered the flute of the glass before him. I could not stop from admiring those fingers, at how deftly he circled the hard planes of the pattern. I started to wonder how they would feel against my skin. The months of strained encounters meant that Louis and I had not spent an evening together for longer than I could count. I missed the sensation of physical contact more than I realized.

Coconnas noticed me staring at his hands, curse the man! I was trapped, and I could not talk my way out of this situation. Years of watching Margot take advantage of sexually charged moments suddenly came to my rescue. "I wonder, Monsieur, why you are not with the rest of the court on your way to Lorraine. Is there a special reason why you are compelled to stay here in Paris?" The double entendre was blatant. I had already gone too far already, staring at him openly. I could not stop now and there was no saving myself or claiming innocence.

He smiled, unwilling to let the fact that I was staring go unnoticed. "Most of the Duc d'Alencon's retinue followed him with the King of Poland and the Queen Mother. I, however, must stay in Paris to take care of the Duc's business. My associate, Boniface La Mole," he glanced at Margot, who looked virtually naked without a male admirer at her side, "keeps me updated daily on the activities in Lorraine."

His knowing glance at Margot told me that she and La Mole were more of an item than I had initially suspected. Margot had not confessed to me who her most recent lover was, but since my mind was occupied with my son's condition, Margot seemed almost embarrassed to regale me with the details of a frivolous love affair.

"Madame de Nevers, it is becoming insufferably hot in this dining room. There are no more courses to be eaten. I suggest that we take in some cooler air." Perhaps the heat had gotten to me, because a cooler head would've stayed rooted in the room, far away from this man's advances. Too caught up in my sudden attraction, I could not say no to him. I simply nodded and followed him out into the hallway of the hotel

Once we were outside, the crisp November air bit at my arms and I pulled my cape around me. In a graceful and sweeping motion, Coconnas removed his own cape and offered it to me. Once again, common sense deserted me, and I accepted it with a shy smile. Bereft of his own cloak, he began to walk directly beside me as we strolled around the courtyard of Claude's home.

"I understand that your husband is a close advisor to the new King of Poland."

"Are you really going to talk politics to me now?" I grinned, once again unable to resist teasing him.

He gave a low chuckle, "No, I'm simply trying to determine how dangerous a seduction will be for me; and for my patron. His Highness enjoys the support of the Protestant and the Malcontents in the court." The Malcontents, a derogatory term given to the Catholics who opposed the idea of the Duc d'Anjou taking the throne upon the current King's death. Both parties would gladly push Anjou from the French succession the moment he left France for his Polish throne.

"As Louis's wife, you think that I am also Anjou's creature?" I shrugged, "The Duc is currently in love with my sister, so it would be to my advantage to support him as well."

"You're being very philosophical, so I assume that you aren't as enamored with Anjou."

I let out a small breath. "I believe that France will get the King that she gets; jostling for position before it's necessary is useless."

He guffawed, "A very political answer, Madame!"

I grinned, "How do you think I was able to become as rich as I am now?'

Before he could answer, a burst of riotous laughter drifted out of an open window. I looked up, distracted by the sound. Coconnas took advantage of the moment to grab my forearm and pull me into an alcove. There, hidden in the shadows, he kissed me passionately. I did not mind his actions one bit.

"Until the next time, Madame Nevers." He tipped his hat to me and led me out of the shadows and back to the dining room.

✣

FREDERICK CONTINUED TO LINGER ON, GETTING NO BETTER. THE expert physician from Turin advised us that a change of environment was the only thing that could save him. "The clear air of the countryside can only heal him. Much of Paris is a squalor," he cleared his throat when he saw the murderous look in my eye and hastened to add. "Of course, the Duc's home is a bastion of luxury, but the air here in Paris is not healthy for a child with a diseased body."

I had no desire to send my only son away where I could not take care of him myself, but Louis was insistent. "If it is the best for him, then we must do it, Henriette." As always, he appealed to my logical side, instead of my emotions. Louis was uncomfortable with the emotional side of an argument, which could make it difficult to argue with him sometimes. It also made it difficult for him to understand the agony I felt at the idea of being separated from Frederick. I had carried the boy inside my body and he still felt as if he were a part of me. As a man, Louis could not understand the bond between mother and son and the pain of physical separation.

We settled on sending him to our home in Nevers, our Ducal seat where he would be treated with every luxury imaginable. "I'll even go with him so I can ensure that he is settled in comfortably."

"I'll go with you, then," I started, but Louis cut me off mid-sentence.

"No, I can take care of our son. One of us must see to our affairs in Paris."

That irked me, Louis thought that of the two of us he was more suited to seeing our son to his sickbed. "Then, I should go with him while you remain here at court."

"Henriette, you're too emotional now and I'm afraid that you'd upset the boy."

"If he's sick, then he needs his mother around him."

"I'll have more authority if I oversee the move to Nevers."

That further infuriated me, Nevers was my own duchy, which I inherited from my father. Louis was Duke only by his marriage to me. Did he really think that now was the time to usurp my authority?

"Louis, you are being unreasonable and furthermore, you are insulting me." My face grew redder with each word. Like my sisters, my pale complexion meant that it was impossible to hide my anger.

He blew air out of his pursed lips. "Anjou has asked me to ensure that you remain close to Margot. He and the Queen Mother are convinced that she and Alencon are plotting to push Alencon to the throne during his absence in Poland."

"And you expect me to spy for them? You really think that is more important than caring for my son?" The idea was absurd. I was shouting, but Louis' lack of emotions made me more determined to display my own.

He sat down wordlessly. Finally, he spoke in soft tones, as if he were trying to calm a spooked horse. "Henriette, I have no desire to upset you, but you must see the bigger picture. You lost both of your brothers and there's a chance that we could lose our son as well. If he is gone, we will have to court the next King's favor so that one of our daughters can inherit."

He was right, of course. The logic of his strategy caused tears to prick at my eyes. "I can't think of the idea of losing Frederick." I looked at my husband, my face a blotched and swollen mess. He looked just as defeated as I felt.

"I will hover over him the entire time that I am there." I could only nod and walk out of the room. Emotions kept me from embracing him and I could feel the gulf between us widening. No matter how dire the situation, we still could not manage to unite in our time of grief.

Thus, by the time that the Advent season began in 1573, I was alone in Paris, bereft of my sisters, my son, and my husband. The loneliness was unbearable.

❦

LONELINESS AND ISOLATION COULD ONLY BE ALLEVIATED BY A pleasurable diversion, and Margot was more than willing to aid me in finding one. "Louis is away, and I think that you should take advantage of the situation to begin an affair." Her eyes sparkled with the prospect of an illicit relationship, one that was very close to her. "Mole will be back in Paris in a few days and I can help you find time with Coconnas." She slapped her forehead, "What am I saying—you have that cavernous house all to yourself, so *of course* you can find time to be with him."

"Marie will be back soon, and I can't kick my own sister out of my home." Margot was cleverer than that, how could she forget that my sister lived virtually homeless with her homely husband away in Picardy? She must have some plan afoot.

"You practically helped Marie and Anjou begin their relationship, so she owes you the favor." Margot was overstating my role in Marie and Anjou's odd flirtation: all I had done was reroute letters between the two and look the other way when they met in person at our home. Margot and Anjou were constantly at one another's throat, so the scandal her brother raised by openly flirting with my sister gave Margot a perverse pleasure. Outwardly, the Queen Mother expected an unapproachably moral court; the reality was that we all took our pleasure where we could find it.

I had resisted the temptation for years, but my attraction to Coconnas was irresistible. Fed up with the strained civility between Louis and me, the passion I felt for Coconnas was the balm I needed while I stretched thin with apprehension over my son. Meeting my lover at the Hotel de Nevers would certainly violate the Queen Mother's double standard of propriety, so Margot and I devised a plan to meet him in the chambers assigned to Alencon's retainers.

Within weeks, we contrived to spend as much time in one another's company as possible. My time with him was the highlight of each day. I once again felt desired and carefree, feelings that lay dormant for too many months. Although I came into this affair determined to be discreet, soon I grew less cautious in our meetings. I'm sure that it was not long before word spread throughout the hallways of the Louvre that we were lovers.

Lying in his arms one chilly December afternoon, we watched the fire lick at the embers in front of us. "Alencon and Navarre are planning to escape from the court," he whispered to me. I rolled over onto my stomach and propped my chin on his chest.

"Are they both mad? The King may spend most of his time in bed, but his guards never take their eyes off either of them."

He tilted his head back, acknowledging my point. "The King vomits up blood with his consumption, meaning that his time is near. Once Anjou hears that he is King, he will race back to France. Alencon plans to be ready to face his older brother with his own army."

Placing my palms on each of his hips, I pushed myself up. "What army?"

"There are troops in Champagne, outside of Reims." Reims, the ancient coronation place of the French kings. Champagne, territory controlled by the Guise family. If Alencon could position his troops in time, he could surround his older brother and force him to forfeit the crown. If the coup succeeded, my liaison with Coconnas would be beneficial, but if it failed, thank God Louis was Anjou's closest advisor outside of the Royal Family.

A second later, I realized that if I knew about the conspiracy, then it was likely that many others in the court did, too. "Does Margot know about this plot?" She had not mentioned it to me, but continued to hide things from me; a misguided attempt to avoid adding to my burdens.

He shook his head. "She's been kept in the dark. Alencon knows that she can't show him favor and that she's torn between her brothers. He needs her as an ally, whether he takes the throne from Anjou or if he later finds himself at Anjou and the Queen Mother's mercy."

He said no more and unwilling to spoil the rest of the day with talk of politics, we turned to more carnal matters. I had thought that the exertion would distract me and calm my mind, but when I returned home that evening, I began to feel unsettled. I had to speak to Margot and as soon as possible.

FIRST THING THE NEXT MORNING, I MARCHED INTO MARGOT'S audience chamber, a small space given to her as a ceremonial favor as

Queen of Navarre. I had hoped to find her alone, but as I entered, I heard a deep male voice speaking. The man was insistent, his voice high and strained. I could not make out the words, so feigning ignorance, I continued to walk into the chamber.

Margot was deep in conversation with her husband's own chancellor, Monsieur de Miossans.

The rest of her retinue were nowhere in sight and a lesser woman would have turned her heel and left her presence to give them privacy. I knew that no matter what the two were conversing about, Margot would prefer that I remain. Miossans and Margot shared a history as he was one of the Protestant men who staggered into Margot's bedchamber and begged her for sanctuary during the bloodbath that occurred on St. Bartholomew's Day. He knew Margot was made of steel and that he could trust her with his own life. We were likely the only two people in France who were assured of such special access to the Queen of Navarre.

"The forces are determined to regroup at Champagne." I could only see the back of his head, but Margot's face was grave. She gave him her full attention and simply nodded. He continued to give her the full story of the conspiracy, all of it the same as what Coconnas had told me the afternoon before.

"You're sure that my brother is determined to go through with this?" Margot was no fool; she knew who to trust and who to dismiss with a wave of her white hands.

"I've heard the same thing, Margot. I came here to tell you the same thing, but I see that I've been superseded." At the sound of my voice, Miossans turned and looked at me, his mouth agape.

"They're been exceedingly careless in the plot and far too many people know about it already. It's best that we do something to save them from themselves."

Margot knew full well how I had heard of the plot, but she kept that detail to herself. Tapping her fingers on the arm of her chair, she began to weigh her options. "Even if they succeed, and it's doubtful that they will, my brother and Navarre will be in open rebellion against the King and Anjou. I've sacrificed too much to allow them to do something so stupid. Keep your ears open and if you hear anything else, let me know. I'll figure out what needs to be done."

He bowed to her, grateful that once again she did not violate his trust in her. Like me, he knew that Margot was a valuable ally. Once he was gone, she turned to me.

"I'll have to prostrate myself in order to get them both out of trouble. I suppose now my husband will expect me to save him from the hangman's noose every time he makes a stupid decision." She rolled her eyes in disgust and rising, began to pace the room. I knew from her actions that she was formulating a plan.

"I have little to bargain with, but can offer the King this promise: if he will promise to spare Navarre and our brother, I will tell him of the plot. It may be the only way that I can save both of them from death."

"What do you need me to do?"

"I need you to go with me to my mother's audience chamber." She signaled for a page, "Send word to the Queen Mother that I must speak to her immediately. It is a matter of life and death."

I stood outside Catherine de Medici's presence chamber as Margot detailed the plot to her brother and her mother. In the end, her plan worked, Navarre and Alencon escaped death by Margot's persuasion.

⊗

WORD ARRIVED FROM NEVERS, BEARING MY HUSBAND'S SEAL. OUR son was improving slightly, which meant that the physician's advice to send him there was sound. Louis wrote that he regretted to say that the physician advised that our son set up his household at Nevers, while Louis would need to return to Paris and to the King's service as soon as possible. I realized that I was prudent in keeping my meetings with Coconnas outside of our home. Once my husband returned, I would not have to go through the intricacies of finding alternative meeting places. The times spent with my lover were too precious to me, and I had no desire to give them up.

By the end of December, a letter arrived from my sister Marie. Catherine had given birth to a stillborn girl and my heart broke for my sister over the loss of her tiny daughter. I hoped that the infant's death was not a portent of Frederick's own demise and prayed that death had touched our family enough. Marie's letter went on to say that instead of returning to Paris, she would leave immediately for Picardy to visit her insufferable husband. I dared hope that my sister had finally grown a backbone and she went to demand a divorce from the Prince de Condé in person. Once rid of her husband, there might be hope of Marie marrying Anjou, or failing that, to become his mistress. A royal mistress enjoyed power unmatched by all but a Queen Mother of a child King.

Margot had wrenched an additional promise from the King that he would not give Navarre or Alencon any indication how he had learned of the plot. The Queen Mother had another tactic when dealing with both men; she assigned Madame de Sauvé to expand her duties in the bedchamber to include a seduction of Alencon. The ungainly and pockmarked eighteen-year-old prince was far too enthralled with the guiles of de Sauvé's seduction to bother to wonder why she suddenly turned her attention towards him. For Navarre's part, I don't know if my cousin bothered to think about his mistress' newfound attention towards his unattractive brother-in-law.

In fact, each man seemed to look upon keeping Charlotte de Sauvé's affections as kind of a game, jostling for her attention, and keeping score as if they were on a tennis court. The scandal and merriment that the two gave the court took attention away from Margot and myself, and we took the opportunity to continue our own affairs without much interference. As far as gossip went, we were much less interesting for the wagging tongues of the court.

My ever-practical husband no doubt learned that I had a lover as soon as he returned to Paris, if not sooner, but if he felt anger or jealousy, he said nothing. My sisters might have husbands prone to fits of jealous rage, but Louis simply accepted my betrayal of our marriage vows as a matter of course. He was too busy playing a diplomatic game of simultaneously serving the dying King and his likely successor, the Duc d'Anjou. Letters arrived daily from Poland, most of them addressed to Louis and the rest addressed to Marie. Using our surreptitious method, I re-routed them to Picardy while I waited for her return to Paris.

29

Guilt-ridden and in search of allies, the Duc d'Alençon stayed close to Margot, which meant that we were able to see an increasing amount of Mole and Coconnas. In fact, the remaining Valois gathered closely together at the Chateau St. Germain, a day's ride out of the squalor of Paris. The King's own physician advised him to stay at the chateau until his health improved. The Queen Mother took a particular interest in improving the gardens of the chateau, making it one of the most Italian of the royal palaces. I took advantage of the new surroundings and took every opportunity to spend time with Coconnas.

The court's move to St. Germain meant that my sister Catherine made her return to court after healing from the loss of her daughter. I was determined to repair our relationship, due in part to my selfish fear that death would take my own child. Death took those under the age of five years all too often in those days and I hung on with the superstitious hope that I could ward off the same fate for Frederick. Although my days and nights were filled with enough activity and concern, if I could manage to make amends with my sister, I hoped I would feel some relief from my guilt.

The lingering resentment over our inheritance meant that our conversations were awkward and that chilly January, Catherine and I stuck to familiar topics, or at least those familiar to each of us. "I have to admit, I was shocked to hear that you had taken on a lover," she remarked one day as we looked out over the gardens of the palace from her apartment windows. Most days, she walked around in a lingering melancholy, but on that day, the color began to return to her cheeks.

"Were you under the impression that I was incapable of doing so?" I tried to make my voice sound teasing and not harsh, but I could still hear the defensiveness in my tone.

She shook her head, chastened momentarily, "No, it's just that in all the years that you've been married, I never heard of you having the least interest in another man. And I," she gave me a wicked smile, "hear everything that goes on in the court."

"I'm sure you do!" I laughed, grateful that we had broken the iciness between us.

"So, what is it, boredom?" Her question was without malice, more of a sisterly concern. Still, it bothered me, unused as I was to the idea of confessing my romantic feelings for another man. Perhaps I still felt some guilt over my actions.

"I feel plagued by anguish and fear these days. I wanted to feel relief for a while. That's what Coconnas does for me." I need not explain any more to Catherine, who daily mourned the loss of a child. Only another mother could understand the apprehension I felt on a daily basis, the nervousness, and the constant bargaining with God to keep my child safe. Catherine knew firsthand what it felt like when God refused to make a bargain.

"Can you really not talk to Louis?" The question hung in the air and I could not answer it. I had asked myself the same question several times before and always came up with a different answer. Catherine pressed on, unnerved by the silence.

"He is a cold fish, I'll give you that. Perhaps he doesn't know how to speak to you." She lifted her eyebrows and inclined her head in my direction. That was my sister, always convinced that there was an easy answer to a problem, if one looked hard enough to find it.

"Catherine, Louis isn't as excitable as your husband. I've seen the two of you going at it, having a row. And he isn't the kind to let things fester. In fact, I wouldn't be surprised if Guise lost his temper one day and you or your lover wound up dead."

She shrugged, unwilling to concede my point. "At least we would have a solution. What good is sitting around in silence?"

Too stubborn to answer her, I stared silently ahead of me. "Perhaps you are ignoring Louis as a way of punishing him?"

"Why would I possibly punish him? Frederick is his son, too."

"Wasn't it his idea to send him to Nevers?" Curse my sister, was there nothing that went on in my private household that she was not aware of? Catherine was becoming a bigger gossip with age. "Having an affair right under his nose would be a particularly effective way of getting him back for separating you from your son."

"You make him sound like a tyrant; and you're making *me* sound like one, too." I was growing tired of her prying questions.

"You are much closer to Nevers here at St. Germain. No one would fault you for riding out to check on Frederick for a few days."

⚜

No matter how much Catherine irked me, I had to admit that she might be at least partially right. When I entered our shared apartments, Louis was in the sitting room, looking over papers. "I'm going to Nevers for a few days to check on Frederick. If there's any change in his progress, I'll write you immediately."

Louis looked up from his work, dazed. "That sounds good." I waited for him to add anything more, a jealous quip under his breath. An accusation that I was leaving to rendezvous with my lover. Anything that might indicate that he might feel jealousy over the loss of our intimacy. He said nothing, and my heart sank.

When I got to my sister Marie's apartments, she was also working on her correspondence and when she saw me, she gave a jump and shoved the papers away like a guilty child. "Ah, I see the post for Poland is coming soon."

"Ah, yes. I wanted to finish this before supper." One of the papers slipped out of the snarled pile she had hastily made and glided onto the floor. Marie pretended not to notice it.

"Really, Marie?"

She cleared her throat and gave me a false smile. I had no desire to know what kind of overly wrought words or devotion she was sending to Anjou, yet her discomfort was fun to watch. If I were not in the midst of packing to see my son, I would stay and see if she would squirm guiltily in her chair for much longer.

"I'm leaving first thing tomorrow for Nevers to see to Frederick."

Her face drained of color. "Is he all right?"

I put my hand up to calm her, noticing that since returning from Picardy, her moods were becoming erratic. I made a note to speak to her after I returned to Paris.

"He's fine, I simply miss him." At that, she smiled, and I returned her goodwill gesture.

"The Queen Mother asked that I stay close to Queen Elisabeth while the King is ailing, so I don't know when I will be back to Hotel de Nevers."

Louis would be in our massive home by himself, left to his own devices. If he chose, he could take on a mistress and I would be none the wiser for it. I felt a quick pang of jealousy at the thought. The feeling reminded me that I would need to speak to Coconnas before I left. I hated to tell him goodbye, but I would not leave without a proper farewell.

"I need to pack. Keep an eye on Catherine for me, will you? I think she'll be up to her usual mischievousness before too long." I could not help but smile at the idea.

"I hope so."

⚜

I STAYED IN NEVERS UNTIL THE END OF FEBRUARY, ENJOYING THE quiet and spending as much time with my son as I could. Every mother hopes for a chubby happy baby, but I only wished for a healthy one. Much of my guilt faded away as I saw that Frederick indeed had the best care possible at Nevers as the Florentine specialist spent his waking hours hovering over him and doing all he could do to bring my son to health.

Eventually, part of my anger at Louis for his decision to send the boy away began to fade. I was able to forgive him for what at the time had felt like a heartless decision. I certainly spent enough hours in Mass and at prayer doing my own bargaining for my child's life. In moments of great self-sacrifice, I offered to give up Coconnas in order to save my child and in others, I selfishly reverted to my desire to remain in Coconnas' arms. Torn between selfishness and guilt, I could not make the decision to keep Coconnas or let him go. Eventually, I decided that whether I ended our relationship or not, it would make little difference to God.

By March, I returned home to Paris and the Hotel de Nevers. Our home was a picture of domestic tranquility. Louis and Marie had managed the household quite handily without me. "I'm quite impressed, Marie. If you ever manage to get a home of your own, you'll be quite the chatelaine."

To my horror, my sister burst into tears. I had only been home for hours and already had an emotional woman on my hands. "Dearest, whatever is the matter?" I led her to a chair in the parlor, where she sank down with a long sigh. For the next several moments, she sobbed uncontrollably while I watched her helplessly.

"I just found out the other day, I'm pregnant."

The full horror of what she was telling me hit before I could pull my face into a blank expression. "Please tell me it's Anjou's child."

She looked at me with a mix of rage and annoyance. For the first time, I realized how much my sisters favored one another. She was the very image of Catherine when she got into one of her emotional states. "No, it's my husband's!"

It's quite possible that my sister was the only woman in France who would be devastated at the idea of having her husband's legitimate child and heir. To be honest, we were all horrified at the idea of her having Condé's child. A pregnancy would prove once and for all to the Vatican that their ill-considered marriage was consummated. If Marie hoped to divorce Condé and later marry Anjou, this could be the end of her hopes.

"How could you? I thought you went to Picardy to ask for a divorce."

"No, I went to, I mean—I had to talk to him and I thought..." she looked flustered and I remembered the day before I left for Nevers and I realized that she was obviously hiding something from me. "I felt guilty about Anjou and I decided to try to fix our marriage." she squeaked out.

There was little I could say to her to make her feel better. "Well, another Prince de Condé is good for the succession, I suppose." It was a weak attempt, but it was all that either of us could think of that was good in her current situation. She was trapped for now until the child came, or she lost it.

"I hope you're doing better with your situation," she attempted a thin smile and I hugged her. "As a matter of fact, I am meeting Coconnas tomorrow at Margot's apartments. Alencon has arranged a little get together in honor of my return."

Officially, the reason for the day's fete was to welcome me back to Paris, in fact, the Duc d'Alencon was determined to ingratiate himself with his sister as much as possible. Someone, most likely Coconnas, had told Alencon that Margot informed the King during their latest plot to escape and Alencon realized that he needed Margot's support now more than ever. Finally, the Queen of Navarre was considered to be a power player in the French court and she relished her newly elevated status.

"I'm being courted by my brother and ignored by my husband. I really can't complain about my situation." Margot strutted around her apartments, relishing the attention. My relationship with Coconnas picked up where we left it, but he stopped talking to me about politics. That was just as well with me since our hours together were the only hours of respite I got from my increasing family issues. I wanted passionate, light-hearted entertainment from my lover and he was willing to provide it. If Alencon expected his man to garner any information about Margot's plans from me, Coconnas declined to do so as we laid naked in one another's arms.

I suppose that was why I was taken by complete surprise one day in April when word spread throughout Saint Germain that a Protestant army was spotted heading directly towards the chateau. Unlike most royal residences, Saint Germain was built more like a country villa, reminiscent of those the Medici built in Italy. Situated on a hill, the chateau had few natural defenses. The menace of an invading army was something that the Valois would not take lightly.

When I heard the panicked shouts, I was bereft of all of my clothing and snuggled closely to Coconnas. Once he heard the word "attack," he jumped from the bed and to his feet. "Those fools! They're too early!"

"What are you talking about? My blonde curls askew as always, I tried to smooth them back into a quick braid. Fishing around for my clothing, I dressed as quickly as possible and rang for my lady's maid. While I waited for her arrival, my lover abruptly exited the bedchamber. With no regard to my appearance, I began to search the frenzied halls of the chateau in search of my husband.

I found him mustering troops. "What on earth is going on?"

"It's the Politiques and the Protestants," he spat. "They've decided not to have the decency to wait for the King to meet his Heavenly reward and simply take the crown now. And since they couldn't break Navarre and Alencon out of the chateau, they'll simply bring an army to them."

An entire army marching towards us! I could not image the carnage. "What is the King to do?"

"He's in no shape to do much of anything. The Queen Mother has ordered out the Swiss Guard." It was so like Catherine de Medici to deal with a crisis by sending out the most fearsome soldiers in all of France. Marie was likely with the Queen Mother, so I would not have to worry about her safety. That left my sister Catherine. "I'll go find Catherine."

"Guise wants her to evacuate as soon as possible and head to safety at Joinville. If you hurry, you can catch her."

"Louis, where should I go?"

He gave me a quick nod, "Go to Nevers and see to our son." It was the best idea that I had heard in months and it took no convincing for me to agree. The weeks we'd spent apart were far too long. But first, I had to check on my sister.

I ran at top speed to my sister's apartments, finding her directing her servants to pack anything of value. "My husband's uncles," she said, referring to the Cardinals of Lorraine and Guise, "are halfway to Nancy by now. The moment they heard we were under attack, they jumped on their horses and ran away like a couple of dowager aunts." Despite her panic, she found the idea of the men gathering up their skirts and running for their lives quite comical.

"Marie is barricaded behind the walls of the Queen Mother's apartments. No one is allowed in or out other than royal messengers. She's safe, though," she added.

"I'll check on Margot and then I'll start packing for Nevers." The chance to see my son again buoyed me and despite the dire situation, I did feel buoyed by the prospect. Now was not the time to celebrate, however, and I tempered my reaction.

Hastening to Margot's chambers, I noticed that there was no rush to pack. Margot stood in the middle of her audience chamber, much calmer than I would have expected. "Are you planning on staying?" It was not a ridiculous question; Margot had survived much worse than this.

"My Mother has the invaders engaged and she's ordered the entire court to go to Vincennes." She rolled her eyes as if the entire situation were nothing more than an inconvenience.

The chateau of Vincennes was the closest and most heavily fortified royal residence within riding distance of Saint Germain. If the court could make it there in time, we could hold out against all but the mightiest army. My heart sank as I realized that I would not be going to visit my son after all. No one would be allowed on the roads for fear of spies or the danger of becoming valuable hostages for the Protestants.

"I don't suppose anyone has bothered to tell the Cardinals of Lorraine and Guise about this plan?" I remarked drily. I was beginning to see Margot's point; this evacuation would quickly become one great inconvenience.

"Those old women! I'm sure they're halfway to Lorraine by now. And good riddance!" She doubled over in laughter at the idea of the two elderly men making all haste to escape an army while the rest of the court went in the opposite direction.

"Margot, you're terrible!" My attempt to chastise her ended in a burst of laughter. She smiled at me like a naughty school girl.

THE MOVEMENT OF A ROYAL COURT, EVEN ONE THAT IS PLANNED OUT in advance, is a chaotic and stressful event. A court running for its life is a nightmare and for the seventeen miles between St. Germain and Vincennes, we sprinted for the safety of the fortress on the outskirts of Paris. No one had time to make preparations for us and once we got to Vincennes, the compound was in chaos as well. With no real apartments or living spaces for the courtiers, we were packed into shared rooms, more irritable than fearful. The entire situation was miserable, and I was particularly annoyed that I had been denied the opportunity to spend the time with my son at Nevers. At least our daughters were safe with their governess back at the Hotel de Nevers.

Catherine and the Duc de Guise shared chambers with us, which was less awkward since we had buried our quarrel months earlier. "I hear that Charlotte de Sauvé is having more trouble than usual keeping both Navarre and Alencon at bay this time. They're both terrified that the King will send them to the gallows any moment." Faced with nothing more to do for the next two weeks, as spring rains came in late March, we kept amused eyes on Madame de Sauvé and her attempts to juggle her two anxious lovers.

In order to save his own neck and stave off exile, the Duc d'Alencon fell to his knees a day after we arrived in Vincennes to confess the entire plot to his mother. The prince and Navarre knew that the odds of being forgiven were against them and we all waited on tenterhooks to see how the King and his mother would deal with their rebellion. Even as jaded and cynical as we all were, none of us guessed the lengths that the two princes would go to in order to save their own lives.

Jammed up against one another, finding places to secretly meet with one's paramour became difficult to manage. The King and Guise decided to make great sport of the situation one day by lying in wait to see if he could catch my lover coming out of my apartments. I may have been reckless during those days, but I was not stupid. Early one cold spring morning, I opened the door on my way to Margot's chambers to find the King and my brother- in- law grinning like idiots.

"May I help you, Sire? Brother?"

"Where is he?" Guise managed to speak, while the King giggled like a young girl.

"If you're looking for Louis, he is not here." I crossed my arms and stared at both of them.

"Madame, we are looking for Monsieur la Mole," the King managed through giggles.

"He is not here, as you can see. Perhaps," a door clicked at the end of the hallway. We all turned to see the gentleman in question tiptoeing out of Margot's chambers.

"If you'll excuse me, I have to attend the Queen." I pushed past both of them, ignoring their laughter. Even when proven wrong, the two could find nothing other than humor in the situation.

Sighing, I strode into Margot's chambers. "Margot, the King, and Guise are at spying on women's bedchambers. They saw Mole creeping out of your chambers." While I was angry and annoyed at the intrusion upon my privacy, Margot simply shrugged her shoulders. "Guise and my brother should be careful if they plan on rifling through someone's private belongings. They never know what they might find."

⬥

By April, we settled in the chateau of Fountainbleu, the Queen Mother refusing to give into the threat of an army and the King annoyed at the idea of a return to Paris proper. Still, the tasteless games and spying continued, carried on by the Queen Mother's Flying Squadron of female agents. My nerves frayed, I took out my annoyance on Charlotte de Sauvé one afternoon as we attended upon the Queen Mother. "I have heard, Madame, that you are spending much of your time sneaking about the apartments of the men of the court. Are your lovers not enough to satisfy you?"

She stiffened, and her face became hard as stone. "My activities are none of your business, Madame de Nevers. I serve Her Majesty the

Queen Mother and answer only to her." Her prim voice instantly grated on my nerves.

"Then, I suppose we should hide all of our valuables, then? I wonder, just what would you do with them?" The accusation hit her hard, her family was newly raised and had no noble blood whatsoever. Her father's title of Viscount and her husband's new title of Baron de Sauvé came through service to the Crown, a reflection of their need to keep a constant influx of money in order to stay at court. Worse still, without the intricate intermarriages of families that established nobles boasted, she had no network of cousins or uncles to speak for her when she was in danger of falling from favor with the Valois.

"My family has not fallen upon hard times as many of the so-called 'noble' houses have." She nodded towards the impoverished Countess de Limourges, who lived only on the charity of her sister, a Duchess.

"Nobility carries with it a certain adherence to propriety. I doubt you could manage to purchase that." At that, I stood up and moved to the window. I was so arrogant that day, thinking that I had scored a victory over her. Little did I know, I had secured a death warrant for the man who made my moments sweeter.

❦

DAYS AFTER MY ENCOUNTER WITH MADAME DE SAUVÉ, WE HEARD A ruckus from the direction of the rooms where La Mole, Coconnas and other gentlemen of Alencon's retinue were housed in the Tuileries. While the palace afforded more room than Vincennes, few of us were afforded much privacy. Outside of my antechamber, I heard the Swiss Guard rushing down the hallway. Thinking that we were moments away from another escape to Vincennes, I asked a passing maid what the cause of the commotion was.

"My Lady, the guards say that there is another conspiracy at the court. The Protestants and Catholics have joined to kill the king." Unable to leave or attack the conspirators had decided to simply rid themselves of the king. I had no desire to follow the growing crowd that followed the Swiss Guard, but at my elbow, my husband's page spoke up. "Madame, they are going towards Monsieur La Mole's quarters."

Knowing that Margot would be in the crowd in order to position herself to defend her lover, I decided that I should join the throng. Reaching for my shawl, I blended into the rush of silks as it passed down the hall.

"I tell you, I am innocent!" Mole's voice echoed from his chambers. Before I could open my mouth, I heard Margot's voice.

"Whatever is going on?" she demanded with all of the haughtiness that came with being born the daughter of a king.

The excited crowd buzzed the word from La Mole's doorway to Margot's position in the middle of the hall, "It is a wax figure of the King!"

One overly excited woman shrieked, "Le Mole means to kill the King!"

"Mon Dieu!" Half of the assembled crowd hastily crossed themselves. As I glanced at those who did not do so, I noticed Charlotte de Sauvé, looking suspiciously calm.

The guard dragged La Mole out into the hallway and we could only watch as they took him away. Margot crooked her finger at me and I quickly followed her to her chambers. We stayed there until late that night when one of her pages finally gave her news of the hapless man.

"It's the same conspirators, including the King of Navarre and the Duc d'Alencon," he blushed and ducked his head in embarrassment, but Margot waved him on. "Mole gave up his accomplices, including Monsieur Coconnas," he nodded towards me and I nodded in understanding.

"Do they have evidence that they planned to kill my brother?" Margot gripped the table in front of her until her knuckles turned white. The young boy put his hands up, wordlessly. "So, it is simply an accusation," she concluded. There was hope for them, after all.

"Highness, it is the third conspiracy against the King in less than a year. I doubt that anything they say will make much of a difference."

"Then, I have to speak to my brother and mother." She pushed herself upright and was silent for a few moments. "Fetch me ink and paper!"

As soon as the boy was gone, I stood next to her, "What can you do, Margot? As he said, the conspiracies keep coming. What makes you think that the King won't simply execute all of them?"

She nodded, "We can't hope to save all of them, but we may save some of them."

"But is it worth the danger to you? Do you really want to save someone who stupidly plots against the King and his successor so much? They'll eventually lead you to prison, too."

She sat and rubbed her eyes, "Navarre can provide me a way out of court and I need to have a cordial relationship with at least one of my brothers. Charles won't last long," she crossed herself at the truth that we were all too afraid to speak aloud for fear of being accused of treason, "and I have no desire to ally myself with Anjou. He'll betray me at the first opportunity."

"Then, how do you save them both? *Can* you save them both?"

⚅

MARGOT SPENT THE NEXT DAY PENNING WHAT WOULD BECOME A masterful response to the accusations against her husband and brother. Mole and Coconnas lingered in prison and we had little hope that either of them would feel the warmth of the sun again. Alencon threw himself on his Mother's mercy, giving up both men in order to save himself. The King would not easily pardon any of them this time and all of the conspirators were thrown into the prisons of Vincennes to await a special commission of five judges.

Alencon proved to be the spineless child that we all knew him to be, choosing to ramble on in front of the court, blaming his part of the conspiracy on a desire to escape to Flanders. Alencon claimed that the Dutch Protestants promised him the governorship of Flanders, a charge that we all found laughable. Given how stupid Alencon had proven to be the previous year, it wasn't that difficult for the commission to believe that he was indeed that naive.

Alencon was not the only one who claimed an incredible amount of stupidity as his defense. Navarre rose to speak and pulled out a paper to read. The statement was extremely well crafted because Navarre did not write it himself. He went on to claim that his escape attempts were necessary because the Valois had treated him so badly that he was all but compelled to escape. He had not been treated like a sovereign king and without her ruler, Navarre suffered. Had the King and his mother treated him with the honor due to his station, he added, he would be the King of France's most loyal vassal and potential ally.

The argument was typical of Margot, playing into the court's assumption that Navarre was a simpleton. It also pricked a sense of shame and guilt in the decision to hold another sovereign hostage, pricking the dying King's conscious. Margot's argument, delivered to the court in Navarre's voice, could not be refuted and both Navarre and Alencon escaped once again with their lives.

Still, the court would not let the incident pass without some form of punishment. While the princes were exonerated, someone must take the blame. The blame fell upon Mole and Coconnas, who under torture confessed to plotting the entire conspiracy. Once they accepted the blame, they were summarily sentenced to death.

"We have to do something!" Margot tapped her fingers on the book in her lap.

"You've managed to get two men off, so what can you do to help them?"

"I'll think of something, we have time before their execution." Both men were sentenced to a public beheading and time was very short if we were to save them.

"I will go to the King, he does love me." She dismissed me, and I went back to my apartment. As I sat, I contemplated on what my life would be like without Coconnas. He was a balm in the ongoing fits of fear that plagued me. Where would I find that same easy companionship that I found with him?

While I mused, from the doorway, I heard Louis discreetly clearing his throat. Annoyed, I had no desire to listen to my husband's self-righteous lectures about my affair with Coconnas. "I am in no mood to hear it, Louis. I have a headache and I wish to be alone."

Ignoring me, he took several halting steps toward the bed where I sat. Wordlessly, he pulled out an envelope, edged with black. For a few moments, my mind could not make out the meaning of his motions.

Then, before understanding could come, I immediately went into denial.

"I came to you as soon as I got the letter." His body shook, and I saw the faintest trace of a tear fall down his cheek.

I said nothing, my head shaking. He proffered the envelope as if my taking it would ease his own pain. I continued to shake my head, refusing to take it.

"It was yesterday. The doctor thought that he was fine, but--" A shaky inhalation cut off his words. If he said anything more, I did not hear it. I did not *want* to hear it.

⚜

I SPENT THE NEXT SEVERAL DAYS FLOATING ABOUT LIKE A WRAITH. Packing my things, I went directly to the Hotel de Nevers where I could have some semblance of privacy from the intrusive whisperings of the court. I allowed no one to see me, save a servant who placed a tray of food at my door. I honestly have no idea where my husband was in those dark days since I cut myself away from all human contact. The world continued, the trees outside my window budding with new blooms. I cared nothing for them since my own life was stripped of color.

After about a week of my self-imposed isolation, my servant told me that I had a visitor, one who could not be refused. Before I could send either of them away, Margot appeared at my doorway. "There really is nothing that I can say to you that can help, I know that."

I stared at her, saying nothing. If I were not still numb, I would be touched by her show of compassion. My feelings were disconnected as a way to handle my devastation, so I could only bite my lip in response.

"I've been an utter failure at espionage without you." She tried a wan smile, one that I could not return. My humor would not return for weeks, if ever. Unsure of how to handle my mood, she pressed on.

"I tried to get Navarre and Alencon out of prison. I was going to visit them with one of my ladies. We would exchange clothing and have one of them walk out of the cell, pretending to be me. The guards never look under our masks or molest us to check our clothing. They wouldn't dare. By the time they did check, the men would be well out of Paris and we would be there to greet them."

"Margot, that idea is pathetic."

She shrugged, pleased to have gotten some response out of me. "I think it would have worked. Sadly, neither man could get together on who would pretend to be me."

"That was the weak point? Really, Margot—you are getting terrible at plotting."

Another shrug, "I do better plotting with you."

I relented and allowed her to try to cheer me up until supper time when she kissed my forehead and returned to her rooms at the palace.

By the end of April, the King was determined to remind all of France that its master and he stood firm in the decision to carry out the execution of La Mole and Coconnas on the last day of the month. Despite her continued pleas, Margot could not convince her brother to relent and spare our lovers.

The morning after their death, Margot came to my house and asked if I would do her a favor. As soon as she laid out her plan, I shook my head. "Margot, I don't think that it's wise," I tried to talk her out of the idea, but she stood firm.

"We'll do it under the cover of night, no one will see us. I can't live with the guilt."

Faced with sitting with my own grief or the distraction of Margot's misplaced romantic whimsy, I decided on the latter. As soon as the city was bathed in moonlight, we took an unmarked carriage to the place where the bodies of our lovers lay. "We should take their bodies and embalm them." She sounded so wistful that I felt sorry for her. My own son lay in the crypt at the cathedral of Nevers and I had been denied the opportunity to bury him during our hasty flight to Vincennes.

"Fine, but we can't possibly take their entire bodies with us. You have to be practical, Margot." I pleaded with her, feeling uneasy at the idea of what she had talked me into doing. To my relief, she nodded.

"Where can we put them?" Her look was pleading, and I realized at that moment that she valued my opinion more than I realized. I also realized that she was more vulnerable than I had noticed before. Mole's death affected her more than I had initially assumed.

"Somewhere out of the way." We talked to the driver, who suggested an unassuming out of the way chapel in the village of Montmare. The village was well out of Paris, and no one would think to look for their bodies there.

Thus, in a small, plain chapel in Montmare we had the heads of our lovers embalmed and perfumed. Margot insisted on this honor for both of them and she sobbed quietly as we had them both interred in the small space. For me, it became the service that I could not hold for my lost son whose body entered his tomb before I could see his face for the final time.

30

Exactly a month after Margot and I slipped out under the cover of darkness to bury the remains of our lovers, the entire country was in mourning. The King succumbed to tuberculosis, making the former Duc d'Anjou, not just King of Poland but the new King of France. Margot was bereft as she detested her brother the new king. At the same time, my sister Marie was thrilled at the thought of having her paramour returned to her.

"It's been misery having to be content with just words. I never realized how much I enjoyed his presence until I lost him." I could not help but feel pity for my sister; Condé had betrayed her and the King by escaping to Switzerland, reverting to Protestantism, and declaring war upon the Valois. He had assembled an impressive number of Swiss mercenaries to fight for the Protestants against the new king. Marie was done with her husband and with the Queen Mother's help, actively petitioned the Vatican for an annulment. Once the King returned and the Pope granted her petition, I had no doubt that she would announce her plans to wed the king. First, however, she would have to endure the birth of her child.

Louis was also pleased to have the new King on his way to Paris. He would now become one of the closest advisors to the new monarch, much more important than he had been to the previous one. My husband spent so much time at the Louvre managing the transition between the rules that I rarely saw him. Louis had plenty of time to make the transition smooth, as the King spent the rest of the Summer dallying in his return to France. "It's due in part to that villain Condé," my sister Catherine told me one day. "He's amassing troops at the border and the King has to spend money he doesn't have in order to find soldiers to fight for him."

She glanced sidelong at me, "But I suppose Louis told you that already."

"He hasn't said anything to me. I don't remember the last time I spoke to him." I knew that I had embarrassed him and hurt his pride with my affair, but I did not care. My grief was so great that I had lost my ability to feel compassion for my husband.

"Guise has offered to raise an army for the King, but the Queen Mother doesn't trust him to shoe a horse these days." Catherine and I walked back from Mass, fanning ourselves in the relentless heat. With no King or Queen Consort to lead the court, we were left to our own devices that summer. Remaining united, Catherine and I kept a close watch over our younger sister and Catherine spent several days at the Hotel de Nevers hovering over Marie.

"If Louis were to offer to reconcile, would you do so?" Catherine's question hung in the air, and I mulled over the idea as we walked.

"I don't know." I really hadn't considered that option. I think that I had grown used to silence and awkwardness. I didn't want the burden of an active relationship with my own husband.

"Will you take another lover, then?"

I shook my head, surprised at my answer. "No, I still feel I lost Frederick because of him."

She rolled her eyes, "Oh, stop sounding like a pious Protestant! Frederick's death was not because you spent a few hours in some other man's bed. Feel guilty for being unfaithful if you wish, but not guilt over causing your child's death. Nothing I did caused the death of my daughter in December."

Catherine was probably right, but my lingering guilt kept me from agreeing with her. I could not stop the constant fear that I had caused

Frederick's death with by betraying my marriage vows. I was terrified that I had caused the fraying of my own family, but I was also too terrified to confess those feelings to my sister.

⚜

BY OCTOBER, THE NEW KING FINALLY ARRIVED WITHIN THE boundaries of France, staying in faraway Lyon. Louis left to meet him as soon as possible, as the court traveled to join up with the new sovereign. Not all of us went to Lyon, however, as Marie was so heavily pregnant that she could not make the long trip from Paris. Catherine and I volunteered to stay with her, and using Louis's absence as a pretext, I moved into the Hotel de Guise to help with the delivery of the child. Catherine was determined to repay Marie for her support in December and I was determined to stand with my sisters.

The time I spent with my sisters, reminded me of my own daughters, who would soon begin settling into the households of their future husbands. Although the tradition was generations old, I finally understood how difficult it was for a mother to send her child away from her. With Frederick gone, I would miss my remaining children more than I cared to admit. I had been so wrapped up in the permanent loss of my son to realize that the loss of my daughters would affect me just as deeply when the time came to give them up.

Marie's due date came and went, and impatient to be rid of any connection with Condé and greet the man she loved, Marie quickly grew agitated. "I'm so glad you're here—she's becoming impossible," Catherine complained to me one morning over breakfast.

"She's just as melodramatic as you are. Now I hope you can appreciate how difficult you can be."

She stopped in the middle of buttering a roll, "I am not difficult!"

"Catherine!" I put my knife down and glared at her. I was about to chastise her when we both heard a loud wail. Marie's labour had finally started.

The delivery was quick and simple, although Marie was terrified throughout the ordeal. Thanks to God she gave birth to a girl, which meant that Condé would not move in to claim the child. Fate seemed to be smiling on my youngest sister finally.

The doctor would not hear of her leaving for Lyon before she had recovered, and she reluctantly stayed abed for the next two weeks. Everything seemed to be going well and we started to make preparations for the King's return to Paris and my return to the Hotel de Nevers. I was glad for the opportunity to return to my daughters and for the time to be by ourselves before Louis returned. As I stood looking over my things, Catherine's young maid knocked on my chamber door.

"It's the Princess de Condé, My Lady." The young girl's face began to drain of color, terrifying me. I suddenly remembered the hours spent by Frederick's bed, weeping, and praying for his recovery. In a daze, I ran behind her to see what I could do to help my youngest sister. At the doorway to Marie's chamber, Catherine stood talking to the doctor.

"It's a tear, Madame. We did not know about it until today when she started to decline."

"How long until she recovers?" They both met me with silence, terrifying me.

"It's bad," Catherine added, "she's lost a large amount of blood. Her maid found her moaning and there was a bloodstain already on the sheets."

"Then what's to be done?" I would not lose another family member, not this soon and not without any forewarning. God continued to be cruel to me for my single discretion.

"I've done all that I can do, I think prayer is needed more than anything. By all means, keep her calm."

Marie lingered on for two more weeks, continuously losing blood and slipping away from us. Between the three of us, she had always had the most delicate health. The stress of the birth combined with the shock of her husband's betrayal sapped what little strength her slender body possessed. My sister had spirit and she held on by sheer will for as long as she could. Eventually, however, she slipped away from us before she could reunite with the King. Catherine sent word to the King in Lyon, whose grief was palatable. Guise wrote to her of how he prostrated himself in the loss of my sister. Together, Catherine and I awaited the return of the new King who would enter Paris behind two coffins.

❧

Spring returned to Paris along with the court, a court much changed from the previous year. My sister would not preside over it as Queen Consort, which brought me much regret. Still, the King needed a wife and an heir, so he settled on a distant relative of the Duc de Guise, a quiet girl named Louise, the daughter of the Duke de Mercoeur. As Louise was a Guise relation, the marriage sent the Queen Mother into a rage, claiming that the Guise were determined to regain power in France.

Most in the court called Louise "unremarkable," but to me, she was quite striking for her looks. Undoubtedly, she was beautiful, but that was not the issue. The new Queen bore a striking resemblance to my sister Marie. Henri III was determined to spend his life with my sister, going so far as to marry a woman who looked enough like her to cause me to catch my breath the first time I laid eyes upon her. Never at a loss for words, Catherine hissed into my ear afterward, "Can you believe how much she looks like Marie! I never thought he really loved her, but if this isn't proof that he did, I don't know what is!" Louise's presence unnerved me, and I resolved to stay as far away from her as possible, so as not to see my dead sister's presence in the new Queen's face.

The King had other plans, however. A week after his wedding, I was called to the Queen's Presence Chamber, where they sat on thrones. "Madame de Nevers, our beloved cousin. I have always enjoyed your loyalty and that of your husband." He inclined his head towards me and I curtsied.

"It would honor me and the Queen," he inclined his head towards her as she blushed mutely, "if you would serve as Her Majesty's Mistress of the Robes." Mistress of the Robes, the head of the Queen's household. The position was a great honor for anyone and if I were not so uncomfortable around the new Queen, I would be extremely honored at the position.

"Sire, I am unworthy. Yet, I feel that the Queen would feel uncomfortable with my presence given my relationship with your Majesty..." the King cut me off before I could elaborate.

"That is why I need you to take on this honor. I will not have the Queen dishonored with talk that she is unworthy of her position. Your presence will signal to the court that her position is without question."

Thus, I was stuck without a way to refuse the appointment. Even more, I could not jeopardize Louis' standing with the king. As we did not currently have a male heir, I could not afford to insult the King. Wordlessly, I sank to my knees.

"Ah, wonderful!" The King clapped his head and I barely heard a "Thank you, Madame de Nevers" from the Queen's direction.

❧

THE PRACTICAL ASPECTS OF MANAGING THE NEW QUEEN'S household were not difficult for me. The massive numbers of maids, pages, ladies in waiting and demoiselles needed a leader, but the duties were not that more complicated than managing my own household. Many of the courtiers spent their lives in service to the royal family, so other than jostling for position, there was little I needed to do in order to keep the household in good order. What bothered me, was the constant reminder I would serve instead of a timid nobody picked from obscurity in Lorraine instead of my dead sister, Marie. Every time that I handled the Queen's jewels, I wondered what they would look like on Marie's neck. Each expensive brocade and silk the Queen chose for her gowns would have flattered Marie better. The court would have run better with my vivacious sister leading the activities. Yet, we were saddled with a mousy girl who spoke barely above a whisper and passively did everything that her husband told her to do.

The King was the Queen of the court in all but name, obsessively detailing complex etiquette rules that we all must adhere to and angrily fuming when we failed to do so. The formality was enough to give me a headache; and as much as possible, I avoided his presence.

His brother's death raised Henri III to the throne and his arrogance raised him even further in his mind. Anyone else would be accused of putting on airs, but as he was the sovereign, no one could criticize him.

The Queen Mother was in a position to temper her son's arrogance, but as always, whatever Henri wanted, his mother smiled and obligingly agreed to. Unchecked, the King's ego grew larger, alienating the long-serving courtiers of France. The King rose to prominence a new crop of courtiers, an overwhelmingly male and attractive group that the court termed the "Mignons." The effeminate dandies, bolstered by the King's generosity and favor, did nothing to ingratiate themselves with us, making the divide between the old families and the new nobles even wider.

"He's becoming insufferable," I complained as Louis and I dined quietly together one evening in late Spring. I would never be stupid enough to say those words in front of anyone. Our marriage might have grown stale, but our partnership was as strong as ever.

He nodded, "He has no idea how much the court is beginning to hate him. He's less than a year on the throne and already the nobility is deserting him."

"And you?" The question and my fork hung in the air.

"I can't afford to desert him. You know that."

"Can you afford to alienate the rest of France?"

"The King commands the army, and I have no desire to place myself or this house at odds with the army."

"So, if you're forced to make a choice, you will back the King?"

"Yes, and as manager of the Queen's Household, *you* will have to make the same decision."

"Louis, France has been divided before, but each time before, it's fallen along lines of faith. Now, even the Catholics are making noise that they plan to desert him. When it's time to make that decision, what will you choose?"

He pushed his plate away from him. "The Catholics do not have a leader and the only backing they can ask from is from Spain. None of us want to be ruled by proxy by Spain."

"What if the Catholics become organized?"

"We'll simply have to make that decision if it presents itself. And," he looked directly at me, "we will make it together."

❧

LOUIS' TALK OF US ACTING IN SOLIDARITY SERVED TO LURE ME INTO a false sense of security. Assuming that any move we made would be made together, I paid little attention to my husband's business decisions as Summer dragged on. The King continued to show his contempt for the established noble houses, threatening the delicate balance of power we had created by generations of constant intermarriages. At the same time, the King grew bolder and more extravagant, wasting money that the country's treasury did not have on his favorites.

I would have remained ignorant of the goings on around me if I had not run into my father's agent in Flanders one day in the halls outside the Queen's audience chamber. "Monsieur Morel, I had no idea that you were in Paris." He gave me a quick bow in reply.

"I'm simply concluding the sale as per your husband's directions." I could not fathom what sale he referred to and at my confused look, he hastened to add, "Your estate in Flanders. The Duc de Nevers was anxious that the funds be transferred to him as soon as possible."

"That's not possible—I have no desire to sell any of my lands in Flanders." I must have heard him wrong. The Flemish estates came directly from my father. They were amongst the ones that Catherine and I spent months arguing over. I refused to sell them in order to help alleviate the Guise's financial woes, despite the ongoing pressure from Guise. The idea that they could be gone was ludicrous. I had to sit down. In shock, I plunked gracelessly on a bench in the middle of the hallway.

"My Lady, I'm sorry. I was under the impression that you had authorized the sale of your lands. The Duc never gave me any indication that he—"

I put up a hand to stop him, "You have to cancel the sale."

His shoulders slumped. "I'm sorry, it's too late. The documents that I came to deliver to your husband are simply a legal formality." My head swam as he continued to offer an apology. But Morel's words were not the ones that I wanted to here just then. I had to hear what my husband had to say.

"I have to speak to my husband, pardon me, Monsieur."

I rushed to the King's study, where Louis usually conducted his business. Usually, the room was occupied by my husband alone as the King preferred to leave the real business of running the country to his advisors. To my chagrin, there were several men in the room with their heads bent over one of the large tables in the study. I had no care for them and scattered them like the vultures that they were.

"Out! I will speak with my husband in private!" None of the men were stupid enough to argue with me, most likely because they saw the expression on my face. As soon as the last of them scurried out the room and closed the door, I turned upon my feckless husband.

"How dare you sell my lands in Flanders!" I spat out every word, boring my eyes into him. I waited for him to blanch or tremble, but my stoic husband never showed his emotions, even when his wife was in a murderous rage.

"The King asked me for a loan and it was the quickest way that I could secure the money."

"Oh, the King asked you for a loan and you immediately went out and started parceling out *my* lands in order to do his bidding? What a good little lap dog you are, Louis!" My voice dripped with venom, yet he did not so much as wince.

"Yes. The King himself asked me for something and I hastened to obey him. That is what I am expected to do as a loyal subject."

"Do not lecture me about loyalty, you who spent your time toadying up to whoever sat on the throne from the moment you came to France."

"You are calling me a whore, wife? I was not the one who spent his hours in another man's bed this year past." His words were a slap. I knew deep down that he held my infidelity over my head, ready to use it against me when the time came. Apparently, he thought that now was just that time.

Yet, I refused to take the bait. I was in the right and I was not about to let him cloud the argument with old sins. "Those lands are

Cleves estates, handed down to me by my father. I am the mistress and I am the one to decide what happens to them."

"Yet, I am the Duc de Nevers and it is my decision that the law honored."

I walked until I was mere inches away from his face. "You are the Duc only by the King's command. You have what you have today because of *me*."

"I have what I have today because the King allowed a woman to inherit. That came from the King's benevolence. Without it, the lands would go to the Guise." He slyly reminded me of our lack of a male heir. This only reopened an old wound. I had still refused to forgive him for keeping me from Frederick. The anger seethed inside me like a tempest.

"You, yourself, told me that we were to remain united in our decisions, but at the first opportunity, you betray me and sell my inheritance. Remember that I am a Bourbon, a cousin of the King and that the Guise can just as easily back me as they could back you. Are you ignorant enough to make an enemy of your own wife?"

"I am not ignorant enough to make an enemy of the King. My wife's anger I can deal with, the King's wrath I cannot."

"Remember your decision today. Today, I learned how easily you will choose Henri Valois over me." I stalked out of the library and past the chastened men who loitered awkwardly outside of the room.

❧

"THERE REALLY IS NO TELLING JUST WHAT MY BROTHER WILL USE THE money for. He may plan to go to war, or he may want gold thread for a coat for that snake Du Gaust." She spat out the name, reminding me that Du Gaust had become her most potent enemy at court. United in our anger, Margot and I fumed over the deal struck between Louis and the King. I thanked God for her loyalty. Unlike my husband, I could always trust Margot to stand beside me and never betray me.

"Louis has plenty of estates from his grandmother that he could sell, the nerve of him to take my lands!" As we spoke, I glanced around the banquet hall to see that Madame de Sauvé was feeding bread suggestively to the Duc d'Alencon, who now was also the new Duc d'Anjou thanks to his brother's largess.

"I have to ask you a favor and the best part is that it will put Madame de Sauvé's nose quite out of joint." Margot smiled and wiggled her eyebrows suggestively.

"Margot, I'm trying to talk to you about something serious, and you're scheming?" Despite her reputation for frivolity, Margot usually knew the line of propriety and rarely violated it in her public behavior.

"This is serious," she moved her lips to my ear so that only I could hear. A couple of men saw the gesture and raised their tankards towards us, misinterpreting it as a sexual advance. "Alencon finally has a plan in place to escape and get to the Netherlands."

"Come on, Margot—every attempt that he's made so far has been a bumbling failure."

"This time, he has a plan, financial backing, an escape route and help along the route. All he needs is a plausible cover story."

"Why should I go along with this?"

"Once it happens, your husband will be humiliated and Madame de Sauvé's stock with my mother will go down precipitously."

Spite caused my interest to spike at her words. "Tell me about it."

"Well, we'll need to start touring monasteries."

⚜

MARGOT HAD A COVER STORY; I WAS GOING TO PRAY FOR THE SOUL of my son and she was going to seek absolution for her sinful ways. Really, the idea of us touring monasteries was absurd and I was convinced that the King and his mother would object as soon as they heard it. I was wrong; they both found the idea of Margot seeking absolution so absurd that neither of them suspected that we were up to no good.

Early on the morning of September 15th, we penitents set out for our tour of the monasteries and religious houses on the outskirts of Paris in my own coach. During lunch, one of Margot's demoiselles complained of nausea and began to vomit. "Take her back to the Louvre," Margot signaled the guards assigned to accompany us for the day. At the Saint-Honore gate of the palace, the poor girl signaled the coachman that he must stop so that she could get fresh air. Moments later, she got back into the coach and in a strained voice pronounced herself fit to return to the monastery. Unwilling to put himself in trouble with the Queen of Navarre, the coachman simply obeyed her instructions and turned away from the gates of the palace.

At the monastery, the girl scurried away while the coachman and the guards loitered. Unbeknownst to any of them, the "girl" was the Duc d'Alencon, who used the lack of care to slip away on the grounds of the monastery in my coach and onto safety. Margot's current lover, a young gallant named Du Bussy, conveniently left him a horse that he used to ride away to safety.

Despite the ludicrous nature of the plan, we had helped Alencon to finally make his escape. With the prince gone, the King had a voice of dissension, one that was far away from the continual surveillance of the court. And for the King, the idea was dangerous.

Realizing that he had a conspiracy unfolding under his own nose, the King sent his most trusted soldiers out to fetch his missing brother. The detachment was headed by none other than my own husband. Unsure of who to trust, the King knew that Louis had demonstrated his loyalty. Margot and I continued to loiter at the monastery, talking at length with the abbot about religious issues. Before supper, the guard led by my husband realized that the Duc made his escape via my coach and we heard a rumbling sound before the doors of the abbey.

"My Lord—how may we help you this evening?" The lanky abbot greeted Louis as he sat astride his horse.

"The King's brother is missing, and we have reason to believe that he stole my wife's coach in order to make his escape." Louis looked around the courtyard as if Alencon would suddenly appear from behind a bush.

One of the priests came to fetch Margot and me, clearing his throat as we sat nonchalantly with the abbot. "Madame, the Duc de Nevers is at the gate. He says that the Duchess's coach is missing."

I rolled my eyes melodramatically. "That's impossible. I set it to the Louvre to deposit one of the Queen's demoiselles. It's probably in the stables as we speak. My husband must be having trouble with his eyesight."

"The Duc seems convinced that it is missing," he shuffled his feet and spread his hands helplessly.

"Well, let's see what Louis is all about, shall we?" Margot rose to her feet, causing the rest of our party to stand. She swept gracefully out of the room and soon we stood at the door of the monastery.

"Louis, what on earth is all of this commotion?" I glanced at the assembled men and horses, careful to show my annoyance at the disturbance.

"The Duc d'Alencon is missing and we have reason to believe that he used your carriage to make his escape."

"The coach is probably right where he should be," Margot adopted the same haughty stance and she folded her arms. "My demoiselle has returned, so the coach should be in the stables of the monastery. Go send someone to check." The delay was timed to ensure that wherever Alencon was, he had more than enough time to make his escape. The longer we kept Louis standing still, the more time we bought for Alencon. Margot and I would stall for all that we were worth.

Margot inspected the trim at the cuff of her dress while we continued to stall for time. "The Duchess' coach is missing, My Lord." At his words, I changed tactics.

"Where is the demoiselle we sent to the Louvre? Merciful Lord, has something happened to her?" I crossed myself piously, causing the assembled group to do the same. If I distracted them with worry over the girl, they would delay even longer.

"The girl has been accounted for, wife. It is the coach that is still missing." Louis's jaw was clenched tightly. He was likely on to my ruse, but Margot and I would play the assembled crowds for as long as we could. We could be the first players in the acting troupe that Margot considered founding.

"Praise God she is safe." At Margot's words, I nodded.

"And you think that the Duc himself took my carriage?" I posed the question to one of the men, knowing that by ignoring Louis, I was further enraging him.

"Without a way to get home, we'll have to find another way back to

Paris." Margot was as adept as anyone in delaying tactics and she put her skills to good use.

"Majesty, you may stay in some of the monks' rooms, although, I doubt that they will be up to the standards that you ladies' are used to." The monks were more than willing to see to our comfort, especially if it meant a sizable donation from Margot and myself. While she inclined her head in thanks, Louis's horse stamped impatiently.

"Then now, that is settled, I must be off to find your coach, wife. We'll send another one for the two of you tomorrow morning." At that, he spurred his mount and the detachment followed. As soon as they were out of earshot, Margot turned to me. "Well, that went well, I think."

The next morning, the guardsmen that had been sent to guard the coach lent to us told us that Louis had located my coach ten miles outside of Paris. The occupant leaped from the carriage and onto a waiting horse. Alencon had made his escape and the King had an unaccounted for rival speeding towards the Netherlands. If Alencon were to meet up with Condé's Protestant forces, the King would have another civil war, this one fought against his own brother and heir.

❧ 31 ☙

Margot and I kept up the ruse that my coach was stolen while under a mission of mercy for an ailing demoiselle. If the King suspected Margot and I had a hand in the plot to get Alencon away, I never heard any remonstration from him. If anything, I think that the King believed that I was as loyal as my husband.

Louis, however, knew better. He met me in the large salon of our home as I watched the September sun set before me. Although I could hear and sense his presence in the room, I did not bother to turn to greet him. Instead, I kept my gaze at the sunset as the orange sun set slowly.

"I told you not to make an enemy of me, Louis."

"I told you not to make an enemy of the King."

"Then, I believe that we are at a standstill." I clasped my hands behind my back and finally turned to look at him. Rather than enraged, he looked tired.

"There was no damage to your carriage or your horses. Apparently, the royal thief treated them quite well."

"Then, I have to thank him for that. Most thieves are not so generous."

"Henriette, this is not the time for us to be at odds. We are more vulnerable than ever."

"If you truly believed that, then why do something so underhanded? Something that you knew would make me angry?"

"I had no choice. The King constantly abandons the men who helped him to the throne for those fawning flops. If I am not careful, then I will find myself on the outside as well."

"So, you do everything to keep the King's favor?

"At one time, so would you." The words were truer than I wanted to admit. But we had lost far too much between the time in which we were united in our goals and that quiet September evening.

"Am I to be forgiven for Frederick?"

"I don't know." I honestly did not know if I could *ever* forgive him. He had made too many stupid decisions in an attempt to appease the new King, not the least of which was sacrificing part of my inheritance. How foolish would my husband's next decision be? Could I count on him to look after both of our interests? Could I even *trust* him?

"I need time, Louis." It was all I could give him.

The next morning, while on an errand for the Queen, I walked into Margot's apartments to find her gripped with terror. "He'll come for me! I shouldn't have done this! What was I thinking, I know him too well!" It was such an abrupt change from the day before that I started to wonder if Margot had gone mad.

"What is the matter? You were fine when I left." I quickly sent word to Queen Louise that the Queen of Navarre had taken ill and gently sat Margot down on her bed.

"I have to stay here. It's the only safe place that's left." Margot began to speak nonsense and her face went white. She tore at the laces in her gown and I worked to loosen it to allow her to breathe.

"Start from the beginning, did someone threaten you?"

"Henri. He'll torment me. He always does. And my Mother will let him do it. He'll beat me, and I won't live to see the next morning." At that, she began crying like a little child and I finally understood the cause of her terror. Anjou had terrorized her since childhood and with the crown of France sitting on his over-indulged head, there was no limit to how he would punish Margot for Alencon's disappearance. She truly was safer in a sickbed. I began making preparations to place her in bed and sent word via her page that she was not to be disturbed. I would do all that I could to protect Margot from her brother's unbridled rage.

As I sat beside her, murmuring words of comfort, I began to realize that a sickbed might be the one place where I was safe as well. Without his sister to take the brunt of his frustration, the King might take his anger out on me. Like two cowards, we hid in Margot's bedchamber and waited out the repercussions of Alencon's escape.

Two days into our ruse, Louis came to Margot's chamber and asked to speak with me. Grabbing me about the waist, he pulled me against his body and whispered in my ear. "Make no motion to startle her. Listen closely to what I say." At his words, my blood ran cold, but I simply nodded.

"The demoiselle you sent to Paris in your coach? The king ordered her drowned to make an example of her. If a group of boatmen hadn't rescued her in time, she would be floating in the Seine right now." The horror of the lengths to which the King would go to avenge himself appalled me.

"Louis, you have to believe now that appeasing him is pointless."

He gave a short sigh, unwilling to concede my point. "We don't have much of a choice. Keep a close eye on Du Gaust, he's the one who helped the King plan this abomination." Du Gaust, the man who Margot had marked as her enemy. If he was willing to plot a punishment on Margot's proxy, what would he have in store for Margot? How safe was *I*?

I did not argue when Louis insisted that I go home with him that night. He did not argue when I insisted that I did not feel safe without him hovering over me. In fact, I began to demand that my husband sleep beside me for weeks afterward in the hope that if Du Gaust came for me, I might have his protection. Our reconciliation, even one born out of fear of my life, came at a fortuitous time. By the New Year, I learned that I was once again pregnant.

Navarre also made his escape and this time, neither Margot nor I aided him in doing so. Margot learned of his escape from the Queen Mother and the King was so incensed that my friend was enclosed in her rooms pending the King's pleasure.

"Louis, I have to see her. She'll think that I've abandoned her."

He shook his head. "Think of how angry the King was in September and increase that anger exponentially. I will not have you at risk for assassination this time." I opened my mouth to argue with him, but he cut me off, "Please, Henriette—I am doing this for your safety." I was miserable without Margot and I spent most of my time in the Queen Louise's presence, sulking and trying to hide the fact that I was sulking. "Madame de Nevers, are you all right?" Louise looked at me with genuine concern, and I felt guilty for my behavior.

"I'm pregnant again, Your Majesty. The nausea is too much for me. Please forgive me, it will go away in a month or two." I gave her a weak smile, hoping that she would accept my excuse.

"Of course, and God bless you for your miracle. I will pray for you." I felt a momentary stab of guilt at blurting out my news. Since the day of her wedding, the King and Queen worked to conceive an heir and I realized that my widening stomach would only serve to rub her failure in her face. Perhaps if I were a younger woman, I would smugly rub the situation in her face. Having lost a beloved child, however, I knew firsthand that children were not trophies to be held over the head of a less fortunate woman.

Thanks to my position as Mistress of the Robes, I had secured a position for my sister Catherine as a senior lady in waiting, which meant that the two of us were able to spend more time together. With the loss of Margot, I cherished the opportunity to be with my sister all the more. Catherine, for her part, cherished the opportunity to gossip with me. "The Queen Mother charged Madame de Sauvé with estranging Alencon, Navarre, and Margot from one another."

I need not ask why, but my curiosity was piqued as to how. Catherine was more than willing to provide the details, as far as she knew them. "Navarre is convinced that the Protestants would not support Alencon intaking the Netherlands unless he came to lead them in person. That's why he was so eager to leave court this time."

She quickly glanced around the room to see if anyone else was listening in. "Madame de Sauvé gave Navarre a note supposedly from Margot to her latest lover asking him to slit Navarre's throat if he so much as tarried from Mass. I doubt he'll try to make an escape. He certainly isn't bothering to speak to Margot."

"That doesn't sound like Margot at all," I pulled my face into a grimace. "She risked her life to save him after their wedding and when Mole and Coconnas were executed. Why on earth would she bother to work against him now?"

She shrugged, "Maybe the letter is a fake. No one knows for sure, but Navarre certainly took it to heart. Word is that he's too scared to even join the King for a hunt." The three were barely speaking to one another at the moment and Margot's isolation from the two men made it easier for the King to forgive his sister, at least momentarily. With a temporary truce between the King and his sister, Margot left her gilded prison a few weeks later.

If Navarre was gullible enough to believe the threats on his life, he soon regained his taste for the hunt. One cold February morning, goaded by Guise into participating in the hunt or risking his masculinity forever, he relented and took off for the forest surrounding Fountainbleu with the King and Guise. Lured into a false sense that Navarre was too terrified to leave the party, Guise and the King stalked off from him and were soon too involved in running the stag down before they realized that their royal party was one person short. Navarre had given the King the slip after all.

Margot need not feign innocence at Navarre's escape; the King and Queen Mother had no doubts that she was left in the dark during this most recent plot. The moment Navarre returned to his own kingdom, he recanted Catholicism and once again became a Protestant. Still, they could not let the loss of both hostages go and Margot remained isolated from the court. Months passed until the King realized that his support amongst the nobility was so eroded that he could not risk further alienating his younger siblings.

LOUIS BENT OVER HIS PAPERS AS WE FINISHED OUR SUPPER. "WE'RE about to be hit with a large tax and there isn't anything that I can do to stop it." At the mention of money, my head snapped up and I dropped the crust of bread in my hand.

"How much does he expect from us now?" My anger boiled within me. If Louis planned on selling any of our properties to pay this new tax, he would bear the brunt of my anger. The past two years had been uneventful, which gave us time to repair our marriage. I had once again grown to trust that my husband would consult me in any decisions that affected both of us.

"Substantial. Villequier convinced him that since the royal treasury is virtually empty, the noble families that are now too wealthy will have to make up for the shortfall." Louis detested Villequier, one of the King's minions elevated to Chamberlain and given the duty of "advising" the king alongside him. With the minions isolating the King, he heeded less and less of Louis's advice.

"I suppose the King is unaware that the missing money is due to the gifts to his minions and those extravagant pageants we have to attend every night?" Determined to keep up appearances, despite the angry court and a continued lack of an heir, the King distracted himself by squandering more money than his elder brother ever had. "And the Parlement can do nothing to stop or at least delay this madness?"

Louis shook his head. "Today, the King personally walked into the Parlement of Paris and laid the edict down in front of them. Before any of them could so much as discuss it, he turned his back on them and walked away. There is no protest in Parlement and the King is determined to keep them securely under control."

"So, he brings us all to the brink of bankruptcy while we are denied the opportunity to check his power?" The endless rounds of evening activities were wearing thin on me. It was 1578, the King had only been on the throne for less than four years and already he had managed to alienate all but the most toadying of his supporters. No matter how much the Queen Mother tried to avoid an oncoming disaster, he pushed us towards it.

I had no desire to stand wildly by while the Mignons ran wild as bucks throughout the palaces, willfully compromising the virtue of the Queen's ladies and making a mockery of the Crown. Queen Louise was in no position to speak to her husband, intimidated by him as she was. She left all of the awkward confrontations involved in running her household to me. I spent virtually every day engaged in arguments with courtiers and creditors in the Queen's name. With a toddler waiting for me at home, I was in no mood to mother a grown woman with no backbone.

The toddler in question ran into the dining room, in a childish imitation of the horseplay I witnessed from the Mignons during the day. On a rosy-cheeked two-year-old, it was endearing. "Papa! Papa!" Francis ran to Louis and beat on his shins, demanding that he take him in his arms. Louis wasted no time in scooping him up in his arms and covering his face with kisses. "Son, I must teach you gentlemanly behavior, I fear the men at court are poor role models."

I smiled, knowing that he had no plans whatsoever to seriously chastise our son. After years spent criticizing Catherine de Medici for overindulging her son who now sat on the throne of France, I now began to understand why she did so. Neither Louis nor I were willing to do anything that would crush the boy's spirit. Unlike our dear Frederick, Francis was fat and robust from the moment of his birth. We both carried a superstitious fear that if we did anything to break his healthy spirit, we would also damage his body. God had given us a second chance with this child and we were determined to do nothing to endanger him.

"Do you want to put him to bed?" Louis tickled him under his chin and he giggled in return. I shook my head. Francis often made a game of running to one of us and demanding attention. As the nurse trailed behind our son, I watched as Louis took him to his bedroom. Before I settled down for the night, I wanted to catch up on my correspondence. Very soon, letters would be all that I had of Margot. Navarre sent word that he wanted his wife to join him in his own kingdom and jumping at the chance for freedom from her brother, she agreed. Led by Margot and her mother, most of the court would depart for a tediously long trip across France to Navarre.

As head of Queen Louise's household, I could not go. Neither the

King or his consort would join the rest of the court to Navarre. I self-ishly wanted my friend to stay with me in Paris and if it weren't for the need to watch over Francis, I would have begged Louis and the King to go with her as far as the border. "It's best that you stay in Paris," Louis confided to me one night as we lay in bed. "Margot and the Queen Mother are traveling to the most divided parts of France. There are declared Protestant towns that will not allow Catherine to even enter and Margot's dowry lands will not allow that heretic Navarre to set foot in them." Undeterred, Catherine gathered her Flying Squadron to entice the humorless men of the Navarrese court into their beds. Chief amongst them was Madame de Sauvé, who Catherine dispatched to ensnare Navarre again in a haze of nostalgia.

Thus, deprived of the people who usually made court bearable, I was forced to endure the Mignons without any buffer between us. Even Claude Catherine had departed Paris to take care of her husband's country estates. The King grew even more erratic, spending more time in selecting the dogs he and the Queen took in their daily walks than running the affairs of the kingdom. The dogs became a point of contention between myself and the Queen. In order to escape being molested by the unchecked Mignons, many young demoiselles ran from them and into the relative safety of Louise's apartments. Eventually, we became a sort of asylum for girls who had no desire to lose their virtue to the Mignons, which meant, I had to find space for them out of sight of the men of the King's inner circle.

At the same time, the King could not be dissuaded from bringing more and more lap dogs into the Queen's apartments. The animals regularly exceeded a dozen flea-bitten and raucous animals. As soon as I managed to quiet the fearful young girls and the yapping beasts, the King would appear to rile up the latter. As always, no one could make the King see reason and the Queen was completely incapable of taking a stand against her husband. The Queen Mother was my only hope for speaking to the King, but with her departure to Navarre, I could not count on her support.

"Louis, perhaps I should resign my position?" As he entered our bedchamber, I noticed that he beamed with the time he spent with Francis.

He sighed, "I'm sorry—I know it's insufferable. But with the King's favorites blocking the way to him, I can't afford to lose any influence within the court."

An idea suddenly came to me. "Perhaps I should leave with Catherine to meet her husband's family." Our eldest daughter was now ten and old enough to join the household of her betrothed, the eldest son of the Duc de Longueville. It would mean leaving her seven-year-old sister, Marie and Francis in Paris with Louis. We had the eldest son of the Duc de Mayenne in mind for Marie, but we still had years before she would also need to leave us for the large nursery at Joinville.

"I doubt that the King or the Queen would fault you for seeing that our daughter is settled in. Speak to Louise and see if she agrees."

As it turned out, Louise was very eager for me to depart for her family's own lands. "Madame de Nevers, if you would, I would like to send these letters to my sister." She produced a stack of letters from her bureau. As I tucked the letters into my cape, I heard an earthly screech from behind me. Louise jumped and fearing the worst, I turned to see if we were being invaded by some unholy demon. To my horror, I saw that we were not that lucky.

On his shoulder, the King carried an animal that looked like an upright dog. I managed to bite my tongue before I asked what manner of animal would join the court this time. "Look, Madame—our ambassador of Venice has gifted us with a monkey!" A smile split across his face and I felt cold horror creep up from my stomach to my head. My escape from the insanity of the court would happen just in time.

"Mama, what will my husband be like?" I looked down at Catherine, who unfortunately shared my frizzy blonde hair. Knowing firsthand how difficult it was to keep those curls under control, I had given my maid, Lydia, the only woman who could handle my own hair, as a gift to my daughter. We had traveled for days in our coach and I relished the opportunity to play childish games with her for the last time. We were accompanied only by Lydia and the girls who would wait upon my daughter. Usually, we would gather a large retinue to demonstrate our importance and that of her husband-to-be's family, but I wanted to enjoy peace and intimacy with my eldest child as long as possible.

"He will be very kind and he will love you very much." My daughter solemnly asked the question, but I did not want to sully the day with talk of reality. Both of my daughters would marry powerful Dukes, ones who would protect them when Louis and I could not. Francis would inherit our lands, but our daughters would be placed in wealthy households where they would want for nothing.

"Will he be handsome?" She persisted and for a second, I thought of my sister Marie.

"All men are handsome in their own way. It is your duty as a wife to bring out his handsomeness and his piety." Her namesake had been married to her first husband at twelve, only two years older than my daughter was now. I could not imagine how Catherine stood the pressure of becoming a bride at such a tender age. I made a note that when I returned to Paris, I would try to be more compassionate towards my remaining sister.

❦

DAYS AFTER I RETURNED TO PARIS, I REALIZED THAT I WAS ONCE again pregnant. Louis did nothing to hide his pleasure at the idea of our having another child. With Francis constantly tugging at my skirts, I grew larger as we awaited the birth of our latest child. We had our heir and two beautiful daughters who would marry well and settle in great noble houses. This most recent child almost seemed a bonus for us.

In April of 1580, my labor began and ten hours later, the midwife announced that we had another son. I heard a joyful whoop from the hallway as the midwife told Louis of the news. Once we were recovered, my husband all but danced into our bedchamber to inspect the new baby. "This is completely unexpected, yet totally wondrous." Uninterested in either of us, our new son let out a long yawn and closed his eyes and began to sleep. We named the boy Charles and began to enjoy the security of having two sons in our nursery.

On the heels of our joy, we experienced once again the greatest loss that anyone can endure. In June, the nurse took Francis outside to play in the warm sunlight. Newly returned to my post in the Queen's household, I joined the court at the chateau of Blois in the Loire Valley. Lost in my thoughts, I did not hear Louis as he rushed into the Queen's presence chamber, or Louise's acknowledgment of his presence.

"Henriette-" he could only choke out my name. Hearing the anguish in his voice, I turned to look at him. Forgetting the strict layers of etiquette, the King enforced at court, Louis dissolved into tears and one of the Queen's matrons grabbed him. He continued to sob for over ten minutes as the sense of horror spread across the room. "I've just received word. Francis was playing, and he fell, and—" he once again succumbed to his sobs and the matron held him as if she were his own mother. I stood alone in the room, seeing nothing. At my side, the Queen embraced me and held me as I sobbed. After the years I spent criticizing her for the sin of not being my sister, the young woman took this opportunity to show me the greatest compassion when I needed it.

Louise continued to show me the kind of support and generosity that I had never thought the quiet woman capable of. She immediately had Masses said for Francis and she insisted that I take time in my chambers to mourn my son. Adding to her kindness, when Louis and I left Blois for Nevers to inter Francis's tiny body, the Queen absolutely insisted that we take her own coach. In the midst of my overwhelming grief, I came to the realization that France had a Queen worthy of the title after all.

❦

IN THE MONTHS FOLLOWING FRANCIS'S DEATH, THE QUEEN remained firm in her insistence that I reduce my duties and concentrate on my remaining children. Unfortunately, I did just that, hovering over Marie and Charles constantly. Less than an hour after I returned to court, my sister Catherine marched in and began ordering me about as if she were our mother. She proved to be the perfect replacement for Margot, who stubbornly remained in Navarre to head its court, while constantly arguing with her husband.

After Margot's departure, three years earlier, our salons with the Duchess de Retz were gone, which dismayed my friend Claude Catherine to no small end. "We really need to gather up what we have left and have a go at it. We need a party and *you* need one in particular." She locked arms with me one morning as we all filed out from daily Mass.

I shook my head, "I don't have time for that nonsense. Marie and Charles need me. What if something happened to them and I wasn't there?" Claude turned to me, exasperated. "Henriette, I will tell you something that no one will, and it is for your own good. There is good parenting and there is obsession. You have reached the point of obsession." A gust of wind flew past us and we turned to see the source. It turned out to be my over-sized brother-in-law, the Duc de Guise. His face was mottled with red and his jaw set so hard, I wondered if he might break it. "Brother, are you alright?"

"It is the King," he said no more, but I knew that there was much more. The King had marked his old playmate Guise as his whipping boy two years earlier when one of the Mignons died in a fight with one of Guise's retainers. Given how many fights the Mignons were involved in, I don't know why this one bothered the King so much. Yet, when Guise shielded his man from punishment in the duel, the King was livid.

The Guise and their Lorraine kin were too well placed in the governing of France, beginning with my mistress, the Queen. The King could not risk dismissing them all without courting open rebellion. So, Henri did the next best thing, causing grief for my sister and her giant of a husband. While most of the court managed to hide our contempt for the king and his gang of criminals, Catherine and Guise openly showed their disgust of the King and his rule. For his part, the King humiliated the Guise clan in small ways that began to add up over the years. Eventually, the Guise would not stand for the constant slights to their honor and would find ways to get revenge on the King.

"Catherine told me that she's tried to enlist the Queen Mother's help in speaking with the King, but it's as if she's virtually retired. I'm sorry, I know how annoying those villains can be."

Guise's greatest strength lay in his affability, "Thank you, Sister. I keep thinking that the King will one day go too far, and his mother will have to step in and curb his excesses. Sadly, that day seems very far off."

"At least Catherine is safe in Louise's retinue," Claude piped up beside me. Guise turned to give her a courtly bow. The Queen remained neutral, generous to her Guise cousins and her royal husband. In fact, Louise's chambers might well have been the most neutral location in all of France.

"And I have to spend each day in the King's presence, which is wearing quite heavily on my patience. If you will excuse me, Ladies." He gave us a gracious smile and swept down the hall.

❦

FROM THAT MOMENT ON, I MADE AN EFFORT TO OBSERVE THE irritation level of my sister and her husband. Louis and I could afford to take a neutral stance, which would benefit us as the gulf between the King and the Guise continued to widen. At court festivities, I kept an eye on the interactions between the two men, always taking mental notes.

One day, as I sat with the Queen, the King strode into her inner chambers and sat talking with the ladies. As the Queen and the rest of the assembled group chatted, the King took my arm and pulled me to a private corner. "Madame de Nevers, I must ask a favor of you."

"Of course, Majesty." The previous "favor" involved the king sending a litter of puppies to Catherine and Charles, so I expected this latest one would be just as harmless.

"I have reason to believe that one of my friends is playing false with me and trying to tempt the Queen." This did have something to do with me; if the Queen's honor was in danger of being besmirched, it was my duty to protect it. Given how much generosity she had shown the past year, I was more than willing to repay her for her compassion towards me.

"Are you sure?" I snuck a quick glance at the Queen, who looked as innocent as ever. The King nodded his head slowly, looking forlorn.

"But, surely you can punish the man or banish him?"

"Sadly, no. But, I believe that you can save your mistress' honor much easier than I can. I think that this man is an adventurer. An affair with one woman at court is the same as an affair with another..."

His words had me confused, "You want me to pick out a woman to carry on an affair with this man?"

"I want you to lure him into an affair with *you*. Now, hear me out, Cousin," he used a term that he always used when he wanted something difficult from me. "I have no desire to make you unfaithful to your husband. I only want you to carry on the facade of an affair."

"And I suppose Louis is to know of this?"

He nodded, "Certainly. I will tell Louis of this great favor that you are doing for me. He will know that you are true to him." He once again adopted a forlorn look. The King had certainly thought this charade out well. With horror, I began to wonder if this was the game that he played with my sister years earlier. Had I been terribly wrong then and he had never loved Marie? Did I unwittingly assist him in using my sister for his own sick games against Condé? The thought sickened me. I had to get to Louis to talk to get his opinion about this. At the same time, I could not risk alienating the King by refusing his request. I was trapped like a fly in his schemes. I had to delay him.

"Sire, I will speak with Louis to ensure that we are united in this plan. I have no desire to embarrass my husband in front of the entire court."

He nodded, "Of course. Say nothing to anyone of this plan, especially the Queen. I promise that in doing this, you will be richly rewarded. As always, you have my thanks for your service to my gentle wife." He kissed my hand and walked away from me. Within seconds, he rejoined the women surrounding his wife and kissed her lovingly on the cheek.

"WHAT DO YOU WANT ME TO DO? HONESTLY, LOUIS—I WILL DO

nothing without your complete blessing." Determined not to hurt my husband and having no desire whatsoever to be unfaithful to him, I would follow along with whatever he decided to do. We had long since moved past our earlier problems in our marriage and he had proven true to his word to make no more decisions without consulting me. We were once again united as a team.

"There really is no way that you can say no to this scheme." Louis shook his head, the realization that the King was becoming increasingly unmanageable sinking in. "I insist that any correspondence you have with that man, I see it."

"See it? My love, you are going to compose it with me. I have no desire to walk into this without you." We sat at the table in his study and I reached across to grasp his hand. He squeezed it gently and smiled at me.

"Very well, that settles your written communication. What will you do when you see him in person?"

I hated to raise the specter, but the truth was that I had the answer in front of me. "I'll carry on as the King did with Marie. I will claim that I am assailed with doubts and that I cannot, for the foreseeable future, consummate our affair. With any luck, by then, the King will have all of the proof he claims he needs and I'll be released from this Devil's bargain."

32

"The air is quite sweet this evening." I slipped close to Monsieur de Levas, the Mignon the King asked me to seduce. I suddenly began to understand the level of anxiety Madame de Sauvé and her compatriots felt when spying for the Queen Mother. Hopefully, I would be as successful as de Sauvé.

"I think that it's the company, especially the ladies." With his arms folded, Levas leaned against a pillar of the ballroom of Fontainebleau. Given how cavernous the room was, it was easy for me to position myself beside him without drawing too much attention from the crowd.

"You do seem to be enjoying yourself." I hadn't used my flirtation skills for a while, but I could manage light banter with anyone. Luckily, he continued to take my bait.

"The court is always a place where I feel welcome." He turned to me with a heated expression. I was instantly ill at ease. The double entendre was not lost on me at all. He was more aggressive than I had assumed. I would have to be on my guard to keep him at bay.

"Tell me, Sir—what duties do you do for the King?" On the surface, it was a safe topic, but given the incessant rumors that some of these dandies spent their nights in the King's bed, perhaps it was not.

"Well, His Majesty has asked me to coordinate the training of our troops in Normandy. The Duc de Joyeuse recommended me. Of course, we are great friends and I would be glad to aid him in the endeavor." Good God, not only was the man vapid and arrogant, he was determined to take any political appointment that he could steal from experienced men. Maybe Guise was right. I wanted nothing more than to get away from this blowhard, but I had to remain near him in order to complete my mission.

"Will you have to depart for Normandy soon?" With any luck, he would do so and the threat to the Queen's honor would be gone with him.

"In two weeks. I will be sad to leave Paris." He sighed and fondled the tapestry behind him as if it were a woman's body. The action made my skin crawl. His crassness also made me wonder if the man might well be stupid. There would be few verbal jousts between us, unlike Coconnas.

"If you would like, I could write to you, Madame de Nevers. The hardships of war are always lightened by letters from a beautiful woman."

"I would love to do that!" I turned to him and tried to adopt the breathless behavior of the demoiselles who flirted constantly at the court.

"Then, I await word from you." He kissed my hand, as he did so, I noticed that he took care to glance in Louis' direction.

Aided quite capably by Louis, I sent regular letters to Normandy, telling Levas how his presence caused my heart to flutter. Sometimes, I thought that the verbiage was overwrought, but Louis would giggle at the naughtiness. A steady stream of letters came from Normandy, most with passages that made me blush. I had Louis read each of them aloud and he often used a falsetto as he read Levas' words to me.

At the same time, I kept a close watch over the letters that came to the Queen. As her chief Lady in Waiting, one of my tasks was to manage the Queen's correspondence. I was relieved to see that there were no letters from Normandy, not even from some of the Queen's Lorraine cousins. I suppose that she could have enlisted another lady to carry her letters to Levas, but that did not sound like Louise at all. As always, the Queen seemed to be irreproachable in her behavior.

◈

MONTHS AFTER OUR CLANDESTINE CORRESPONDENCE BEGAN, I sat with Claude at the banquet given by the King for the court to celebrate the end of the long Summer. Claude continued to try and enlist my help in reviving our salons, but without Margot's presence, they seemed almost pointless. "After this banquet is over, I plan to go to bed and sleep for hours." Popping a grape into my mouth, I stared at Claude with a mock-threatening expression.

She burst into laughter at me. "Henriette, you have become the worst type of woman: a boring one!" I joined her in her laughter, but I shrugged in my own bit of defiance. She continued to pester me as the banquet continued around us.

After the majority of plates were cleared, the King rose. All noise in the room stopped and we turned to hear what he had to say. "I continue to be concerned with the level of morality here at court." I glanced at Claude, thinking that he would promise to put a stop to the unbridled frivolity that his favorites indulged in on a constant basis. I was sick of constantly monitoring the safety of the demoiselles of the Queen's household. If he were finally listening to his councilors like Louis, I applauded the King.

"As you know, my beloved Mother has tried to set an example of behavior for the ladies and gentlemen at court." At his words, several raised loud toasts to the Queen, who held her own court in the Tuileries. Once the clamor died down, the King resumed his speech, with all eyes upon him. He was clearly enjoying the undivided attention.

"However, I cannot sit idly by while certain members of this court engage in immoral behavior that violates their marital vows." Beside me, Claude snorted; if the King wanted to lecture his courtiers for taking on lovers, he would have a very steep battle to fight. As the crowd leaned forward to see who would be singled out for the King's admonishment, the silence was unnerving. "The Queen and I have worked hard to set an example of marital fidelity for all to follow." At the mention of Queen Louise, I looked at her seat at the King's table. When I did not see her, I began to rise to see if she needed my help.

"I have here letters which make me very sad to see the state of our court as it stands today. And as your God-anointed sovereign, I will not allow such lasciviousness in my court." He pulled out a stack of letters from his doublet, which as always was woven with shining golden thread. Like his sister, Margot, he had a flair for the dramatic and he loved to use it whenever possible. Unfolding the pages, he began to read.

"My dearest," he began, and I noticed that the room sat rapt with attention at his every word, "I cannot tell you how much it pains me that you are not with me tonight in Paris." Eyebrows wiggled, and several tried to stifle giggles. The gossips of the court were having quite a night.

"When you return from Normandy be assured that I will be there to greet you." At those words, I froze. Those words sounded too familiar. It was possible any number of married women were writing men who were away at the Norman campaign. Surely, I was imagining things. The King's next words removed any doubt.

"I spend too many nights virtually alone, lying next to a cold husband," those words were ones that Louis himself wrote, but taken completely out of context and read in front of the court, they were humiliating. My head began to spin, and I could only see a white light. I could not face anyone at the banquet, but none of them knew why. No one knew that those words were written by me.

"Madame de Nevers, you have brought shame to this court." The King looked me straight in the eye as if he was a wolf about to take down his prey. I have never seen a colder look in anyone's eyes and I will never forget it. I have never been at the loss for words, but the shock and humiliation he heaped upon me at that moment were unimaginable.

He held the letters above his head, "Those are your words, are they not?

"Those letters were sent by me, but as you know, Majesty--"

"This is unacceptable. I have given you and your family every honor possible in this court. You live on my largess. Your husband is one of the finest men in France and you," he pointed a long, elegant finger at me. I was still so shocked at the absurdity of his behavior that I could not utter a response, "show no gratitude for either of us."

The entire room pivoted to look at me. I heard an awkward cough, the clatter of silverware as it dropped onto a plate. I had heard of the Valois children viciously tearing at one another, but the experience of seeing it firsthand, of being the victim of such behavior, was horrifying.

A second thought came to me. Had the King inherited the madness of his older brother? Henri III had never had the fits that Charles IX suffered from in the past, but was it possible that his madness surfaced much later in life? Had the King lost touch with his senses? Did France have yet another mad monarch? Whether I had been set up or not, I would choose that as my excuse for the King's erratic behavior that night. In my heart, I knew that it was due to his inherent cruelty.

"Majesty, I believe that I have been falsely accused. I will ask for your mercy, but if you will excuse me, I think that I should leave." I curtseyed, determined that if he was indeed mad that I would show no disrespect to the Crown.

"I believe that you should leave, Madame de Nevers. There is no place in my court for your kind of loose morality." Taking that as my leave I fled from the banquet room and hailed my coach. I told the coachman that he was not to stop until he arrived at the door of the Hotel de Nevers. The second the door closed, I collapsed into tears.

❧

"PLEASE TELL ME THAT YOU KNOW WHAT IS GOING ON WITH HIM." I looked at Louis, searching his face for some answer. He only shook his head slowly. "I wish I knew, Henriette."

I had spent the night before sobbing and when my husband made it to our home at dawn he immediately came to see me in our bedchamber. He held me as great tears overtook me, and I shook with the effort. Cooing to me that everything would be all right, he simply held me until the chambermaid came to bring our breakfast.

"I need to leave Paris. I cannot stand it here." Before I left, I would send word to the Queen that I must resign my position as her Mistress of the Robes effective immediately. I hated to leave the Queen, but I could not continue to function as a member of the King's court. Nothing could convince me otherwise. As soon as possible, I bundled myself and my daughter Marie, barely ten, into a coach and sped with all haste towards Nevers. Louis and our son would remain behind in Paris. The ducal palace had suffered from neglect with Louis and I constantly in Paris and it was as good a time as ever to see to the upkeep of the house.

⚜

"Papa says the King was unkind to you," Marie looked at me with compassion that tears formed in my eyes.

"He was, dearest. We are never to speak ill of the King, especially in public, but what he said to me was very cruel."

"So, that is why we are going to the country?" She tried to hide her excitement at the idea of our trip. I did not blame her for her excitement, Nevers was a wonderful antidote to the machinations and cruelty of the court. The last two trips that I had taken to Nevers were cloaked in mourning and as a result, I had no recent happy memories of my time there. I was determined to change that.

"Yes, we are going so that we will not be underfoot of the King and so Papa can get work done without worrying about me. But we will have fun while we are in Nevers, I will make sure of that." At that, my daughter smiled at me. I was looking forward to spending time with her before we made arrangements to send her to her eventual in-laws. The Duc de Mayenne was keen to finalize my daughter's betrothal to his son and heir, and my sister encouraged the match. We would have even stronger ties to the Guise, but no matter how furious I was with the King, I still worried that if we joined in open rebellion against him, we were dooming ourselves. Louis had his own doubts about allying with Mayenne because the week before I left Paris, he openly quarreled with Guise and Mayenne over the King's policy of handling the Duc d'Alencon. Louis started to question the motivations behind both of the brothers. Because of this, I had hesitated in finalizing the betrothal.

We took two days to reach Nevers, starting with the congested road out of Paris. The first evening, we stopped at Gien, where we met the Loire River that would follow us until we reached our home in Nevers. My vassal, the Seigneur of Gien met us at his home, where we stayed the night. At supper, he turned to speak to me. "I am told, My Lady, that the court has grown disgusted with the King's rule."

I nodded, admitting to myself that speaking of the unrest was not speaking against the King, so I could hardly be faulted for doing so. "He listens to few men outside of his dandies and favorites. Even the Queen Mother has lost so much influence that she spends almost all of her time holding a separate court at the Tuileries."

He raised his eyebrow. "The Tuileries stands facing the Louvre; are they now in opposition with one another?" We had long since accepted that the King was his Mother's favorite child and that their bond was unbreakable. Now, even Catherine de Medici found her petted son unmanageable and unreasonable.

"I should warn you, that here in the countryside, men are more given to talk. And many of them question why they should continue to support a King who taxes us into poverty and squanders the money on a few favored dandies."

"I do hope it is only talk; I do not encourage open rebellion of my vassals and I certainly do not wish to betray the King." If he wished to lure me into a rebellion, I would not fall into that trap. I came to the countryside to escape danger, not to sow seeds of it wherever I went.

"At the moment, yes. There are many loyal Catholics in France who wonder what good loyalty to a King who betrays us will benefit them. As he has no heir other than Alencon, they also worry if the county will immediately fall into heresy once Henri III is no more."

Marie and I continued on to Nevers, looking out towards the Loire as it wound southward. On the second evening, we saw the towers of Nevers and I knew that we were home. As we pulled up to the ducal palace, I felt a swelling of pride. Nowhere else did I feel more the Duchess of Nevers than our family seat. At the top of the stairs leading to the front door, a tower enclosed a spiral staircase, commissioned by my grandfather. The same architect who had designed a more elaborate version at Blois had repeated the exquisite feat for our family home. It was a particular favorite of mine as a child, a place to run and hide while whispering secrets around the winding slabs of stone. A hoyden, I had played with my siblings as we wound down the steps of the staircase, hiding from one another as we did so. I snuck a glance at Marie and I realized that she was thinking of doing the same thing. Only without a brother to play with, she would have to find a companion.

I had no desire to take Charles with us because the landscape of our home only served to remind me of his precarious position. Directly behind the palace stood the Cathedral de Nevers, where the bodies of his brothers lay. I vowed to spend as little time looking at the cathedral while I was home as I dared. I had no desire to remind myself of the fragility of our lives.

❧

A FEW DAYS AFTER WE SETTLED INTO THE PALACE, I RECEIVED several letters from Paris. The first was from my sister Catherine, filled with her indignation at the King's decision to publicly humiliate me. "Now you know what my husband has been forced to endure," she declared. "At least in his case, the King has the decency to do it in private. Only an animal would be crude enough to do that to a lady in public. And in full view of the court! My dear, I cannot imagine how you felt!"

The second letter came from Claude, equally appalled at the King's behavior, but since she had witnessed it firsthand, she was more concerned with how I was dealing with the public humiliation. "I have heard that you resigned as Mistress of The Robes and I completely agree with you. No one should have to see that insufferable man every day, given how vilely he treated you."

The third came from Louis, who opened with asking how I was faring and asking after Marie. The King, he wrote, made no reference to his treatment of me, acting as if it never happened. So far, he had said nothing to Louis about my resignation and withdrawal from court.

The rest of the letter caused me great concern. The Plague had come to Paris, spread this time from Spain. After taking the Queen of Spain's life, it quickly swept into Paris the Summer of 1581 and Louis began to fear for Charles' life. I was just as fearful that our son was in danger. Quickly pulling out pen and paper, I wrote a quick letter to Louis that I as much as it pained me to separate him from our children, perhaps he should send Charles to Nevers to stay with me. Calling for a page, I sent the letter to Paris posthaste.

"Madame, you have a visitor." My chambermaid appeared in the doorway and bobbed a quick curtsey.

"Who is it?" I had no plans to see anyone that day. If anything, Marie and I were to spend a quiet day walking in the palace gardens. I was relishing the opportunity to play mother to my remaining daughter without the demands of the court pulling at my sleeve.

"The Bishop of Nevers." I frowned; like most Bishops, he rarely spent time tending his own flock in person and tarried in Paris to solidify his personal interests. I could not fathom why he was in Nevers.

"Madame la Duchess!" He swept into the room and gave me a quick kiss on the cheek. Settling into a chair next to me, he began to speak.

"Forgive me for intruding, but I was just informed that you are here. I heard of the King's behavior in Paris." I groaned inwardly—if word had traveled to Nevers so quickly, it had spread everywhere. I would do well to remain unseen for a while.

"That behavior is beneath a Christian King and I am appalled by it. I am especially appalled that it happened to my own liege lady. If I may say, this does not sound like the woman I have known since she was a babe."

"May I confess something to you?" At that, he nodded. "The King himself asked me to write those letters, claiming that he wanted to catch his Mignon in an attempted seduction of the Queen. I agreed to do so, and Louis worked hand in hand with me in writing those letters. In fact, Louis wrote most of them."

"That romantic fool! Forgive me, this is no laughing matter." He leaned forward as if to convey to me his deepest secrets. "I have been a staunch supporter of the King. When he took the throne, he made a spectacle of himself, flagellating in the street and attending services. I was under the impression that he was a Godly man."

I raised my eyebrows, "And now?'

He excelled a long sigh. "I have read several reports that the King engages in sexual relations with these male favorites. In this, he is flaunting God's teachings. As a man of the cloth, I cannot support a man who flagrantly flouts the Church's laws."

I nodded again, "I understand." Still, I did not want to encourage rebellion or to be seen caught up in inciting one.

"Yet, I wish that this behavior was the only thing that worries me about this King. He has shown his contempt for the noble families of France by promoting these base men. The taxes he has raised are ruining our treasury. Madame," he looked directly at me, "I fear that this King may bring about the ruin of France."

"Do you think that he is as mad as his brother was?" I had not broached the subject with anyone other than Louis. The Bishop simply shrugged in response.

"I do not know if I am fit to judge the soundness of any man's mind, but I do believe that this prince is not fit to rule. Despite his mother's desire to put him on a throne, I do not think that he is fit to sit on any Earthly throne."

"Bishop, I understand your fear, but as the wife of one of the King's most important counselors, I have no plans to put myself in open rebellion against him. Louis and I could not afford my doing such a foolish thing."

"My Lady, there are many people who would tell you that the man who sits on the throne and the kingdom are one and the same. However, this King has shown that in his misrule, he will do all that he can do to destroy that kingdom. I believe that our loyalty is first to France and secondly to the man who sits on Her throne."

"But, did not God, Himself, put the man on the throne?" Louis and I both believed in the principle that God chose our sovereign and that to rebel against our king, we were also rebelling against God, Himself. Despite our growing disenchantment with this particular king, our belief in his right to rule was unshakable.

"Perhaps Satan, himself, has poisoned his mind and now it is the duty of Christians to help him to leave it." Those words scared me; was I looking at the beginnings of a true rebellion against the king?

⚜

A WEEK LATER, A COACH APPEARED AT THE COURTYARD OF THE palace, bearing two occupants, my sleepy son and his nurse. "The Duc is terrified that the Plague will continue to ravage Paris and he told me that I was to come to you as soon as possible."

I pulled Charles into my arms and he gave a sleepy whine. "I'll send word to the Duc immediately to tell him that you've arrived safely."

She curtsied, and I noticed that she looked uncomfortable. "What is it?"

She wrung her hands, "People in Paris are saying that the Plague is God's punishment for the King's sinful relationships with his favorites."

So, word of the King's unnatural activities had made it to the masses and the superstitious amongst them were already blaming things on him. Previously, I had thought that the threat was limited to a few disgruntled nobles. The anger was more widespread than I had assumed.

"What else are they saying?" I led the girl into the house and towards the nursery.

"That they need a man who will stand for Paris. They are looking for a champion. Many of them are asking that the Duc de Guise stand up for them."

⚜

"I WILL DO NOTHING THAT WILL JEOPARDIZE LOUIS' POSITION AT court; I want to make that perfectly clear." I glanced at the women assembled in my salon that January morning of 1583. To my left sat my sister Catherine, determined as always to play an active role in opposing the King. Her mother-in-law, Anna, the Duchess of Nemours, formerly the Dowager Duchess de Guise, sat beside her.

On the other side of Catherine sat the Duchess of Montpensier, Anna's only daughter and the biggest firebrand of criticism against the King's rule. For moral support, Claude sat at my own right, ready to give her advice and hopefully balance the extremism of Montpensier.

"Henriette, you are practically one of us," Montpensier leaned forward to take a cake from the table in front of us. "Other than my brother, few have suffered under the King as much as you have."

"And I plan to suffer as little as possible in the future." I turned to Anna, who like Louis, was an Italian and one of the closest friends of the Queen Mother. "Are you sure that Catherine can do nothing more to reason with her son?" I mourned the old days when the court quaked at the sight of Catherine de Medici's shadow crossing a threshold. To think that it was her pampered favorite son who neutered her power was galling to all of us.

Anna shook her head, "We have both done everything that we can to address the King in a maternal fashion, he is well beyond reason." She shot a harsh look at Montpensier, who was about to interrupt her mother. Montpensier wisely shut up as soon as her mother looked at her.

"I have to raise this issue and I'm sure you're all in particular tired of hearing it. I will be seen as fully putting in my fortunes with the 'Guise faction.' I mean no disrespect to any of you, but you do know that any criticism you all face for being power-hungry will also fall on me. I had planned on taking a neutral stance." I glanced at Anna, who by right, led the female portion of the 'Guise faction.' To her credit, she did not look offended.

"France needs a strong leader and ultimately, we all serve France, not a man." She echoed what the Bishop had told me in Nevers, which still made me uncomfortable. That the Malcontents and the adherents of the growing Catholic League parroted a single line made me wonder if they were fewer patriots and more fanatics. I started to worry about Marie, who had left for Joinville to get to know her own betrothed, Mayenne's heir and Anna's grandson.

The granddaughter of King Louis XII, Anna was conscious of her royal lineage. It was her tie to the older Capets, who ruled France for centuries, combined with her genuine friendship with the Queen Mother that made her such a valuable ally at court.

"Tell me, if Henri were to lose the throne, who would take his place? My cousin Navarre?" At the mention of Navarre, Montpensier winced. This time, Anna could not stop her from speaking.

"France is a Catholic nation and it will continue to be so. As a heretic, Navarre is barred from inheriting the throne. As we all know, His Holiness will soon bar him from the succession." I lifted my eyebrow at that. While all Catholics owed the Pope loyalty, kings and nations were not very keen on the Pope making pronouncements on the succession of their monarchs. The Pope was reaching too far, but I kept that opinion to myself. Besides, Navarre had changed religion once and nothing stopped him from doing so again in order to take the throne.

"Henriette, we only want you to open your home to members of the court, just like the salons that you held at Claude's home." Claude groaned at the mention of her home; the building was a virtual dust pile while renovations to store up rotting wood stretched on. Catherine had volunteered my home as a replacement, which was why the group were assembled in my salon that cold morning.

"I will not allow political speeches or talk of rebellion against the King. This is Louis' home and I will not endanger him by doing something stupid." I looked directly at Montpensier, who gave a flippant shrug.

"Very well—you can simply provide entertainment, while the political discussions continue at my home. The orators are more than welcome there, anyway."

"Do you think that Margot will attend?" Catherine would love to have the King's sister give her blessings to our activities through her presence. I, however, remembered the terror in Margot's eyes years earlier, when she realized the King would blame her for Alencon's rebellion. Margot's position was even weaker since Alencon began exhibiting the signs of tuberculosis the previous June, the second of Catherine de Medici's sons to suffer from the illness. Without Alencon, Margot would be bereft of influential allies at court and I had no desire to place her in any sort of jeopardy either. "If Margot feels comfortable, she will come. Knowing that we won't be witness to seditious talk at my home will make it easier for her to attend."

"Well, then, it's settled. You will provide the lighthearted entertainment for the court, while I provide a haven for its deserters." Montpensier popped another cake into her mouth.

"That reminds me, I want to make sure we do nothing to usurp the Queen's position as the first lady of the court." I would never forget her kindness to me when Francis died suddenly, and she had earned my lifelong amity for what she had done for me.

"Henriette, Louise has no desire to be a social leader," Anna interjected. "Given how that horrible woman"—she set her jaw at the mention of the Queen's step-mother—"shut her up like a housemaid, it's no wonder Louise wants to withdraw to the quiet of her chambers."

I looked at Anna. "Then, it's settled, no humiliation of the Queen."

ॐ

"YOU WERE ADAMANT THAT THESE WERE NOT TO BE POLITICAL gatherings, right?" Louis glanced at our salon, which was packed with people.

"Yes, I looked Montpensier right in the eye and demanded it. If this gathering turns political, you are to escort them out into the street."

"Let's hope it doesn't." He glanced over to a corner where the Spanish ambassador, Mendoza, chatted with nobles known to be sympathetic to the gathering Catholic League. I groaned inwardly, hoping that rumors would not reach the King's ears that I was supplying money to Phillip of Spain and his Catholic League. Phillip was eager to pick up support from any disgruntled Catholics, no matter where they lived in Europe. Just to be safe, I would spend Mass the next morning on my knees, praying for protection for myself and the rest of my family.

I felt another strong gust of wind and looked to my side to see my brother-in-law, the Duc de Guise stride into the packed salon. "Do you always walk accompanied by so much wind, brother?" At my teasing, he laughed. "It's the outcome of being so tall. I control the elements, I'm afraid. This is a wonderful gathering," he added.

"Just be sure that it is not filled with political dealings. I still want to keep this neutral ground."

He nodded, "I do enough meetings at the Hotel de Guise and at my sister's house. You have my word on it." Despite his reputation, I began to earnestly like my hot-headed brother-in-law. He always kept his word to me. While he and Catherine were always having a row, he treated me with the utmost respect. As he walked away, I turned to listen to the poet I had hired for the evening. I stuck with love as the theme, thinking that it was one of the safest.

Holding court in the midst of the audience, Margot sat, her hair adorned with a long ostrich feather. Fed up with her husband's philandering, she had returned to the French court to try her luck as an exiled Queen. So far, my friend found my home a safe haven from her brother's boisterous court. At Margot's hand, a handsome man whispered to her. From the look on his face, he found her utterly irresistible. "Oh, no, Margot. Not again," I shook my head, but I knew that it was pointless to try to dissuade her from a new love affair. With enough money from her dowry and loans from friends like Claude, Margot set up her own household in a hotel near the Louvre, which meant that she enjoyed more freedom than she had seen before in France or in Navarre.

❧ 33 ❧

Margot has suffered the same humiliation that I did. On a hot August night, she made her way to the Louvre, to preside over a banquet as was her due with Louise and the Queen Mother absent. As the King had done with me, he spent the entire evening luring his sister into a false sense of security. Near the end of the evening, he railed against her, accusing her of conceiving her latest lover's child. He had the audacity to claim that her "excesses" were ruining his Mignon's "morals." As if those criminals ever had any morals! Never one to give up without a fight, Margot employed her considerable letter-writing skills to defend herself. The King responded by banishing her from France.

To her credit, as soon as the Queen Mother heard of this charade, she went to her son and demanded that he work to reconcile himself with his sister. Navarre also came to Margot's defense, unwilling to allow his own Queen to endure the humiliation of a fellow sovereign. Navarre's pride had been wounded, but he had no desire to admit his queen back into his own kingdom. Margot sat in limbo, unable to leave France but unable to enter Navarre. A lesser woman would have bemoaned her situation; Margot used it as an excuse for revelry.

The Queen Mother finally employed her skills at reconciliation and took an active hand in their King's behavior. Now the King had gone too far, humiliating his remaining sibling, and alienating an ally against Spain. Catherine de Medici, more than anyone, recognized how vulnerable the King's position was. Cracks were openly forming between the King and his Catholic supporters, which led them to add their support to the Catholic League openly. Now Catholics had a legitimate alternative to remaining loyal to the crown.

Plague returned to Paris that summer and to escape the illness, the King moved the court to St. Germain. Louis and I were unwilling to take any chances, so Charles and I joined him at St. Germain. I hooted with laughter when Louis told me that the King sent men across France to hear of their concerns. "If he really cared, he would have asked in 1574."

At St. Germain, the Cardinal Bourbon and Duc de Guise began a friendship, one motivated by Bourbon's belief that he should be the next Dauphin. "My husband has another candidate," Catherine confessed to me one day as we walked amongst the Italian gardens of St. Germain. There was not a soul within earshot, so we could talk freely.

"Who?"

"The eldest son of the Duc de Lorraine. As Princess Claude's son, he is Henry II's grandson. The Queen Mother cannot say no to her own grandson."

"But, will she say no to a cousin of the Guise?"

She shrugged, "Henri plans to make her see that the boy is the only candidate."

"So, the League plots against itself?"

"No, my husband believes that the League can ally itself with the King and avoid open conflict with him if he accepts his own nephew as his heir. It would avoid bloodshed. That is what you and Louis want, isn't it?'

"Catherine, do you really think that given the League's rhetoric, that it exists only for the purpose of putting a boy on the throne? I doubt it; it goes much further than that."

She put up her hands, "Sure, there are some that want open warfare, some that want to rid the world of Navarre and others who would be happier if Phillip of Spain were King of France. There are so many who have united against the King that they have different ways of getting rid of the King."

"It's this disorder and squabbling that makes me hesitate in supporting it. That and the danger of being thrown into the dungeons for treason."

❧

"I AM LEAVING FOR ROME," LOUIS SLID THAT BIT OF INFORMATION to me while we were preparing for bed as August turned into September.

"Are you on a mission from the King?'

He nodded, "Officially, it is all that my trip is for. I have another reason for seeing the Holy See. I want to ask the Pope to weigh in on whether this Catholic League is legal."

"You mean, you want to know if their plans to usurp Navarre are legitimate?"

"That, too. I also want to know if the Pope would actually support Frenchmen who support the Spanish king in opposing the King."

"What will you do if the Pope gives the League his blessing?"

"Officially, I will still support the King, but my true alliance will be with the League. I can't remain neutral for much longer. Guise confides in me constantly and I've begun to see the wisdom in his reasoning."

"Catherine does the same to me, but I admit I've got my reservations."

He nodded and gave me a small smile. "There is another reason why I want to go to Rome. My brother has no heirs and I want to ask the Pope for his support in naming me Duc de Mantua."

"Do you think there's a chance of him doing so?" Louis was a male heir, but given the fact that this title was Italian and not French, a different law applied. We did not have substantial Italian holdings since Louis was the designated heir of his family's French holdings, so we had little experience in dealing with the inheritance laws of

Lombardy. There was no more powerful ally in Italy than the Pope, however.

"What should I do while you're away in Rome? Should I cancel the salons?"

He shook his head, "Continue our policy of neutrality. It's been the best one for us so far and I think that it's wisest if we continue with it."

A week later, four-year-old Charles and I stood in the courtyard of St. Germain, where the court stayed to avoid the plague sweeping across Paris, and we bid adieu to my husband. Our family was down to two people. I hoped that he would return soon and with news that would decide our own position on the succession of France.

❧

Louis' trip to Rome meant that we spent more than half that year apart, united only by our letters. Papal politics were an art unto themselves, one that few were brave or patient enough to enter. When Louis had mentioned that he wished to go to Rome, I assumed that he felt he had a strong claim to his older brother's Duchy. As the months passed on, however, Louis and I learned firsthand just how slowly things progressed at the Holy See.

Louis' letters told of his ongoing frustration. *"I have approached the Pope several times about Mantua; he somehow manages to talk for hours, yet say nothing. I thought that the King was difficult, yet the Pope is more exasperating."* He hoped to get more encouraging news about the legitimacy of the League, but without solid victories, the Pope held on endorsing it until it was politically expedient to do so. Other than lavishing my attention on my son, letters were all that I had of my family. Catherine wrote to tell me of her deepening friendship with her betrothed. As I had hoped, the Orleans were an excellent match for my eldest daughter and they did nothing to try and damper her spirit. I had worried that Marie de Bourbon, our kinswoman, could be a liability as years before the King imprisoned her for harboring Protestants. Given how nebulous the future of France's leadership and religion were, I soon realized that a family friendly to Protestantism would be a good thing for my daughter. I sternly cautioned her not to attend Protestant services, however. There was plenty of time in the future for her to question her faith as my sister Marie did.

My daughter Marie wrote me from Joinville, where the entire Guise clan had descended to mourn the loss of the first Duchess de Guise. Antoinette de Bourbon, another of our distant relations, had finally succumbed to old age and the Guise were bereft without their matriarch. Catherine spent her childhood at the Dowager Duchess's knee and saw her husband's grandmother as her own family. The loss of her surrogate grandmother hit her hard. Generations of French girls grew up in Joinville where they learned the skills of becoming noble wives, while the Duchess worked to secure matches for each girl under her care. As a result, many noble women in France owed their loyalty to the Guise from an early age and that loyalty was embodied in the Dower Duchess de Guise.

I continued to keep a watchful eye on Mayenne and his sister, hoping that neither of them did anything to cause me to regret my younger daughter's betrothal. So far, none of the Guise had done anything to cause me alarm. If anything, we were growing closer to the Guise cause by necessity, while the King continued to alienate even his most ardent allies.

❦

WHILE LOUIS PUBLICLY DECLARED HIS LOYALTY TO THE KING FOR all to hear, in private, we both maintained close ties with Guise. We were firmly in agreement with the League but could not afford to offend the King. Marie continued to flourish at Joinville and we set her wedding date for a few months after her eighteenth birthday. In Paris, I remained close with the band of Guise women and when asked, I simply responded that the King's treatment of me drove me to find friendship with those who were most injured by him. In those days, I scarcely think that the King cared that I did not support him. He probably thought of me not at all.

I continued to enjoy the camaraderie of the Guise women and the freedom of responsibility of managing the Queen's household. My current position was perfect for me, with all of the respect that came from my family and my marriage without any obligations at court. I was free to come and go as I pleased. While Louis played the politician in Rome, I straddled the two camps of Catholic retainers and enjoyed my stated neutrality.

Being a silent part of the opposition to the King meant that I could still afford to watch the activities of the League as an insider and as a detached observer. Realizing that he could not make a claim for the crown openly, Guise continued to put forth our kinsman, the Cardinal de Bourbon, as the heir to Henri III. Unlike me, my sister Catherine had no reservations about speaking her mind openly, as she often did while sitting beside me at Montpensier's salons.

"He dotes on the Cardinal. My husband stands next to him, hat doffed and in his hand, and refers to him as 'Monsieur.'" As soon as Bourbon leaves, he calls him 'the Little Man.'"

"Does Bourbon even know that he's laughing at him behind his back?"

"No, it's become an open joke amongst us. Oh, that reminds me," she snorted before she could stop herself, "Henry actually suggested to the Cardinal that he marry Catherine of Navarre. And he is actually considering it! What an imbecile!" She fanned herself, more so from the exertion than shame.

"Wouldn't they need a dispensation?" Catherine was his own niece. The practicalities of such a marriage made me dizzy.

"Probably, but no one seriously plans on going through with the plan. Bourbon is the only one stupid enough to think that they're serious." Truth be told, no one in our family could stand my Uncle. In addition to being incredibly gullible, he was also selfish and incredibly vain. According to my nurse, I hated him the first time I saw him, choosing to bite him rather than greet him. Unfortunately, as my mother's only remaining brother, he was the next in line to the throne.

"Catherine, if he takes the throne, he'll need an heir."

"If he has no one, then the crown will fall to..." she rolled her eyes in a mock-innocent gesture.

"Surely you don't think that the country will accept your son as the Dauphin." Perhaps the Leaguers' ideas were more absurd than I'd feared. If they expected the young Prince de Joinville to become the next Dauphin, they were stretching too far.

Catherine dropped her fan in her lap. "Henriette, someone has to be King! My son is a Bourbon and as a Guise, he is a Capet. His pedigree is impeccable, and France needs a King of royal French blood. Surely you don't want to give Spain a pretext for taking the throne of France!"

"With all of the money Phillip is pouring into the League, doesn't he own it already? Your husband should be careful to whom he owes money. Phillip will ask for his due eventually."

"Phillip has been asking for many things recently."

"Oh, how is that?" I knew better than to take the bait when Catherine had my curiosity aroused, but I always fell into that trap.

"He's been corresponding with Margot recently. She's thinking of divorcing Navarre and becoming Phillip's next Queen."

I had not heard of this, even when Margot and I were alone together. "You have to be mistaken about that. Why would Margot agree to marry her sister's husband?"

Catherine shrugged, "She is married to a heretic. Phillip would likely ally with the King, at least in public, if he were once again married to his sister. It might elevate Margot in her brother's eyes." I could not fault Margot for trying to outsmart the King; his cruelty towards her was the only thing worse than his cruelty towards me. After Phillip's fourth wife had died of the plague five years earlier, he had yet to find a fifth. Still, the idea of marrying his dead wife's sister sounded repugnant.

"Where do you hear such things, Catherine?" If she was conspiring, I would have to try to reason with her. I had no desire for my sister to implicate herself in a conspiracy and languish in prison at the King's pleasure.

"Not at court. Since the Queen Mother gave up hope of influencing her son, she spends most of her time writing letters at the Tuileries. This information came directly from my husband's spies."

The Queen Mother's palace sat directly across from the Louvre, yet the distance between her and her favorite child might have been an ocean's width. The Mignons, led by the Duc d'Epernon, whispered in the King's ear that his Mother had also turned against him. Faced with few allies at the heart of power, Catherine de Medici had turned to making an alliance with the Guise. My sister's star was in ascendancy just as her husband's was, and she knew it.

❦

THE SUMMER OF 1584, THE FORTUNES OF THE ENTIRE VALOIS FAMILY changed for the worse. The Duc d'Alencon, the King's younger brother and heir, died of tuberculosis. Before his death, Catholics across France held out hope that our childless King would be succeeded by a Catholic monarch. Henry of Navarre was previously just a worst-case scenario, a contingency plan if all of the Valois princes died without an heir.

The League went into action, working to do anything to keep a Protestant from ascending to the throne of France. As Catholics, our worst nightmare would soon come true and with the King's death, we would descend into heresy.

❦

EVENTUALLY, EVEN THE KING BEGAN TO NOTICE THAT HIS SUPPORT outside of his sycophantic Mignons was dwindling. In September, a letter arrived from the Louvre, bearing the King's own seal. As my page handed it to me, I could not stop a groan from escaping my throat. I placed it on my desk and resolved to dally as long as I could before opening it. I managed to fill my day with empty activities until supper. Eventually, a macabre sense of curiosity overtook me. I opened the letter to see what the King had to say.

"Ma Cousine," he must want something since he resorted to addressing me as "Cousine" once again. *"Having found an opportunity to write to you, you have me hopelessly in your hands; not, however, to trouble your repose, but to assure you that the affection I bore you before you quitted the Court has not diminished;"* I snorted at this. His definition of "affection" was clearly not the same as mine. *"on the contrary, it has gathered strength;*

so that as long as I live, I vow to bear you all honor and love, and to demean myself as your very faithful relative and good friend."

Oh, God help me, the man wanted my "friendship?" What kind of trickery was he about? The languid joy I had felt for the past four years melted away. Despite the flowery words, he wanted something from me. The question was just how much he wanted from me. The letter continued with more flattery, enough to make me feel nauseated. I scanned the rest of the letter, looking for the favor that I knew he would eventually ask of me.

"Adieu, ma bonne cousine, I am yours entirely; and say the same to M. de Nevers, as you will both soon experience. Return hither soon; for it is not seemly that you should both be absent from the court for so long a period. I kiss your hand, ma cousine, a thousand times. HENRY." Ah, there was my answer. The King was terrified that Louis would desert him. I had no idea if he had spies telling him that Louis was considering joining the League. I knew that Louis wanted to continue playing a middle way as long as possible, although hopefully, the King did not know that. Flattering me was his best hope for also flattering Louis.

About a week later, Louis returned from Italy. He strode into our bedchamber, covered in dirt from the road, but I cared little for how he looked or smelled. I simply wanted my husband in my arms. For just a moment, I wanted to forget the court and have him all to myself.

"The King has been busy writing me." At that, Louis' eyebrows shot up.

"What did he say?"

"He gave me vague promises that he admires me and begged me to intervene with you on his behalf. He must be getting desperate."

Louis expelled a deep sigh. "He is. He's sounding out the loyalty of everyone, including me. I've assured him several times that I will back him, but he's like Charles when he thinks that we aren't paying attention to him. He needs assurance from everyone around him."

"And being King, he will neither apologize nor take responsibility for alienating his nobles." I rolled my eyes.

"Exactly. He's offered me a governorship as soon as one becomes available."

"Available! They're not 'available' because he's already given them to his friends!" I shook my head, marveling at the King's arrogance.

"He's done worse, much worse. Or at least, his friends urged him to do so. He's allowed them to pen an edict stating that the King of France is not subject to any acts by the Pope that he disagrees with. And," he looked at me, "that includes a Papal bull, interdict or even excommunication."

My mouth fell open. If the King were to issue such an edict, it would mean that he placed himself above the Holy Father. "But that would mean that he would basically be--"

"A Protestant."

"Will he be stupid enough to go through with such an act?"

Louis shook his head, "I don't know—but if it were to be issued, it would pave the way for Navarre to rule. Perhaps in some way, the King would be making his rule official."

"But he would lose the support of virtually every faithful Catholic in the kingdom."

"Starting with Guise."

The Guise were well aware that the idea of such an edict was possible; in fact, they used it as propaganda against the King as soon as word leaked out of St. Germain that there was the merest whisper of it happening. No Catholic cleric in France would dare address the edict in the pulpit and emboldened with this latest development, the Cardinal de Bourbon began loudly declaring his support for the League. Catholics were splintering faster than the kingdom at large and only the King was unable to see it.

"Any commitment from the Pope? Or any progress on Mantua?" Louis shook his head and I began to see how tired he was from his journey.

"Now, they see me as a foreigner. I followed Catherine to the French court and I accepted my grandmother's French lands. Those two acts alone have branded me a Frenchman. Now, no man in Lombardy wants to accept me as Duke." He exhaled a long sigh.

A selfish part of me felt relieved that we would not be taking over the lands of Mantua. I understood Louis' desire to take over what should have been his birthright. I had taken over my lands for my brother James after his death. Louis should have been allowed to do the same thing. Yet administering foreign domains was not easy, as I had learned when Louis made the decision to sell my lands in Flanders without my consent. Lands out of sight were all too easily given to another.

Unlike my husband, I considered myself thoroughly French and had no desire to reign as Duchess in Italy. France might be splintering under a foolish monarch, but I was determined to stay and fight for her.

$$\maltese \quad 34 \quad \maltese$$

A few days later, Louis departed for St. Germain in an attempt to reason with the King and counter the nonsense his favorites were whispering in his ear. If nothing else, surely Louis could convince the King to avoid insulting and alienating the Vatican. Without the Pope's help, faced with Phillip II's deep pockets and surrounding Protestant nations, the King was politically isolated.

"I scarcely know which way to place my own allegiance," he confessed to me at the end of another long day. "The Cardinals Guise and Bourbon keep interrupting the meetings, arguing over points of theology one minute and precedence the next." My uncle, the Cardinal of Bourbon was growing increasingly stupid in his behavior. The Cardinal de Guise, the younger brother of the Duc de Guise, was a powerful member of the same League that put forth Bourbon as the strongest Catholic candidate for the heir to the throne. Alienate the Cardinal de Guise and Bourbon would lose his allies, but only my uncle would be foolish enough to not realize the danger he caused.

"Another 'vital' issue to the kingdom, was the issue over how extravagantly the women should dress. "He still occupies himself with issues of etiquette in lieu of actual decision and policy making. The Queen herself caught Madame de Neuill, wife of the President of the

Parliament of Paris buying fabrics reserved only for the nobility. The outcry took days to resolve. This is what our government is distracted with! Sometimes, I think that I would get more done sitting on the floor, playing with Charles."

"Now more than ever, I know that it was wise to strike a middle road between the King's supporters and those of the League's. Neither of them seems capable of putting together a viable plan for the future of the country. France is becoming increasingly vulnerable to invasion."

At least the absence of the Ducs de Joyeuse and d'Epernon meant that the King was available to meet with Louis on a regular basis. *"The King confessed the d'Epernon was in Pau to lure Navarre back to Catholicism. If he could do so, then the League's power would be minimized, and I would have no reason to ally with Guise. I pray more than most that d'Epernon will succeed. Joyeuse is at home, convalescing, so we are spared his presence for the moment. Once they return, however, the King has decreed that each shall be treated as Princes of the Blood. All rules of deportment are suspended for them and they are to approach his apartments at any hour."*

The King had elevated his favorites to the level of his own brothers, treating them better than he had ever treated his own siblings. Previously, the complaints of the nobles against the King made them look like children squabbling over precedence. With this elevation, it was becoming apparent that the King was determined to undermine the structure of the nobility of France.

❦

THE MEMBERS OF THE CATHOLIC LEAGUE BEGAN TO DRAW LINES against the King, first by recruiting loyal clients in the Northern and Eastern reaches of the kingdom. Fearing that the Spanish would attack France from the West, the King began looking for foreign sources to lend money to the royal treasury. The moment the King's royal envoy entered Lorraine on his way to beg for money in Switzerland, however, the Duc de Lorraine stated his determination to openly rebel against the King. The envoy was promptly arrested and detained, pending payment from the King.

No talk of politics mattered to me as Charles was struck down with a fever. It has spread throughout his body, at first causing him to scream with pain. As the days dragged on, however, exhaustion sapped his strength and he rarely slept without becoming fretful. *Dear God, he is only five-years-old—will God take him away from me*, I wondered? Were I a more pious woman, I would race to the chapel in the Hotel de Nevers and plead to God for his life. Luckily, word immediately came to my sister Catherine and the Queen Mother in St. Germain, and the two spent hours on their knees praying for my son's life. I cared not one whit for politics; Guise and Valois prayers were the same when my son's life was at stake.

They were not the only ones who pleaded with the Almighty to spare my remaining son. The Guise women, the Duchess de Nemours and Montpensier also sent prayers to Heaven to save Charles. With their fingers on their rosaries, their efforts freed me to spend my hours at Charles' bedside, wiping his feverish body down and singing to him to calm him.

I had a cot brought into Charles' room so that I could attend him constantly and be at his side whenever he needed me. "Madame, I am not sure, but I think that it could be contagious," the physician Mouzon warned me. With no faith left in the men who could not save my two older sons, I had sent for a new man to tend to him and Monsieur Mouzon came highly recommended by the Duchess de Nemours.

"If God sees fit to take me, then he may have me. My husband can raise our son and I have no desire to continue living with a third son buried in our crypt at the cathedral in Nevers." I snapped at him, not caring for manners at the moment. I am sure he had seen his fill of worried mothers hovering over a sick child, and he only placed his hands on my shoulder and left the room without uttering another word.

I spent the month of November tending to my son, willing him to eat and drink, and hoping that all the effort would convince God to allow this son to live. I scarcely noticed when the Advent season brought on the chill of December to Paris. The King allowed Louis to leave St. Germain for the season and to help me tend to Charles in Paris. While I read each of Louis' letters, in my state, it was difficult to remember when Louis would return. I was too ensconced in my ever-shrinking world of anguish.

On the fourth of December, the door to Charles' room quietly opened. Thinking it was the physician or a maid, I did not turn to see who stood behind me. Louis' large hand cupped around mine and I realized that my husband was finally home. Turning to him, I allowed him to hold me while I wept.

"The Queen asked me to give this to you." He placed a small rosary into my hands. As tears slid down my cheek, I fingered the small beads, hoping that they would keep me from fully giving in to my emotions. They failed to keep me from doing so and I began to wail like a wounded animal.

"Don't fret so, Henriette. The physician told me that he is through the worst of it. The fever has broken."

I shook my head. Two tiny coffins told me otherwise. I could not relax until my son was on his feet and up to his old antics once again.

"You dare to argue with me? Your own husband?" He was teasing me and the idea that he would do so in the midst of my worry caused me to snort despite myself.

"Louis, you are inappropriate." I glared at him, but he was determined to break my mournful mood.

"Look, he's sleeping. Walk with me for just a few moments, please?" It was a small request and I did need a break from my seated position. I nodded and allowed him to pull me from the room. He held my hand as we walked along the corridor to our own bedchamber.

"Joyeuse has allied himself with the Duc de Lorraine." At his statement, my mouth dropped open. Together with the Duc d'Epernon, the two men virtually ruled the King and France. The King allowed them to style themselves above the rest of the court, which was at the heart of the grudges the Guise and Lorraine relations bore against the King. Joyeuse was married to Queen Louise's sister. There were no other men in the kingdom who owed more to the King's largesse. If one of the Mignons had deserted the King, what did that mean?

"Does that mean the King will desert his favorites? What about the Guise?"

"d'Epernon continues to cozy up to the King. In his case," Louis rolled his eyes in disgust, "there really is no change. The King continues to listen to his counsel as much as he listens to mine, sometimes more. But the King does realize that he will have to keep his loyal advisors close to him. It's why he told me to come home for Christmas and I hate to tell you this at such a time, but he drew up papers for Catherine to inherit the Duchy of Nevers at my death."

I nodded, thankful that Louis had been looking out for our children's inheritance. If, God forbid, we lost Charles, we would not lose everything, and our eldest daughter would become the next Duchess de Nevers.

"I probably don't have to tell you that this largess comes at the cost of my continued loyalty to the King and his cause." Of course it did; nothing from Henri Valois came for free.

"What will you do, Louis? Where do you stand?" Now that I had him in front of me, I could ask him about his plans directly. We could debate our options in real time without the waiting for the post to send his responses.

He looked down at his hands, "I haven't really decided. Guise has asked to meet with me tomorrow morning. He's been at his headquarters in Chalons-sur-Marne."

"Headquarters?" My head snapped up. My isolation from the politics dividing France meant that I was woefully uninformed about the maneuverings around me. If Guise had men that close to Paris, he was less than a day's march to the city. "Did he tell you what the men are for?"

Louis nodded, "Officially, they are at the King's disposal until the money from England comes to hire more Swiss mercenaries. The king is frantically trying to raise the money to get his envoy out of France, which will cut deeply into royal funds. Once he has Swiss money, the King is determined to use Guise's troops to pursue a siege on the city of Antwerp.

His face darkened. "Unofficially, they are there to ensure that the King behaves himself." We both knew that there was little hope that the King would do so.

※

THE NEXT MORNING BEFORE BREAKFAST, MY HULKING BROTHER-IN-law strode into the front salon of the Hotel de Nevers. "Sister," he enveloped me in a warm hug. Guise was born with the personal touch that drew the common people to his standard, bolstering his popularity while alienating the people from the King. The common people had made their choice and Guise was the leader they wanted to lead France. Once Guise chose to use that charisma against the King, the people would immediately follow. At the moment, however, he was simply offering his support for Charles.

"How is the boy?" He looked into my eyes, the eyes that had lost a child before and felt compassion for my situation.

"He is better. The physician thinks that if he continues to improve the next week or so, he may well survive this."

Guise nodded. "I think that if he does so, Henriette, you should both go to Nevers."

His statement grabbed my attention. Guise had never held a secret from me, his respect for me, even when we argued over money years before. He respected me too much to try to deceive me. His respect was due to my position as his sister-in-law and one of the most influential women in France. I had always appreciated that fact, and I pressed the issue further.

"Henri, I know that you are here to talk to my husband and forgive me for being a little behind in the maneuvering in the coming war against Spain, but I would like to know your mind at the moment. Are you here to fight against the Spanish or against the King?"

He pursed his lips. "I only want to save France from heresy. It's touched my family too much for me to sit by and allow it to destroy the country. My wife was married to a heretic. My grandmother almost gave her life in the misguided belief that the heresy was legitimate. Your sister was married to one of the worst heretics in France, one who almost overthrew the King before he could even sit on his throne." He glanced at me, worried that in mentioning my cousin the Prince de Condé he had gone too far. I shook my head, determined to reassure him.

"No, I have more reason to hate Condé than you do. In fact, I'm grateful to you and your late grandmother for taking my niece in and keeping her safe from her father. How is she?"

He smiled, the wrinkles in the corners of his eyes deepening. "Just as magnetic as her mother was," he crossed himself in the memory of Marie. Catherine de Condé was almost ten and almost of an age to marry. I had made the right decision in placing her in the safekeeping of the Duchess de Guise.

"Catherine and I will have to arrange her marriage soon. I trust you have a candidate in mind?" I lifted my eyebrows and he nodded his head.

Guise scratched his chin, "I think that she would be a good wife to the son of Lorraine. Catherine de Medici may not have had Marie for a daughter-in-law, but she might have Marie's daughter for her grandson."

I looked at Louis; the King had no heirs and the eldest son of the Duc de Lorraine would be the strongest candidate for the throne. As the son of the king's elder sister, Claude, the boy was an attractive candidate. "Wouldn't you want a more illustrious candidate for Lorraine?"

"Actually," he crossed his legs at the ankles, "I would want a girl who has grown up at Joinville and who understands the needs of the houses of Lorraine and Guise." He raised his eyebrows at me, his charm becoming infectious. I realized why Catherine often forgave her husband and why she had given him so many children over their marriage.

"But aren't you placing your alliance with the King of Spain in jeopardy?" It was an open secret that Guise took Spanish money to lead the League. Following the King in going to war against Spain was one thing; it was simply following royal policy. Taking an extremely eligible prince away from a Spanish princess might well be going too far in the powerful Spanish monarch's eyes.

"Phillip knows that I do what I do for the good of France. Where Spanish and French interests diverge, I will have to serve France. No amount of Spanish gold can change that."

"Henri," I leaned forward to look him directly in the eye. Knowing full well that nothing I said could change his impetuous nature any more than I could successfully do so with my sister, I decided to speak. "I know that you think that you have Phillip and the King balanced well, but you must be careful. Even the weakest of Kings can strike out when you least expect them to. And they may very well prove to be lethal to you."

He gave me a tight smile. "I understand, Sister. That is why I have no desire to start a war with Spain. Wars rarely end the way that we expect them to. I have little desire to spend expensive men on a war with Spain when they can be of better use elsewhere."

❧

I RETURNED TO CHARLES' BEDSIDE WHILE LOUIS MET WITH GUISE. I knew that Louis would give me a detailed report of what the two men said, so I was not worried about being excluded from their meeting. To my delight, my son began to babble at me, something that he had not had the strength to do so before.

"Would you like to go back to Nevers, my beautiful boy?" As I watched my son, Guise's warning came to me suddenly. Going to our ducal palace there would separate Louis from us, an idea that I found distasteful after his weeks away from us at St. Germain.

"Can we run up and down the staircase?" The elaborate spiral staircase was irresistible to any child. I understood his desire to play on it as soon as possible. I also understood that if he wanted to play there so badly, it was a sign that he was recovering from his illness.

"I will make a promise to you: if you get well enough to run by New Year's, you may run up and down the stairs as much as you wish." At that, his eyes brightened and for the first time, I had hope that my son would not be taken from me.

At supper, Louis and I dined quietly together, while I waited for him to tell me the details of his meeting with Guise. "He wants me to return to Rome." Louis looked forlorn as he spoke. A trip to the Vatican meant that he would be even further from us.

"Why on earth would he ask you to go to Rome? And would the King allow you to leave so soon?" A departure so quickly after Joyeuse's defection would look suspicious. Now, more than ever, we needed to ally with the King's suspicious nature. As I had warned Guise, even a weak King could strike when we least expected.

"Guise wants me to ask the Pope directly if the League has the Pope's blessing. Guise worries that without the Pope's support, our fight against the heretics will have little basis. The papal blessing will cause more nobles to flock to our cause without feeling conflicted."

"What will you tell the King? How can you keep him from finding out your true purpose in going to Rome?' Fear for my husband caused my blood to run cold. I had no desire to lose his presence and I was not willing to allow him to place himself in jeopardy with an accusation of treason.

"I will tell the King that I want the Pope's support to succeed to Mantua. I still haven't lost hope that I can manage to do so. I will also tell the King that I will take his case for war against Spain to the Pope. Phillip has had the favor of the Papacy for far too long. It is time that we broke Rome's favoritism towards Spain."

I nodded; Louis' reasoning was solid. "I don't want you to leave France, but if you think that you should do so, then you will go with my blessing." Louis took my hand and squeezed it. If he left me, I would miss him more than I wanted to admit.

With his potential trip to Rome in our minds, we spent Christmas 1584 in Paris together quietly, just the three of us. The only dark spots were the absences of my daughters. While I knew that custom dictated that they live with their future in-laws, I wanted to have all of my children sitting around me. To my delight, Charles continued to recover, taking tentative steps on Christmas Eve that proved to be the best Christmas present that I could have hoped for. I wrote letters to the Queen Mother, Queen Louis and the Guise women thanking them for their prayers and support. Finally, God did not see fit to take my son from me. As New Year's Day dawned, my son burst into our bedchamber and tried to leap onto our bed. The motion woke Louis from a sound sleep and laughing, he tried to admonish Charles for his behavior. As our son climbed into bed between us, we savored the moment that we were together, and fortune seemed to be smiling upon us.

35

"Mama, you promised!" Charles bounded from the carriage and into the frigid January air on his way towards the Ducal Palace of Nevers. The promised spiral staircase lured my son in and I had no chance of stopping him before he reached it. There was also no chance of standing on ceremony as the staff of the palace stood before us. While my son screamed and ran up and down the polished stone steps of the staircase, I directed my Parisian maids in settling in for our stay at Nevers.

As soon as I could, I checked my correspondences. I had two letters from Louis, who, for the moment, was with the King at the Louvre. The King would not give him leave to go to Rome, which meant that he could not aid Guise and the League in their efforts. Unbeknownst to the King, Louis and Guise continued to correspond, with Louis giving Guise advice on the proposed war in the Low Countries. The King planned to send Guise and his army to Antwerp to besiege the city, while my brother-in-law lobbied to change his mind. Guise was forced to appease both Henri and Phillip on an ongoing basis.

"As you warned him, Guise is torn between two royal masters," Louis wrote to me from his apartments at the Louvre. *"If he does not proceed to*

Antwerp with his men, he defies the King. Phillip's ambassador, Mendoza, has threatened to deliver a copy of the terms Guise submitted to at Joinville if he does attack Antwerp. Guise is paralyzed, and he begs for my help if I ever make it to Rome." Guise had signed the treaty saying that upon the death of Henry III he would accept Spanish troops to promote the Cardinal of Bourbon as heir to France, displacing Navarre. This agreement amounted to treason and showed for all that Guise intrigued with a foreign power behind the King's back. Louis faced the same choice of maintaining his stated loyalty to his King or his secret loyalty to Guise. He asked for my counsel in what to do and I readily gave it to him. I could hear his growing frustration with the vacillating King. Before coming to the throne, Henri III was a decisive soldier, but now, it was a rare occasion when he made *any* decision, good or bad. I hoped that Louis's enormous store of patience never ran out.

I continued my personal policy of finding a middle way, advising Louis to remain at the King's side at the Louvre, advising him alongside Epernon. As long as he stood beside the King each day, he could hardly be suspected of being a traitor. While at the Louvre, he continued to ask the King for permission to depart for Rome to ask for Papal support for the war and for the Dukedom of Mantua. The trip to Rome would take days, during which either Guise or the King could gain the upper hand. Given how recalcitrant the Holy Father proved to be to grant anything to Louis, he could hardly be faulted for the time in which it took to get an answer from the Pope. Once he arrived in Rome my husband would be far away from the looming civil war between the Guise and Valois factions. Hopefully, tucked away in Italy and the French countryside we were both safe from danger.

That February, Catherine began sending my anxious letters, determined to convince me to compel Louis to go to Rome. *"Mendoza showed himself at Joinville, threatening in person to expose my husband to the King. As if he were a naughty boy to be brought before his father for punishment! Without the Guise, Phillip would have no support in France and he well knows it. Henriette, you must prevail upon Louis to take the League's case to the Pope!"* Unwilling to place myself or my husband in the midst of the upcoming fight between Guise and the King, I placed the letter under a pile of papers and promptly went outside for a walk.

By March, the Valois began to cause splinters amongst the Guise and Lorraine cousins, threatening to split their generations-old alliance. Christine, Lorraine's eldest daughter, also happened to be the Queen Mother's favorite grandchild and as with the King, she favored this child to the exclusion of all others. Calling on a grandmother's privilege, the Queen Mother called Christine to the Tuileries to wait upon her in person, which gave Catherine de Medici a bargaining chip against the Guise faction. With his beloved daughter ensconced within the Tuileries, Lorraine was all but neutralized and Guise lost one of his most powerful allies.

Heeding the King's wishes and my advice, Louis continued to linger at the Louvre, waiting for a sign that either faction would soon gain the upper hand. Louis wrote me daily, reassuring me that he was safe and that he would make no moves to openly support either side. Daily I thanked God that I had heeded Guise's advice and retired to Nevers where I would not be brought into the conflict. In my absence, Montpensier continued to agitate the populace of Paris and speak against the King's alliance with the Protestant Elisabeth of England. Rumors spread across Paris that any extremist priests willing to speak against the king from the pulpit were on the Duchess de Montpensier's payroll.

IN APRIL, HOWEVER, OUR IDYLLIC EXISTENCE IN NEVERS BEGAN TO dissipate. Even miles away from Paris, rumors reached us that Guise was planning to eschew war with Spain in favor of civil war against the King. Unbeknownst to the Queen Mother or his own daughter, Lorraine accepted Guise's offer of the towns of Metz, Verdun, and Toul, marching onto them with the troops earmarked for Antwerp and giving control of the Champagne region of western France directly to Guise. If Guise thought that the King would surrender the towns easily, he was mistaken; Epernon rallied royal troops to Metz and throughout April and May the city held out against Guise's forces. Now there was no doubt that Guise was in open rebellion against the

King. This moved far beyond rhetoric; lines would have to be drawn amongst the nobility and choices made.

As soon as I heard of Guise's defeat, I wrote in alarm to Louis. *"Pray that the King does not think that you are loyal to Guise or that you will flock to his banner."* Louis responded by writing that the King spent his days roaming Paris, strengthening the city's fortifications, certain that Guise would turn his well-placed army toward the city that was a short march away.

While the King sent reinforcements to Metz, Guise split his troops in an attempt to incite rebellion across France. Gambling that Catherine de Medici would not harm her favorite grandchild, an emboldened Lorraine went north towards Calais to siege towns across the region and to cut off any supply lines crossing the Channel from England. Suddenly, the King's alliances with the Protestants began to pay dividends as Navarre and his troops were amongst the few loyal troops to come to the aid of the King. Years of consolidating possessions in the north meant, however, that the Guise and Lorraine cousins had a virtual lock in the north and Navarre could not manage to break that lock.

In hindsight, Guise would have been better served to strengthen his presence in the north and be satisfied with it. A lifelong man of the people, however, Guise assumed that wherever his allies went, so did the support of the people and he began to feel overconfident. The city of Lyon gave itself over to the League without a shot, disregarding its history as the first city the King visited at the start of his reign. With no encouragement from the League, the people of the city tore down their own citadel and offered the keys to the city to the League. This rebellion was motivated instead by personal grievances. The city's governor, a man named Mandelot, used the rebellion to take revenge upon Epernon for appointing a new loyalist commander at the citadel. With Lyon's show of disloyalty to the King's man, the King faced the problem of his subjects openly rebelling against him even without incitement from the League. The uprising showed that remaining favorite of the King could be defeated with the proper motivation. The people were finally punishing him for his partisanship of his newly raised nobodies.

By late March of 1585, the League troops decided to control the southern ports along the Mediterranean, in an effort to control all French ports that were held not by the Protestants. If the League could control the northern and southern coasts of France, they would have a virtual embargo against Spanish and German commerce across the Mediterranean. The temptation of such a dominant position proved to be too much for the League to resist.

To compensate him for his support, the League offered Louis the governorship of Provence, which would make him the most powerful man in southern France. *"As always, I told Guise that the honor would be mine, but I could not openly rebel against the King. If the southern campaign were to fail, the League would need a loyal man in the King's service to negotiate the League's surrender. Guise would not hear of a potential threat, of course, and he scoffed at the idea. I may be portrayed later as a coward, but I believe that by holding to our middle way we will be safest."* Reading those words, I breathed a sigh of relief that Louis continued to honor our pact.

Reassured that Louis had both our best interests in mind, I wrote to my sister and suggested that Louis would be the best ally if the League were to meet with any resistance. I suggested that his diplomatic skills would be the most effective no matter what the outcome.

Now, I thank God that I did so. At the close of March, as Charles bounded in front of me in the palace gardens looking for flowers to pick, a message came to me from Paris. "Madame, the Duc de Nevers asked that you open this at once."

I scanned Louis's letter, which he had hastily scrawled in his own hand. The southern campaign had proven to be a disaster. Overconfident that the King had pulled his troops to Paris to defend the capital, Guise had assumed that Marseille was ripe for the taking. With no large force commanded by Epernon to oppose him, Marseille had few defensive fortifications, only an open port. The League forces marched into the city, ready to "liberate it from heresy." Never a hotbed of Protestant activities, the city looked like an easy victory for the league. One alert merchant, however, gained advance notice that the League was on its way and organized a resistance comprised of Protestant residents to face the men marching upon the city. Just as with Lyon, local resistance decided the battle with little interference from either Royal troops or League forces. Marseille demonstrated that the Protestants could be underestimated, and the League used it as proof that the heretics were better armed than Navarre would have the King believe.

Once he heard of the defeat at Marseille, Louis declined the offer to serve as governor of Provence. *"I have assured Guise that I still hold to the ideals of the League to destroy heresy, and that I only hope this defeat is a temporary setback,"* he wrote to me. *"I must confess, however, that the endless back and forth between the League and the King's troops worries me. I hope that the King will not place me on the battlefield."*

His last sentence worried me. Louis had sustained an injury before our marriage falling from a horse. Thanks to his injuries he walked with a slight limp that excused him from participating in active battle. If the King grew desperate enough, he might force Louis to return to the battlefield. I found another reason to worry as I read the rest of his letter. *"I have been given permission from the King, however, to travel to Rome to present his plans for a war to His Holiness. I will also take Guise's case to the Pope."*

The End

Get the final book in the trilogy, Fate's Mistress, *now.*

FATE'S MISTRESS

HOTEL DE GUISE, PARIS, JANUARY
1586

❦ *36* ❧

CHAPTER 1

H otel de Guise, November 1586

"HENRI, FOR GOD'S SAKE—SLOW DOWN! I CANNOT KEEP UP. MY legs are too short!" I watched as my husband's wide shoulders trailed down the hallway before me, his enraged voice booming from the thick, stone walls. I scurried behind him, doing my best to keep pace with him. When he was in one of his rages, there was no reasoning with him. Yet, that fact had never stopped me before. I was in the third month of my latest pregnancy, my twelfth, and could still scamper behind my husband.

His hulking legs continued to put him further away from me, taking one step to match my two. I was far from the shortest woman at court, but Henri, the Duc de Guise, was a giant of a man. No man in France could measure up to his height, the blond giant towered over every man at court. Unfortunately for me, he had a personality to match his oversized body.

"Henri!" I screeched at the top of my lungs, taking my turn in the game we had perfected in the two decades of our marriage. Neither of us would fit a priest's view of a Godly or virtuous man or woman, but then, neither of us had attempted to pretend that we were anything other than what we were. This arrangement made it easy to be honest with one another. Our determination to be brutally honest with one another that we found ourselves in screaming matches with one another, but on this one occasion, I was not the person who had enraged my hulking husband.

The person in question was his August Majesty, King Henri III of France, Duc d' Anjou and only surviving son of Catherine de Medici. Last summer, my husband and his Catholic League had successfully compelled the king to agree to place him in charge of the armies of France. My husband immediately appointed his younger brother, the Duc de Mayenne to attack the Protestants that swarmed across France. When the terms were set in the heat of summer, we breathed a sigh of relief that the king had finally come to his senses and protected France from invasion and the threat of heresy from the Protestant queen of England and my heretic cousin, the King of Navarre.

Today, however, my husband received word from his spies in Normandy that the king had spent the last three months in secret negotiations with the Protestants behind his back. All the work that Mayenne did on the battlefield was for nothing. Worse still the king casually broke his promise to the Guise brothers to follow their advice in leading the armies of France.

I continued to catch up with him, but he stormed out of the front door of our house and onto the courtyard below, where a saddled horse always waited for him. Watching him so, I seethed. I knew where he was going. He would see that strumpet.

Do not misunderstand me—I am no moralist who chafes at a philandering husband. I have had my share of lovers myself. I am too lively to be satisfied with a single man, even if that man is my husband; even if he is arguably the most handsome man at court. I have never begrudged Henri for his mistresses as he has rarely objected to my lovers. I object to the idea that he is going to take out his frustration with another woman, while ignoring me. I have spent too many years in service to the Guise family to allow them to shut me out today.

I storm back to my own rooms, passing one of the many retainers who have sworn loyalty to the Guise and the Catholic League. Our cavernous home, the Hotel de Guise, purchased by the previous Duke and my mother-in-law, has more than enough room to house the people necessary to sustain a rebellion. Every person in this house has been a party to the seditious acts against the king and his favorites. As one of my husband's most ardent allies, I do not take well to being shut out of his council.

Once at my desk, I pulled out a pen and paper and composed letters to allies across France. My husband might not want to acknowledge my usefulness to the League, but there were many people who would. After he finished having his sport in bed, we would have words.

"Every time I think Henri Valois cannot sink any further, he surprises me!" My sister-in-law, the widowed Duchesse de Montpensier, sat her wine on the table before her, careful not to spill any on the intricate lace cloth before her. Her wording was deliberate; while the rest of us still continued to refer to the man on the throne of France as the King, she insisted on insulting him by referring to him as "Henri Valois" as if he were an ordinary citizen. If Montpensier had her way, he would soon become an ordinary citizen. Amongst the noblewomen who ran the female contingent of the League, she was the most ardent. There was no moderation in her tone or in her actions. If she ran the League, Catherine of Lorraine would gladly march upon the Louvre and burn the King in his bed as he slept.

"You would think for his own survival, he would take advice from someone other than that useless fop Épernon." As soon as the man's name was out of my mouth, I ground my teeth. Épernon enjoyed the place that rightfully belonged to my husband and the members of the Guise and Lorraine families. As the highest-ranking nobles of France, their place was at the king's hand. Yet, Henri III had raised up virtual peasants to the lucrative posts that kept the nobles from going into virtual bankruptcy. It had forced far too many of our retainers and allies to sell land and assets to make up for losing offices that were rightfully theirs.

"If he had common sense." She absentmindedly picked at the ruffs at her wrists. "He would listen more to your brother-in-law." I groaned inwardly at her accusation. My brother-in-law was the man who had risen with the king's ascension to the throne; and a man who had long-served the Valois kings of France. Louis Gonzaga, who took over my father's title of Duc de Nevers by marrying my older sister, was the only voice of reason left in the king's privy chamber. Louis' continued presence there gave us hope that eventually, he would get through to the king. Yet, judging by the king's past decisions, he would ignore Louis as soon as Épernon whispered into his royal ear.

I shook my head, "I never know what is in Louis' mind. I know that part of him agrees passionately with the League. He is as loyal a Catholic as we are. Yet, he works to remain as neutral as he can. It's as if he's terrified to stand up and decide."

She shrugged, "Then speak to Henriette. She is your sister." *I can no more control my sister than my husband can control his*, I thought, as I avoided Montpensier's gaze. As controlling as the woman who sat before me was, Henriette was just as nebulous. I never knew her mind either. Sometimes, I felt as if my sister was a cold, calculating fish.

"I have a relationship with my sister, and the king himself made it so." Henriette was once the most senior woman in the queen's household, as well-placed in the king's court as her husband. In a characteristically stupid move, however, the king decided one evening to trap my sister in a fake affair and "expose" Henriette before the court. She fled from the court in humiliation and has barely made any effort to return. If I wish to see her, I usually have to drop by the Hotel de Nevers and make a sisterly visit. Even though it is selfish, I am very put out by her self-imposed exile from court. Without her, I have few real friends to rely upon, save my radical sister-in-law. Montpensier is quite a handful, angrily railing against the king at every opportunity. I count myself as a radical, but her extremism gets on my nerves regularly.

"Catherine, you mentioned the new printing blocks—would you show them to me?"

She clapped her hands. "Of course! I was afraid you would never ask. Come!" Standing, she pulled me up from my chair and dragged me outside as I struggled to put on my heavy cape. The damp cold settled on Paris this time of the year, bringing with it a heavy fog over the river. With an almost gleeful bounce in her step, she led me to the stables of her Hotel de Guise and at an empty stall, she glanced both ways and opened the padlock.

"Here they are. The carvers finished just last week. I paid them well for their silence." Throwing back a horse blanket, she showed the wooden printing blocks. One of them depicted the King of France as a priest, shorn of his hair and shorn of his crown. "The price of betrayal of Gaul." the inscription screamed in bold lettering. Another featured a Protestant army, marching upon the familiar walls of Paris, with babies hanging aloft on pikes. I glanced at Montpensier, "Isn't that a trifle much?" My stomach lurched at the sight and the wave of nausea caused by my pregnancy.

"Innocents suffer in war, and if the Protestants and their mercenaries from Germany and Switzerland march across France without opposition, there is no telling what horrors the city will endure. It is best we acknowledge the danger and do something before this image comes true!" Her eyes shone with the passion of a fanatic. In those brown depths, I saw a touch of madness. Still, I knew that I had few friends and allies in Paris, and given how Henri had pushed me away a few days before, I could not afford to alienate his sister. Instead, I turned to look at another plate.

"This one doesn't have an image," I frowned, trying to make sense. She made a reverse nod, acknowledging my confusion.

"This is blank so we can create pamphlets from it. The lines are there to make the sentences straight. Here," she rummaged around in the hay until she found a small sack, "are the individual letters that the printers will use to make the pamphlets. The beauty of this is that we can use many combinations of letters. We can make several pamphlets and we can do it."

"And are you certain you want them taken from your house? At least there, you can have complete control over the printing process." Something told me that the wooden blocks in front of me were a portent of trouble, but I did not know just how troublesome they would later prove to be. For the moment, my main objection was the added activity they would bring to my home.

She shrugged, "Henri promised. As I am a widow, it would not do for someone to see me instigating rebellion against the king's policies." My mouth snapped open in shock. Was she serious? There was no woman in Paris better known for instigating and fermenting rebellion against the king! Why would she bother to stop now? Had she finally realized that she had gone too far? Did she know that the blocks were too dangerous? Yes, her sex would cause the king to have mercy on her if someone found the blocks at her home, but it was not a given. She faced just as much danger as the rest of us.

Still, I wanted to show my usefulness to my husband. Having control of the words printed by the League across the city of Paris carried with it an irresistible amount of power. Despite my earlier sense of foreboding, I turned to her.

"I'll see that Philobert finds a place for him at the Hotel de Guise." At least inside my home, they would be under my control. I would see to that.

◈

LIFE AT THE COURT WAS TAXING FOR ME. SINCE 1579, MY HUSBAND and the king openly quarreled, and the king constantly took pains to make little insults towards my husband and every member of his family. Once the two were playmates, a reflection of the vaunted position that the Guise and my mother-in-law, a granddaughter of a king, enjoyed at court. Soon after the king came to the throne, however, he allowed other men to poison his once close friendship with my husband.

Never at a loss for ambitious men to fawn over him, the king had selected a man named Quelus and another, Charles de Balsac, Sieur d'Entragues. as his particular favorites in the fashionable sport of dueling. This dueling was not a method of satisfying honor, more play-acting to amuse the king and his close friends. Having the king's favor made a man reckless, none more so than Quelus. The men were stupid enough to engage in a duel, killing both of them. The king mourned Quelus so much that the city came out in droves to mock him. Entragues sought and received sanctuary at the Hotel de Guise.

Thinking he was doing his old friend a favor, my husband readily tended to the king's favorite, working in vain to keep the man alive, despite his injuries. To our horror, the king turned on both d'Entragues and my husband.

Demanding the body of d'Entragues, the king raged against my husband, accusing him of rebellion against him. When my flabbergasted husband replied that he was doing the King's will, the King went to even more extremes. He stated that d'Entragues came to our home because he was carrying on an affair with me and he sought my aid. I have never been faithful to my husband, but even I would never be desperate enough to lie with one of those effeminate favorites. I would sooner lie with a peasant from the fields of Navarre. My husband did not fall for the ruse and buried the man without releasing his body to the king. From that point on, we became a continuous target for the king's ire.

As if this ongoing unpleasantness were not enough, there are enough base individuals at court to make me question the standards of the court. At the forefront of these individuals, is the woman I know to be my husband's current mistress.

Charlotte de Beaune-Semblancy is nothing more than the descendent of a silversmith and the great-granddaughter of a known traitor. By her first marriage, she became Baroness de Sauve. By her second marriage, she had finally ascended to the nobility to become the Marquise de Noirmoutier. She is coarse and with no breeding at all. Every time I am forced to see her, I feel the bile rising in my mouth.

It is easy to blame my hatred of the woman on her common origins. Yet, I have many more reasons to hate her. She is the Queen Mother's creature, one of her Flying Squadron who spends their days and evenings in various men's beds, coyly plying information from them at the Queen Mother's behest. While most women at court choose their bedfellows for passion or for sport, these women do it for money. Charlotte is one of Catherine de Medici's most accomplished whores, managing the feat of juggling two lovers at once. Even in France, that was quite a task. At her mistresses' command, she jumped between the beds of my cousin, the King of Navarre, and the king's younger brother and heir, until she had alienated the men to a degree they barely trusted one another. I blame her for alienating them from the king's youngest sister and my sister, Henriette's close friend, Queen Margot of Navarre. Thanks to Charlotte's machinations, the king stripped Margot of her allies at court and left with few friends at court, save my sister.

This behavior was despicable enough, but no act is too shameful for that Circe. I hold Charlotte directly responsible for breaking my sister's heart over a decade ago. While Henriette mourned the sudden death of her only son, she found solace in the arms of a lover. Charlotte schemed to find evidence that sent Henriette's lover to his death. My poor sister endured those losses within a month of one another, at the time when I thought she might die as well of heartbreak. For these reasons and more, I have no reservations in admitting my hatred of Charlotte.

As I attended the Queen Mother, I kept a wary eye out for Charlotte. I was in no mood to deal with the snake. "Madame de Guise, please hand me my ruff," the Queen Mother gestured towards me and I moved forward.

"Here, your Majesty." I spread my hands over the foamy folds, doing my best to straighten them so they would sit high around her fleshy neck. The Queen Mother nodded her approval of my efforts and I stepped back from her.

"Someone is missing," I heard a sly voice whisper behind me. It was one of the sharp-tongued Mademoiselles. Most of the women my age and older in the queen's household knew better than to engage in gossip directly in front of her. She publicly decries any hint of scandal, while meeting with her Squadron behind closed doors. It is one of the many hypocrisies that Catherine de Medici has created during her long years at the French court.

"It's Madame de Noirmoutier.! I wonder where she is!" A giggle spilled out from a mouth behind me and I fought the urge to turn around and slap the offender.

"I think it's better to ask where she's been!" This time, the laughter is louder, drawing the queen's annoyance.

"If you girls have anything to say, I suggest you say it out loud so we can all hear. No? Then, I suppose you are gossiping. That is a sin and you are both to go to confession to absolve yourselves of your sin." Catherine directed her words at the two offenders and I felt impressed with her ability to hear. Craning my neck around to witness their humiliation, I saw one girl's mouths snap open. The other girl only blushed furiously. Wordlessly, they both curtsied and made their escape from the Queen Mother's privy chamber.

⚜

I avoided Charlotte's presence until that afternoon, as the ladies of the Queen Mother's retinue sat and played cards. I exhaled loudly, annoyed as she floated into the room and made her reverence to the queen. "Forgive me, Madame. My son is sick, and I was attending to him."

Catherine searched her face as if looking to detect a lie. "I will pray for your son's health. See it does not happen again, Madame de Noir-moutier." The Queen Mother's behavior surprised me; was Charlotte acting independently of her Mistress' instructions?

Like the other ladies of the court, I was smart enough to avoid an open quarrel with Charlotte, which meant that it forced me to be civil to her in the Queen Mother's presence. Away from the sharp eyes of Catherine de Medici, however, the woman was fair game. I would have to bide my time. Spying my mother-in-law across the chamber, I rose and took a seat next to her. She was reading a book in Italian. Like the Queen Mother, she was an Italian, and they often spoke in their native language to ease their homesickness. While I could speak and read Italian, I was far from a native speaker.

"What are you reading?" I gazed over at Anna d' Este, the Dowager Duchesse de Guise and Nemours, who smiled to acknowledge my presence. She gave me a quick motherly squeeze on my forearm.

"Plutarch." Anna was one of the most educated women at court and she had imparted her love of history to her son. While my husband preferred reading the history of warfare, his mother preferred the philosophers. Her taste in reading material made it much easier for me to talk to her.

"How many times have you read it?'"

She shrugged, "Not enough. I get more out of it each time I read it. You look uncomfortable."

I shifted in my chair and tried to sit without pressing against the nerves of my back. I was carrying my twelfth child, proof that my marriage had been a fruitful one. Our children provided the Guise family with plenty of sons and daughters to marry across France. Five of our children lay buried in the family crypt back in Joinville, close to the eastern border of France. Losing a child was a common event, but losing each one was an agony for me. After carrying a being who depended upon me for almost a year and caring for it after its birth, the sudden loss was excruciating. I never got used to the threat of losing a baby, no woman ever did.

Of our healthy children, most lived at the nursery in faraway Lorraine, where my husband's formidable grandmother had raised generations of children. Most noble families in France entrusted their daughters to Antoinette de Bourbon's capable hands. A year ago, the aged Antoinette died, which meant that my youngest, Renee, lived with us at the Hotel de Guise. It thrilled me that my daughter was with me in Paris and hardly missed an opportunity to tend to her myself.

"I understand my daughter is off making mischief again." Her sharp eyes missed nothing. It was not my place to shield Catherine of Lorraine from her own mother; if Anna planned on upbraiding her for her actions, that was her prerogative. Still, I did not want to implicate myself and put myself in an awkward position with my influential mother-in-law.

"She's still dealing with Louis' estate. She's cleaning out his personal items, finally." That was partly true—the elderly Duc de Montpensier had crammed their home with items and now, Catherine faced the overwhelming task of dispensing with them. We packed many items off to the far corners of France to her step-children as part of their inheritance. Others were collecting dust until Catherine could sell them and make a profit. Overall, she was luckier than most of us— her husband had left her quite a fortune and she did not have to handle paying off the taxes from her father's death over a decade ago. That duty fell to his heir, a burden Henri faced when his father died suddenly in 1563.

"I doubt that everything in that house qualifies as a priceless antique. Some of those items might bring another kind of price, no?" She continued to scan my face, and I squirmed.

"This child will not get off of my back!" I cried out loudly enough that the entire room could hear me, hoping to change the subject. The matrons in the Queen Mother's entourage gave me tight smiles of sympathy. Anyone who had carried a child before knew the daily discomforts that came with the condition. Beside me, Anna snorted but let the subject drop.

ჯ 37 მ

CHAPTER 2

The next morning, I heard a commotion in the courtyard
below my chambers. Considering how frequently troops
rushed in and out of our home, I barely noted it. After
breakfast, however, my husband strode into my chambers. "Catherine,
I'm leaving for Normandy."

"Why would you possibly need to go to Normandy?" It was on the
tip of my tongue to ask if he would spend time with Charlotte de
Sauve, but I stopped myself from saying it. I had no desire to sound
like a clinging, jealous wife. That wasn't in my nature.

"My spies in England just reported that Elizabeth plans to send in
more English troops to aid the king. Apparently, they've become closer
allies than I'd feared." The thought made me nauseous, if the king was
cozying up to the English Queen, then he really was planning on
allying with the Protestants.

"Are those troops going to fight Spain or Frenchmen?"

Henri sobered, "Frenchmen. I'm going with Mayenne to shore up
Eu." Eu was my county, one precariously close to the English coast, in
the heart of Normandy. If Henri wanted to build fortified strongholds
in Normandy, it could only mean they were there to protect France
against English invasion.

"You could be taking a gamble; if those troops coming from England are there to fight the Spanish and you engage them, you are openly committing treason. Your spies might not be as loyal as you think they are. They could set you up for a trap."

He shrugged; for years, he'd been all but committing treason, but since last July, he had control over all French forces. As General of France, he had the right to defend the country, but this could lead to an open declaration of war against the English.

"What does Mendoza say about this latest adventure?" The Spanish ambassador had virtually moved into our home, constantly dictating to my husband what Spain expected him to do with French forces. Henri had long since grown tired of being treated like a puppet of Spain. When he first solicited Spanish help, he needed the money to finance his campaign against the king. We were now financially insolvent thanks to the income from his late grandmother's estate, so his dependence upon Spanish money was not as strong as it once was.

"He says Elizabeth Tudor will slaughter my cousin Mary Stuart and then kill every Catholic in England." *Slaughter every Catholic*, Henri and Montpensier loved to use that apocalyptic threat to scare people into allying with the Catholic League to save the church from its enemies. I'd grown tired of the same threat thrown against anyone who wavered in their support of the League. I had yet to see any slaughter coming from England.

"Your cousin is being reckless and stupid, plotting out in the open against Elizabeth." Mary, Queen of Scots and the daughter of Henri's only aunt was being held under close guard at Elizabeth's pleasure. Anyone could see the danger Mary was in with her claim to Elizabeth's throne and her male heir. Anyone, that is, but Mary. She'd been foolhardy since her youth as France's Dauphine and later, Queen to the king's older brother, Francis II. Once she returned to her own kingdom of Scotland, however, she became a lethal threat to Elizabeth, challenging her for the English throne.

"I've decided to set up a school for the sons of Catholic nobles from England. They're fleeing in terror and someone needs to show them that there are loyal Catholics somewhere in Europe."

That got my attention, "And just where will you put that school?"

"At Eu. If anyone asks, I'm helping refugees from England to get settled in France."

"You plan to set up some kind of spy factory masquerading as a charity home on my territory?" I turned on him, completely at the end of my patience. "I am not about to let you use my inheritance to ferment a rebellion against the crown! If you plan to do so, there are many Guise properties you can use to defy the king!"

He rolled his eyes, "Legally, they are *all* Guise properties."

"Law be damned! I will not allow you to trample all over me!" The insufferable lout had the nerve to turn and walk away from me. I was not about to let him end our conversation like that. "How dare you walk away from me! You will not touch one timber of my chateau; do you hear me? Henri! Henri!" He sped up his pace until he was so far ahead of me I could not keep up. We raced through the halls of the Hotel de Guise until we were outside in the courtyard. Henri raced, while I waddled as much as my expanding body would allow. The assembled crowd turned to watch the spectacle we were making, but I could not have cared less.

"Are you really going to ignore me and ride out of Paris without a word?"

He mounted his horse and turned to face me, his expression droll. "Goodbye, wife." Before I could respond, he turned around and rode out of the courtyard.

❧

LOATH AS I AM TO ADMIT IT, I WAS WRONG. IN THE SPRING OF 1587, as I rocked my newest daughter Jeanne, a messenger appeared at the doorway of the nursery. The letter he carried stated that Elizabeth of England had finally signed the death warrant for Mary Stuart and that they had beheaded her less than a week ago. I never thought Elizabeth would take the drastic step of killing another anointed monarch, no matter how many stupid intrigues Mary carried out under Elizabeth's nose. Mary's death would be a blow to the French, not only had she been Queen of France, she was a Guise. Henri would feel her execution as a direct challenge to his family.

Sighing, I stood and swept the dust from my skirt. Montpensier would soon likely be banging my door down in disgust over Mary's untimely death. No matter how much the empty-headed woman deserved her death, she would soon become a martyr to French Catholics. Before I could make plans to leave to speak to Montpensier and my mother-in-law, a message came from the Louvre. The Queen wished to see me.

Queen Louise was easily the least problematic person of the Royal Family. A member of the House of Lorraine, she was another of my husband's many and well-placed cousins. Unlike Mary Stuart, however, this queen gave no one a moment of grief with her behavior. I had been part of her retinue since the previous July when Henri wrestled command of the armies from the king's favorites. In passive-aggressive spite, the king removed me from serving his aging mother and into the Queen's household. Since Louise had no public presence, the king thought to wall me up in the Queen's rooms where I would do no harm. If the king thought I would feel slighted by the assignment, he was mistaken. Serving Louise took up so little of my time I had plenty of extra moments to aid my husband and his family in promoting the League in Paris. As my mother-in-law continued to serve the Queen Mother, I was always welcome to visit her in her apartments. If anything, the king made my life much easier.

I found Queen Louise in her privy chamber, directing her maids in packing. "Madame de Guise, I'm sure you've heard the horrible news about Queen Mary." She crossed herself as a reflex. For many people, the gesture was a perfunctory move, but for the pious queen, it was an earnest expression of her compassion for a fellow queen.

"Yes, Madame. I have not spoken to my mother-in-law or the Duchesse de Montpensier, but I'm sure they the feel by the news." Hysterical and milking it for all that it was worth might be a better way of putting things. The longer I avoided speaking to Montpensier, the more dramatic she would be by the time we met. We could reason with Anna with since she had actual memories of her shallow and often empty-headed niece.

"I have told the king that I wish to go to Abbey d'Ardenne to pray for the deliverance of Queen Mary's soul." The abbey was an odd choice. Although it was one of the many that counted Louise as its patron, the location was what caught my attention. Located outside of the town of Caen, it was firmly in Normandy. Since storming out of our home several months ago, my husband had worked to secure Normandy as League territory in an affront to the king.

"Madame, are you sure that such a trip would be safe? The English have taken the life of a Catholic queen, and it may put France in jeopardy." Besides, I could not imagine the king allowing his wife to travel to Normandy where rumors swirled her Lorraine and Guise relations were building up an armed resistance. Was the king oblivious to the resistance building up against his rule?

Caen was also temptingly close to my county of Eu and close to my husband. Going there would give me an opportunity to speak with him in person and see what his plans were now that Mary Stuart was no more. At one time, before the birth of her son, James, Mary had named Phillip of Spain as her heir to the Scottish throne. What would Phillip's reaction be to her death? I could learn little in Paris, but in Normandy, I could speak with Henri in person.

"The king feels I would be safe if you accompanied me to the abbey." Although the queen said this with no hint of artifice, I detected behind-the-scenes machinations of the king giving her permission to go. I would accompany her as a warning to the League she was not be kidnapped or held for ransom. I would go as insurance she would return to Paris without the king being forced to ransom for her release. If the League were stupid enough to attack the queen on the way to the abbey, it would smoke out the traitors for all to see. As a result, the League would not dare make any attempt on the queen during this pilgrimage.

I dashed off a quick letter to Anna, telling her of the queen's desire to make a pilgrimage and of the king's hand in ensuring that I would accompany her. Anna was astute enough to know that the king was positioning me as a pawn in this trip to Caen. I planned to take time out during our trip to Abbey d'Ardenne to make the short ride to my chateau at Eu. True to his nature, my husband had defied me and set up a school under the Jesuits for the "poor Catholics driven out by the English heretics". My husband might have thought he had outmaneuvered me by hiding his activities in Normandy, but he hadn't counted on my determination to check on those activities.

❦

As I'd predicted, I found Montpensier moaning the tragic death of her cousin, Mary Stuart. "That snake Henri Valois just sat there and did nothing! He had it in his power to save her, and he sat by and let her die. If *that* isn't proof he is on the English payroll, I don't know what is. France has to do something about him. This goes far beyond consorting with heretics. Before long, they'll rule us, whether it's Navarre or Elizabeth herself!" Since the king's younger brother died two years earlier, France faced with the prospect of Henry of Navarre being the only heir to the throne which meant inevitably, a Protestant would rule us. The Catholic League found the idea of France ruled by a heretic was an abomination and no one thought that more than Montpensier.

I sometimes wondered if her passion came from a true devotion to her religion or some other reason. She often gave me the feeling she was mentally unbalanced, giving into one fit of hysterics or another. Perhaps, she thrived on melodrama and the thrill of inciting rebellion. Whatever her motivation, on some occasions, she could be too much to handle; and on this afternoon, she was just that.

Anna, thank God, was there to mediate her daughter's behavior. "Dearest, it's probably best not to work yourself up into a bother. Mary knew full well that smuggling letters out of her chambers would be a risk. Only she would be naïve enough to think those letters weren't being read."

"And you think that for *that*, she deserved to die? Many have done much more to Elizabeth and lived. She died for who she was, not for what she did." Her face shone with tears and her body shook as she spoke.

"How is the family going to react to her death?" Weary of Montpensier's theatrics, I asked Anna directly.

"There should be a memorial service, one fitting a Dowager Queen of France." From her purse, Montpensier pulled out a delicately embroidered handkerchief. Blowing her nose in the most ladylike manner possible, she remained silent for a moment.

Anna was also silent for a few moments. "We cannot make any public statement; only the king can speak about her death. We have the option of holding a quiet memorial service for Mary." Although she chose her words carefully, I knew that Anna felt relieved that her royal niece was finally no longer proving so troublesome on the international scene. The political future of France was precarious enough without being called on to help the Scots.

"My brothers will have to come to Paris for the service," Montpensier cut in. Neither Henri nor his younger brother, the Duc de Mayenne, had returned to Paris since my husband stormed out of our courtyard a year ago, taking the bulk of the French forces with him. His prolonged absence was disquieting for me; we had spent long periods apart since we married seventeen years earlier, but *this* absence had the ring of permanence.

"I must leave with the queen, she's planning a pilgrimage to the Abbey d'Ardenne, and she's ordered me to accompany her." At this, Montpensier's eyebrows lifted in surprise.

"Louise is going to Normandy? I can't believe the king would allow it."

"I'm to go as a hostage, guaranteeing her safe passage. If the League dares attack her, I'll be at risk."

Montpensier rolled her eyes and the handkerchief in her hands balled up into a wisp of material. Her knuckles went white, and I stared at her hand in fascination. "Now, the Guise are being used as human shields. Whatever will Henri Valois think of next, Mother?"

❧   38   ❧

CHAPTER 3

The trip to Abbey d'Ardenne was a short one, lasting just over a week. Even with my presence as a hostage, the king seemed loath to risk Louise's life out in the Guise controlled northern reaches of his kingdom. By the twelfth, we were back in Paris, nearly dead with exhaustion. I trudged up to my chamber at the Hotel de Guise to find a message from Montpensier waiting for me. The family had arranged a public memorial and they would hold it the following morning. As the Duchess of Guise, it required my presence. I collapsed into bed and slept the sleep of the dead.

The memorial for Mary Stuart was nothing short of a canonization of a saint. They extolled the late queen's virtues, conveniently omitting any of her faults or propensity for scheming. No one, for example, bothered to mention that many people believed that she had been behind the murder of her second husband, Lord Darnley. Darnley had sired her son, who was now the very Catholic heir to the English throne. Priest after priest pointed out Mary's unswerving loyalty to the Catholic church and her determination to bring Scotland from heresy in following the scoundrel John Knox. Had Mary taken the English throne, they argued, England would have a faithful Catholic monarch and they would not threaten France with an invasion from the English.

As Mary's closest French relatives, Montpensier and her brother the Cardinal de Guise stood and accepted the condolences from the people who packed the church. When I first heard of the service, I assumed that it would be a private family affair. When I lifted my veil to see the assembled crowd, I noticed that many of them were strangers and that many of them were of the merchant and lower classes. This service was much more than a remembrance, it was a rally to the Catholic cause and a recruiting tool for the League. As I had suspected, neither my husband nor his brother, Mayenne, bothered to leave the field to come to Paris for the service. Montpensier used the opportunity to speak with every person she could, working the crowd like a master politician.

"I cannot believe neither Henri nor Mayenne are here," she hissed at me after the service once the crowds had thinned. In a corner, I saw two priests accepting coins from mourners. Not only was the service, raising support for the League, it was also raising money.

"They're busy commanding the army, Catherine. They can't take a day off to ride to Paris on a whim."

At my last word, she bristled. I immediately regretted saying it, since it would set her off. "My brothers are the leaders of the League in France, are they not? They lead the people since the king failed to do so."

"And if your brothers don't lead, who will take their place? You?" Had I expected her to demure and claim to be just a background actor, I was sadly mistaken. She instead straightened her spine and looked around us with pride. "Every son or daughter of Lorraine does their part in helping the family. Am I to do less because of my sex?" There was her naked ambition, on display for anyone to see. Henri's sister was becoming more dangerous and I would have to warn him he was in danger of a coup within his own house.

MY HUSBAND MUST HAVE SENSED THE COMING SCHISM WITHIN THE Guise and Lorraine ranks because, in May, we were all called to Joinville for a family conference. These family conferences were a regular occurrence, happening frequently to ensure that the family acted with one voice. The family worked to ensure that each member, even the youngest daughter of the youngest son, felt as if they were as important to the family's success as the heir. The sense of camaraderie and appreciation made it easy to ensure loyalty generation after generation. Unlike most great families, who squabbled over scraps of inheritance, the Guise ensured that each member felt well taken care of. This ensured loyalty and had so far, kept the family from breaking apart.

After the death of the first Duchesse de Guise, my husband's grandmother and the woman who virtually raised me, that assurance of family loyalty was in danger of splintering. If the Guise were to challenge the king for failing to provide leadership for all of France, we could not afford to disintegrate into petty squabbling. Thus, I approached the opulent chateau of Joinville with trepidation on that warm May morning. Returning there was bittersweet for me because although I had been the Duchesse de Guise since my marriage in 1570, I was the mistress at Joinville in name only. Every man and woman in France knew that Antoinette of Bourbon ran the chateau and that fact was perfectly fine with me. I had no resentment for my formidable grandmother-in-law; she was virtually my grandmother. Along with a slew of young French noblewomen, I grew up under her care and I learned everything I knew about being a woman and wife at her knee. I was closer to Antoinette than my husband, who barely spent time at Joinville, or in his grandmother's presence.

In the long colonnade, I found my hawking husband slumped over the tall windows. "How did you arrive here before I did?"

He gave me a brilliant smile, "My horse was faster. Plus, I didn't have a retinue and furniture slowing me down." I had missed his gentle teasing. We had an unusual relationship, one that had allowed us to weather two decades of marriage. Neither of us came to our marriage bed an innocent, and neither begrudged the other for finding companions outside of that marriage bed. Unlike most wives, I did not trail after my husband in hysterics when I discovered him cheating. Nor did I follow the dictum I must act a prude and suffer in silence when news of my husband's infidelity reached my ears. I truly did not mind

Henri's affair with Charlotte de Sauve, but for the danger she posed in acting as a royal spy, she did not threaten me.

The danger that concerned me, however, was Montpensier's behavior the past few months. "I think you should do something about your sister."

He snorted, "Can you do something about your sister?" He had a point; my older sister Henriette and her husband Louis had refused public committing to the League for years. Henri had done all that he could to convince both of them, writing to Henriette several times to ask for her help. My sister feared if they declared for the League, it would spell the end of Louis' career as an advisor to the king. Given the fact that it composed the rest of the king's advisors of his toadying Mignons, Henriette might have a point. It was not in either of our natures to moderate, but perhaps, in the event of a disaster, we would need a moderate to plead before the king on our behalf. I hoped that we never came to that point.

"She's becoming more radical with each passing day. I think your mother has lost her ability to reign her in."

He turned towards me, his eyes betraying the weight of his responsibility of leading the Catholic League. "I need someone with her passion in the capital. Paris is the king's city, and she's much more effective than I am in subverting his policies." At my cocked head, he held up his hand, "As a woman, she can always plead she is of the weaker sex if the king comes after her. What kind of tyrant would he be if he threw a widow in the dungeon of Vincennes? The backlash would be more than the king could counter."

"She's whittling away your control of the League. She's too emotionally unstable to control its activities in Paris."

"And I cannot afford to be in Paris. If I leave the field, the king will immediately put Joyeuse or Épernon in charge of the army and I'll lose command forever. Besides, the king would not hesitate to throw me in prison. I don't have a woman's constitution to save me." At those words, his eyes raked over me. I had missed that part of our relationship, too. Taking a few steps, I laid my head on his shoulder. He encircled me with his arms and we made our way towards his chamber.

THE BALLROOM OF JOINVILLE BURST WITH LORRAINE AND GUISE cousins, with parents standing with their families. With so many of us crammed in there, the buzzing noise was deafening. "Aunt, my governess says it's time I retire." My younger sister, Marie's daughter and my namesake, Catherine, placed her hand softly on my forearm. I searched her face for any trace of her homely father, the Prince de Condé, but luckily, I only saw my late sister in her features.

"It's family only, I'm afraid. But next time you may be over there, seated behind the Duchesse de Lorraine." It was a tempting prospect, linking my niece in marriage to the heir of Lorraine. So far, we could not come to terms with Lorraine, but Catherine was only twelve. There was plenty of time to settle her future. Unlike me, I would not force her to marry as soon as she turned twelve, packed off to marry a complete stranger who followed a heretic faith.

I sighed at the thought. So far, she had shown no affinity towards the Calvinist teachings of her father. Marie grew up in a heretic household, under the care of our Aunt, Queen Jean of Navarre. Marie had escaped in time and converted to Catholicism and I would do all in my power to ensure that her daughter remained loyal to the church. There was no family in France more dedicated to the church of Rome and that was why the assembled Guise cousins were here for this most recent family meeting.

As I took my seat, I noticed a conspicuous absence in the room. "Where is Aumale?" The Duc of Aumale was one of my husband's many first cousins and one of his most trusted lieutenants in the League. In his youth, he served as the master of the king's Hunt and his tracking skills made him one of the most effective men in Henri's confidence.

"He's staying in Boulogne," the Duc d'Elbeuf cut in. He was yet another of my husband's first cousins and had I not grown up amongst the Guise, I would never have a chance of keeping them all straight.

"Why?"

"To win and hold it for the League. When the English try to invade France, we can defeat them at Boulogne." The port stood at the northern border of France, facing the English coast. If the English could capture the city, they could quickly make inroads towards the interior of France. Holding Boulogne meant stopping an English incursion before it started.

Even amongst family, Henri and his subordinates never spoke of a strategy so openly. They must be confident they can capture Boulogne and hold it. I glanced at Henri, who swept the room with a long glance before straightening the papers in his hand. "We have little time to tarry here in Joinville. I'm glad you could all take the time out to be here." A murmur of agreement rumbled across the room. None of the Guise were much for speeches and it did not surprise me that my husband immediately got to the point of the meeting.

"We need to hold every beachhead in Normandy. Phillip of Spain has done what Henri Valois will not do, avenge the death of our cousin, Mary." The entire room stopped to make the sign of the cross in unison. There was no more devoutly Catholic family in France than the Guise. "Phillip is building an armada to invade and conquer England. With Elizabeth as his prisoner, we will finally be able to stop the Protestant threat against France."

Behind me, I could hear astonished gasps for a few seconds. A thunderous applause quickly replaced those gasps. The Lorraine and Guise relations stood firmly behind the idea of justice for the Queen of Scots. Once the room had quieted down, Henri got to his next point.

"Aumale and I have promised Phillip that France will provide any safe harbor for beached Spanish galleons. While the king may balk at assuring Phillip of his support, the houses of Lorraine and Guise will stand with Catholic Spain."

"And does Phillip envision many ships running aground during this endeavor?" A deep male voice asked from the middle of the room.

"Nothing is certain, but in case of a shipboard accident, we and our allies are to give them succor. Be sure to tell all the men in your counties and duchies that. All the Guise will aid Spain in this holy mission."

"If Spanish troops run aground in France, there is no guarantee they will not loot and attack our lands," another male voice shouted from the back of the room. At this, Henri sighed.

"To make it to the Channel, they will have to sail around the

French coast. Spanish galleons are too well built to encounter much trouble. I doubt that we'll see much of the Spanish troops. This is simply to give Phillip a guarantee of our friendship."

"And what will Phillip give us for our 'friendship'?" Henri had not expected this many suspicious questions. His skin was getting mottled at the neck and around his ears. Two decades of marriage had taught me he was close to exploding from annoyance.

"Phillip will break the back of England and stop the Protestant troops that threaten to sail to France. The Swiss march from the east, which I need not remind you is close to here." He was right, Joinville was at the eastern edges of France and dangerously close to Switzerland. If Navarre and Condé wished, they could march into Champagne and threaten the city of Nancy. There were far too many Lorraine and Guise relations living in Champagne, and the thought of invading Protestant troops sent a shiver of terror through all of them.

"Then, who will protect us in the East? At least leave Mayenne here to guard his own family!" At that, panic swirled around the room and Henri put up his hands to stem it.

"Henri Valois will interpret any large force of troops in Champagne as a revolt against him. Since I have legitimate control over all French forces, I will station them in a manner as to protect all of France, not just us. Besides, once Aumale secures Boulogne for Spain, he will block a third of the troops threatening to land on French soil. With our forces strengthening Boulogne, the Spanish can afford to send troops in case Navarre or Condé attack. That is why we have to protect and hold Normandy: if we secure our shores, the Protestants cannot penetrate the heartland of France. That," he looked pointedly around the room, "is why we are all here. We have to display the unity that France itself has failed to show. We are the front line for our church and for our nation. The king and the Valois have betrayed their responsibility towards the nation. As Frenchmen and descendants of the Capets, it falls to us to defend France."

At that, the room fell silent. For the rest of the meeting, the Lorraine and Guise relations closed ranks and made plans to maintain their unified front against Protestants within the country and those threatening from without it. Before I left, I went to the wing of the chateau that had housed generations of noble girls across France. I had grown up there and now my goddaughter, Catherine occupied my old chamber. I found her sitting quietly, reading at her window.

"Isn't it still too cold to sit there?" The mid-March sun gave sufficient light, but not much warmth. She had placed a shawl that my sister Henriette sent from Paris around her shoulders.

"Probably." She gave me a smile and scooted over to allow me to sit next to her.

"I hear that my father is threatening to head towards Nancy, is that true?" Catherine rarely asked about her father. After Marie died, days after her birth, we could not bother Henry Bourbon with the newborn girl she left behind. She had never even seen her father and I wonder if he ever spared a thought for her. My husband had asked her to call him "Papa," which helped both of us recover from the loss of our daughter months before Catherine's birth. As a result, we thought of ourselves as Catherine's true parents.

I cleared my throat, stalling for time. Deciding that truth was the best policy, I turned to her. "We don't know where or when the Protestants will attack. Every report the Duc, your Papa, receives, tells him they plan to meet up with the troops coming from Switzerland. But don't worry," I placed my palm under her chin and realized that she was crying, "if that horrible man comes near you, your Papa will save you."

"I don't want to see that man," she shook her head and sobbed harder. I pulled her into a hug and held her, while she continued to cry. "No matter what they say, I don't support him. I don't want him to win. I'm a good Catholic, just like you and Papa taught me. I'm not a spy."

She dissolved into heaving sobs and my blood ran cold. Suddenly, I remembered myself at her age, married to a rabid Protestant. My first husband had tried to make me promise that I would never marry Guise. I refused to make that promise. Still, months after my marriage, there were Guise relations who looked down at me with suspicion. Someone accused me of being a spy for the followers of Calvin. I took years to win their trust and my heart ached at my niece facing the same torment.

"Are there people here who are questioning your faith or your loyalty?" She was silent and her refusal to answer me told me all that I needed to know. Fury ran through me. I held her for a quarter of an hour, refusing to leave her until I felt satisfied that she was better. Closing the door to her chamber softly, I padded down the hall to the chamber occupied by the governess, Madame Longrais.

❧

I FOUND HER SITTING AT A TABLE, PLAYING CARDS WITH ONE OF THE upstairs maids. When they saw me, they both leaped to their feet. "Madame, I will speak with you. You," I gave the maid a withering look before she could scurry away, "will report to the Chamberlain." After she made her retreat, I whirled on Madame Longrais. "How long have you served at this house, Madame?"

She swallowed, "For ten years, My Lady."

"And how would you rate your term here as a governess?" She trembled before me. I may have a quick temper, but I am not fond of playing with another woman as a cat plays with a mouse. Still, the knowledge that the other girls had been tormenting my niece under her own nose enraged me.

"I would think you and the Duc feel pleased with how I have been managing the girls since the death of Duchesse Antoinette." She fell silent.

I would get right to the point, "My niece tells me that the other girls accuse her of being a heretic and a spy for the Prince de Condé. Are you aware of this?"

"No, Madame," she shook her head violently, her voice barely above a whisper.

"Yet, it is your duty to supervise the girls, is it not?"

"My Lady, I cannot watch the girls every minute of the day or night. It's possible they are harassing your niece at night after Vespers. You and I both know how sneaky young girls can be."

I knew all too well. Charlotte de Sauve skulked around France, winding her white limbs around my husband's body every chance she could get. I had no evidence that the woman was purposefully shirking her duties. The girls at the dormitory of Joinville were more covert than I had imagined. They could have picked Catherine out as a weak girl and saved their torture for when there were no adults around.

"I will ask for you to send reports of my niece's progress every month. I expect to hear of no more incidents of teasing and name-calling. Any girl caught doing so will be sent home. I don't care how valuable a client she is to the Guise family, there is no room for an ill-mannered girl in my home." I made a note to have Catherine send me regular reports and through a system that Madame Longrais would have no access to. I would not give her the opportunity to dictate what Catherine said in her private correspondence.

❦   39   ❦

CHAPTER 4

Before Summer ended, I saw Montpensier's point of view. While most of my previous dealings with the movement of the Protestant forces had been theoretical and far removed, as fall came, their presence became all too real. I felt the panic and terror of their presence the other Catholics had felt for months. In the sultry heat of July, the king and my husband met at Meaux, in the middle of France, to discuss the advance of troops across France. Many of the generals thought the Protestants would attack in any corner of the country, putting every Frenchman at risk. Others, including the king believed the Protestants were hellbent on marching towards Lorraine to strike at the heart of Guise holdings.

I was only four months into my latest pregnancy. This would be the twelfth time I would carry Henri of Guise's child within my body. While I was far from a fragile woman, the constant strain on my body was getting to me. I was almost thirty and had spent far too much of my life with child. This child would likely be my last pregnancy. I had five living children, more than enough to carry the Guise line forward for many generations. If I had thought I could sit quietly while my child grew inside me, I was very much mistaken.

On the afternoon of September 2nd, I sat beside the king and

Queen Louise, while they listened to a lecture about philosophy from an Italian orator. The irony of the king sitting and listening to a lecture about something so frivolous while he ignored counsel about the state of his nation, infuriated me, but years at court meant that I could hide my anger behind a mask of tranquility. Half an hour into the lecture, one of the king's Swiss Guards crept in and whispered in his royal ear. The king rose and left the room abruptly. As the orator looked help-lessly towards Queen Louise to see if he should continue, she indicated that we were to take a break. Thankful for the respite, I excused myself to attend to my toilet.

As I walked back along the corridors of the Louvre, I saw Char-lotte de Sauve coming in my direction. I tried to alter my course to avoid her, but she appeared to be seeking me out.

"The king is on his way to arrest Montpensier's creatures I hear," The words sounded casual, but I could tell she was baiting me.

"Creatures? Whatever are you talking about Madame de Sauvé?"

"It's Madame de Noirmoutier. Perhaps you haven't heard of my recent marriage." She had married the Marquis de Noirmoutier, elevating her status at court and making her a richer woman than ever before, yet she still saw fit to pursue my husband.

"Ah, yes—I think I heard something about you buying a new husband. Perhaps this one won't steal from you." I hoped that this little dig would cause her to leave in disgust, but I was not so lucky.

"Aren't you afraid that I'll implicate you in Montpensier's schemes?" Charlotte batted her long eyelashes at me. Unlike most of us, she was a natural blonde. She never had to dye her hair to achieve the delicate coloring that men at court found irresistible. Feeling bloated at my pregnancy, I felt ungainly beside her, flaring my anger even further.

"Madame, you never have bothered to tell me what your personal politics are. Do you support the church that nurtured you since birth, or do you continue to consort with Heretics?"

"Me?" her voice dripped venom. "I have always remained loyal to the same faith, unlike you, who changes religions like you change husbands." The old taunts from childhood came back the lifelong Catholics insinuating that I was a traitor to both sides. Common sense told me to hurry back to the queen's side and away from a further confrontation with the tart standing in front of me. Unfortunately, I used none of my common sense.

"Ah, loyalty. I suppose that you remain a Valois spy. Tell me, who do you work for? The Queen Mother? The king? When you're rolling around in someone else's sheets, who pays your bills?"

She opened her mouth to respond, but a matron told us that the queen required our presence. She denied me the chance to learn who was pulling Charlotte de Sauve's purse strings.

⁂

DAYS LATER, I RECEIVED A LETTER FROM MY HUSBAND. THE KING had ordered him to move all French troops to Gien, a village within my sister's Duchy of Nevers. "The king believes the Protestants march straight for Joinville," he wrote in a hastily scrawled note. "You will be safe as far away from Champagne as you can get, either at Eu or with your sister at Nevers." His letter gave me two options: return to my chateau in Normandy or visit my sister at our ancestral home in Nevers. Since Henriette had resigned from Queen Louise's service eight years ago, we rarely had time to spend with one another. I was still in the early days of my pregnancy before the added weight made me unwieldy. I decided that it was the perfect time to make a sisterly visit.

After a long, bumpy ride over muddy roads, I finally pulled into the courtyard of the Ducal Palace of Nevers as Jeanne buzzed excitedly beside me. Renee had outgrown the nursery, and I had sent her to Joinville. The last time I was at the Palace, I was about to marry Antoine de Croy, the Prince de Porcien. Barely out of childhood, all I could think of was the brilliant life I was about to partake upon. On that warm afternoon, however, I had returned there for protection.

Henriette met me at the top of the steps and embraced me. "Guise was smart to send you away from Joinville. From what I've heard, the king expects there to be a major engagement outside of Joinville. There are German and Swiss mercenaries camped outside of the village. He's hoping that Guise will fall during the battle and all of his worries will be over."

I snorted, "He really thinks if my husband dies, all of his worries will be over? What a naïve man! If Henri falls, there are plenty of League members ready to avenge him. Phillip will still plan to invade France, but he will solicit a less reasonable man to aid him. At least my husband knows how to keep Spain at bay. A traitor may take a small Spanish payment and sell us all out."

We came to a small boy, one who looked as if he could be my son, Charles. The thought brought a pang of longing to see my firstborn who waited out the Protestant threat behind the safety of abbey walls. Henri and I had moved him to an abbey deep within Lorraine, where his uncle, the Cardinal de Guise, could keep a watchful eye on him. This Charles was Henriette's son and heir, who was all of eight years old.

"Charles, would you like to play with your cousin, Jeanne?" Henriette's voice showed that she expected him to say a quick yes and leave the two of us to speak in private. Charles foiled her plans, however, by vehemently shaking his head.

"She's too small." He curled his upper lip in disgust at the task asked of him. Henriette rolled her eyes in response.

"Show her the staircase, please. It is the birthright of every Cleves child to run up and down the staircase until exhaustion sets in. You would not deny your young cousin the pleasure of doing so, would you? What kind of gentleman would you be?"

The maternal guilt worked its way on Charles and chastened, he nodded. "Okay, Mama. Here," he held out his hand to Jeanne, who looked at me in confusion. "Go ahead, you'll love it." She slowly let go of my skirts and walked towards her cousin. With our children gone, we sat in the palace's solarium to speak in private.

"Louis tells me that the king thinks all the Protestant incursions are attacks against the League, not him."

"Does he think he has no enemies then? That this is just another battle between warring faiths? This is not another St. Bartholomew's Day. The same people who would not think of betraying King Charles have no problem with rebelling against the current king."

"The king sees himself as the embodiment of Catholicism in France. You know how publicly he wears his faith, self-flagellating and going on as many pilgrimages as possible."

"Spectacles are hardly a way to prove that he is a loyal Catholic," I rolled my eyes at the thought of the king working so hard to convince his Catholic subjects he had the situation well in hand. Everyone knew that there was a schism between the throne and the rest of the Holy Church. He was fooling no one.

"He'll ignore his Catholic critics and when it comes time to place the blame, he'll claim that they're Protestants determined to undermine his reign." She stopped and looked at me, "As far as Louis and I are concerned, the only rebellion against the king is foreign and Protestant."

I settled into my ancestral home in Nevers, determined to make as little trouble for my sister as possible. Hoping to call little attention to myself, I had only taken Jeanne and two of my maids on my trip from Paris. If Henriette saw I was not there to stir up dissension, then there would be little about my visit to object to. Her household was a small one, a holdover from the time she left court service. I envied her simplicity; our household comprised refugees, dissidents, soldiers, and radicals who flocked to the Guise banner. Those hangers-on meant extra expenditures, straining the paltry pension we received from Phillip of Spain.

While I worked to avoid Henriette's bad temper, others did not. The city of Nevers was much more compact than sprawling Paris and the cathedral was directly behind the Ducal Palace, allowing Jeanne and I to attend Mass daily. As we exited the cathedral, a young man dressed in the simple garb of a Jesuit stopped to speak with us. "Madame de Guise, I heard that you were here in Nevers and I wanted to thank you personally for your patronage of our order in Normandy."

Henri's Jesuit mission in Eu was his idea and one I strongly disagreed with, but the fresh-faced boy standing in front of me need not know that. "We see it as our duty to help those who are fighting to preserve the sanctity of our church." I turned to walk past him, but he stopped me.

"Would it be too much to impose upon you to visit at the palace tomorrow? There is something I need to speak to you about." The request seemed innocent enough, so I gave him an indulgent shrug. "Meet me tomorrow afternoon."

The young priest was punctual, appearing at the palace gates well before our appointment. Interpreting his punctuality as a sign of respect, I welcomed him into Henriette's salon and we settled into small talk. Father Jean began his career in the church in a small village in Normandy, hoping to improve his family's fortunes by joining the Jesuit order. A quarter of an hour into our interview, he came to the point of his visit.

"My Lady, I realize I have no right to take advantage of your charity, but I am desperate. I need your help."

Lured into a sense of ease, I lifted my eyebrows and urged him to continue. "I have two younger sisters remain trapped in England. My parents sent them abroad with me when I went to England to minister to the Catholics there. We were lured in by Elizabeth Tudor's promises of toleration of Catholics, but now–"

I held up my hand, horrified at the thought of two vulnerable children at the mercy of the English Protestants. "Are you not able to send for them?"

He shook his head vehemently. "No, with the Spanish threatening to attack the English coast at any moment, the sea captains are charging ten times what it usually costs for a voyage across the Channel. Once I have them safely in France, I can relax, but I can spirit them out of England."

"And you would like me to give you the money for their passage?" The after effects of Mass made me more charitable than good sense would have allotted, but I felt moved to pity for his plight.

"No, my Lady—I would only ask to *borrow* the money. I will pay you back in full." He looked so earnest and so naively hopeful for his family I could not say no to him.

"Very well—I will advance the money to you. Repay me when you can."

He stood and took my hand. Kissing it, he bowed his head to my hand. My pride was stroked at his reverence. By the end of the week, I had sent the money to the young priest, and he was back on his way from his order to Normandy.

Flushed with the elation of having done a small part to help the English Catholic refugees, I found it easy to sit with my sister. Freed from the endless demand of court duties, we could sit and talk as long as either of us wished. As Jeanne and her cousin Charles played in the palace's foyer, Henriette and I read over our niece, Marie's letters from Joinville.

"You're certain she's safe?" Although the Dowager Duchesse had supervised Marie's upbringing, each of us took our duties as surrogate mothers to our niece seriously since her birth. Nothing changed that fact.

I nodded, "Joinville is well-protected, it's just the road is at risk. Henri would not hear of my traveling along it from Paris. That man and his troops camp just outside of one of Lorraine's isolated abbeys." At the mention of "That Man," we both rolled our eyes in disgust. Time had done nothing to lessen our shared hatred of our former brother-in-law and cousin, Henry, Prince of Condé "He has another daughter now and I'm sure she'll be raised as a proper Protestant. Even if he did remember Marie, he's long since replaced her in his heart."

"He has a submissive wife now to do his bidding. He sequesters her in his chateau and refuses to allow her to court."

I shrugged, "She's really not missing anything by not attending court. It's dull without you." At that, Henriette gave me a small smile. When Henri Valois took the throne thirteen years earlier, it was a foregone conclusion that our youngest sister, Marie would sit beside him as his queen. He was a man in love, a king who would have made a strong ally. Today, we could only sit and remember the sister who left us thirteen years ago. "I sent Marie some silks for her birthday. She's a teenager this year, which means she's ready to be betrothed."

"Who does Guise want for her husband?" If Marie's mother was alive, she would lead this conversation. If her father had any honor or sense of decency, he would have already planned an advantageous marriage for his firstborn child.

"He still wants to marry her to one of Lorraine's sons. I support the match and if she's at Nancy, she won't be too far from us."

"Louis and I are thinking about one of Lorraine's daughters for Charles." I glanced at my nephew, who had taken to his duty to watch his younger cousin with a seriousness that was touching. A husband with such a protective nature was a find. There was a seriousness about the boy that seemed well beyond his years.

"I'll have Henri speak to Lorraine for you."

❧

ON SEPTEMBER 11TH, BEROU, THE CHAMBERLAIN WHO HAD SERVED the Ducal Palace of Nevers for longer than I could remember, came into the garden, holding a scrap of paper. Henriette and I were watching our children play and enjoying the cooler weather of early Fall. "Madame, I've bad news I'm afraid." He handed the message to Henriette, who let out a groan of frustration.

"What?" I turned from Jeanne, who struggled to use her dress as an apron for transporting pebbles.

"There's been a battle." At that, my blood ran cold. The Protestants had attacked Lorraine and could then turn directly towards Joinville. This would be a disaster for our family and the many retainers who sent their noble daughters for education at the chateau.

"It was at Coutras," Henriette clarified. I frowned; the name meant nothing. There was no place in the entire Champagne region named Coutras.

"It's in Burgundy, southeast of La Rochelle. Condé double-backed with most of his troops and headed towards the coast. They engaged royal troops under Joyeuse's command." I sent a quick word of thanks up to Heaven that my husband and his troops were safe.

"Well, that's good, isn't it? One of the king's favorites is dead. The bulk of the army is safely in Lorraine. How is that bad?"

Berou cut in, "My Lady, I'm sorry to say the Protestants had a rousing victory. They cut down Joyeuse's troops. And the army has not been in Lorraine for over a week. The king ordered them to march to Gien."

It dumbfounded me. "Why are they in Gien? That makes little sense." I searched Berou and Henriette's faces and he tried to explain the ramifications of the battle. "The king wanted to hold the Loire, so he chose Gien as the staging ground for the rest of the army a few days ago. Joyeuse's troops were a small portion of the army and most of them were young, untrained troops. Condé's men were too experienced for them. Someone injured Joyeuse so badly that no one expects him to live."

"And what of Lorraine? Is it safe?"

"The king purposefully left Lorraine exposed to Swiss and German troops. He would sacrifice Lorraine to the Protestants. It's likely that he hoped someone would kill Guise in the effort." The extent of the king's betrayal hit me, stoking my ire. He had purposefully tried to expose my husband to danger and deprive him of his own troops. I had not heard from Henri for days and suddenly I knew why.

"That's not all, I'm afraid." I looked at Henriette, who looked as if she could hear no more bad news, either, but she nodded, urging him on. "The Prince de Condé was injured and taken from the battlefield. Someone shot him off his horse, but the Protestants took him to his Chateau at St. Angely."

If I were a better Christian, I might offer thanks that my former brother-in-law was safe. Instead, I felt annoyed that this longstanding thorn in our side was still alive and capable of doing more harm to us.

"Well, at least Joyeuse is gone. That's one of the Mignons out of the government." Joyeuse was governor of Normandy, an honor usually given to princes of the blood, men far above his station. Men like my husband, who would have been a much more effective administrator of northern France. With Joyeuse dead, now perhaps the king would see reason and appoint Henri to the post. If the king would do so, I would feel safe in returning to my chateau in Eu without the threat of molestation from the king.

As soon as possible, I scribbled a letter to my husband in Lorraine, thinking he was deep in the western reaches of France. It was weeks before he replied, and I soon learned why. After learning of the debacle in Coutras and the king's betrayal, Henri had doubled-back towards Paris to rejoin the bulk of the army before the Protestants could destroy all French forces. Navarre, even without Condé at his side, was only days away from joining German reinforcements and creating a Protestant force so great that no royal troops could match it. Before Coutras, Henri could only shadow the Protestants near him in Lorraine and watch their movements. When the king took the bulk of his troops off to Gien, my husband was even more shorthanded than ever.

The advantage of having such a small force, however, was a greater mobility and Henri could outpace the Protestants until he could find a place to cleave their forces in two. He found that place halfway between Paris and the sacred city of Chartres just before November turned into December. Besides cutting down two-thousand Swiss mercenaries, he successfully plundered their supply train, one that destined for Navarre's troops. Holding the Swiss troops captive, my husband lay in wait for Navarre to reinforce the Swiss, but no help came for the invaders. As was typical of my cousin, Navarre, something much more appetizing than a victory distracted him; his newest mistress. For weeks, he delayed in his paramour's arms while waiting for Condé to recover. Navarre's dalliance gave my husband more than enough time to provision his troops and provide payment for them.

The bulk of the spoils in the Protestant camps came from the French countryside, mostly Guise and Lorraine lands. With his victory near Chartres, Henri could return many of the items plundered from his retainers, increasing the debt owed to him by the people of Lorraine.

As I read his letter, I beamed with pride. My husband had cut the main source of heretic troops from the West and they would be on their way back to Switzerland with nothing more than the clothes on their back. During their long march back, they would have to face the wrath of the common folk they had stolen from. He cut Navarre off, and the people turned against the Protestant marauders. This victory was enough to prove to the king that this use of German troops was ruinous to France. Doing so had turned the common people against him.

I had two short days to savor my husband's victory in central France, during which, the baby inside me became increasingly active. This latest child was due in the New Year, likely before the end of February. Many women hated to give birth in the coldest months of the year because the ice and snow made travel hazardous. With twelve births already behind me, I much preferred to go to my childbed during the winter. The swelling of my limbs and the stress on my body were too much to bear during the heat of the Summer. Unlike many women, I considered Winter to be the most fortuitous time of the year to bring a child into the world.

I still had a third of my pregnancy to endure and I was already waddling everywhere I went and the slightest exertion tired me. I likewise waddled into the dining room of the palace at the end of November to sup with my sister. My sister seemed distracted, but given her propensity to lose herself in her thoughts, I paid little mind to her odd behavior. After the servants cleared the dishes, she rose to her feet and strolled towards me, clutching a piece of paper.

"What is this?" She laid it beside me and I could only stare at it in confusion.

"I do not understand."

"You're right, you probably wouldn't know, so I'll tell you. It's a note from the forces stationed at Gien saying they've captured the spy you sent to Eu."

I could only stare at her, my mouth agape. "Spy? Have you lost control of your senses? I sent no spy to Eu. I sent no one, even a servant to collect rent." Knowing how greedy Joyeuse had been during his lifetime, I assumed that any of the money sent on the road from Eu his troops would raid to Nevers and immediately placed into his own pocket. The odious man knew nothing other than greed. Delaying my payment of the rents turned out to be a costly decision since my income had dwindled since he became governor of Normandy.

"Really, Catherine? You deny that you've been carrying out a rebellion against the king right under my nose the entire time?" Her face became darker and flushed with red as she spoke. Neither of us was blessed with olive complexions and the slightest amount of anger showed immediately on our skin. It terrified most people of the court when my sister became enraged, but most people were not her younger sister. I could easily hold my own in an argument with her. This time, however, I knew that I was innocent of whatever scheme she accused me of.

"Do you have any proof of any rebellion I've been carrying on? The only people I've seen since I got here are you and Charles. I suppose your eight-year-old son is my co-conspirator?" At the mention of Charles, she flew into a rage. I had gone too far, but it was too late to take back what I said.

"Proof?" she all but screamed the word at me, multiplying her anger. "Follow me and I will show you proof." She stormed out of the dining room and towards the study. I struggled to keep pace with her. In my state, walking was becoming difficult, and I had to stop frequently to catch my breath. Without a child in her belly, Henriette easily strode into the room before I could follow her. Once in the study, I took a seat to calm myself. While I did so, she rifled through a drawer until she found a stack of papers. "Here," she tossed them at me.

I scanned the papers, unwilling to believe what I was reading. Amongst my letters to the Father Jean, who had begged me for money to help spirit his young sisters from England to France were detailed reports between the Jesuits of Gien and Eu, exposing how the money was being funneled to pay for the League's defiance of the king. I had seen none of these letters, but as I read them, I realized that not a single sou of what I had sent would help innocent girls escape religious prosecution; it would instead pay for ammunition and supplies. My signature sat prominently at the bottom of every letter I sent to the young man.

"I am sorry, Henriette. He has exploited my charity. I did not understand what he was really doing with the money I gave him."

"You never asked for an accounting of the money? You're usually more careful than that. What has this League done to you?"

Likely, the League had made me as reckless as Montpensier. Yet, unlike her, I had the stresses of pregnancy to influence my bad decisions. The young man had preyed on my emotions when he spun a yarn of helpless girls looking for a savior. A pregnant woman was entirely too easy to exploit, and I had fallen for his scheme. He had successfully played me for a sentimental fool. I was ashamed at how gullible I had been.

In his letters, he expounded me as his patron and begged for more contributions in my name to add to what I had unwittingly donated to the cause. What I had contributed to the cause was a sizable sum, but according to these documents, the Jesuits had raised a considerable sum to finance their activities from Nevers to Normandy.

She sat beside me an exhaled a long sigh. "If it's any consolation, I believe you."

I nodded, unable to speak for a few moments. We sat in silence, neither of us able to break the awkwardness between us. After several moments, she spoke.

"I've spoken to Louis about this. Since it involves the king's troops in this, we really have no choice. I have to banish you from Nevers, or the king will see the two of us as being complicit in this scheme."

It horrified me at how easily she and Louis would throw me to the wolves. I was her only surviving sibling. "Banish! You must be joking with me. Where could I go? The Swiss troops have laid Lorraine to waste while Normandy is still rife with men loyal to Joyeuse."

"You should go to Paris. There is no threat of invasion there. The king is planning on returning to the Louvre within the week. You can go to plead your case to him in person. Louise will probably do all that she can to help you." She shrugged, "Well, all that Louise can do, anyway."

Return to Paris in disgrace, accused of conspiring against the king? And with no one to plead my case? I shook my head, "No, you're asking too much of me."

"Catherine, this is the second Jesuit conspiracy that has occurred under my roof. Neither Louis nor I can afford to anger the king before he suspects us. I have my son to protect. I cannot protect you too this time."

My sister was right; I had placed them all in danger with my naivety. The honorable thing would be to leave Nevers as soon as possible for Paris. Spite caused me to rebel against her, however. "Are you two still going to continue to play both sides? How much will that cost you in the long run?"

She whirled upon me. "You and Guise have already taken the part of radicals. What other parts are left to the rest of us? While you quarrel openly with the crown, the rest of France has to take sides and hope we make the right one. Do you really think if you were in our position, you would not try to travel a middle road?"

"No choice *is* a choice, Henriette! When are you and Louis going to realize that?"

"Catherine, Louis and I have made our decision. Nevers is our duchy, and this is our home. I expect you to honor our decision."

The next morning, with Jeanne beside me, I began the long journey towards Paris. Within the silent carriage, I had plenty of time to ponder my situation. In the past, I had watched as Montpensier stroked the fire of rebellion, all the while thinking of her as little more than a radical. Now events outside of my control branded as another radical, although I was innocent. They would know me for being a radical and a rebel, even while I had tried to tread my version of a middle way for myself. In a way, I had followed the same philosophy that Louis and Henriette had espoused for years. I had warned Henriette that no choice was a choice and my words were coming back to haunt me.

It was time for me to take a more active role in promoting the League. It was too late to turn back. Henriette showed me I had no other option. It was time to enjoy the perks of being a radical leader. At those thoughts, the child within me stirred, and I felt a mother's guilt wash over me. With one daughter not yet out of the nursery and a child coming in a few months, I had no business contemplating an active rebellion against the king. As a childless widow, Montpensier had that luxury. I had children to protect and their future to safeguard, just as Henriette had banished me to safeguard her son's future. Sighing, I laid my head back on the upholstered bench and tried to lure myself to sleep. I would have trouble enough once I reached Paris.

40

CHAPTER 5

I spent several days nursing my wounded pride before I ventured to leave my chambers at the Hotel de Guise. Henriette might well have a point I would have to grovel before the king eventually, but I had no desire to head to the Louvre to see if the king had heard of my supposed seditious activity. Still, with the Advent season, my presence at court was a requirement. The more Guise women were absent, the more the king would think a conspiracy surrounded him.

I found Queen Louise in her privy chamber, as serene as usual. She had none of the excitable fervor of most of the Lorraine dynasty and this was one occasion that I was glad for that fact. "My Madame de Guise—how was your trip to Nevers?"

Before I could stop myself, I blurted out, "Someone framed me for committing a conspiracy. My sister banished me from her home." I don't know why I said such a thing to her, I can only think it was because of pregnancy moods. I shamed myself immediately afterward by breaking down and crying like a fishwife. The matrons in the room rose to cluck over me and Louise took my hand. "Catherine, if someone falsely accused you, that is terrible. Tell me what happened; maybe, I can speak to the king for you."

I told her the truth of the young priest who preyed upon my

sympathy and the discovery of his notes. She nodded and rubbed my forearm as I blubbered on. The more of the tale I told, the more emotional I became. I hope to God that this was only because of my pregnancy. "I'll talk to the king at supper. Don't worry about this and don't let it spoil the miracle of your coming child."

I could only bite my lip as I tried to compose myself. Louise pressed further, "If it would make you feel better, it would honor me if you would name me as the child's godmother."

Her offer was touching, but Henri and I had already talked about the naming of a godmother of our next son or daughter. "Queen Margot has already agreed to serve as godmother. Please don't think I am in such severe straits."

She smiled, "Then, this little one will have two queens for godmothers. He or she will be twice blessed." I could not refuse her offer to be an additional godmother for my child and as godmother, she would have a greater stake in intervening with the king for me. I nodded and thanked her for her generosity.

Louise was true to her word, going against her usual reticence to convince the king that someone had framed me in the payments for the English emigres. The king, usually an aloof man, even took the time to be solicitous throughout the Advent celebrations. Perhaps, it was the celebration of the birth of our Lord that put him in such a charitable mood. Whatever his reasons, I was thankful for it.

❧

DECEMBER WAS NOT PEACEFUL FOR EVERY MEMBER OF MY FAMILY, however. Henri remained in the field, trying his best to stem his frustration with the king's behavior. Behind my husband's back, the king gave the Swiss mercenaries extra money to slink back to Switzerland unmolested by Guise troops. Money that should have gone to provisioning Henri's army, went instead to paying off foreign heretics. My husband's fury was so great I was thankful I was not there in person to see it. He wrote long letters raging over the king's betrayal. In a little of bittersweet revenge, Henri took the Duke of Lorraine's son with him across the Swiss border where the two set fire to as many Protestant villages as possible before returning to the safety of a devastated Lorraine.

My belly continued to expand and other than light duties for the queen, there was little I could do, whether purposefully aiding the League's activities. Montpensier more than made up for me in vexing the king. She had been living on borrowed time since the previous June when she and her coconspirators put up the mural damming Elizabeth Tudor. I suppose the king ran out of Christian charity after forgiving me because he chose December 1587 to bring finally Montpensier to heel. When I was on my journey back from Nevers, the king attempted to rout all the men on her payroll, raiding houses of Leaguers across Paris. The raid was a complete failure and the people of Paris flocked to the bridge over the Seine connecting the Sorbonne to the Ile de Cite. If Épernon had his way, they would fill the scaffolds with the hanging bodies of conspirators, but the king instead, banished most of the priests and men who had been acting in Montpensier's name. She found herself with few people surrounding her, but the population continued to be restless. In December, the rector of the Sorbonne declared that it was within church law to depose such princes who acted in a way that endangered the church.

This was pushing the king too far. On December 16th, as we were about to sit to listen to a Christmas concert, the king strode into the room, his face as heated as Henriette's had been when throwing me out of her home in Nevers. Before taking his seat beside Queen Louise, he fixed a cruel stare directly at me. "Madame de Guise, I assume you have heard of the scheming going on here in Paris. My beloved wife," he nodded to Louise, who blushed in return, "tells me you are innocent of these rebellions, but I cannot say the same for other members of the House of Lorraine."

Dear God, please let this have nothing to do with Montpensier, I prayed. I hadn't spoken or written to her in weeks. This time, not only was I innocent, there was no written proof in my hand to damn me. If someone implicated me in Montpensier's latest activities, the worst that could happen would be to place me in the dungeons of Vincennes. Even if the king was guilty of the abominations, the most radical League members accused him of, he would never stoop so low as to harm a pregnant woman. If there were any who were undecided about their loyalty to the king, such a heinous act would make their decision for them. He and I knew that.

"I am told that Montpensier pays the curates of Paris to speak against me during their homilies. They say I was so jealous of your husband's victories I agreed with the Heretics who invaded our nation. Do you believe what they are saying, Madame?"

I folded my hands in my lap. Or at least, where my lap used to be, and tried to adopt the pose of a serene Madonna. "Sire, it is probably best to remember that Montpensier has none of the comforts of marriage you and I enjoy. She lost her husband, and you cannot imagine the sorrow of losing a spouse." I glanced at Queen Louise, my voice heavy with innuendo. "Even worse, she has no children of her own. There is no one in her vast home to provide her with comfort or companionship. I assume she does what she does because she wants to put her passions into something. She is misguided, but then, as a woman, I know how difficult it is to resist the being swayed by emotions." I lifted my hands and shrugged, hoping that the king would see her as a harmless woman shouting from her salon. It was a long shot, but I felt determined to do anything.

"There is also talk of your husband taking a trip to Rome. Has he spoken to you of such a thing?" His words shocked me, I had heard nothing of Henri leaving France. As commander of French forces, it would be career suicide to leave the troops for someone else to assume command.

"Rome? No. Our child is due in two months. Henri wouldn't dare leave me for such a long journey with another child on the way." It was a weak excuse; the king was afraid that Henri would go to Rome to beg to have him deposed just as the rector from the Sorbonne was preaching to the crowds. I had to convince him that the rumor was nothing more than poisonous gossip.

"At any rate, I plan to go to Normandy once the child is born. I would like to show him or her my chateau at Eu."

"I hear it is a lovely structure you are building. I shall advise The Duc d'Épernon he should visit once he settles in as governor of Normandy." I inwardly groaned; we had just gotten rid of Joyeuse and now the king was installing his remaining favorite in his place? No sooner than Joyeuse's body was cold, the king had named him the Governor of Normandy. Would the king never learn that his actions had no consent from the people he governed? My husband deserved the governorship of Normandy. No one in France was better qualified to rule the north. This was a punishment for the Guise dominance in the North. The king was determined to break our backs.

CHRISTMAS AND THE NEW YEAR CONTINUED WITHOUT MORE discord between the king and the Leaguers. I assumed that the king had forgotten Montpensier and her agents until I heard rumors they were comparing the king to Edward II of England and his lover Piers Gaveston. An accusation of sodomy was going entirely too far and the first week of January 1588, the king once again called Montpensier to his presence at the Louvre. Anna offered to accompany her daughter, hoping that her presence there would soften the king's wrath, but Montpensier refused to take her with her into her private audience. Anna and I walked with her as far as the great doors to the king's audience chamber. "Ah, the Queen of Paris is here," the king's chamberlain snorted at her with derision. Not a woman to fall prey to be intimidation Montpensier looked at him without saying a word.

"I believe we need to get some fresh air," Anna declared loudly, as the heavy door closed in front of us. She gently tugged me beside her, doing her best to support my swollen body as we walked towards an alcove.

"I've done all that I can do to beg the king's mercy; I'm out of options at this point," her voice edged with anger, as she whispered in my ear while we walked past curious courtiers.

"Has the Queen Mother been able to make any headway with the king?" Anna and Catherine de Medici were friends from their earliest days in France. Despite both having noble French heritage, the French nobles saw them both as Italian interlopers after decades at court. Their shared battles for legitimacy at court made them lifelong allies.

It was this friendship that kept the Guise and Valois from tearing each other apart for years.

She shook her head, the strain of dealing with her only daughter written on her face. "Even they are more estranged than ever. The king refuses to listen to her counsel, and he disregards her experience. He'd rather listen to those hayseeds from the wilds of the provinces. Country folk are so adept at handling statecraft." She rolled her eyes in disgust and was silent for a few moments. Desperate to break the silence, I turned to her.

"I think your daughter is the most extreme example of how weary we all are of the king's favoritism towards these nobodies. We are all suffering while the country is being run by inept governors. Meanwhile, we're dealing with enough droughts and crops to ruin us. I can't blame her for her frustration."

She arched an eyebrow, "You sound like you agree with her methods."

"Not so much her methods as her sentiments." I let out a long sigh. "I do, however, agree with her frustration. Paris has been boiling for months." A guard walked by and I lowered my voice so only Anna could hear me. "When the city goes into open revolt, we have to have a family capable of ruling and directing the people so that the country won't fall into chaos. The moment France falls into chaos, we're easy pickings for Spanish or English invasion."

"Take care how you say things like that. You sound like you're advocating a Guise-led rebellion against the throne."

"Me?" I turned to her in shock, "I'm the size of my house and I can barely move around. What can I do in this condition? Have you ever heard of a revolution being led by a heavily pregnant woman?" I rubbed my aching back, which refused to let up and give me some relief.

"At the moment, I'm worried about my daughter attempting to lead a revolution. If the king--" she stopped as the doors to the Presence Chamber swung open and Catherine of Lorraine, Duchesse de Montpensier strode out, barely concealing a smug smile. "Mother, Sister." She greeted us as if we were simply standing idly by at a ball.

"So?" Anna hissed in her ear and strode behind her, trying to match her pace. Catherine gave a delicate shrug in reply. Left to myself, I waddled behind them as quickly as I could manage in my state.

I finally caught up with mother and daughter in Anna's chambers, where they were deep in an argument. "You assume too much weakness on the king's part. It doesn't matter how weak he is he can have your head removed from your body with just a flick of his hand." Anna paced as she lectured her daughter, who looked unmoved by her mother's words of warning.

"That's just what you don't understand, Henri Valois knows that if he were to put a Guise in prison, the revolt he fears will begin immediately. He can't afford to do anything. That is how weak he has become. With every noble in France alienated from him and the populace convinced he is consorting with the Antichrist, he has no one to come to his defense."

I took a seat, determined not to receive any of the anger that existed between the two women. As I sat, the weariness spread over my body and I exhaled another long sigh. Neither woman noticed that I was even there.

"That rabble-rousing as you've been calling my work has more than paid off. The king has been doing more than just checking on the physical defenses of the city walls this past year. He's been taking the temperature of the Parlement, the church, and the people. None of them will follow him. He knows that now. You didn't see the trembling fop I saw just now. He shook every time he spoke to me. He fears me, fears the League." Montpensier's eyes began to shine and something in her demeanor reminded me of those tales my governess told me of Jeanne of Arc as a girl. Was that religious fervor I saw in them? Or increasing ambition?

"Do you really not understand how dangerous a fearful monarch can be? If the king becomes frightened enough, he will pick off Guises to take care of his problem. You are a widow and the second wife at that. You have no children to defend you, which makes it much easier for the king to send men to take you from your bed and carry you away."

Montpensier snorted, "My brothers will rescue me. If you really think I scare that easily, you know me little, Mother." If Montpensier hoped to sound defiant, she failed. She reminded me more of a petulant adolescent than a revolutionary. While she was excellent at stirring up emotion, she had few skills in leading men. It would take Henri to make a final step in revolution against the king.

⚜

NOT LONG AFTER MONTPENSIER'S ESCAPE FROM ROYAL PRISON, I had my reprieve from politics, giving birth to what would be my last daughter on a chilly February morning in 1588. Unwilling to spend my last weeks of the pregnancy amidst the scheming and machinations of Paris, I left with Queen Louise for the Chateau de Blois to have my child in peace in the Loire valley. My departure also gave me a chance to escape the deteriorating relationship between Anna and Montpensier.

There were few places that felt like home as 1588 dawned: the Spanish planned to launch the Armada in May and my husband offered Normandy as a safe haven for the Spanish galleons. This defied the official word from the king, who refused to insult either his English allies or his Spanish ones. Henri Valois waited out the result of the Armada in case he backed the wrong sovereign. My husband showed no vacillation, however, and although the Duc Épernon was the new governor of Normandy and officially controlled all traffic across the region, the League promised to come to Spanish aid if needed. No matter who ruled Normandy I was not safe at Eu and could not travel there.

There was no chance of returning to Nevers, either. Since banishing me in September, Henriette refused to speak to me. Month after month, my letters went unanswered. I even resorted to writing Louis in Picardy to see if he would intervene between my sister and me, but Henriette would not see reason. The last time Henriette and I were estranged, we were fighting over money; now politics separated us. I felt isolated from my family and during my pregnancy, the timing could not have been worse.

My husband continued to refuse to return to Paris, due in part to his fear that as soon as he abandoned his troops, the king would award their command to his remaining favorite. We knew the king would make good on his threat to arrest him for seditious acts if given an opportunity. It was as if the king sensed that something was in the air, because in February, he forbade Henri from entering Paris, even to see me and our newborn daughter. Life in the field was hardly more hospitable; Épernon was Admiral of France, making it impossible for my Henri to command any French ships to come to the aid of Spanish galleons if needed. In February, the Guise returned to Nancy to decide what to do about their limited options. I did not know it at the time, but at the meeting, the Guise and Lorraine cousins made plans to assassinate Épernon and take the king hostage. Had someone had taken if Épernon care of that winter, it could have helped to reconcile my sister and I. My husband could have prevailed upon Henriette to see my side and forgive me.

I had no time to think of those things because in early February, Louise Marguerite finally came, a little past her due date. When she made her appearance, she was wrinkled and large for a newborn, but she was healthy. I was thankful that at least I had a healthy child during my time of isolation.

A week after my daughter was born, both Anna and Montpensier came to see my daughter, despite the ongoing awkwardness between the two. Anna brought gifts and congratulations from herself and from Henri's stepfather, the Duc de Nemours. Montpensier brought something besides gifts for the new child. As I sat coddling baby Louise, I noticed my sister-in-law's dress had a golden chain dangling from her belt. "Have I been so busy that I've failed to notice the current fashions? Amulets dangling from belts haven't been popular since the 1550s." I raised my eyebrows, hoping to show that I was lightly teasing her. I had no desire to incite her and have to deal with a surly sister-in-law.

Instead, she clapped her hands, "Ah, it's more than an amulet. It's a talisman!" Louise gurgled, and I turned to check that she was not choking. When I returned my attention to Montpensier, she was holding a small pair of golden scissors. I frowned, unable to imagine what she could need a pair of scissors for.

"It's for the king. I am preparing him for his third crown." The tone of her voice made me hesitate. I knew that I did not want her to elaborate, so I tried to change the subject. She refused to be swayed, however, and continued to speak, her hands jabbing at the air while she spoke.

"He has two crowns, one of Poland and one of France. He is so devoted to his church I think he needs a third crown on his royal head —that of a tonsure." She smiled triumphantly.

I had heard nothing of the king joining a religious order. True, he had taken part in extreme religious activities since taking the throne in 1574. Many of his confidants followed him in religious processions where they self-flagellated. I had heard him speak of spending time at a monastery in the spring when the ice melted, and the weather was milder. Queen Louise was also extremely devout, but neither of them had spoken of their desire to retire to a monastic life.

I opened my mouth to speak, but Montpensier cut me off. "The king will need to shave his head when he enters religious life. No one would want to defile the body of the king by killing him. We will remove him from his throne and sent to live out his life in quiet contemplation. It's perfect for a scholar like him. He's not meant to govern, only to feed his soul. Don't you see? It's the perfect solution for France!"

"Is that what they decided in Nancy?" Henri was guarded in his news of the decisions made in Nancy. He knew that the health of our child distracted me too much to even bother with external politics. Now, with a child on my knee, I was no longer saddled with the physical demands of pregnancy. If I wished to take an active part in the League's activities, I could afford to leave Louise in the care of a nurse and devote my time to promoting the League in Paris. The thought was appealing. I had resented the feeling of being sidelined while events swirled around me. I was also nearing thirty and would be at the end of my childbearing days.

She shrugged. "The king is inept, and we should place him where he can do good. France would be stronger with a Regent popular with the nobles and with the people."

I lifted my eyebrows, intrigued. "Henri would serve as regent? But who would become king? France cannot be ruled by a Regent for long."

She cocked her head to the side. "Well, we Guise are descendants of the Capets. We have royal blood in our veins. The Valois came to the throne when there was no other option available."

"But by law, Navarre is the heir to the throne."

She shook her head, "The Pope has already issued a bull of Excommunication. Navarre can not take the throne. Without the Vatican to support him, he will never be king."

That meant that my eldest son would be the heir to the throne. I would become Queen Mother. The idea immediately appealed. "Tell me more."

"Well, Henri has promised to give the king a distraction in May when the Armada sails. The king will be too busy with this 'distraction' to worry about the Spanish."

I lifted my eyebrows, completely seduced. "Tell me more about this 'distraction'."

❦

BY SPRING, MONTPENSIER AND I WERE WORKING IN TANDEM TO head the Parisian Leaguers, she taking the role of the public face of discontent, while in public, I wrung my hands in the king's presence and wailed about my inability to reign in my excitable sister-in-law. My husband and I exchanged letters, with him promising me that Spain would send three-hundred-thousand ecus to fund a revolt against the king in May. We had only to fan the flames of discontent until then.

I opened the doors of the Hotel de Guise to any English emigres looking for sanctuary and for onlookers to see the strength of the international Catholic cause. "Monsieur," I nodded at Nicolas Poulain, one of the most dedicated members of the League in the city. He had spent the past three years supervising the surreptitious movement of weapons to the hotel and safe houses across the city. He had just returned from the countryside, where he encouraged supporters across Paris to do the same thing.

"Madame la Duchesse," he nodded at me and I noticed that he had a thick pamphlet in his hand. "I wonder if you've had a look at this. It's fresh off the printing blocks."

Entitled, "The Tragic and Remarkable Story of Piers Gaveston," the pamphlet told in both English and French the story of the English king and his perverse relationship with his male lover. "I suppose our English brethren are familiar with the story, no?"

He nodded, "And now, the French will know about it. Even the basest peasant will know what happens to a king who commits sodomy and consorts with rabble." I had heard whispers of the king engaging in sexual relations with his favorites, but I had witnessed nothing inappropriate between them. From the moment he married Louise, he took pains to remain faithful to her. The rumors seemed more like spite, but sodomy was a serious charge for a faithful Catholic. It would be enough to excommunicate the king and turn his subjects against him. A pang of guilt rose in me. I knew the king was likely innocent, but by that point, I had gone too far in my own rebellions against him.

"Sir," a page came up to Poulain, a note in his hand. "Madame, I'm afraid I have some bad news." He read the missive, his face growing dark. "I'm afraid that the king's troops have taken over several villages in Picardy from Aumale. It forced him to fall back into the countryside."

I held my hand up to my throat. This was a huge loss for the League. With no promise from Épernon and the king, the Spanish ships had only the League's guarantee of a safe port. Even worse, if the Armada were to fail, the English troops might come spilling over French soil, starting with the Boulogne that we had lost months earlier.

"Not to worry, My Lady. I'm sure they can fix it. If you'll excuse me." He bowed and strode away from me. Moments later, Montpensier was at my side. "We're losing more villages to the Protestants." She gasped and at the sound, my shoulders sank. They shrank further when I looked up to see Mendoza stalking towards us.

"Madame, soon your husband's forces cannot hold any location they guaranteed us. King Philip has risked so much for the Guise cause, I would think one section of the country would be no problem. Even a small seaport was too much for them."

"I think you've underestimated the determination of French forces, Señor," I snapped at him so quickly that it shocked even Montpensier.

Well, let her be; she was not the only firebrand in the family. I would play second to her for no longer.

"Phillip has had my county of Eu at his disposal for months. If it is not enough, then I question the might of the Spanish fleet. Is Phillip so unsure of his victory over the English he needs a guarantee from France?" Henri would berate me for baiting the Spanish ambassador later, but my temper was up, and I wanted to take my anger out on someone, preferably someone who challenged my family.

Instead of retreating in shame, Mendoza instead stepped close to my ear. "Be careful, My Lady; kings do not take kindly to treason and you and your family are at the forefront of just such activity."

"We are standing for France, for her strength and her future. If Spain is so strong, then I wonder why you spend so much time skulking around our country looking for friends? From my perspective, Phillip looks to be weak."

"You will regret those words come this summer, My Lady. Oh, and I'd advise you to get rid of that traitor you're welcoming into your house." Throwing on his cloak, he left the room without so much as asking my leave. Fine, I was more than glad to be rid of him. Beside me, Montpensier exhaled loudly. I blinked; I had forgotten all about her presence. "I'd forgotten how terrifying you can be when angry, Sister."

Mendoza's mention of a traitor unnerved me. There were untold numbers of men moving in and out of the Hotel de Guise. How was I to know who was loyal to us and who was using our hospitality as a ruse?

۞

FOR THE NEXT TWO WEEKS, EVERY PERSON WHO WALKED INTO MY home was suspect. Every note I sent to Joinville went under coded message. When I spoke to my husband, it was only to talk of our children, including Louise who grew more robust by the day. In my paranoia, I hired and dismissed servants at will, including ones who had served the Guise family for years.

Unable to discover the false friend in our midst, I started to lose hope. Looking back, I should not have lost hope so easily. On April 11th, fifteen members of the sixteen came to my home, caps in hand.

"Poulain has betrayed us." One man ran his hand through his hair, the wrinkles in his face deepening as he spoke. "We've been strengthening our militia, to prepare for May. We knew that the king had stationed men in each quarter as spies. We were arrogant enough to think we'd identified all of them." He turned to the others, raising his hand in surrender. "We missed one, the biggest traitor of all."

I sighed, the words I'd said to Mendoza within Poulain's earshot reverberating in my ears. Enough words to damn me. Enough words to put me on a scaffold if Henri Valois wished to do so. "Was he always on the king's payroll? Or did he turn his coat these last few days?"

Another spoke up. "We don't know for sure. All we do know is that the first chance he got, he slipped away and ran to the Louvre to warn the king that we were arming. We have to tell the Duc that the king knows of our plans. He has to come to Paris to rescue us."

"But, how can he come now? The king will be waiting for him." Even more dangerous were the spring storms, which would make the roads between Nancy and Paris a quagmire. One determined man on a single horse could make it to Paris, but not the leagues of men Henri would need to confront the king.

"He must come. It's likely that the king will pick off Guise allies to break his power. We've got to depose the king and do it as soon as possible. To do it properly, we'll need your husband in Paris."

Two weeks later, his words came true. Seeing the Duc d'Elbeuf as the most vulnerable Leaguer, the king sent the bulk of French forces were not under my husband's control into Rouen. This time, however, the king overextended his forces. With his own army in faraway Normandy, he left the capital open to invasion. Days after the army marched westwards to Normandy, I received a triumphant letter from Nancy. After two years away, my husband was finally coming back to Paris and back to his family.

41

CHAPTER 6

As a girl, I used to scoff at stories of women who lingered at home, waiting for their men to come home. I thought those women weak and passive, merely sitting by as the world passed them. I suppose after months apart, I could be forgiven for my excitement on May 9th when a messenger came running in, crying that the Duc de Guise had finally returned to Paris.

While Henri made his triumphant return to the city that loved him, a crowd swelled around his horse. Crying, "Long live the Guise—the pillar of the church!" they proclaimed their loyalty to our family. As we had hoped, we had the loyalty of the populace firmly on our side. As the news spread, the hotel turned into a hive of activity. Months of speculation and weeks of preparation were finally a reality. Like a romantic ninny, I stood at the top of the great steps of the second floor of the hotel, waiting to see my husband. A part of me held out the hope he would stride into the hotel, laughing at his victory over the king.

After half an hour of standing and waiting for my husband to wander into our home, a small figure appeared in the doorway. Seeing it was Montpensier, I felt bitter disappointment she arrived before her brother. "He's gone to the Louvre," she announced as she took off her cloak.

"Already? Is he gone to depose the king then?" I frowned; the pace of this uprising was much faster than I had expected.

"He's with the Queen Mother. He figured it would be safe to claim he was here at her behest. Even with no army, Henri Valois can be slippery as an eel. Guise figured that if he put out the word, he wanted to make amends with the king, he could walk into the Louvre without so much as a shot being fired."

"And how did he get Catherine de Medici to go with him?" My husband had a silver tongue but convincing the king's mother to accompany him on his way to depose the king took incredible skill.

"She's going in her litter and he's walking beside her. It's so gallant! He's keeping the angry crowds off the old woman." That was wise, given the crowd's growing dislike of the Queen Mother. Without their golden champion to tone down their emotions, they might tear the diminutive Catherine de Medici to shreds.

I called for food and with Montpensier sitting beside me in my salon; I learned the events of the day as they unfolded. I soon realized that I would not see my husband until nightfall, or even later. As he and the Queen Mother slowly made their way towards the Louvre with a crowd of thousands, news reached the king and his council that the Duc de Guise had defied royal decree and entered Paris. "Henri Valois was furious! He stood there with his Privy Council debating what to do next. They were just like a bunch of boys, pissing themselves at hearing the lord of the manor had returned. They took so long debating on what to do, that my brother was at the door of the council chamber before they could decide. So, there he walked in, with Catherine de Medici as his escort."

She dissolved into giggles. I could only imagine the awkwardness of the occasion. Still, knowing the king's paranoia, I knew that my husband was in danger, the Queen Mother's presence notwithstanding. Playing for the time, the king drew my husband into Queen Louise's chamber, a place I would normally be, but on that day, I had begged leave to attend to personal business. "My brother told the king that the present estrangement between them was because of Épernon. He's determined to make it clear to the king that everything is because of the favorites, not a quarrel he has with the king."

"Did the king take the bait?" I knew that he would not, but I had to know how the king took this latest ruse. My husband had marched confidently into the Louvre itself and now, had to talk his way out of there alive.

"No, he quoted the saying that 'he who loves the master should love his dog.'" At that, I rolled my eyes. If the king had not surrounded himself with such common mutts, no one would have reason to love them.

"How did Henri answer him?"

"He responded, 'Provided he does not bite.'" I snorted at that; it sounded like him.

"So, now where are they?" I glanced around, noting that the evening sun was slanting in the windows.

"Henri will do his duty as Grand Master of France, presiding over a supper at the Louvre."

I rolled my eyes, "I suppose that means I won't see my husband until Midnight?"

I DID NOT SEE MY HUSBAND UNTIL WELL PAST MIDNIGHT. Following him, dozens of retainers flooded into the courtyard of the Hotel de Guise and I spent the long hours getting provisions set up for the extra mouths I was to feed. My Henri stayed close to the king and the Queen Mother for hours, knowing that if he was beside them, they could hardly withdraw to plot against him.

Flushed with exhaustion, I finally heard the thump of my husband's boots as he came into the house. "Henri!" I shouted, taking the two stories of grand stairs as I rushed towards him like a lovesick young girl. Embracing him, I noticed a tear in the linen of his shirt. "Are you injured? What happened?"

He glanced down and grabbed at his right forearm. "Ah, it's nothing. A woman pulled at my sleeve and she refused to let go. I suppose this shirt is a little old." He looked at me and gave me a shrug.

"It's unseemly. Here, come with me." I pulled him behind me and marched into my bedchamber. Once inside, I tugged his shirt off and carefully inspected him for wounds. "Well, I suppose you are all right."

"See, I told you I was fine." He gave me a sunny smile, one completely out of place with the situation at hand. To my shame, that smile melted my heart and my long months of missing my husband rose to mock me. I was too weak to resist, and we spent the night in one another's arms.

෴

THE NEXT MORNING, MY HUSBAND ROSE TO DRESS FOR MASS. "I promised the king I would attend with him. All of Paris will be watching." I knew that it was only an outward show, meant to cool down the fevered pitch the city had risen to the day before. If I had any common sense, I would have stayed at home. Naturally, I had no common sense, and I decided I must accompany him.

"I am a lady-in-waiting to the queen, it would be best if I sat with the two of you." Unwilling to start an argument, he shrugged his shoulder in agreement. Bundled into the Guise coach, we made our way through the crowded streets to the church for the service.

Flushed with the wave of emotion we felt at his return, I basked in the adulation in the church. Hundreds of curious onlookers came to the church to see the king and Guise reconcile before the Host. Reveling in my position as the wife of the triumphant Duc, I became too overconfident that morning.

During Mass, I looked at the assembled crowd to find an unwelcome blonde head amongst the worshippers. Charlotte de Sauve was in the congregation. I hadn't seen the woman since Christmas and something convinced me I had seen the last of her. Had she been in Paris the entire time, or did she trail behind my husband like a camp follower? Where had that damned woman been the entire time? My mind raced with explanations as the Mass droned on. My anger gnawed at me, fueling my apprehension minute by minute. Her presence was an offense, and it spoiled the triumph I felt in having my husband returned to me.

I wanted to go to her, to snatch the pious lace veil from her head. I fantasized about grabbing her by the hair and pulling her out of the church, exposing her as a spy and a traitor. I would learn that day who she was working for, why she was so determined to attach herself to my husband. She reminded me that no matter how many victories the League earned, there would always be those in the shadows, acting for unknown agents. She was danger incarnate.

Once Mass was over, I rose to confront her, the consequences for my husband be damned. Before I could do so, Henri took my arm and guided me towards the king. "Henri, I need to speak to you about that woman." I glanced to see her retreating shoulders as she moved steadily away from me. I would not have a confrontation with Charlotte de Sauve. At the door, her current husband, the Marquise de Noirmoutier, took her forearm and whispered in her ear.

"Not now, the king is waiting." He pulled me towards the king's party and away from my perch spying on the woman warming my husband's bed. A churlish feeling of rebellion swept over me.

"I see the entire Privy Council is here." Noirmoutier was amongst the few men the king added halfheartedly in response to the allegations that his favorites had taken over the upper echelons of power in France. I wondered if the man was a cuckold or if he was complicit in his wife's infidelity. Many men used a comely wife as a weapon to climb further up the social ladder. Was he playing both sides, sending his wife to Henri's bed? If that were the case, she was even more dangerous than I had feared. She could prove to be more dangerous than the traitor Poulain.

"Are you really so stupid as to be consorting with that woman here in Paris?" After he had spent the night in my arms, no less. Jealousy tinged with anger rose within me. As I seethed, Henri turned to accept the welcomes from well-wishers. His determination to ignore me and play the politician further stoked my anger.

"Catherine, now is not the time to indulge in jealousy. We'll talk about this later." Once again, he was sweeping away my fear for his safety, labeling it as jealousy of a woman scorned. I couldn't take any more of his behavior, so I turned and stalked out of the church. On the carriage ride home, I fumed at the thick-headed husband they had cursed me with. He might have all of Paris at his feet, but he remained blind to the dangers wrapping their perfumed white limbs about him as he slept.

As I climbed out of my carriage, I noticed a young officer shouting directions to the surrounding men. "Madame," he tipped his hat, and I nodded in response. "Not to worry, Paris is safe in Guise hands. The city is not in danger of invasion."

I frowned, "Why on earth would it be in danger?" I had heard nothing of a danger of invasion.

"Well, the city has the sacred right to arm itself. By law, the king cannot send troops in to quell an uprising. We're safe from any reprisals from the king." His last words chilled me. Was there a danger of Henri Valois taking his revenge on my husband for coming to Paris in defiance of his order? Would he send in troops, despite the city's traditional rights? There were many royal troops embedded in the League troops across the city. I glanced around and tried to see if I could detect a traitor before my eyes. Alas, like Poulain, I could not guess which might be a Judas amongst us.

"Madame la Guise, are you all right? I'm sorry to have scared you. We really are safe behind the walls of the Hotel de Guise." I felt safe behind the walls of the three-story complex, which since January, had become less a home and more of a fortress. They quartered men amongst the stables and outbuildings, and I even heard rumors that some of the youngest amongst them were sleeping in our Orangerie. I craned my neck and peered towards it, vowing to check in on the boys, who were no older than my eldest son.

"Besides, with Condé gone, the Protestants are no threat to us." At that, my head jerked up. "What? What happened to Condé? Did he go back to England?"

He shuffled his feet and looked around for someone to pass me onto regretting his decision to talk. "Word just came through—the Prince de Condé died at the hands of his wife."

The ground spun beneath me. Once, Condé's wife was my sister, Marie. He had married his second, wealthy wife less than two years earlier. So, the wife he had shut up in a golden cage had relieved him of his earthly burden? I had to laugh at the irony. Our irascible brother-in-law was gone. Seconds later, I realized that this meant my niece Catherine was now officially an orphan. Although she had never met the garlic-faced man, the news would pain her. I strode into the main house and into my chambers. As soon as I could, I would write to Catherine and give her my sympathies.

❦

HENRI DID NOT COME TO MY BED THAT NIGHT. I DO NOT KNOW where he spent the night, although I suspect it was in some home used by Charlotte de Sauve. I went to bed that night furious with my husband and resolved to seek him out in the morning to confront his lackadaisical attitude towards his latest mistress.

My mind was reeling as I rose that morning, but I wanted to do my duty towards my family before I confronted the situation with Madame de Sauve. At six that morning, I sat down to write a letter to Catherine, reassuring her of our love as her true parents. Although she was now of an age to be betrothed, I avoided the topic to respect her time of mourning for the father who had abandoned her before her birth. Once I finished the letter and posted it to Joinville, I sent a second letter to Henriette, telling her of my plans for our niece. Hopefully, she would put aside her anger towards me and answer this letter for the sake of young Marie.

Just before eight, I heard a commotion in the courtyard below. This was nothing new since additional troops had been quartering in our home and the surrounding buildings of our section of Paris for weeks. Thinking it was a drill, I turned back to my letter,

The door opened with a crash and I looked up to see my lady's maid, Suzanne, her face ashen. "Madame, the king!"

"What, he's here?" I blinked, unable to understand what had her so upset. "Why would the king come here?"

She wrung her hands, "No, he's ordered troops into Paris! We're being attacked by the royal army. The king has sent his troops out against the people of Paris!" She grew more hysterical with each word and by the time she stopped speaking, I could barely understand her. Coming to my feet, I decided to seek out my husband and see what was going on.

I found him leaning over a large map of the city, men hanging onto him like a nest of ants. He seemed calm, which told me that there was no reason to panic. Until he took to his own horse and unsheathed his own sword, there was no danger. "What is going on?"

He looked up at me and expelled a long sigh. "The king brought in troops, including some of his Swiss mercenaries. They've been sneaking into every street of the city since before daybreak."

"Then, we really are being invaded? The king violated the city's right to be free of troops?" Henri Valois continued to indiscriminately violate every civil liberty that his subjects enjoyed. I rubbed my mouth with my hand. This was what a panicked king could do when cornered. "What are you going to do?"

The men looked at me, unused to hearing such questions from a woman. "Stay here by all means. Where the invaders are, there is little resistance. It caught too many people unaware and unable to put up a defense. There is no telling how many women and children are vulnerable to these villains." He crossed himself and the rest hurriedly did the same.

"What about the ones who *could* defend themselves?" I would ask before it hung longer in the air between us.

"The troops we could station can hold off the invaders. We have loyal men across the city, so we can hold our positions there." Henri straightened and cleared his throat, a typical signal he was busy with other matters and could bother no longer to explain things to his wife. None of them bothered to mention that many of those men stationed by the man who had given up the plot to the king and betrayed us all. A sudden fear struck me, could Poulain be in league with Charlotte de Sauve? Was that why the strumpet was back in Paris?

"As there will be many innocent victims of the king's betrayal, I think I should organize relief efforts." My husband gave me a curt nod of dismissal and I nodded in reply. In the hallway, my Suzanne met me. "Madame, my son is young, I should be with him."

I did not want to send her out into the street with little to defend herself, but before I could protest, she pulled a knife from her skirts. "My husband is loyal to the Duc and to the League. Once I get to our home, we will barricade ourselves in and defend our home. I cannot do that here." Her eyes pleaded with me and I knew that I could not refuse her. She was only a few years younger than I and it terrified me at what she could face once she left the safety of the hotel. Still, there was no way I could stop her from leaving.

"Go, but be careful as you go." I turned to the rest of the staff and commandeered any space in the hotel not used by my husband's men for relief efforts. We compiled any supplies we could find, bandages for injuries, blankets and all the food we could spare. The last item was scarce since it stretched us thin feeding the men billeted within the hotel. I sorely missed having Montpensier at my side. Marshaling relief efforts was exactly what she could manage, but her hotel was outside the city walls, within the faubourgs that encircled Paris. I could not risk the lives of my pages to get a message to her. I would have to wait until the League troops surrounded and disarmed the invading troops.

I continued my work until just after noon, using my vantage point just outside of the study to monitor my husband's activities. Suddenly, my husband marched out of the study on his way out of the front door. Running after him, I caught up with him at the steps to the ground floor. "Where are you possibly going?"

"I will address my men," he spat, impatience straining his voice. "The king has ordered me to leave the city at once."

"Are you actually going to play the coward and leave?"

He laughed, a deep sound that echoed across the courtyard. "Hardly. I've been sending messages to the king and to my troops. Only I can negotiate a cease-fire between these invaders and my troops. If the king wants to avoid a massacre, he needs me to stay in Paris."

"How benevolent of you, to create a conflict and emerge as the man to end it." He smirked at me enjoying his role as peacemaker. "I have to go now, wife. Stay inside," he held up a single finger, bidding me to stay rooted at the spot as if I were a hunting dog he was training. With that, my husband walked out of the courtyard like a madman, waving and doffing his hat as the crowd roared their approval. For most of that afternoon, he paraded down street after street of League held areas, basking in the peoples' adoration. I could only shake my head and wonder if my husband had taken leave of his senses.

His overconfidence was a folly, of that I was certain. Catherine de Medici had weathered enough riots and uprisings in the middle of Paris and this one would be no different. She had trekked to the Louvre at my husband's side out of necessity, but given the slightest opportunity, she would turn the situation around to her beloved son's advantage. As the afternoon wore on, the king's troops proved to little more than fodder for the populace. Citizens raised makeshift blockades to trap the men in the streets of the city, streets that the foreigners and Frenchmen from across the country did not know of. Once trapped, they easily picked them off as the people fired at them from balconies and windows. By sunset, there were dead soldiers lying in every street in Paris. The king had risen against his people and his people responded by rising against him.

◈

LATE THAT AFTERNOON, THE HOTEL ONCE AGAIN WAS ABLAZE WITH the word that we were about to receive a royal visitor, the Queen Mother herself. This was hardly a social occasion but, befitting her status as the king's most respected negotiator, we had to scurry to prepare the hotel for her visit. While I supervised the domestic aspects of the visit, Henri rushed around to prepare himself. The two would meet in private, with no other visitors in the room. I placed my hand on my husband's forearm and looked into his eyes. "What are you going to ask of her?'

He pursed his lips, "I want the king to do more than just dismiss Épernon. They must banish him and the rest of the favorites from court. I want those brigands, his Forty-Five disbanded. What kind of coward needs a personal guard? He is not the Emperor of Rome. And," he held up his pointer finger, "He must immediately ban Navarre from the succession."

I folded my arms, "Do you really think she will agree to that?"

"We hold Paris at this moment. She has no cards left to play. Or, rather, her son has no cards to play. We have finally won Paris for the Church."

"If she agrees to bar Navarre's succession, are you going to put forth Cardinal de Bourbon as the heir?" My uncle was too old to marry and produce an heir, we all knew that. Louis XII had in his desperation married Mary Tudor to produce a male heir, but he died within months of the marriage. The next in line would be our eldest son or the eldest son of the Duc de Lorraine. Either son would put our cause on the throne, but I would prefer my Charles to become king.

"Yes. If I show that I'm solidly behind Bourbon, they 'll see me as promoting a man of the church, not my family. Neither of us can predict when your uncle will meet his Lord." He smirked at the thought.

"Navarre could still come to the king's aid. He can't waste time in the countryside, whoring around and mourning Condé's death forever."

"That is another reason I need to have the king agree to my terms as soon as possible." Before he could finish, he jerked his head up, indicating that the Queen Mother was in the courtyard. The woman who walked through our door looked like a gaunt version of her former self. Gout had sapped most of her energy and she looked a pitiable shade of gray. "Madame," I sank to my knees in reverence.

"Madame de Guise, it would seem that we are at a dark day for France. Here I am, speaking for my son's throne."

"I believe that we are all speaking for the French throne. My husband only wants to remove the bumpkins who have infiltrated--" she cut me off with an upward tilt of her head. I curtseyed, looking my husband in the eye as I did so.

The two spent the better part of three hours negotiating, with the sounds of their voices carrying far outside of the study walls. At last, we heard "I will carry your terms to His Majesty," and we scurried from our listening perches before the door opened. A few moments later, Catherine de Medici swooped out of the door and made her slow, torturous way back to the Louvre.

"THAT DAMNED FOOL!" MY HUSBAND BURST INTO THE DINING ROOM early the next morning as I was quietly having breakfast with Montpensier. His face was flush with blood as he entered, a sure sign he was on one of his emotional rampages. To calm him, I delicately placed my fork on my plate and looked up at him, hands folded in my lap.

"Dearest, what is it now? Is it Mayenne?" The two brothers had been at odds for months, arguing on tactics for dealing with the Swiss mercenaries in the field. Hopefully, it was just another fraternal argument.

He placed his hands on the chair next to Montpensier, his knuckles turning white. "No, it is the king. He fled the city last night and we still don't know where he plans to go."

"Perhaps to a monastery." Montpensier could not hide a smirk as she piped up beside him.

"I couldn't be that lucky. It's likely that while I was squandering my time 'negotiating' with his Mother, the king was busy planning his escape."

The story poured out of him, as his anger rose. Yesterday, the Queen Mother had invited my husband to meet with her again at the Louvre, where she would give him the king's response. Before Catherine could leave her rooms at her own hotel, word had already leaked out that the king left on a stroll at the nearby Tuileries and slipped out a side door to freedom.

"Both of they had duped me. The damned Valois, they're slippery as eels! Where I to--" a page whispered in his ear, breaking his mood for a moment. "Really? Here? Ha—then, by all means, send her in!"

Before I could ask him what was going on, Catherine de Medici appeared in the doorway of our dining room. We rose to our feet and curtsied, never forgetting our stations. Henri, so battle-hardened by years in the field and in the royal court, recovered far faster than either of us women could.

"Madame, you have deceived me. While you have kept me talking, the king has left Paris and gone where he can stir up more trouble for me."

Her face blanched even further. Never had I seen anyone give Catherine de Medici such a dressing down. If she were she anyone else,

I would think her a vulnerable old woman, too fragile to endure this verbal assault

"My son told me none of this. I swear to you, I went to the Louvre and presented your demands to him, as you asked. He said he would need time to consider them. He promised me, his mother, that he would give an answer today. He never hinted that he would do something so cowardly."

Her voice shook as she spoke. She looked bewildered. For a woman who spent most of her adult life outmaneuvering and always staying two steps ahead of everyone, she looked very much out of her league. And afraid. Even my husband must have sensed her fear because he softened his tone towards her for the rest of their short conversation.

THE NEWS THAT THE KING HAD FLED PARIS IN DISGRACE, PROVED TO be all too true and that news spread across Paris like wildfire. The few men left of the invaders the king called into the city, quickly disbanded and fled towards the countryside. With no need to defend themselves, the populace removed the barricades, and the city became Guise territory. Within three days, my husband and his allies in the Sixteen commanded all the main fortifications of the city: the Arsenal, the Bastille, and the chateau of Vincennes. There were no troops in Paris loyal to the king left to defend his reign.

In the absence of a royal government, Paris made its own government under the guidance of the Sixteen and my husband. They would base offices of every level on merit, not through bribery and nepotism. The king had violated the city's civil liberties and with him gone the people were eager to restore them.

On the sixteenth of May, Montpensier could no longer contain her glee over the king's withdrawal. Taking advantage of a newly abandoned Hotel de Ville, she threw open the building's doors for a victory celebration. She packed the salon with bodies, including several Spaniards. Chief amongst them was Mendoza himself, who could not keep himself from bragging about this present to the King of Spain.

"Madame de Guise, France has given Spain perfect peace. Our

Armada will sail to England on her Holy mission with no impediments. I owe your husband my thanks." He raised his glass in a toast and unwilling to get into a debate with him, I raised mine. Judging from his appearance, he was three glasses of brandy into the night already.

"I hope this demonstration proves to Phillip that France is more than capable of defending her borders and the Holy Church." Unlike me, Montpensier had no qualms about provoking the might of Spain. Also, unlike me, she had no children to worry about if our relationship with Spain took an ugly turn. Luckily, Mendoza ambled off to receive more congratulations and more drink.

"Isn't it a little reckless to be taunting Spain like that? By autumn, they'll be ruling England and knocking at two of our borders." I hissed in her ear, as she took a sip of her wine.

"You' doing not see the larger picture. Now they have humiliated the king, the Estates-General will rule France. That means it will unite us nobles, instead of marginalized. We will go from a weak king to a strong rule by the nobles. Plus," she took a pastry from a proffered tray, "my brothers control our military. If Spain were foolhardy to attempt an attack, they will cut them down on the battlefield."

She was blind to her overconfidence, but once again, I held my tongue. As much as I prayed she was right, I still had my doubts that the king was truly brought to heel. As that thought filtered through my mind, I looked up to see the diminutive figure of Catherine de Medici enter the room.

All conversations stopped. She was no stranger to hostile gatherings, but this evening, things were different. Her son had been all but deposed. It shocked me that she would appear at such a gathering, yet there she stood, right in front of us swathed in black mourning garb like a crow. She stood for a moment, stock still. Seconds later, the pain from her gout returned, and she called for a seat. Acting the solicitous hostess, Montpensier called two servants in to bring the Queen Mother of France her chair.

She settled down in her chair, all eyes upon her. Eventually, the musicians returned to their songs and conversations resumed in the hall. In a silent battle for territory, Montpensier refused to withdraw from the Queen Mother, earning her older woman's irritation.

"Catherine of Lorraine, do you really think it's proper to hold a fete when the city is in such a turmoil?" The Queen Mother arched an eyebrow and turned to glare at Montpensier. The Matrons in her royal entourage turned to stare at my sister-in-law in curiosity.

Montpensier burst into laughter, the high sound resounding like a dinner bell, "What would you have me do, Madame? I am like a brave soldier with a heart swollen with victory! We have driven the Swiss invaders back and Paris is safe!" She threw out her hands in a melodramatic gesture. Beside her, the Queen Mother "harrumphed!" in disgust, saying nothing more. An awkward silence followed, with Montpensier, for once, failing to find the words for a comeback. As much as I wanted to see the rest of their showdown, a tug at my elbow held my attention.

I turned to see my maid, Suzanne, who I had hadn't seen in four days, beaming up at me. "I'm sorry, Madame—I could not get back to you earlier. There was a small company of Swiss held up in my brother's home. We've been hiding from them until the men loyal to the Guise could free us." They had opened the gathering to all levels of society, with jubilant nobles rubbing shoulders with the lower classes. The entire city belonged to the Guise, and we would celebrate that fact with all of them.

42

CHAPTER 7

The next two months filled with moves and countermoves between the Guise cause and a divided Valois household. Paris remained solidly declared for the Guise and the Catholic League. Catherine de Medici spent the Summer in Paris, going to the Hotel de Guise so often that she soon became a fixture at our dinner table. The King continued to cower in fear, holding out in the city of Chartres. In his absence, his bewildered mother did all that she could to hold the government of France together.

We continued to celebrate the liberation of Paris and her people from the foreign Invaders, with the people flocking to our banner. Less than two months after the day of liberation, which the people later called the Day of the Barricades, I learned that I was once again pregnant. A child is a particular blessing, and I have loved all of my children dearly but learning I would be with child for the fourteenth time made me despair. I had harbored a secret hope I would be past my childbearing years and to learn that there was another baby growing inside me, made me quite upset.

Henri was quite pleased. My Henri ways always good with people.

He had a particular touch with children, whether they were his own or not. My news delighted him, "Ah, so I see we celebrated more than we realized when the king fled." I did not find his jest particularly amusing. By my own calculations, I would give birth for the second time during the chilliest part of Winter, most likely in February. My youngest, Marie-Louise was barely walking, her older sister Jeanne not much older and I would have another child in the nursery.

In August, Henri saddled his horse and left south for Chartres to parley with the king to make provisions for a convention of the Estates-General. Riding alongside him were eighty well-armed men, the Cardinal of Bourbon, fifty archers and my Mother-in-law, the Dowager Duchesse de Guise, and the Dowager Duchesse de Nemours. "It's best you and the child remain back in Paris where it's safe," Henri warned me. He was right: outside of the walls of Paris, the king still ruled France and we were at risk.

They accomplished little during those talks. While outwardly, he and the king displayed every pleasantry, their rivalry still simmered just beneath the surface. A few days after Henri's party arrived at Chartres, Bernardino Mendoza virtually danced into the cathedral of Chartres and announced to the Guise party that the Armada had cut the English navy to pieces. For a few moments, it seemed as if everything we had worked for had come true. A Spanish victory would cut the heart of English Protestants and their supplies to the French. Less than an hour later, the king appeared and informed Mendoza that he had left Paris without hearing the whole report of the Armada. The king had heard the terrible news that had been sweeping across northern France that day; the mighty Armada of Spain lay at the bottom of the English Channel. Now the way from England to Calais lay unchecked and vulnerable. Henri's invincible patron had finally suffered a devastating blow.

IT WAS UNSEASONABLY WARM IN THE SALLE D'ESTATE OF THE Chateau de Blois. One might expect October to give us a break from the relentless heat of the past Summer, but we were not so lucky. It was if the cavernous room echoed the king's fury in being called to hold a representative meeting packed with men who opposed him. The buzz of barely concealed contempt competed with the humidity, making it a miserable afternoon for us all. My condition excluded me in the meetings in Chartres, but I could not miss a meeting of the Estates-General. I had not seen Henri since Chartres, as he took every opportunity to return to the king's side when not out in the provinces. The king even extended his courtesy towards Montpensier, insisting that the Guise woman occupy the best rooms at Blois.

The ladies of the court packed the gallery facing the throne. Not since the days of the king's grandfather, the jovial Francis I had the court seen so many glittering ladies assembled in a single place. Facing beside her husband, Queen Louise looked pale and withdrawn, the only Guise woman who did not share in our triumph. Fifteen years of balancing her family's disdain for her husband and her spouse's erratic behavior had finally worn her down. My heart went out to her. Her sister, Marguerite, widow of the Duc de Joyeuse, sat with her, clothed in black and constantly weeping for her husband. The two spent most of their waking hours in prayer.

More upsetting was the absence of my sister, Henriette. Although due to arrive in October with the rest of the court ladies, she had made one excuse after another to delay coming to court, to avoid seeing me. A year after banishing me from her home, she had still not forgiven me. I had all but given up hope she ever would.

Taking his place as Grand Master of the Court, Henri had finally realized his dream of recognition as was his due as a Prince of Lorraine. Finally, the years of working to remove the king's dandies and unworthy men looked to be over and they restored the Houses of Lorraine and Guise to their place in the governing of France. Joyeuse was dead and Épernon neutralized, the king suddenly seeing reason had dismissed his former ministers. Relief spread over our faction. I stood at the women's gallery of Blois, fighting nausea, but still flushed with pride for my husband. Henri's place was in front of the king, the traditional seat of the Lord High Steward. Yet, placed as he was, in front of the king and with his back turned towards the beleaguered monarch, the symbolism of their placement lost on no one in attendance that sweltering day in October. He preceded Henri Valois in the assembly and in the hearts of the French people.

Rising, the king addressed the assembly in eloquent words and I held my breath as I watched Henri's face to see his reactions. Stating his continued devotion to the mission of the Holy Church, he continued for several moments to extol the Queen Mother and her skills in negotiation. I looked over at Catherine de Medici, who looked old and frail. Her granddaughter Christine, a Lorraine princess, would marry a Medici in two months' time and the Estates-General session at Blois was in part to celebrate their nuptials. Suffused with the heat and finding my fan incapable of keeping me cool, I drifted off as the king continued his speech.

Suddenly, his tone changed. "Some of the greatest princes of my realm have entered unlawful leagues and associations; but in the exercise of my accustomed clemency, I desire to obliterate the memory of the past; and to relieve the natural fear which assails many of my loving subjects, that after my demise they may fall under the dominion of a heretic prince, I have caused this august assembly to be convoked to remedy this evil and to restore order, justice, and submission to the laws throughout my kingdom." I glanced over again at Henri, who remained as still as a statue.

Would the king attempt to punish the League for treason despite his speech of reconciliation? His words were a direct attack on my husband, yet the king knew he held no cards. They packed the Estates-General with League adherents, with little to no men allied to the king. Henri had been part of the game for too long to panic at the slightest hint of danger. Nor was he gullible enough to fall for honeyed-words spoken to a room full of nobles. As my mind raced with possibilities, the king stated that he would accept the demands of the League.

I FOUND MY HUSBAND AT THE DOOR OF THE CARDINAL DE Bourbon's lodgings. Pleading an indisposition, the Cardinal had missed the opening session and had not heard the king's speech. "Henri," I clutched his doublet in terror.

"Come," he pulled me into the Cardinal's antechamber. Glancing over his shoulder to see that no one was watching at the door, he shut the portal and ushered us well inside the room before he spoke. Before he could, a knock sounded, and he opened the door to admit the Cardinal de Lyon and his younger brother, the Cardinal de Guise. Fastening the door behind him, his brother hastened to the middle of the room with us.

"The king has inferred that we are traitors, Gentlemen," his deep voice shook with anger.

"We get that passage stricken from the records before it's printed. Once it's dispersed across Europe, they 'll know us as traitors," his brother responded.

"Yet, he said that he planned on imparting his clemency. Perhaps he is just trying to scare us." Lyon, one of the most affable of the group, tried to calm the others down.

"Not in his present mood. He's back to being as unpredictable as ever. We thought we had him in our palms and now, he's taking control over the proceedings." Unbidden, he looked over at me. Not liking what he saw, he squeezed my hand in reassurance. Unfortunately, a gesture that gave me no reassurance, nor did it calm me; instead, my anxiety continued to increase by the second

Bourbon shook his head, looking as if he were on the verge of losing his nerve. "We could speak to the Queen Mother. If anyone can temper the king's feelings, it's her."

They stood silent, silently debating their next move when another knock sounded. I jumped at the sound, hysteria causing me to think the king's Forty-Five guards were at the door, determined to arrest them for treason. Instead, it was two of Montpensier's most outspoken priests.

"The king has branded the populace of Paris as traitors! Surely you don't think his words extend only to the 'Princes of France,'" he snorted in anger.

"I can't allow the people of Paris to suffer at the hands of the king. I'll go to the Queen Mother myself in the morning to beg her to help us." Henri ran a hand through his hair, his exhaustion written on his face.

"Henri, if you had listened to me and refrained from doing things halfway in May, we would have no king to deal with." the Cardinal de Guise shook a finger in my husband's face. Horrified, I realized just how close we had come to an assassination the night he left our hotel with the Queen Mother to meet the king at the Louvre. I shuddered; my husband was no murderer. Like Montpensier, he would rather shove the king into a monastery and allow him to live out the rest of his life in disgrace. He had heeded calmer counsel and spared the king's life. Would Henri Valois do the same in his place? I prayed we never had to find out.

AFTER THAT DAY, AN OMINOUS GLOOM DESCENDED UPON THE Chateau de Blois. Two days after our impromptu meeting in Bourbon's apartments, the king met with the members of the Sixteen present at Blois and promised that he would do nothing to avenge the Parisians' behavior in May. Still, something was missing. I noted that the king never made a promise to forego any punishment for the Princes of Lorraine who took part in that day. That evening, the king conferred command of the army in Poitou to my brother-in-law, the Duc de Nevers. The king made a special provision they would never force Louis to hand over his command to my husband. In the event of an uprising, the king would always have a division of the army was not under Guise control.

The Queen Mother had refused to speak with her son about censoring the lines marking my husband a traitor, so I decided that I would have to take matters into my own hands. Days had passed, and Henri grew more agitated at the thought of the rest of Europe branding him a traitor. On All Saint's Day, I rushed into her chambers and begged an audience. Sighing, she waved her attendants away.

"What may I do for you, Madame de Guise?" her voice was soft, lacking any of her typical vitriol.

"I want to ask your Majesty's help."

"How can I possibly help you? The Guise have their Assembly, your husband is in control of the Army and the Court." she sounded bored, as if she resented the burden of going through the motions of another intrigue.

"Yet, the king branded him a traitor. What he did was in defense of your son's throne. This is not the work of a traitor."

She scoffed, "Paris is in Guise hands—how is that not the work of a traitor?"

I shook my head, "Henri offered to broker a truce between the populace and the Swiss invaders." I deftly left out the French troops that the king sent pouring into the streets. "He offered several times to help the king recapture Paris. That shows his loyalty."

"People purchase loyalty cheaply these days. I have information that your husband is more loyal to Phillip of Spain than France. With the Armada destroyed, that loyalty may be up for sale again."

"Madame, it does France no good to splinter and fight. We are both threatened by Heresy. The king swore to protect his people and the church, should we not be united under those banners now?"

She waved her hand, "Perhaps. What would your husband do if of my son died?"

"We would support the only legitimate heir, my uncle, the Cardinal de Bourbon."

"Henri of Navarre has the stronger claim," she pointed a long, bony finger at me. Frailty be damned, she could still command strength when she wanted to.

"He has taken up Protestantism and refuses to acknowledge the True Church. The Edict of Union forces the king to make war on Navarre. You and I both know that makes him unworthy of the throne. His Holiness has already excommunicated him. Without the support of Rome, France could be easy pickings for invaders."

"Perhaps you are right," she stood, and I sank to my knees in obeisance. "I doubt that your cousin, Navarre will earnestly embrace the True Church as you did once. God knows that I have tried." She half-sat, half-stumbled back onto her seat. "I will speak with the king. Publicly airing factions will not help in the long run." With that, she dismissed me.

As I walked along the hallway, I saw Charlotte de Sauve coming towards me. Flushed with my victory with the Queen Mother, I had no desire to ruin my mood by engaging with my husband's whore. Henri had not spent every night at Blois with me and I was not naïve enough to think it was due to fatigue. I still held rank over a lowly Marquess and I resolved to ignore her as we passed.

"Madame la Duchesse." She, however, refused to let me go unnoticed.

"Madame de Sauve," I nodded stiffly. She bristled at the slight. "Madame de Noirmoutier. I have been so for almost two years."

"Ah, I forgot your husband, as I'm sure you have forgotten yourself."

"I see that you are with child, Madame de Guise. It is your husband's is it not? Ah, but you'll be leaving soon to give birth no doubt. Blois is bursting with people now that the Estates-General is in town." Her dig hit me, they forced us to vacate our rooms to make room for Christine of Lorraine's Medici fiancée and his family. The slight stung, but even more so when I considered it would place me far away from my husband and drive him into Charlotte's languid arms.

"I'll be leaving soon to give birth to my child, yes. I've been so blessed with children during our marriage." It was common knowledge that Charlotte had only given birth to a single healthy child. Gossip abounded that she had aborted Navarre's bastard during their liaison years before. "I would assume that you would take the time to visit your child instead of skulking around hallways looking for a lover."

She giggled, the high peel reverberating on the stone walls. "Madame, I have no need to 'look' for anything. I'm quite pleased with what I have." Anger and a wave of nausea hit me simultaneously. I would not humiliate myself by vomiting in front of a common whore. Sticking my chin out, I rushed past her and out to the courtyard. Once there, I was sick for ten minutes.

I spent the next four days packing, churlish at the thought I would leave Henri at the mercy of the king and Charlotte de Sauve. I had failed to learn who she was working for, but my instincts told me she was the king's creature, as much as she had been his Mother's. Before I left, however, the king called Henri into his presence and as the fog rolled in on an early November morning; he struck the offending words from his speech and gave him his reprieve.

⚜

"THIS RAIN IS MISERABLE. I THINK I HEARD SLEET," MONTPENSIER whined at my side. I was not thrilled to have her with me, either. Whereas I was going to Paris to settle in before I had my child, she was leaving for very different reasons. During her brief stay at Blois, she had stirred up the king's anger with her words. Henri begged me to bundle his sister into a carriage and spirit her away from the king before she wound up in a cell. "The weather is miserable, and I'm so far gone with the child I can hardly think straight. Now you want to saddle me with your sister?" I whined at him, exercising a pregnant woman's prerogative. Neither of us would spend Christmas at Blois, it seemed.

"Please," he took my hands in his and looked deeply into my eyes. Filled with the conflicting emotions of pregnancy, I could not say no to him. "I can't stand something happening to her. My mother would never forgive me if it did."

"I shall never forgive you for forcing me to ride the road from Blois to Paris with her." He kissed the top of my head and helped me into my carriage. I sighed and leaned my head back onto the head cushion as the carriage took off. I was so annoyed with him I did not bother to look back at him.

"At least we're away from that gauche, Charlotte de Sauve. She's been at every dinner since October."

"You mean the ones where your sharp tongue got you into so much trouble?" I added archly. I truly was trapped. She would crouch on my frayed nerves throughout the trip.

"I think 'Father Henri' is a good name for Henri Valois," she replied tartly. "He should take it as a compliment, considering how many pilgrimages he goes on.

"Anyway, Charlotte's looking for new prey, have you heard? She's tried sinking her claws into Mayenne. The absurdity of it all!" She burst into laughter. "She's not even the woman Charles finds attractive, but does that stop Charlotte? No!"

I had no desire to hear the latest gossip about my husband's mistress, but she pressed on. "Charles and Henri got into a huge argument over her, Charles telling him he was making a fool of himself. Henri ordered him to the yard so they could fight it out. When they got there, Charles just waved his hand and told him he was wasting his time." She gave a small shrug, "My brothers."

The season of Advent was one of the loneliest times of my life. Without the court, my husband, my remaining sister, or even my mother-in-law for company, I spent the month of December in a dark mood. My one bright spot was the time spent with Louise, who would soon be a year old, and her sister Jeanne, would all too soon grow out of being a precocious toddler. The extra time alone gave me time to reflect and quietly prepare for the new baby.

Montpensier moved into the Hotel de Guise to spend the holiday with me and we spent the day of December 23rd playing with baby Louise. "She's so serious, sometimes I can hardly believe that she's a Guise." She removed her necklace and gave the beads to Louise to suck upon. I wanted to protest, worried she would ruin the shape of her mouth by constantly sucking, but I decided that just for Christmas, we could indulge my tiny daughter.

ON THE MORNING OF CHRISTMAS EVE, I WOKE EARLY TO START celebrations with my daughter. Minutes after I finished my breakfast, a sharp knock sounded at the great door of the Hotel. I knew immediately that the message must be from Blois. Sighing, I admitted that even on the day of our Lord's birth, it could not spare me the intrigues of the court.

One of Henri's teenage pages huffed into the door, his breath smoking up the hallway. "Forgive me, Madame. I rode as hard as my horse would allow." He winced as a stitch in his side caught, forcing him to take a shallow breath.

"Come by the fire and warm up. It's Christmas. I'm sure your

Mother would not forgive me if I allowed you to freeze to death." I raised my hand and tried to usher him into the antechamber, but he shook his head rapidly. He glanced around nervously, as if he would rather be anywhere else but in my presence. "Someone told me the Duchesse de Montpensier was living with you, is she here?"

My blood ran cold at his question. Why would a young man fear being alone with an emotional pregnant woman, unless he was there to impart bad news? "She is in her rooms; I will send for her." We passed the next ten minutes before Montpensier's arrival in stone silence, neither of us wanting to break the agonizing quiet. When we heard the swish of Montpensier's velvet skirts, he rose to his feet with a clatter. "Forgive me for being the one to tell you and this on the day before the celebrations of our Lord's birth." He crossed himself vigorously. I rolled my eyes and braced myself for whatever the vacillating king had laid out for Henri this time. "It's the Duc de Guise, he has..." He shook with the effort. "He is dead, Madame." Tears formed in his eyes and despite my shock, I knew that he was serious.

I blinked and clutched at the bottom of my stomach, a spasm echoing my surprise. "How? Was there an accident?"

He shook his head once again, "You should sit for this news." With him on one side and Montpensier on the other, he settled me gently into a chair. From somewhere, my lady's maid, Suzanne appeared, and she did her best to hold me until Montpensier could take over the job of consoling me.

Holding a hat that rapidly melted with snow, he told me of the horrors that had occurred the past two days. "They assassinated him, Madame, under the king's orders. We had heard murmurings that the king planned to do him harm, but no one thought His Majesty would spoil the festivities of the Duc of Tuscany's wedding. He would never dare to face the wrath of the Queen Mother." He gave me a wan smile and paused for several minutes before continuing.

Given her bouts of emotion, I expected Montpensier to gasp or fly into a rage. I do not know what passed over her face because I could not bear to look at her, but I heard only silence from her. I could not stand to sit idly by, passively accepting that my husband was gone.

Hefting all of my weight, I rose to my feet. "I want to know the details! What has that cur, Henri Valois done to him?"

The boy gulped, "He invited the Duc for an early morning meeting after breakfast. After eating his meal in the king's antechamber, they ushered the Duc into the king's most private chamber. Likely, my lord assumed it was an assurance he was being admitted into the king's most intimate confidence."

How like Henri to think he had finally achieved his goals and follow blindly into a trap. "He had no warning? No idea that his life was at risk? How could you surround him with such paltry intelligence?" The boy was blameless in this plot against my husband, but I had no care for that fact. I would lash out at Christ himself if I had been able.

"No less than five people warned him of the danger, Madame. The Duc de Mayenne warned him before he rode to Paris a week ago." I snorted, had Henri not been too busy arguing with Charles over his whore, he could have picked up on the danger surrounding him. "God damned Charlotte de Sauve! She had him ensnared in Henri Valois trap from the beginning!"

"She was one of those who warned him. If she was working for the king, she betrayed her master in the last minutes. She tried to warn the Duc of the danger he was walking into." I turned to look at Montpensier; if Charlotte was not working as a spy for the king, then who was the strumpet working for? Now was not the time to worry about her sympathies, however. I had a husband to bury.

"When will the body reach Paris? We will have to have a funeral. The people will want to mourn him." Tears pricked at my eyes and I suddenly remembered the last time I sat behind my husband's coffin. I was so young then, but then, I was not great with child. My heart ached at the thought; beneath my heart, Henri's last child lay sleeping. He or she would never be chucked under the chin by their charismatic father.

"I am so sorry, Madame. The king ordered the bodies disposed of. They burned them. They scattered the ashes into the Loire."

Montpensier snapped her head up. "What bodies? What has happened?"

"It's not just the Duc de Guise, my Lady. They also assassinated the Cardinal de Guise. You have lost two of your brothers." Her face became for a few minutes vividly suffused, although she sat motionlessly. After an interval, her cries of despair, horror, and rage resounded through the entire vast hotel. She tore her hair and in words of appalling purport, cursed the tyrant.

⚜

I SHOULD NOT HAVE STOOD UP. IF I WERE IN A BETTER STATE OF mind, I would have long since taken a seat. As it was, I was still standing. Those were the last thoughts I had before the entire world went black.

⚜

WHEN I WOKE, IT WAS AFTERNOON. THE THIN COLD DECEMBER SUN barely shone through the windows of my bedchamber. Montpensier came to check my forehead, placing her hand against my skin as if checking for fever. "Don't sit up," she barked at me. Defying her, I raised my head to see three of my women sitting by the bed. They had left their own families to come to my bedside.

From outside, I could hear shouting and the noise of a foaming crowd. "What's going on? Is there a riot?" One of my ladies shook her head, "No, the people wish to see if you and Madame de Montpensier are all right. They know you are here alone and they come to give their condolences."

Their concern touched me. The crowds of Paris had always been our supporters, an affinity that the Valois had never cultivated. The people warmed towards authenticity, not a feeling of entitlement. Henri Valois had thought it entitled him to end my husband's life, and the crowd rushed to see that his widow was all right. "I should go to them."

One woman shook her head, "No, the physician says you're too weak." I looked over at Montpensier, who looked just as drained as I felt. Since leaving Blois, she had experienced swelling in her extremities and now, she looked as if the condition would overwhelm her.

"Help me up, I will go to the balcony." One of them looked as if she would defy me, but I was in no mood for debate. "Up! Or I will do it myself. Would you have the people of Paris see I am bereft of my husband *and* my women!" Their shoulders slumped, and they struggled to help me to a seated position.

I could hear the angry shouts well before I opened the doors to the balcony of the hotel. Women called Henri and the Cardinal de Guise martyrs, men devoted to the survival of the church. Others shouted that the king was the antichrist. I wondered if they could hear me when I took the balcony. I needn't have worried because when the crowd saw me; they took on a hush like that during Mass. I cleared my throat, determined to gain control over my emotions.

"My heart is broken. I have lost my husband and the father of this helpless babe, who lies within me. Like you, I planned to celebrate the birth of our Lord in peace and like a good Frenchwoman. That right was taken from me just as they have taken the rights of every Parisian for the past fifteen years. Before today, I did not wholeheartedly believe that it was right to oppose an anointed king. I believed that God put Henri Valois on the throne according to his will."

I looked at my hands, realizing that at that moment, I no longer believed in anything that they had taught me my entire life. The realization took the fight out of me, draining my life essence slowly. Revolution had seemed like such a radical idea, one reserved for the mentally unbalanced and the disgruntled. Now, in that moment, I fully became one of them.

"I cannot forgive a man who ruthlessly takes the life of The King of Paris. I cannot sit idly by while he drags France into constant heresy and warfare. I know that none of you can sit idly by either." At that moment, a plan formed in my mind, but I could not give words to it. Not yet, not in front of the crowd. Unable to express the feelings inside of me, I collapsed and out of the corner of my eyes, I saw the women reaching to steady me. I barely heard the roar of the crowd as they blessed me. I meekly let them lead me from the balcony and back to my bedchamber.

As I made my way back, I heard Montpensier haltingly drag herself to the balcony. I heard snippets of her speech to the crowd, one that inflamed them further. She repeated the words she used earlier that afternoon, cursing Henri Valois. Her anguish had a reviving effect on me and for a moment, I thought to go through the streets surrounding the hotel and stir up the populace.

THE FOLLOWING DAY BEING CHRISTMAS, PARIS WOULD USUALLY BE under a dreamy spell of reflection. Christmas Day of 1588, however, was not such a day. None of us would leave the hotel to attend Christmas Mass, a break with a lifelong tradition. Instead, my personal confessor came to celebrate Mass in the Chapel of the Hotel where we said prayers for the dead through our sobs.

After our luncheon, Montpensier retired to her rooms to write her remaining brothers, chiefly Mayenne, who would inherit the role of head of the Guise family. My son was still not fifteen and not yet in his majority. He remained at Blois, under close guard, until he could escape the king's eye and find his freedom. Although I cared not one whit what happened to military power in France, the king gave my brother-in-law, Louis command of the army to keep it from falling under Mayenne's command.

The day after Christmas, Paris sprang into action to defend itself against the king and his army. I had avoided speaking with the Sixteen earlier, but they insisted on greeting me at the hotel that afternoon. I could no longer put off speaking with them, so as I sat in my black-draped drawing room, I received the men who governed Paris and for years had been close allies of my husband.

"Madame, we cannot imagine the anguish you are going through today." At his words, I inclined my head. He looked familiar, one of the indistinguishable men I had met during a salon in the rooms of this same building. Today, we reunited for a more sorrowful occasion. "No doubt His Holiness will Condémn the king for his actions at Blois. It is a shame for every Frenchman that the Princes of Lorraine are no longer with us."

"I thank God that there are still some princes left to us. My son is safe, and the Duc de Mayenne is still at liberty." From the corner or the room, I saw one of them shift his feet awkwardly. Ignoring him, I pressed on. None of them could know of the plan I was planning. There had been too many spies in their ranks before and I would risk none of them running back to the king for payment and telling him of my plan for revenge.

"My Lady, have you not heard the latest?"

I shook my head, weary of the influx of bad news from Blois. Each day, the news grew worse, and I had stopped bracing myself for even worse tidings.

"Just this morning, the king apprehended the Guise faction living in Blois. They have placed the Dowager—excuse me, your mother-in-law under guard." His slip of the tongue reminded me I was now the dowager Duchesse de Guise, not Anna.

"But, Anna d'Este is a close friend of the Queen Mother, surely the king would not dare hurt her?" At those words, I realized how ridiculous the idea sounded. Any man who ordered the slaughter of Henri de Guise would not hesitate to put his own cousin under guard, no matter how close she was to the Queen Mother. I raised my eyebrows to show my disgust at the news.

"There is more," he faltered, and another man took up the burden of telling me the rest of the news from Blois. "The king also put your son the Prince of Joinville under guard. For now, he is safe, and we don't think he is an imminent danger."

I sank back in my chair in despair. I had hoped that Charles would make it to Normandy to fortify himself at Eu. With the Jesuits residing on the estate, he could plan his next move in safety. Now, he was at the king's mercy.

"I'm sorry, I meant the *Duc de Guise* is under guard." Until the man spoke, I had not still not realized that my eldest son was now the new Duc de Guise, a boy with no real experience in leadership, but already the weight of his family's inheritance on his slim shoulders. I was the Dowager Duchesse de Guise, a title I had associated with Anna for so long it felt as if she had always held it. Now it was up to me to take up the Guise legacy and honor my husband.

"My Lady, you seem disturbed. We have come here to assure you you will always have the support of the people of Paris. We have resolved that we will take responsibility for your and the Duc's children."

It sounded like an empty promise coming from these men, these would-be politicians. I had felt this sentiment, a sincere expression of sympathy, from the people the other day on the balcony. In that moment, coming from these men, it sounded hollow and easily discarded at will. Unwilling to let them know of my true feelings, I inclined my head. "That is very generous of you."

"That is not all. If, God willing, your child is a boy, the city pledges to stand beside him at the baptismal font and serve as a godparent."

I lifted my eyebrows, "The entire city. Your charity is remarkable." Weeks ago, I had hoped to repair my rift with Henriette by asking her to become my child's godmother. Her silence made that wish seem unlikely to come true.

"We are striving to free those dear to you. The Cardinals of Bourbon and Lyon are also under guard. The king has sequestered himself behind his chamber walls with the queen and the Duchess of Tuscany. The Queen Mother," he hesitated and glanced around at his compatriots, "is in declining health. No one expects her to live out the year."

I crossed myself at hearing the words. My last audience with Catherine de Medici came to me, my desperate negotiations to save Henri's reputation. She resigned herself to the inevitable that day, knowing that her life was rapidly ending. Even enveloped in my grief, I mourned the demise of the woman who had led the court for thirty years. With her death, the ing would lose his one remaining ally.

Realizing that, I knew that with her death the king was even more isolated than before; if that were possible. After alienating himself from the bulk of his subjects, he had few real friends left to mourn his own demise. Still, every time I had thought the king defeated, he came back defiant. I would never underestimate his power again.

43

CHAPTER 8

The king crowed in his chambers he was finally master of France, but as the vast Guise relations planned a revolt and his mother's life drained from her, he also lost his own vitality. The men remaining at Blois remarked that the king seemed lesser each day than the one before. Yet the king worked to keep his enemies under close watch. They transferred my eldest son and mother to the stronger prison at the Chateau d'Amboise. Anna could not get any letters to us, but her women reported that she spent the days in prayer for her dead sons and for the draining life of Catherine de Medici.

The young Duc de Nemours, alone, escaped the transfer from Blois to Amboise and he reached Paris on the 13th of January. The king had toyed with releasing Anna, but once he realized her son was at liberty, he kept her under key, to keep her from conspiring with Mayenne and Montpensier. By the sixteenth of January, the king dismissed the Estates-General and the experiment of democracy was over. We lay in wait for the king's next move that would likely involve striking at Paris.

A day later, I awoke to find that I was bleeding. Terrified that I would lose my child, I took to my bed and prayed for a safe delivery. I could not stand the heartache of losing Henri's child so soon after losing him. My body could never withstand the stress of a stillbirth. Unable to do anything more, I resolved to stay out in my rooms and remain patient until the child came. When he was safely in his crib, I would resume plotting.

On Monday, January 30th, they performed a grand requiem in Notre Dame for the Duc de Guise and his brother. They hung the churches of the capital with black; and for the entire day, Paris remained prostrate, fasting, and weeping the demise of her hero. There were no bodies for us to bury, only ashes floating in the Loire. Still fearful of losing my child, I could not attend and Montpensier and the Duc d' Aumale attended in my place. It was just as well I was not there; I would have shamed myself by dissolving into tears.

At Amboise, the king alienated himself even from the captain of the Forty-Five and du Gaust, the jailer of the Guise dynasty. At the beginning of February, he finally gave my mother-in-law her freedom. His timing could not have been more fortuitous because my child would enter the world at any moment.

On February 7th, my labor finally began. After bringing thirteen previous children from my womb, the experience of childbirth no longer caused me anxiety. I still worried that the horror of December would be an ill omen for the child. Twelve hours after I felt the first stirring, the midwife pronounced that I had a son. He was small and gave out a small cry, but otherwise, he was healthy. The people would have you believe that he came into the word with his hands clasped in supplication and with eyes raised to heaven. That is a silly myth meant to stir up the people, I can assure you. He came into the world wiggling, just as any other babe before him.

The next day, the people of Paris fulfilled their promise to act as godparents for my new son. Henriette, unwilling to communicate with me, the Duchesse d'Amuale stood as his godmother. At the altar of St. Jean de Grève, the place of worship for the Guise family, I named him Alexandre Paris. The christening completed, several men rose to expound on the behavior of the tyrant who ended this child's beloved father's life. To show their regard for me, many stopped to give presents to my son. One, in particular, held my interest. "Ambassador Mendoza." He took my hand once I could free it from under Alexandre's wriggling body. Kissing it as if I were Queen Louise herself, he took his own hand and pressed it on top of mine.

"My great Lady, words cannot express how I feel at your loss." Although I had little time to waste on pleasantries, for Alexandre's sake, I accepted his condolences. I also pressed my case. I had plans for Mendoza and the Spanish.

"I would like to meet with you at the Hotel de Guise." Despite his years of subterfuge at the English and French courts, he could not hide his surprise at my request.

"It would honor me." He made a show of bowing to the Dowager Duchesse de Guise and her fatherless child. France and Spain united, that was what I had in mind.

❧

AT THE END OF THE WEEK, MY CHAMBERLAIN USHERED MENDOZA into the study. "I won't delay you; instead, I will come right to my point. I want to arrange a marriage between Phillip's daughter, Catalina and my son, the Duc de Guise." It was perfect timing, as Charles' previously betrothed had died of the plague last summer. Burdened with the issues of statecraft, Henri and I had delayed arraigning another match for our heir. The solution came soon after I heard of the slaughter of my husband.

"I will send word to His Majesty immediately. He is entertaining several matches for his daughter."

I snorted, "I am sure he is. With Bourbon in captivity, he is hardly a suitable candidate to succeed as King of France. Catalina is the king's niece, carrying both Valois and Hapsburg blood. Along with my son's heritage as a direct descendant of the Capets, there are few who could match his pedigree."

"His Majesty has asked that the Infanta Catalina be put forth as the League claimant to the throne." There had been plans in motion to remove the Salic law that forbade women inheriting, along with specific language barring Margot from inheriting after her brother's death. Taking advantage of this, Phillip had put forth his unmarried daughter as a candidate take the throne.

"The French people may not accept a Spanish princess as their queen, but if she married a French prince, I cannot see any reason they would reject her. Convey to Phillip that this marriage would be to both our advantage."

He took a sip of the wine in front of him, "Madame—I believe it just might."

❦

"THE NERVE OF THAT CLUMSY, DIRT-COVERED BUMPKIN!" I THREW down the paper and stomped on it to stop it from offending me further. Determined to push his case for the French throne, Navarre opened the month of March by decrying the movements of both the king and the League. As ever, the king hid in his chateau at Blois, too timid to return to Paris. Reeling from Henri's death, the remaining leaders of the League tried to rally their troops under Mayenne's command.

My brother-in-law was proving to be a less than inspiring commander. Dawdling in Paris and gorging on food, he refused to expand the League's control over the south and center of the country. In this vacuum of power, marched Navarre, solidifying the south under Protestant rule throughout that spring. France was in danger of splitting into two nations, one in the south, ruled by an absolute king, and one to the north, ruled by a burgeoning constitutional government. While the king feared the damage a constitution would do to his rule, he did not act to curb the League's power in the north. This made getting messages to and from Eu easier than they had been in a decade.

Between his own whoring and soldering, Navarre had taken the time to print and distribute a proclamation decrying the Spanish support of the League and the push for representative government springing up across France. While his fellow Protestants might structure their religious meetings in a democratic flavor, make no mistake about his designs for ruling France. Navarre would rule as one and over all of France once given the chance.

I wanted to keep him from doing so. Once Charles and the Infanta married, France would have two strong Catholics on the throne and two who not influenced by unworthy bumpkins as Henri Valois was. Spanish stock may have plummeted since the destruction of the Armada the previous Summer, but Spain was still a powerful ally. A powerful ally I wanted to win to our side.

There was virtually nothing left of the Parlement of Paris, which officially ruled the city. Everyone knew that the Sixteen ruled in theory and practice. Still, I went to the Parlement in late March to present an official petition to begin proceedings against all the men responsible for the death of my husband and his younger brother. I knew that the trail would immediately lead them to investigate the king, and I relished the image of them squirming when presenting a warrant against the king. To my surprise, the Parlement was more than willing to grant a petition to such an "illustrious widow" and they sat about appointing commissioners to start proceedings against Henry Valois and his co-conspirators. I hoped that I would receive justice.

The Parlement went even further than granting my petition; in January, we learned that the Pope had granted absolution for the murders of the Guise brothers. The idea was abhorrent and to any right-thinking Catholic in France. With his actions, the Pope had made clear his decision to move towards the king and betray the League he himself had supported for years.

❧

IN APRIL, MENDOZA FINALLY RECEIVED AN ANSWER FROM PHILLIP regarding my offer of marriage between Charles and the Infanta Catalina. As I read Mendoza's response, anger boiled up inside me. "His Most Catholic Majesty is not convinced that an alliance with the house of Lorraine is the best match for his eldest daughter. He wishes to unite her with a Hapsburg prince, under the tradition of the House of Hapsburg. In addition, as the League is unwilling to commit to preserving the Catholic faith, he wonders if the house of Lorraine is as strong as it once was."

I gritted my teeth—of course, the house of Lorraine was not as strong as it once was. In November, it had a strong leader, and a committed commander who could lead it to glory. Now, reduced to a corpulent third son who was showing himself to be a complete coward. My son might not be old enough to lead the Guise family, but within three years he would be. He would show himself to be just as effective as his late father had been. He would be another military giant, a man worthy to be called the son of Guise.

Grabbing a piece of paper, I jabbed at it until I had composed a response to Mendoza.

"Might I remind Phillip that Spanish power has diminished since last August? Marriage to another Hapsburg will mean that a hostile France remains between Spain and Austria. Such an alliance would yield no advantage to Phillip, only maintain the status quo. France hungers after a strong leader and one who has not dedicated himself to the Heretic cause."

Wounding Phillip's pride and reminding him of the spreading cancer of Protestantism might well be enough to scare the Spanish king into a commitment. I hastily sealed the letter and sent it on to Mendoza's house.

I immediately composed a missive to Eu, demanding that the priest who caused the rift between Henriette and I come to my house in Paris as soon as possible. It was time to put my plan into action. Navarre felt the crown of France sitting upon his dirty head.

In April, Navarre and the king formalized an alliance, putting down their arms and signing a treaty outside of Tours. Without the two men opposing one another, there was only one enemy left for them both to face: the Catholics of the League. Once the two armies combined, there was nothing to stop them from marching upon Paris. Henri Valois would take his revenge upon the city, and now he would do so with the help of hundreds of Protestant troops under Navarre's command.

There was nothing left to stop those troops but Mayenne. Finally, he had to admit that his laziness had led to this watershed moment. Had he acted months earlier, as so many had begged him to do so, the job might have been easier. Gathering up as many men as he could, he began a slow campaign to clear the road between Paris and the city of Tours. Although I was angry at Mayenne for not acting sooner, I felt safe enough in Paris with the wall of men between us and the king's combined army. Mayenne would keep the fighting well away from us. Alexandre was still a symbol of pride for the League and I felt justified in keeping him and his sisters, Louise and Jeanne with me in the city. Besides, only a coward would run away to either Joinville or Eu.

Even more so, I had a plan for breaking the king and his newfound alliance with Navarre. To carry out that plan, Father Jean came from Eu to repay his longstanding debt to me. "Father, I trust your 'sisters' are happily settled in France?" As with the Sixteen, I sat in state under a drapery of black, emphasizing my status as Duchesse de Guise. Until Catalina married my son, I would continue to use that title to my advantage. Given how much this man had cost me, I would make sure he quaked before me.

Recognizing his status, he looked down at his feet in shame. "I am sorry, Madame. I should not have deceived you."

"No, you should not have. Since you already have, you will now make up for your sins against me."

He gulped, fear written across his face. "How so, My Lady?"

"I understand that the Jesuits are skilled in combat and taking care of problems. I want you to take care of a particular problem I have had recently." I needed say no more, he knew what task I had set for him.

"This is for the survival of the Holy Church. I will see to it someone forgives you for your deed." If Rome could absolve the king, then His Holiness could do the same for the man who avenged Henri Valois' crime.

❧

ALTHOUGH THE GUISE CAUSE REVELED IN THE ABSENCE OF THE KING, eventually cracks appeared within the family. The unity that Henri cultivated for so long was splintering after his death. I blame that fully on Mayenne's lack of leadership skills. Unlike his older brothers, he was indecisive, lazy, and more invested in furthering his own means than that of the family. His behavior caused many of them to wonder if he was worth following at all.

As it was, he could barely install a stable government within Paris itself. The men he installed to govern the city immediately passed legislation cutting taxes. While the poor reveled in the break-in taxation, eventually the middle-class lost money. Within months, the city's economy started a slow ruin.

The women of the family wedged divisions between ourselves. Previously, Anna d'Este had been available to curb her daughter's fits of emotion, but after the death of her eldest sons, she retired to her country estate to hover over her eldest son by the Duc de Nemours. Determined to avoid watching another son fall to an assassination by making up for the years of lost motherhood, she smothered her son at the expense of tending to her Guise children. Her absence led to building resentment.

No one resented her absence more than her only daughter. Montpensier continued to rail against the king, and amid her complaints against the king, she spoke against her missing mother. Somehow, she found the time to badger her brother into taking up arms against the king and marching towards Blois. Had it not been for her, I doubt that he would ever deign to leave Paris.

Once he did, she changed her tone to praising him in the highest notes. "With him goes the strongest chance for a united France," she faced me one warm day in the middle of April.

I shrugged, "*If* he goes all the way to Blois. He seems half-hearted at best."

"He's a worthy successor to the crown. He should take it the moment he defeats Brother Henri." I bit my lower lip; if she honestly thought the king could peacefully enter a monastery after his crimes against the Guise, she was mistaken.

Anger flared at me. Was she truly going mad? "Mayenne? The third son? When he has several nephews who have a better claim to the throne? If it goes to a Guise, it should rightly go to my son, Charles." I ignored the superior claim of the son of the Duc de Lorraine, who was also a grandchild of Henry II and Catherine de Medici. Given the city's love for Henri, his son would be the sentimental favorite.

"He seems very un-kinglike. He may prove to be an effective soldier, but he, in general, is unremarkable." She waved her hand as if debating the merits of a pastry.

"Your own nephew, the Duc de Guise, you dare call him 'unremarkable'? How dare you? You, a woman with no children, have the nerve to call my son 'unremarkable'?" I shouted at her, venting my full wrath. Anyone else would quake at my yelling, but Montpensier was nonplussed.

"I'm only stating a fact. The people will see it, too. Eventually." She gave a small shrug. So, this was the extent of Montpensier's loyalty—once her beloved brother was out of the picture, she owed it to no one.

"I think it's time you retired for the faubourgs." I snapped at her, unwilling to stand her presence one second longer.

By the end of the week, people overheard Montpensier making the case for Mayenne to take the French throne. As she had with me, she smoothly disregarded my son's stronger claim as the eldest son of the eldest son. With the throne up for grabs, we could disregard any pedigree.

To my amusement, she also threatened the king's safety, in words so inflammatory, that the king sent a gentleman of his bedchamber to tell her that her words were treasonous. If she were wise, the message read, to retire from Paris and thus save herself from death by fire.

Montpensier stayed put in Paris, to mine and the king's disappointment. At a party held in the Paris City Hall, she shouted that she would do anything to prevent the king from returning to Paris. I did not temper her speech; she was proving to be more helpful than she knew.

CHAPTER 9

At the end of April, a letter finally arrived from Henriette. Louis rejected at an alliance with the Protestant troops and had retired to Nevers in protest. Finally, Louis and I were in agreement about something and I took it as a step towards reconciliation. I hoped that my sister would never learn about my plans for the king, but if we could repair our relationship, I would be grateful.

Louis' departure from Blois meant that the king turned to his habitual advisor, the Duc d'Épernon. Hearing the news, I seethed. Henri had worked for years to remove the sycophant from the king's council and now that Louis had left in disgust, Épernon was back.

"I've been too quick to judge you and now I cannot think of you in Paris without Henri. As much as we often disagreed regarding the king, I regarded him as a friend. His loss is immeasurable." I teared up as I read Henriette's letter. I finally had my sister back. Letters also arrived from Blois, carrying the king's seal. The Guise women, including Montpensier and I, would immediately leave Paris and lodge at Blois. I could see through the king's words. Unlike in the past, this would not be an invitation to serve at court. We were to go under guard, just as Anna had been during the chilly months of winter. She had barely escaped and there was little chance I would.

I laughed as I read the letter from the king. This ruse reminded me too much of his meeting with Henri at Blois in December. I would not need five people to warn me that to leave for Blois was suicide. I would rather die than allow the king to put me under custody. Nothing would compel me to leave Paris and the support of the people. I was safe in Paris and so were my children. If Mayenne failed, Paris would defend itself against an army headed by Navarre and the king.

Another letter arrived the next day, written in Queen Louise's own hand. In it, she begged me to ride to Blois so that the king and his guard could ensure my safety. They had received word at Blois that Paris was collapsing under a ruined economy. The royal troops would march into the city soon to restore order and chaos would result. She could not guarantee my safety in Paris, but under guard at Blois, I would protect my youngest children and myself. I shook my head at her words. Previously, Henri Valois had not used the queen to entrap her own family. She had been off limits in attacking the king. Now, he stooped to using her as a weapon to capture the remaining members of the Guise family. The letter Louise sent to Anna was even more manipulative; she addressed her as the mother of two dead sons and inferred that her remaining children from her Guise and Nemours marriages were now in peril.

Thank God, Henriette and I had reconciled, because even in Nevers, she was not immune to plotting. At the end of April, a fanatical preacher ascended the pulpit in the cathedral of Nevers and preached a sermon filled with the foulest abuse against the king. The words were familiar, sounding like the priests Montpensier patronized in Paris. Louis sat the sermon out, then sent for the monk and forced him to return to the pulpit and contradict each of his previous assertions. Regardless of his issues with the King, Louis would allow no one to incite a riot under his nose.

To my relief, after Louis stormed into the palace in fury, Henriette sent a letter urging me to remain in Paris. My sister knew full well that my life was in danger if I were to take the king's offer and head towards Blois. I thank God that she knew that I was blameless this time in the plotting.

ON THE FIRST WEEK OF MAY, MAYENNE FINALLY MARCHED UPON the outskirts of Tours. The city was the traditional Viscountcy of Charlotte de Sauve's family, ruled over by Charlotte and her latest husband. The former whore of both Navarre and my husband, now stood to lose her lands, an ironic touch I found amusing. She had been so arrogant for years, parading her charms and her ability to lure men to her bed, and now, she was powerless to stop the army outside her city. If Charlotte was among the dead, I would not mourn her loss one bit.

As I sat in Paris, awaiting the result of the campaign against Tours, a knock sounded at the door of my chamber. "Madame, there is a priest waiting to see you." Wrinkling my brow, I waved the man inside. It was Father Jean. I held my breath, willing him to give me good news.

"Madame, I have been thinking about the task you set for me." I curled my fingers, biting my palms with my fingernails. He would back out of the task.

"While the Jesuits do not shirk from their duty to defend the Holy Church, I think there is a flaw in your plan."

"A flaw? How so, Father?"

"The king well knows that the Jesuits are allies of his enemies in the League. To pass undetected, I would need to shed the clothes of a Jesuit."

"I see." His logic was sound. Sending a Jesuit into the king's camp might arouse suspicion. I did not want to fail in my plan. Relieved that he was not backing out of the task I set before him, I will listen to his argument.

"The king has been generous towards the Franciscan friars, staying with them for several of his pilgrimages. We know his affinity for their order." I nodded, finding no logic with his argument.

"Dressed as a Franciscan, I could avoid suspicion. The king would easily admit me into his private accommodations. After the tragedy of the Duc's death, I would expect the king's guards to surround him closer than ever. It's not out of the question to expect that there will be a plot to avenge the Duc's death."

"I want nothing to ruin my plan. Get into the king's confidence however you can. If someone catches you, then say you do what you're doing for the League."

He gave a curt nod and left. I wondered if I would see him before he left Paris. Mayenne's troops had secured the road between Tours and Paris, so he should have no problem reaching the king's encampment.

I spent the rest of the day waiting for the post and the message that Mayenne had surrounded the king's forces. Although he and Navarre had signed an informal truce, they would still separate their forces. Navarre camped far from the king, for his own safety. None of the Protestants trusted the man suspected of orchestrating a massacre of Protestants in the St. Bartholomew's Day Massacre in 1572 with the life of their remaining military leader. Condé might have died under suspicious circumstances, but the Protestants would not allow the same tragedy to strike them twice. In the event of a disaster, the alliance with the Catholic, Henri Valois would quickly dissolve.

After supper, I went to visit Alexandre at the nursery. He dozed peacefully, but I wanted to hold him, to remind myself of why I had done what I did. I was the only parent left to care for him and the rest of our children. Henri could no longer negotiate with fathers to make great matches that would keep him and his descendants safe. That was my duty as his mother. This was my attempt to keep him and his siblings safe.

❦

EARLY THE NEXT MORNING, A MESSAGE FINALLY ARRIVED FROM Tours. From the boy's crestfallen face, I knew that the news was bad. "The Duc could not capture Tours, My Lady. The Protestants sent for reinforcements and they arrived before he could penetrate the city."

"And the hing's troops?"

"The king and his troops remain camped in Tours. There were heavy casualties on our side, but the king is still master of Tours."

I groaned and rubbed my eyebrows with my hands. Depending on how bad the casualties were, Mayenne could fall back and regroup.

There was every chance he could make up for this debacle later. If Henri were still alive, he would know how to avenge this disaster, just as he had in November after Coutras. Henri cut down the Protestants, scattering them all the way back to Switzerland. His brother could do the same. I smugly realized that with this defeat, the shine dulled on Mayenne in his candidacy for the Crown. A recalcitrant leader with a stinging defeat would be less palatable than an untried teenager. Charles had yet to prove himself on the battlefield, but unlike his uncle, he had no stinging defeats attached to his name.

THE DAYS FOLLOWING MAYENNE'S DEFEAT IN TOURS; HE FELL BACK and besieged smaller towns to encircle the revived Royal troops. His efforts were for nothing. Frenchmen daily arrived to join the royal standard, and expressions of sympathy and promised aid reached the king from England and eastward from Switzerland. Allies, who would not have dared touch the king, finally came to rally to his standard. Make no mistake; these new supporters did not declare their affiliation because of the king's chances of keeping his crown. No, they believed that Navarre would succeed him to the throne. With the two allied, supporting one meant supporting the other. More and more people accepted that Navarre represented the future.

Not our family. We would never accept my heretic cousin as our next king. As the Royalist army made its laborious march from Tours to the gates of Paris, we dug in and made plans to defend the city at all costs. At the end of May, Anna came to my home to see how Alexandre and his older sisters were progressing. Too innocent to understand the catastrophes that threatened them, they provided the only respite I had from my anxiety that summer.

"It's quite a contrast to see a nursery within such heavily fortified walls." She glanced out the window to see the guards watching over the courtyard. Although she tried to keep her voice light, it shook with concern.

"I can't remember the last time that this was a noble home. It feels as if it's been a fortress for years." It had, starting in 1586, when the king's remaining brother died, and we realized that Navarre was inching closer to the throne. Henri had done everything he could to keep Navarre from becoming king. He had given his life to the cause of keeping an unworthy man from ruling France. Only we remained to pick up his cause, one that was faltering since his incompetent brother lost his best chance to take the king hostage.

"To be honest, I'm worried what the constant warfare is doing to you and the children. I think you should send them to Joinville." My shoulders slumped at her suggestion. Only weeks earlier, it would have been an easy feat to send them from Paris to Lorraine on the main roads. Mayenne had held that same road wide open for the League. Now, however, the king and his Protestant forces were inching closer to Paris, making travel in and out of the city hazardous.

I shook my head, "Alexandre is a powerful symbol of hope for the people. If I send him away, it will all but be admitting defeat. That will betray everything that my Henri stood for. I will not tarnish his legacy by acting a coward."

"Then, at least send Louise from Paris." I looked at the gurgling toddler. She placed her fingers into her mouth, sucking on them. Mundane issues crowded my head, none the least was my annoyance at the thought she would become a thumb sucker if I did not take things into my own hands. Could I spare Louise and send her to Joinville and away from me?

"Do you think it's come to this?" Dread settled over me like a heavy blanket.

She nodded, her face clouded. "I think we've waited too long to counter the king. He took the time to add to his army. It's getting harder every day to find financial support for the League."

Playing upon my public role as the shattered, cloistered widow, I had neglected to keep up with what was happening with the League's finances. If the cause was not attracting donors, then they were rapidly losing faith in our ability to prevail. That was a powerful symbol of the temperature of the feeling of the country.

"I've done all that I can as the mother of the martyrs to raise funds. I've sold a few jewels from my Grandmother." My heart sank at the desperation and wistfulness in her voice. The jewels she inherited from her mother, Queen Anne of France were invaluable. If she had resorted to selling them, then even she was out of options.

"You should take Louise and Jeanne, then. Keep them safe in Joinville. If I'm captured, I must face the consequences. Both of the children would be safe in their grandmother's care." Although I knew that, I could not sever the tie I had with Alexandre. He was all that kept me from descending into radicalism. If they discovered my plot, I would face a sentence of treason.

Weeks earlier, the king had threatened me if I did not leave Paris for his custody at Blois. I had laughed in derision at being taken to Blois in disgrace. With Mayenne licking his wounds and barely able to regroup, I had lost my only chance to escape the king's revenge. If I fled to Joinville or tried to take the king's offer and go to Blois, I would lose my opportunity to avenge Henri's death. I could not risk telling Anna of my plans. I had to remain in Paris and play my last card in this game. Yet, this game was so lethal I could not justify exposing my newborn son to danger.

"Take all the children with you. I will remain in Paris. They may criticize me for sending Alexandre away, but will tell the people it is because the king has allied with a heretic and endangered even the most innocent of us."

❦

PARIS WAITED, HOLDING ITS COLLECTIVE BREATH THAT SUMMER. June brought superficial victories, the capture of small villages by Mayenne and his troops. It also brought a new wave of Catholic refugees, fleeing the destruction wrought by Navarre's Protestant army. The heat of Summer settled in, turning the city into a cauldron. Heartbroken, I packed up the children with their nurses for the flight to Joinville. "They'll be safe away from the city. It's obvious that Navarre is dead set on besieging the city," Anna tried to reassure me, as she settled the children into her carriage. At the sight of me bursting into tears, she took me in her arms and hugged me tightly.

"Have faith. France will never accept a Protestant as her king. God himself will save us and the country." Although she meant to calm me, her words sent me into a fresh fit of sobs. She gently disentangled herself from me and stepped into the carriage. I watched through tears, as they rolled across the courtyard and through the inner gates of the hotel. I had neglected to watch Henri the last time I saw him, and I refused to repeat my mistake.

A letter arrived from Nevers, another one from Henriette. Neither she nor Louis would fight alongside Navarre and his Protestants, a decision that led to many Catholics across France to flee to safety with us in Paris. I was angry to learn that these cowards would not fight with us against the king. As far as it concerned them, he was their lawful sovereign and they would keep their stated neutrality.

The one bright spot that June was the capture of two royal advisors in a small village outside of Paris. The Sixteen thought the two men were spies and once they apprehended them, announced that they would publicly execute them. With their capture, I saw an opening for Father Jean, one I could to capitalize upon. I ran to the home of Monsieur Caravans, the new President of the Sixteen to plead to pause their executions.

"Monsieur, I need to speak with those men."

"Madame de Guise, it is not my desire to deny you anything. Yet, I must know, why would you need to speak with them?"

"They told me that these men helped to plan my husband and brother-in-law's murder. I want to speak to them in person. It's the only way I can process my husband's death." Lies, but I had vowed long before, to never trust the Sixteen with any confidences.

"It's likely that anything they would tell you would be inappropriate for a noblewoman's ears."

"Still, my soul won't quiet until I can look in the eyes of my husband's murderers."

Finally, he relented, unable to say no to a grieving widow.

GETTING INTO THE CELL WHERE THE MEN WERE BEING HELD WAS easier than I had hoped. Few people in Paris would dare cross the wife of the slain Duc de Guise. When I went to see the first man, he had the decency to look at his feet in shame. "Madame de Guise, I am sorry for your loss."

"Spare me your sympathy, had you advised the king to take another path, you would not need to give me any condolences." I fixed a cold stare upon him.

"I have spoken with a confessor with the Franciscan order. He has advised me I should forgive the king. I have written to him to tell him of my forgiveness. I need you to write the king that I have forgiven him.

"His eyebrows shot up, but he did not deny my request. A few hours later, I had a letter from two of the king's remaining advisors. As soon as possible, I sent for Father Jean. Now, he had the means of getting into the king's confidence without arousing suspicion.

⚜

THE LEAGUE WAS RUNNING OUT OF SUPPORT OUTSIDE OF FRANCE. The Pope refused to absolve the League from damnation if of the king's death. I worried if this would destroy my plot. Would Father Jean disappear with the money I paid him and refuse the risk of damnation for ridding me of the king? If so, I would lose my chance for revenge.

⚜

AT MASS ONE SUNDAY IN JUNE, MONTPENSIER STOOD BY MY SIDE and glanced nervously at the crowd. "It's time to rid ourselves of that tyrant. Only his death will suffice."

I raised my eyebrows, shocked that she would speak so vehemently in a house of God. "Are you ready to put the king into a monastery now?"

She snorted, "Past time. We need a more permanent solution." To my horror and delight, she said the last sentence loud enough to cause the surrounding people to turn their heads towards us. She did not know of my plans against the king and she was unknowingly implicating herself before the people.

I would continue to play the moral and grieving widow. Mustering as much shock as possible, I turned to her, "I do not think it is very Christian-like to advocate killing the last Valois. Haven't we had enough bloodshed as it is? I, for one, am tired of it all." I crossed myself and pinched the underside of my elbow to make myself cry. At my side, Montpensier sighed in annoyance.

I felt no guilt in throwing Montpensier to the wolves. She had already earned my anger for doubting that my son could lead the Guise family into the future. Everyone in Paris had heard her rail against the king on multiple occasions. If the priest implicated me in the plot to kill the king, I would declare to all that I was only a grieving widow. I felt no guilt over framing her for the king's demise; she had earned it. She had no children to grieve her if the king put her to death.

THE KING AND NAVARRE CONTINUED TO ADVANCE TOWARDS PARIS, surrounding the city the last week of July. The city could not hold out more than a few months. Out there somewhere, was the man who would exact my revenge and rid me of the king. I had to be patient for him to know the right time to make his move.

On a sweltering second day of August, I was listless, endlessly pacing the hallways of Hotel de Guise. Something told me that the world had changed, but I would not celebrate just yet. I had to know that my instincts were right. At mid-morning, a messenger came galloping into the courtyard, yelling the news. "The king is dead! Henri Valois is no more!" I clapped my hands in relief, then crossed myself. I could not appear to be too excited at the prospect of the king's demise.

The assassin had made two attempts to kill the king. Turned away the first day, he returned to speak to his sovereign, claiming that he had letters from traitors to the League who would offer to swing Paris' gates wide open to him. Unable to resist the temptation of an easy victory, he led the man in. Handing him the letters written by the two advisors, he gained the king's confidence quickly. I don't know if he bothered to mention my gesture of reconciliation, but I suppose, it was best they not attach my name to the plot.

Flashing a blade in, what I hope, was a scene very much reminiscent of the murder of my husband, he stabbed the king, finding vital tissue with his first attempts. The king grabbed the blade to disarm him, but the damage was already done. Henri Valois, king of France, had only hours to live. As much as I worried about Father Jean giving me up as a co-conspirator, the Forty-Five took care of that problem for me. In seconds, he lay dead, unable to tell anyone about his motives. Unless he had told his mission to anyone else, I could walk away from this deed with no repercussions. I would later learn that his name was not even Jean, yet another lie he had told me. His real name was Jacques Clement and the fact I could not give even his real name meant that my alibi was even stronger than I had hoped.

Arrogant to the last and unable to accept the reality of his situation, the king immediately dictated a letter to Queen Louise at Chenonceau, telling her he was only injured and that he would live. As the day wore on, he called Navarre to his bedside. There, Henri Valois violated French and Church law by naming the heretic Navarre the heir to the throne. When the League's leaders heard of this abomination, they were livid.

Henri Valois bled to death, lying like the coward he was in his own bed. The man who masterminded the slaughter of the Huguenots in 1572 and was directly responsible for the death of my husband, finally lay dead himself. I could finally rest now I had eliminated the threat of the last Valois. The threat of the Bourbon was negligible; no Frenchman would accept Navarre as his king.

EPILOGUE

Virtually from the moment she heard of the King's death, Montpensier took credit for hiring the man to do the deed. I needn't bother denying my guilt; she was more than capable of framing herself with no help on my part. The printers in Paris went with her story, depicting her as the avenging angel, who killed the King in her grief over the loss of her brothers. If anything, it bolstered her celebrity status across France as she became known as the killer of the King. The more she sought the spotlight, the more I took strides to avoid it. Although there was a push for Navarre to become King, his wife languished under lock and key, so there was no court to speak of. I had ample time to tend to family affairs.

With the need to reunite with my children as my excuse, I quietly slipped out of Paris much as the King had done a year earlier. I traveled to Joinville, to see my children. Rumors said Navarre would march for Paris next, but it would take time before he could position his troops to attack us. I would be in Lorraine by then. I left Paris with only months to spare. Navarre began a long and unsuccessful siege that lasted longer than anyone would have imagined. He would not enter the city as its King until 1594.

Charles and I hoped he would marry the Spanish Infanta and

become King in Navarre's stead until 1593. As rulers of Lorraine, the reformed Parliaments of Paris deemed the Guise foreigners and thus, barred from the French succession. The ruling also meant that a Spanish princess was not an option, so the young Duc de Guise married a daughter of the Duc de Joyeuse. Checkmated, I returned to court in 1593 to find that Navarre planned to make his mistress, Gabrielle d'Estrees, Queen of France in Margot's stead. Relieved that there was finally a royal court in Paris once again, I returned to Paris to seek our fortunes once again. In a few years, even Louise Marguerite and Alexandre Paris would need to marry. Without a father to guide them, I was all that they had left.

THE END
of
FATE'S MISTRESS

Join Laura du Pre's mailing list to receive a **free book**, the latest news about upcoming releases, and special offers just for subscribers.

Read on for more books by this author, historical notes, and contact information.

ALSO BY LAURA DU PRE

<u>Coming Soon</u>

The French Mistresses Trilogy

The Valois Mistress

The Uncrowned Queen

The Queen's Nemesis

ABOUT THE AUTHOR

Laura du Pre is a historian turned author. The Three Graces Series is her first foray into historical fiction. Laura holds a Master's Degree in History from Middle Tennessee State University. Before writing full time she worked as an archivist and a contributor for historical publications. She continues to live in the Deep South with her cranky elderly cat, Owen.

You can learn more about Laura at her website. Stop by there for a **FREE** copy of *Safe in My Arms: A Three Graces Story*.

Connect with Laura
www.lauradupre.com
laura@lauradupre

RESEARCHING THE RENAISSANCE

I'm indebted to the historians and biographers who came before me.

- Borthwick, Robert Brown. *History of the Princes de Conde in the 16th and 17th Centuries.* Vol I &II, 1872.
- Carroll, Stewart. *Martyrs and Murderers: The Guise Family and the Making of Europe.* 2009.
- Goldstone, Nancy. *Rival Queens: The Rival Queens: Catherine de Medici, Her Daughter Marguerite de Valois, and the Betrayal That Ignited a Kingdom.* 2015
- Knecht, Robert J. *The French Renaissance Court,* 2008.
- —— *The Rise and Fall of Renaissance France,* 1483-1610, 2001.
- Freer, Martha Walker. *Henri III King of France and Poland.* Vol I-III. 1888.
- Marsh, Ann. *History of the Protestant Reformation in France.* 1851.
- Strange, Mark. *Women of Power: The Life and Times of Catherine de Medici.* 1976.
- Williams, H. Noel. *The Brood of False Lorraine: The History of the Ducs de Guise.* Volumes I & II.